SUDDENLY one p
molding, then anoth
for a moment, and t
shaking the car. Mu............ stood by,
moving their eyes from the pulleys and gears
to the quivering loop of rubber over their
heads.

Then, crisply, and with surprisingly little noise,
the cable snapped. "Oh, my God," Toscani
said, crossing himself. The car dipped into the
trees and hung, dangling, from the broken
cable, swinging gently in the breeze. . . .

"GOOD, FAST-PACED ADVENTURE
. . . Well-plotted and logical to the intelligently conceived finish."
—*Publishers Weekly*

"MR. NATHAN HAS DONE A MASTERFUL JOB, not only of storytelling, but of
revealing fascinating inside information
about a world few people know."
—*Helen Van Slyke*

AMUSEMENT PARK

A NOVEL BY

Robert Stuart Nathan

FAWCETT CREST • NEW YORK

AMUSEMENT PARK

THIS BOOK CONTAINS THE COMPLETE TEXT OF THE ORIGINAL HARDCOVER EDITION.

Published by Fawcett Crest Books, a unit of CBS Publication, the Consumer Publishing Division of CBS Inc., by arrangement with The Dial Press.

ISBN: 0-449-23960-8

Printed in Canada

10   9   8   7   6   5   4   3   2   1

For my mother and,
in loving memory, my father and for
Rosemary and Arthur Hagadus

ACKNOWLEDGEMENTS

The author thanks Elaine Markson, for constant good cheer and encouragement; Joyce Johnson and Joyce Engelson, for instruction and patience and enthusiasm; and Lewis Chesler, who shares an enthusiasm for amusement parks, and whose idea this book was and without whom it would not have been written.

There are only the pursued, the pursuing, the busy, and the tired.

—*F. Scott Fitzgerald*

1

The city was still asleep, but Everett Morgan was running late. He packed his tools. First, the transformer, freshly oiled and painted with black lacquer. Morgan held it, caressed it with nearly sexual pleasure. The Breiter clips, German. The Germans were best at electronics, he thought, better than the Japanese. Of all the parts Morgan had removed from the warehouse of A. W. Albright & Company, the Breiter clips would certainly be missed first. He carefully laid in cable, terminal caps, lug bolts, alligator prongs, and a Tersa spring-forced timer accurate to within four seconds a day. He surveyed the remaining parts spread out on the bed, then lifted each one, meticulously examined it, and set it into the green wooden case.

Rain falling in a fine translucent sheet slapped on the bedroom window. Second Avenue was dark. The black pavement glowed as red taillights receded down the block. Only one street lamp burned. The day before Morgan had watched a Puerto Rican boy methodically shatter, one by one, first the glass shields in the street lamps and then the bulbs, using steel pellets in a rubber-thonged slingshot.

The street was empty. Silent.

Morgan stepped into the kitchen and turned on the hot water faucet, then watched until the water grew hot. He measured two tablespoons of instant coffee into a cup and dashed the cup under the running water. Lips poised over the cup, he breathed. Steam rose, fogging his glasses. He gulped the coffee, dribbling a bit onto his overalls.

The raw floorboards in the dingy tenement creaked as he returned to the bedroom. On top of the tools, he placed the toy train he had bought for his son. Soon, he thought, they would be far away. Out west. Matthew would like the west. Kansas. Wyoming. Holding the toolbox in his hand, Morgan tested its heft, then tucked it under his arm. He turned, looked back at the empty bed. He wondered if his wife were awake in her parents' house in Brooklyn, pacing her bedroom. Louise paced; she had never slept well. Once more he glanced around the room. Every drawer in the dresser was open and empty. Hangers littered the closets. Across the floor flew puffballs of dust. He was leaving not a trace of himself behind. He was never coming back. Stepping into the hallway, he patted the bulging pocket over his left thigh. Three wallets held $10,000 in cash. No, he was not coming back.

Searching like a mountain climber for a foothold, he walked down the steps as if uncertain they were there. On the third-floor landing, he stopped. Through the window, open against the muggy summer morning, he saw the rain letting up. A cat screeched and pawed at the door behind him. Somewhere in the building a radio played loud Spanish *salsa*. Morgan negotiated the remaining steps gingerly, then stepped out of the building over a pile of debris in the doorway. A Bustelo coffee bag, half-spilled. Chips of brown glass: beer bottles. A sopping roll of toilet paper.

Thin and stoop-shouldered, Morgan took short, rapid steps toward his car, carrying the toolbox under his right arm. The only sounds he could hear were the rain and the hum of air conditioners and the distant rumbling of trucks on the pavement. Occasionally a wailing horn broke the stillness. Perhaps a third of New York's eight million were gone this Saturday, Memorial Day, off to weekend retreats, sunshine at the Long Island shore. Only the poor and a few shopkeepers stayed behind.

Against the bleak, craggy facade of buildings, Morgan saw a toothless woman of indefinite old age crawl from the half-light of a garage entrance, pulling behind her a tattered gray blanket. Glaring at Morgan, she snorted, gathered her rags and torn shopping bags into a loose bundle, and shuffled away. Across the avenue, another solitary figure disappeared behind a row of green industrial containers overflowing with construction refuse, bulky poles of black lumber veiled in white plaster dust and leaves of tar paper.

Stopping in the middle of the empty avenue, Morgan peered downtown, past stores shuttered and barred to intruders, city tombs, toward the horizon marked by the thirties Deco crenulations of the Empire State Building. With the toolbox squeezed under his arm, he pulled his wristwatch close to his pale, lined face and squinted. Two diesel trucks rounded the corner of Eighty-ninth Street, moving in tandem as they roared by, passing him within inches. They shook the pavement and blew a sooty newspaper against his legs. Morgan bent over and peeled the paper away, then wiped his hands on his green overalls with the long, slow stroke of a man who is accustomed to dirt.

Thickly clouded, the sky showed the barest outlines of a full moon. Abruptly Morgan set his toolbox on the roof of his battered white Pontiac. He fumbled with his keys for a moment, then opened the door and, handling the toolbox like a case of fragile crystal, gently pushed it across the vinyl-covered seat cushion. He leaned into the car, opened the box, rummaged through it. After a few seconds, he climbed in and inserted the key in the lock without looking, a tic of familiarity.

The engine failed to turn over. He looked at his watch again. Three-fifteen. Muttering, he threw the door open. Rain, leaking through shriveled weather stripping, had finally rusted the ignition switch. Morgan unhooked the hood, but the latch jammed, engaged, and he cut himself.

"Shit," he said, surprised at the echo of his own voice in the darkness.

The hood popped open. With a short strand of wire, Morgan connected the alternator and distributor to the starter motor, touching the wire for a fraction of a second, and the engine groaned. Again he touched the wire; the engine turned over, backfired. With little pleasure, Morgan slammed the hood, took the wheel, and eased the car

11

away from the curb with a single turn. A pair of lucite dice swung like a pendulum from the shaft of the rearview mirror.

Laying his hand protectively on the toolbox, pulling it closer, he started downtown. The street was barren, the lights synchronized, allowing a steady pace. As he turned the corner of Thirty-fourth Street, heading crosstown, an ambulance sped by, eerily flashing lights without a siren. Reaching for cigarettes on the dash, Morgan caught his sleeve on the gearshift and, leaning forward, accidentally pushed the accelerator to the floor. He braked hard to avoid hitting a dog.

Trailer trucks crowded the entry lanes to the Lincoln Tunnel. Craning his head out the window, Morgan saw police barricades blocking the way.

"Tunnel open?" he called, perhaps too loudly, to a Port Authority policeman near the tunnel entrance. He would never make it if he had to drive up to the George Washington Bridge and then down the turnpike.

"In a minute, bud," the policeman answered. "Six-axle trailer broke down."

"What about the other lane?" Morgan shouted, his voice booming in the narrow corridor leading to the entrance.

"It's open," the policeman said, walking up the ramp toward him. "Careful there swinging around." He waved his flashlight toward the sawhorse barricades. Morgan pulled his car wide to avoid a panel truck beside him. In his mind's eye, he saw a snapshot of the sun rising, and he feared he would be short of time. Zigzagging through the barricades to the adjoining tunnel, he watched the policeman retreat, shake his head, and wave his flashlight.

Morgan took the center lane south on the turnpike, through the crowded industrial zone lining the Hudson River basin. He drove steadily at the speed limit, his left hand gripping the steering wheel tightly, his right resting on the toolbox. In the glare of the highway's mercury lights, his narrow face and reedy hands turned a sickly green, his brown hair a dirty gray. Pollution tinted the black sky ominously yellow. Smoke spun from puffing stacks, gauze in an open wound. Oil tanks, brightly lit, flowed by in rows. By the time Morgan reached his exit, trees had reclaimed the countryside. He was deep into the New Jersey Pine Barrens, raw stands of pines and oaks and maples so dense a man could hardly walk through them. The numbers on the tollbooth clock, circled in blue fluorescence, were unreadable, and Morgan came to a full stop to check the time once again. Eighteen minutes before five. He was behind schedule. The tollbooth light reflected the orange enameled letters on the toolbox: A. W. Albright & Company, Electrical Contractors.

"Morning," the toll collector said, hobbling out of his booth to the car. "Going to be a scorcher today, huh?"

"What?" Morgan asked, irritated, digging into his wallet.

"Scorcher, I said. A hot one. Going to be real hot today." The old man looked down, satisfied with his pronouncement. He stroked his chin. "Yep, a hot one for sure."

"Right," Morgan said, passing the man a dollar bill and three nickels.

"Drive careful, now," the toll collector said.

The road off the highway was illuminated only by the moon breaking through clouds. Towering pines, bending in the breeze, lay against the sky. Although Morgan had driven the road before to learn its landmarks, he forgot the steep bank to the right and swerved to stay on the pitted tarmac. The bumps shook the toolbox and he pulled it against his side. Easing off the accelerator as the road twisted left, he remembered where he was. Just over the next ridge, he thought.

At the intersection ahead, the sign—OLYMPIC ADVENTURE—leaped out, blue and brown neon letters seemingly suspended from the forest wall. Morgan pulled onto the shoulder and flipped his headlights off. It was five minutes to five. At most, half an hour remained until sunrise.

He lifted the toolbox, this time by the handle, and

stepped out onto the shoulder. Crickets chattered in the trees. His heavy breathing sounded unnaturally loud. A mosquito buzzed in his ear, and he slapped wildly. At what he thought was the sound of an approaching car, he spun around. But there was nothing. He stood, lit a cigarette, puffed jerkily, then crushed it out on the dirt with his boot. The moon faded from the sky again, and the neon letters shone more brightly, phantoms in the forbidding cloak of darkness. Hushed sounds from the woods swelled in his ears. At the entrance to the amusement park, chains rattled across the roadway. Morgan peered north and south along the three-lane blacktop, then darted across. Standing in the gully bordering the shoulder, he lowered the toolbox to the ground without a sound and clasped his hands behind his neck. He pulled his arms tight, trying to relax his constricted neck muscles. On his knees, he crawled into the bristly underbrush. He heard a car arrive at the entrance, looked up, and saw a guard unlock the chain.

"Morning, Mr. Masters," he heard the guard say.

"Morning, George," came a muffled voice from the car, hardly audible over the engine.

"Big day, huh?"

"Sure is. Anybody else in yet?"

"Mr. Toscani," the guard said. "About twenty minutes ago. Said he'd be down checking the northern aerials if anybody wanted him. Down at the big wheel."

"That's Pete for you, working harder than the rest of us."

"How many people are you expecting today, Mr. Masters? Got any idea at all?"

"No way to tell, George. We're praying for a big start this season. Seventy-five thousand, maybe. If we get lucky. The rain's clearing. At least the weather's with us."

Headlights zoomed past Morgan and he ducked his head. It was nearly light enough to see the road. The guard strolled by him, his shoes glinting with dew. Morgan eased farther down the road along the gully. Burrs dug into his legs. His ankles itched. Fifty, perhaps sixty yards away,

14

his car was visible on the shoulder. A truck passed, speeding in the opposite direction, and Morgan was suddenly aware that its headlights were out. He looked up. The sky was a lighter shade of blue.

The sun crested the horizon.

2

The spidery clouds lifted and Ken Masters watched the sun rise high above the Pine Barrens. He stood at the center of Olympic Adventure, the largest amusement park in the world. From his vantage point, at the top of a tower two hundred and ten feet high, Olympic Adventure spread out in all directions as far as his eyes could see—more than three thousand acres of glossy toys. To the south, the main arcades. To the north, the Olympic Safari. The tower itself was the tallest toy of all, a gigantic glazed ice-cream cone, designer Gabriel Bloome's most whimsical accomplishment. A stiff, warm breeze rolled through the tower windows, a breeze that had traveled more than a thousand miles of Atlantic coast.

In its fifth season, Olympic Adventure was indisputably a legend. Arabian potentates traversed the ocean to see it. Movie stars brought their children to play. Fantasists celebrated it. And on those rare occasions when Ken Masters could forget the responsibilities of his job, even he succumbed to its thrall. But now he wished only that Brad Hawkins would show up.

Masters was staring at a series of sixteen-inch television screens, ten green, blinking windows ablaze with numbers. The time was exactly 9:30, the monitors told him, and 72,512 people had each parted at the gate with seven dollars and fifty cents. The computer system displayed continuous gross gate figures ($543,840 at that moment), population density for the park's four main arcades (on a scale of ten, an unbalanced 7.13), the number of staff currently on the grounds (354 permanent, 931 temporary, plus assorted vendors), shipments arriving at and supplies leaving for the park from the services-support center in nearby Glenwood, the amount of electric power being drawn, the number of cars in the drive-through safari

(3,111), and a host of reports on machinery which Ken Masters only partly understood.

The throngs poured up the midway, fanning out across the park's natural greenery, the gardens and manicured lawns, into the Pine Barrens. Spectacular, Masters thought. Damn spectacular. And what amusement park wouldn't be spectacular with one of the country's oldest and most exquisitely developed forests as a backdrop. The scenery overpowered the mechanical toys, overshadowed them, exactly as Gabriel Bloome had planned.

Seventy-two thousand people. Masters found the numbers improbable. More paying customers than on any other day in the park's history, and it was only 9:30 in the morning. Opening day of the season. His first day as assistant general manager. Masters compared the computer's figures with the manually tabulated amounts for each individual entrance gate, and saw that the computers were not mistaken. The scanning devices at the turnstiles were accurate, according to the manufacturer, within one-half of one percent. Seventy-two thousand people—more than they could have hoped for. By noon, if the pace kept up, it would be one hundred thousand. Where the hell was Hawkins? How the hell did Hawkins manage not to be here on opening day? Masters wondered if this were some sort of test. Had Hawkins stayed away just to see how he would handle the pressure? A damn stupid time, Masters thought, for a test. This crowd, this unexpected boon, would tax the park's resources as never before. Masters had only one satisfaction: at least Olympic Adventure would operate at capacity for a change. Yes, he thought, they would make money this year. Hawkins had seen to that.

Fresh from five years at Disneyland, Masters knew how important the crowds were this weekend. If Memorial Day was good, if the tens of thousands of dollars spent on advertising filled the park for opening day, then you could expect a strong season. Olympic Adventure needed more than a strong season, needed, in fact, capacity crowds all summer and into early fall. Only a few people knew why

17

this season was so crucial, and the reason would have surprised a casual observer. The world's largest amusement park—what its creator, Gabriel Bloome, had once insisted be titled "The Eighth Wonder of the Modern World"—was losing money. Close to half a million dollars a week. Eleven million dollars in the previous season alone.

The financial facts were supposedly secret, and Ken Masters would not normally have been privy to them. But Brad Hawkins, the park's general manager, had told him the truth, emphasizing how precarious was the park's survival. An American institution, Hawkins had said, and it could wash right down the drain. Masters had only the dimmest idea of how uncertain the future actually was, but he did know that for him no tragedy could be greater than the failure of Olympic Adventure. At Disney, he'd been secure, but there he was only a concessions manager in one distant corner of the giant enterprise. Ordering a quarter of a million hamburgers was nothing compared to the responsibility he had now.

His whole life had changed the day Brad Hawkins hired him to be assistant general manager of Olympic Adventure. With his wife Sarah and their two children, he had moved from a tiny California apartment in Long Beach to a twelve-room farmhouse in rural New Jersey where George Washington reportedly once slept (or so the real-estate agent said). Away from the Movieland Wax Museum and Knott's Berry Farm, away from dreadful Anaheim and speed roadsters. Now he had two new cars, a new mortgage, a new way of living. At twenty-nine, he was earning $45,000 a year, and even to him that seemed a great deal of money. The future looked bright *if*—if Olympic Adventure succeeded.

For that reason, the crowd below, whatever problems it might cause, pleased him. It meant, as Hawkins had predicted, that average people couldn't spare the money to rent cottages for the long weekend, that many couldn't pack the children into the car and set off for three days in the Catskills. It meant, most of all, that this period of hard times had wrought its debilitating havoc on the family budget: a one-day trip was all most people could afford. Olympic Adventure, the corporate experts said, would benefit from dreary economic conditions. The trip *did* cost almost ten dollars a person, and it *did* only last a day, but it cost far less than a weekend in the mountains. And for the majority, that would simply have to do. Olympic Adventure was as much of a summer vacation as they would get.

But while the surge of bodies and ringing cash registers pleased Masters, it also worried him. More than a hundred thousand people would be a strain. Lines would be long. Supplies might run short. And crowding caused accidents. And *he* was managing it. *He* was responsible. Where the hell was Hawkins?

Masters couldn't help imagining the worst. He saw only chaos for the next fifteen hours, chaos breeding in the thousands of acres crammed with people, chaos growing like the gathering wind before a storm. But chaos would not do. Customers came to escape, to live in a dream world for a day. How little they know, Masters thought, what it takes to make dreams come true. For a moment, he believed that by concentrating hard enough, he could will Hawkins to appear.

Added to his fears about the park, it did not much help Masters to consider that his position as Hawkins's assistant was accidental. He suspected that Hawkins would have preferred Jock Constable, who had already worked at the park for three years, who had run its concessions with apparent success. After all, Masters thought, Hawkins and Constable were old friends. They had gone to law school together. Men who know each other that long take care of each other. Guessing at higher intrigues, Masters assumed that Constable had offended the park's owners, Gabriel Bloome and Cole Cunningham. Maybe it was Jock's drinking. Jock was never really drunk, but you could tell when he'd had a few too many. And so Masters thought himself Hawkins's second choice, and he felt compelled to prove himself.

Heat rose in the booth, and he closed the tiny, rectangular cantilevered windows one by one as he walked around the room. He could not help admiring the Olympic Adventure advertisements hanging on the walls—miniatures of billboards, magazine layouts, illustrated storyboards from television commercials. His favorite was a billboard with a collage of animals grouped about the ferris wheel, all the same size, superimposed on a hazy sunset and a cone of treetops. When it was finished and installed on the turnpike, the lights of the ferris wheel were actually lights—individual bulbs.

The electronic chime on the control board sounded, and Masters reacted so instinctively that his hand reached the phone before the tone faded from the air.

"Masters, station one."

"Kenny, my boy. How's the weather up there?" It was Pete Toscani, the park's chief engineer.

"Crystal clear, Pete, and getting clearer. Quite a crowd you've got down there." Masters had a sense of warm familiarity with the one man in the park, other than Hawkins, whom he completely trusted. It was from Pete that Masters had learned what Toscani called "the details."

"We got crowds all right, and we also got a sixteen-cylinder engine cooking, and if it don't cool down pretty soon, it's going to melt. Where the hell is Hawkins? He promised me high-grade oil this morning, and it ain't here."

Calliope music faded in and out through the phone as Toscani fiddled with the volume controls of the walkie-talkie. A burly fifteen-year veteran of amusement parks—he had worked at them all and helped design Disney World—Toscani could tear down an engine and put it back together in an hour, but he was mystified by the new voice-activated radios carried by all senior park employees.

Ken jabbed at the control board to bring onto a screen a list of shipments received that day.

"Just a second, Pete. Let me take a look."

The board showed that the order had been expected the previous morning—sixty cases of special lubricant. Fortner & Sons, Chicago. There was no indication that the cases had arrived.

"Pete, the oil's not here yet. Supposed to be in yesterday."

"I *know* that, son. I just told you I haven't got it. I told Hawkins I needed that stuff a week ago. Now what the hell do we do?" Toscani's voice, sharp and direct, left no doubt as to his anger.

"Hawkins is in the city, Pete. Some damn meeting with Bloome and Cunningham. Don't ask *me* why he's not here, but I'll bet it's important, whatever it is. Look, I'll try to find out about the oil. Where are you now? What's the immediate problem?" Toscani had failed to announce his location at the beginning of the conversation, as the park's wireless regulations demanded. But Ken didn't dare reprimand Toscani for a minor infraction of the rules.

"Sorry, kid. Station C-fifty-one." He was on the Mt. Olympus side of the Sky Chariot at the northeast corner of the park, more than a mile away. "Kid, the engine on Chariot number one is steaming hot. We're okay for the time being with number two, but they're both running real slow. And there are long lines here, kid, halfway back to the damn flume. And if I run the friggin' cars *too* slow, we get slack in the cables. The cars just pull 'em down. It pisses me off, I can tell you that. I told that idiot Cunningham I wanted to replace the damn cables last year and he said nothing doing." It amazed Ken that Pete could call the park's owner, Cole Cunningham, an idiot. Masters had met the man only a few times, and while he didn't like him, he assumed he was nobody's fool—he did, after all, own Olympic Adventure.

"I don't understand, Pete. Why do you have to run the engines slow?"

"Look, Kenny. Cunningham bought these damned engines used. Now I don't want a snapped cable sending thirty kids flying into the trees, but if I don't get some oil into engine number one, the sonuvabitch is going to seize. And if I don't run it slow, it'll seize. You get it?"

Masters did not understand elementary mechanics. His

21

specialty was concessions. For a moment, he was afraid to admit his ignorance to Toscani, but decided this was no time for bravado. "Sorry, Pete," he said, "explain it to me."

"Look here, son, I can't give you a lesson over this damn radio, but this is it straight and simple, so listen up. Oil keeps the moving parts from building up too much friction. Friction—you know what that is. Makes heat. The parts I'm talking about are valves and pistons, just like in your car, only these pistons are bigger and there are twice as many of them. Without oil that'll stand up to the heat of the engine, the stuff just evaporates and the whole damn thing gets so hot the engine seizes. It has . . . let me see. Well, it has a sort of heart attack. The rod, that's what connects the pistons, see, it separates. The engine throws a rod. You ever see a rod come through an engine block?"

"Never, Pete. Don't know if I'd recognize it."

"Damn straight you would. A sad sight. A real ugly sight. The valve comes up and the rod just keeps on going. You got one dead engine on your hands. And if that engine seizes up while I got a couple of cars in the air on those cables—" he spoke softly now "—we not only got ourselves a dead engine, we also got ourselves a couple of dead people."

"I get the message, Pete. You need the oil."

"I needed it yesterday, son. Yesterday."

Masters contemplated telling the engineer to just shut the ride down altogether. No use taking risks. Where the hell *was* Hawkins? I just can't shut it down, he thought. Not on opening day. Not so early in the day. What would Hawkins do? Masters reproached himself for indecision. *Dead people.* The words echoed in his head.

"You want to shut it down, Pete?"

"You crazy, son? We've got a thousand people here and they're already getting edgy. They'd ask for their damned money back. Or start a small riot. You just get that oil for me and get it quick. And I don't care if you drive out to Glenwood yourself, okay? Just get the damned oil."

"Right, Pete. I'll start looking. Masters, out."

As the sun climbed higher, above the clouds, into clear sky, the control room grew hotter. Masters boosted the air-conditioning as high as it would go, and the noise of the fan blotted out the sounds of the crowd below. Again it seemed to him the Chariot should be shut down if there were any danger of mechanical failure while the cars were in the air, crossing the park. But the Chariot was one of the park's focal points. Not only did it give riders a view of the Pine Barrens they would never forget—and would, hopefully, talk about to their friends—it was also the single most efficient mover of people from one end of the park to the other, from Mt. Olympus in the Land of the Gods in the northeast, to the scale reproduction of the Eiffel Tower in Parisian Paradise in the southeast. The two elaborate monuments were each two hundred feet high, ten feet higher than the ferris wheel, itself the world's largest. Together they bounded the Land of Monuments. How could he shut down this ride? He would risk destroying the park's reputation in one stroke. There would be reporters here today, newspaper photographers. And why did the crowds come; why did they suffer the two-hour drive from Delaware or New York or Philadelphia? To stop time for a moment, to be suspended outside reality, to forget for a brief moment the pressures of daily life. They did not come to be reminded of failure, of things that did not work, of accidents, mistakes. For seven dollars and fifty cents, they wanted escape from the mundane, from the real. For seven dollars and fifty cents, they wanted dreams.

Masters reached for his console phone to call the services center in Glenwood. The sun, moving higher in the sky, shone directly through the window with refracted shadows of russet, purple, and green. Ken hesitated. Perhaps Pete had overreacted. Engines didn't just explode. Or did they? He castigated himself for his ignorance. Hawkins understood machines. Shouldn't a man know about pistons and rods?

Before his hand reached the console phone switch, the

elevator behind him opened. He had not even heard it coming. Turning, he saw Jock Constable framed in the parted panels. Broad, tall—he was six foot three—Constable appeared to fill the entire elevator. His gray-streaked red hair capped a wrinkled, splotchy face that was not quite the texture of a prune. By his size alone, Constable was intimidating. Even Constable's age seemed an insult to Ken, an accusation, and in the few seconds it took Constable to cross the room to the console, Ken shaped an image, not altogether consciously, of his own appearance contrasted with the older man's. Ken's face was smooth, bronzed, taut. His thick, dishwater-blond hair was so uniform in color it might have been dyed. Aside from a slightly crooked nose—the result of hastily performed surgery following a car accident on a reckless drive from San Francisco to Palo Alto the year before— his face conveyed the soft insouciance of Californians which Easterners joked about. Were it not for the heavy bags under his eyes—a trait inherited from his father— Ken could have been mistaken for a high school cheerleader. He knew it. And it annoyed him. Against talent or toughness or drive, a man might match himself. Against age, he had no defense.

"Morning, Jock," Masters said, hearing his voice sound higher, more childish, more diffident than it actually was.

"Good day, little fella," the larger man said cheerfully.

"Knock it off, Jock, will you? I don't need your crap today."

"Sorry, fella," Constable said, a little too exuberantly for Masters's taste. "I keep telling you, that's how I talk to everybody." At least that much was true. Constable called Hawkins big fella. But Ken didn't like the diminutive, especially from Constable.

"Are you just passing the time, Jock? Or is there something I can do for you?"

"I don't get up to your nest often, you know. Opening day, though, I wanted to see the crowds the way you see them." Constable wheeled a chair from behind the console desk to a window and sat with his back to Ken. He rested

24

his chin in his hands and pressed his face against the glass. "Packing them in, I see. How many have we got?"

Masters looked at the television screen. "Pushing eighty thousand."

"Bless me," Constable said with a snort. "Bless me and the Virgin Mary. Where in the sweet Lord's name do they all come from? And at seven fifty a throw. Good work, Kenny. You've brought us luck all the way from California. The Hawk is going to be real happy. Where is the main man?"

"In the city for some damn meeting," Ken said angrily, instantly regretting his tone.

"What's the matter, Kenny? Can't handle the pressure?"

"Nothing's the matter, Jock. Except that I have work to do. What about you?"

"All square, Mister Assistant General Manager. No, I think I'll just sit here a bit and watch. Take the edge off a long day. If that's okay with you, little fella. If I'm not bothering you."

"Make yourself at home." Masters refused to be annoyed, knowing Constable wanted to watch him stew. Provocation was a game of the weak.

Calling the park's eleven lookout stations, he spoke briefly with the largest concessionaires. The staff was handling the load. He checked the telephone-activated paging devices worn by all junior personnel; all twenty-seven supervisors responded to the call within three minutes. He checked through his worksheets for the day, preparing to make his rounds on foot, waiting for Constable to get bored and leave. But Constable stayed. He would have to deal with the missing oil in Constable's presence. He punched the button for the Glenwood center, six miles north on the road from the park's main entrance.

"Operations, R-forty-one. Dexter here." Ken recognized neither the voice nor the name. Six months of this, he said to himself, and you still don't know these people. Well, five hundred people was a lot of names and faces, and other duties had demanded his attention.

"Dexter, this is Ken Masters, station one. Pete Toscani

tells me he's been expecting a shipment of oil all week. From Fortner in Chicago. You have any word on that?"

"Sir, could you give me a waybill number?"

Masters looked at the screen. "Airbill. Trans World. It's B as in boy, Z as in zebra, one-six-five-nine-five."

"Hold just a minute, sir." Masters was a bit surprised by the man's deferential tone, and then he remembered his own prominence within the park. Either Dexter had recognized his name or the station number told him that the call originated at the top. Despite, or perhaps because of, Constable's presence, Masters enjoyed the recognition, took satisfaction in it, regardless of the problem with the oil. He had wanted that sort of recognition all his life.

The phone rang behind him—his private line. Which meant that either his wife or Brad Hawkins was calling. He hoped it was Hawkins. Cradling the console phone on his left shoulder, he answered the direct line.

"Masters." He tried to sound businesslike, severe, unruffled.

"Hello, love. How's it going?" It was Sarah, and somehow he was relieved to hear his wife's voice and not Hawkins's, eager as he was to hear from his boss. Maybe he was worried Hawkins would notice how nervous he was. He needed Brad, and he needed him now, but he hated having to pretend everything was fine.

"Just peachy," he said to Sarah sarcastically. "Marvelous. The engine on the Sky Chariot needs oil and we don't have it. Pete Toscani is hopping mad and Hawkins is in the city for some damn meeting and was supposed to be here already, and at this very moment there are"—he leaned over the console screen—"there are exactly seventy-eight thousand, two hundred and eleven people inside this damn zoo."

Sarah whistled. "Amazing. You didn't expect that, did you?"

"No, and I didn't expect to be stuck here alone with them, either." Masters noticed that Constable had leaned back in his chair. He was listening to every word.

"Come on, honey," Sarah said. "You can handle it and you know it."

"I guess so," he said. Masters was glad to have his wife's reassurance. He'd married Sarah during their senior year at Berkeley and he was one of the few people he knew from college who was still married. He loved his wife and children. To him, it was no more complicated than that. Of course, there had been rough times. The children came earlier than planned, before Sarah realized how time-consuming and expensive they could be. Moving from California, leaving friends and family behind, uprooted their emotions more than their possessions. But still he found it strange that so many of his old friends were already divorced. Why hadn't they made a go of it? Wasn't that what marriage was all about? Making a go of it. Taking the good times with the bad. Wasn't that what love was all about? That, at any rate, was how Ken Masters felt.

"I hate to bother you," his wife continued. "I know how busy you are, but Tommy's been pestering me since he woke up this morning. You haven't seen much of them lately and they don't think it's fair, especially since you're gone in the morning before they get up. Kenny, I just can't listen to them complain anymore about not seeing you. Tommy's sulking now. He won't even talk to me."

As much as Ken didn't like to admit it, his wife was right. But he'd thrown himself into his job because he wanted to do well—because Hawkins was giving him more responsibility, more power, than he'd ever had and was paying him to take charge. Hawkins had no use for people who refused to devote themselves to their work. Well, that's okay for Brad Hawkins, Masters thought, because he hasn't got a wife and kids waiting at home. But today was the wrong day to have the kids out. He had enough problems.

"Out of the question, honey," Masters said, already feeling guiltier. "This just is not the right time. It's crowded and it's going to get more crowded and it's incredibly hot. Alan'll cry his head off." His youngest son was only five.

". . . . and Alan slept late," his wife was saying.

Masters found it impossible to listen. "He'll be fine. I think you've got—"

The other phone came alive.

"Mr. Masters, that oil shipment is—"

"Just a minute, Dexter." Ken set the console phone down, hesitating a moment. Forbidding Sarah to come was bound to start a fight. Damnit, he had no choice.

"Honey, take the kids to the club. It's madness here today and I don't have the time. *Period*. I can't swing it."

"Kenny, *I* have to see you. There's something I have to talk to you about."

"Christ, what is it?"

"I don't want to talk about it over the phone, Kenny. I've got to see you."

"What the hell are . . ." He was losing control. He stopped, lit a cigarette. The morning had barely begun and his wife was on the phone and Pete Toscani needed his damn oil and someone he didn't know named Dexter was waiting to tell him about the oil and probably listening to him swear at his wife and he was weary. He had been awake since four o'clock that morning and he felt a pain in the back of his neck, a headache coming on, his muscles pounding with tension. Somehow this was not turning out as he imagined it, but exactly what he'd imagined he couldn't be sure. Constable shifted his weight in the chair, and Masters thought he was straining to listen.

"All right," he said to Sarah. "Bring them out. We'll have lunch, then I can go back to work. Call me from the gate when you get here. It'd better be important, and in the meantime I've got another call. Bye, honey."

Constable looked over his shoulder. "Trouble with the little woman?"

"Stuff it, Jock," Masters said, and returned to the problem of the missing oil. "Well, Dexter, what's the good word?"

"Well, we haven't . . . I mean it's just that . . ."

"Come on, man," Masters said. "Spit it out."

"Sir, the supplier didn't ship because we haven't paid some old bills. I told the accounting department to send a

28

check, but Fortner just got it yesterday. We'll have the oil by one o'clock. It's coming into LaGuardia on TWA. The plane's scheduled to land at noon."

"Thanks, Dexter. Call me as soon as it comes in. Masters, station one, out."

Hadn't paid their bills! So that's how bad it was. Now Masters understood, for the first time, why Hawkins was so agitated. Now he could fathom why Hawkins was in New York this morning and not at the park on opening day. He suppressed a wave of nausea. Behind his eyes, the headache was coming on again. Tension.

He signaled for Toscani.

"Yeah, Toscani here," the engineer said gruffly. He was still angry.

"Pete, this is Ken. You'll have that oil by one o'clock." He paused, thinking he should tell Toscani why the oil had been delayed. No point, he decided. Only make him angrier. "The shipment got misrouted somewhere between Chicago and New York. They're sending it by air."

"Is that right?" Toscani's voice betrayed his disbelief. "What do you take me for, son? Was I born yesterday or what? We probably didn't pay the friggin' bill and the bastards wouldn't ship. I know how Cole Cunningham operates. Pay 'em when they threaten to sue and not a day sooner. I've been here awhile, remember?"

"Okay, Pete. You made your point. Sorry."

"That's okay, kid. But play it straight with me from here on out. That's the way Hawkins wants it." Toscani waited to let the message sink in. "Anyway, I've changed my mind. If that engine gets much hotter, I *am* going to shut it down. You can send word to the kids that Zeus had a bad night and is taking the day off."

"Whatever you say, Pete. I leave it to you." He signed off, glad to leave the mess in Pete's hands. It was hard to tell who Toscani meant by kids, though: the children waiting in line or the students who ran the rides. High school juniors and seniors were cheap labor, but Hawkins thought the park should spend more money and get full-time, responsible operators. *Responsible,* Cole Cunningham had bellowed. *You mean drunks and dope addicts and anybody else who wants seasonal work. I'll take those kids any day.* Perhaps Cunningham was right. Disneyland had full-time mechanics on most rides, but Olympic Adventure ran only a five-month season. Seasonal mechanics were either too expensive or simply not available. At first, even Ken had thought the number of permanent employees ridiculously small. But he discovered that the summer help, hired before the season started, suffered rigorous training programs. For three weeks, he and Toscani had marched them through the park, drilling and questioning them constantly on the location of every restroom, every restaurant and its menu, each ride and its entrance, the time and content of the performances in the three Arena shows. The students were expected to memorize the details of the park's grounds so well that they could walk through them blindfolded, pointing out sights along the way. And they were taught to smile. Smile always. Smile everywhere. Smile at everyone. Make people feel happy. Let them know you care. Answer every question politely and get the right answer if you don't know it. Treat the customers as if they were guests in your home. For three weeks the rules were repeated daily, and by the time Memorial Day came it was as if they were surgically implanted in each guide's brain. Breaking the rules led to a simple, strict penalty: immediate dismissal. And that was a rarity.

Masters himself had instructed the park's private police force, mostly industrial security guards who worked seasonally anyway, or who had retired from other jobs on full pensions. Of all the staff, Ken thought, the police were most important. Nothing gave people more confidence, made parents feel more secure with their children, than the sight of ever-present, blank-faced policemen, their green uniforms blending in with the background.

Ken's hand was lying in direct sunlight on the counter, and with a start he realized how hot it was. Even though the air-conditioning churned harder, the small booth did not get cold. The sun had moved to the top of an azure sky, casting long waves of heat on Olympic Adventure.

The morning was slipping away and Ken had yet to start his rounds. He called the gate and left word that he should be summoned when Sarah and the children arrived, reminding the guard that under no circumstances were the children to be given special treatment. Most important, they were not to be taken into the ice-cream-cone tower. It would destroy their illusions. They might as well have their illusions, Ken thought, as long as possible. That's what childhood meant. And if Ken sometimes regretted growing up, occasionally thinking of himself as a child, his responsibilities sent another message. No, he thought, my illusions faded years ago.

He considered calling Hampshire Industries' corporate headquarters to look for Hawkins. But then Hawkins would only want to know why Ken couldn't take care of the park himself. He could hear the rough Southwestern patter, Hawkins's thick voice alternating between clipped precision and folksy drawl. Hawkins was tall, big-boned, broad-shouldered, and Masters knew why he admired him. When Hawkins walked through Olympic Adventure, every member of the staff nodded in recognition and smiled—and it was more than good training. The circus clowns dancing among the children, passing out flowers; the blue-smocked girls sweeping the sidewalks; the guards and concessionaires—everybody knew Hawkins was in charge, in control. How Masters envied that respect; he wanted the respectful nods, the smiles.

"Wife and kiddies coming out?" Jock Constable said.

"Yeah, Jock. What's it to you?"

"Nothing. I just figured you'd be too busy today to find time for the family. That's terrific. A real hard worker and a family man, too."

"You bet, Jock. I'm your basic All-American type. I help old ladies cross the street, too."

"Give this boy a merit badge," Constable said.

Masters understood how a man might overcome the forces of civilization and revert to an animal of pure instinct. With very little effort, he thought, he could have lifted Jock Constable out of his chair and pushed his paunchy body through one of the narrow tower windows without stopping to think. The console phone buzzed again.

"Masters, station one."

"Kenny, I'm glad I caught you." It was Sheila Richardson, head of the park's guest-relations office. A dark, attractive girl who turned heads and generated whistles, she had one of the most important jobs in the park. Masters had always wanted to know whether it had more to do with her good looks or her efficiency. Some front office types gossiped that she was having an affair with Hawkins. That, Masters was certain, had to be a rumor with more jealousy behind it than truth.

"What's the problem?" Masters asked.

"Have you heard from Brad?"

"Not a word."

"I've finished the visitors' schedule for today and I want to make sure Brad's available to meet the governor. He's arriving by helicopter with his staff around two. And he'll have plenty of reporters with him. Brad should be there."

"I don't know when to expect him, Sheila. But if you told him two o'clock, I'm sure he'll make it."

"That's just it. I didn't tell him because I didn't know. Now what do I do? What do I tell the governor's office?"

Masters chewed his calloused knuckles, an old habit he tried breaking from time to time. "Tell them to leave it set for two o'clock. If Brad isn't here, I'll handle the governor."

"You know we've also got a group of diplomats' kids coming from the United Nations school and they'll have some local television crews. Do you want to lead any tours?"

"No way, Sheila. Can you handle them?"

"Sure. But I thought you might need an excuse to take a break."

"I wish I could. But I've still got rounds to make this morning. Later in the week, maybe."

"Fine. Ask Brad to call me, will you, as soon as he gets in."

She signed off and Ken prepared to survey the park on foot. It could take anywhere from an hour to two hours, depending on who needed help and whether or not he could give it. Masters covered only the main arcades and the largest rides, along with the Olympic Safari; his department supervisors did the rest. He lit a cigarette and riffled through the papers on the console table, looking for his logbook. Already behind schedule, he decided to skip the safari. For one thing, he had little affection for Alfred Windsor—the Commodore, as he preferred to be called. Nor was he much enamored of the Commodore's assistant, Chuck Graham. The British director of Olympic Adventure's game preserve and his Scottish assistant were condescending and arrogant. They seemed to be staring down their noses at you, Masters thought, even when they were sitting. Masters didn't doubt for a second that they were indispensable. The Commodore had personally supervised the gathering of the African animals and the building of the safari preserve, just as he had for the major wild-animal parks in Europe. But that didn't mean Masters had to like him. And he didn't.

He grabbed his walkie-talkie from its recharger and dropped it into a holster hanging from his belt, then checked his logs and the television screens one last time.

"I'll ride down with you," Constable said, rising and rolling the chair back to the computer console. They descended to the ground without exchanging a word. Ken stepped out into the park first, sucking in a deep breath. The warm air filled his lungs and instantly he felt calmer.

"Have fun," Constable said, ambling down the main arcade. Good riddance, Masters thought. From the entrance to the park, at the top of the arcade, down to the ferris wheel and souvenir shops, the sidewalks were so crowded it was difficult to move. Masters watched as Constable made his way past the Olympic Bazaar toward the Land of Monuments, and decided he would have to control his attitude toward the man. It was not so much anger

33

that he felt. Jock's childish hostility was so blatant and so misplaced that Masters actually pitied him. If I didn't pity him, Masters thought, I'd hate him.

Resolutely he headed across the arcade, mentally attempting to prepare himself for a long, difficult day. The more he thought about it, the more he realized that if he was angry at all, it was at Sarah for forcing him to let her come and at Hawkins for not speeding up his meeting. When he reached the bottom of the steps and stepped onto the tiled plaza, a college student Masters had hired as a clown rolled toward him on skates and slowed to a halt. Ken did not recognize the face under the bright yellow makeup.

"Howdy, Mr. Masters. Having a good time?" Now Ken recognized him. Johnson. Tim Johnson, a drama student at Cornell.

"Not bad, Tim. How's it going down here?"

"Mighty fine, sir. Got a big crowd and they're loving every minute of it."

"Have you been down to the Chariots, Tim?" That oil was still on his mind, much as he tried to forget it.

"Yes, sir. All the clowns were down there about half an hour ago. They had long lines and lots of kids were crying, so we went down and did a little juggling. Cheered them right up." Johnson turned abruptly at the sound of a screaming mother and her crying daughter. "I see a kid over there who needs some help," and with that the affable young man skated down the ramp to the little girl, who was crying and choking. He pulled a flower from behind his ear and put it into the child's balled fists, then played "Yankee Doodle Dandy" on his kazoo. The child's face lit up and the grateful mother smiled.

Long lines at the Chariot. Masters worried again about the wisdom of letting the ride continue to operate. Damnit, Pete's in charge. That ought to be good enough.

Despite the crowds, the arcade sidewalk remained virtually spotless. Not a cigarette butt or candy wrapper marred the view. Keep the park clean, the psychology went, and the hordes will do the same. And the psychology worked. People who might have stubbed their cigarettes out on railings or on the ground instead walked to sand-filled canisters placed every few feet on the grass islands lining the walkway. The lawns and the forest, elaborately landscaped and assiduously maintained, were equally pristine. Disney's reputation for cleanliness set the standards, Masters thought, but Hawkins's troops topped them. In fact, Masters wondered if they shouldn't stage a publicity stunt in which a six-course dinner was served on the ground. Good for pictures in the suburban papers. Well, perhaps not, but it was worth thinking about.

Masters eased through the gates to the shops in the Olympic Bazaar, noting the arrangement of the merchandise and the location of the clerks. Shoplifting wasn't common, but losses the previous season had been abnormally high. Hawkins had hired more clerks for just that reason. When Masters entered the Crossroads of the Mediterranean, he saw a young, long-haired man in the far corner of the store, shuffling toys on a counter top. He doesn't look like the type to be buying, Masters thought, not sure of why he felt that way. A sixth sense. Something in the man's manner, something distracted. Ken motioned to the supervisor with thumbs up, a sign to watch for shoplifters, and the manager immediately moved to the rear of the store.

The man at first took no notice that he was being watched.

"Can I help you?" the manager asked him.

"No thanks," the man said. Then he seemed to become aware of Masters at the end of the aisle. He set down a stuffed animal and walked past Masters out of the store.

"Strange character," Masters said to the manager. "Call B-eighteen and C-twelve and warn them to be on the lookout. They ought to be on their toes anyway with a crowd this size."

The manager picked up the phone and Ken left the shop, heading for the calliope. Even Ken, who had passed the ride hundreds of times, who had once ridden the glittering, bejeweled horse that stood out from all the others, was struck by its garishness. Thousands of four-inch-square mirrors covered the canopy of the revolving platform, reflecting sunlight during the day and colored lights from the roof at night. Each horse was hand-painted; no two were alike; polished brass stirrups gleamed at their sides. The carousel had come from Austria, where in the 1820s it had been handmade by a team of artisans on the instructions of a mad baron for his six children. Gabriel Bloome had discovered it in storage in a Vienna warehouse ten years before. After finding the bank that controlled what little was left of the baron's fortune, Bloome bid on the machine. One day it would be useful, Bloome had thought, for even then his vast fantasy was taking shape. Masters marveled at the eccentricity that would lead a man to buy a carousel before he had a place to put it. But then again, if you had Bloome's money, maybe eccentricities always turned a profit. And then Ken remembered: Olympic Adventure had yet to turn a profit.

The sun broke through the remaining clouds. Ken looked up and saw the Sky Chariot across the park. Still running. So Toscani had not shut it down after all. Ken passed the Temple of Heavenly Delights and the strong odor of frying potatoes and hot dogs wafted by him. As he circled the Fountain of the Gods—a foamy spurt of green water soaring more than a hundred feet into the air—small chunks of bread floated past along the fountain's porcelain rim.

"This is roving station one to operations."

"Operations, L-fifteen. Zimmer," came the reply.

"Zimmer, Masters here. Would you send somebody over to the fountain with a net? There's crap floating in it. And make it fast, okay?"

"Yes, sir. On the way."

Well, you couldn't stop kids from throwing bread. Or maybe it wasn't kids. Olympic Adventure attracted a goodly number of college students—the long-haired variety which, as far as Masters was concerned, spoiled the view. But paying customers were paying customers. At least Hawkins had been smart enough to veto popcorn at the concessions. Too easy to throw around, he said. Let them eat cake.

Stopping at the ferris wheel, Ken strode to the entrance and asked for the inspection records. The clean-cut young girl running the engine smiled smartly, looked at his badge, and slid the clipboard out of the case hanging on the control box. Doors and bolts on every carriage had been checked the day before. Toscani's bold signature showed that he'd personally inspected the engine that morning. Turning toward the Bobsled, the park's longest and most hair-raising roller coaster, Ken noticed that two hedges were badly torn; he marked his log so that they would be replaced. Then, finally, he headed for Mt. Olympus, to see what Toscani had done with the long lines. Crossing one of the six bandshells—a Latin group was scheduled to play in an hour, according to his log—he saw Toscani approaching. The man had a long, confident stride; his shoulders were thrust back as he walked.

"Kenny, my boy," Toscani shouted. "Just the man I want to see. Heard from Hawkins yet?"

"Not a word, Pete. He must have gotten held up in the city."

"Yeah, held up. And mugged. And beaten, probably." Toscani lived in Princeton, a New Jersey suburb. Having grown up in New York's Little Italy, he'd always longed to live far away from the city. Anyone who lived there was, to Toscani, a candidate for the nearest mental hospital. Why Hawkins insisted on living in New York—his Fifth Avenue duplex notwithstanding—was a mystery to Toscani. The filth. The crime. The traffic. Who needed it?

"You're probably right, Pete. Any minute they'll fish him out of the East River. What's up at the Chariot?"

"I told Davey Thompson to keep an eye on the engines. At the slightest knock, he'll shut them down."

"Thompson? Who's he?"

"One of the few bright kids they saddled me with this year. Christ, what I wouldn't give for six top-notch mechanics." Toscani scowled.

"You trust Thompson?"

"I guess," Toscani said. "Sure I trust him. I ain't got a helluva lot of choice right now. There's a busted wheel at the flume and I've got to get over there and fix it before there's a riot. How the hell many people do we have here, anyway?"

"Must be over eighty thousand by now."

Toscani whistled.

"About the Chariot, Pete. It's all right, you think?"

"Thompson will do okay. Don't sweat it."

"If you say so," Masters answered. "I'm going over to the Western Arena show. Keep me posted on those engines."

"Yeah, and keep *me* posted on Hawkins. I want to give him a piece of my mind."

You'll never do it, Masters thought. Hawkins wouldn't listen. Idly he wondered how people like Hawkins were made. Why were some men leaders and others followers? It was true that Ken Masters was ten years younger than Hawkins, but Masters suspected that Brad Hawkins had always been successful, that the breaks had come easily for him. He knew nothing of the man's past, but it seemed obvious: Southern oil money, prep schools, connections. Like most people from middle-class backgrounds, Masters assumed that rich, successful young men *must* have been connected—well-wired, they called it—to have done so well. Hawkins never talked about his life, and Masters had heard that somewhere in the dim past was a bad marriage, the only blot on an otherwise impeccable existence.

The buzzer sounded on his walkie-talkie. "Station one, roving."

It was Sheila Richardson. "Sarah and the kids are here."

"Tell her I can't see them now. I've got to check the Western Arena. I'll meet her at Heavenly Delights in about twenty minutes. Call over there, will you, and have them hold the back table for us."

"Ken, you know Brad wouldn't like that."

"That's tough," Masters said. "Just reserve the table, will you?"

"Sure, Ken, if you say so. Richardson, A-seventeen, out."

To hell with the goddamn rules. Democracy. He'd be damned if he and his wife were going to stand in line for a table. It was bad enough that Sarah and the kids sometimes seemed like millstones around his neck, responsibilities to be met instead of people he loved. Today, especially, he felt that way.

The sign for the Western Arena needed a daub of paint. He marked his log and heard the announcer for the cowboy show begin warming up the audience. "Folks, you are about to witness one of the most spec-*tac*-ular rodeos in the world . . ." Indeed, it was a superb production. Hawkins and Masters had debated why the cowboy extravaganza was such a success. Of all the entertainment arenas, none drew crowds as large as the Western Arena. It was described more glowingly than the others in newspaper stories. Invariably all seats were occupied at showtime. Maybe cowboys represented, as historians often explained, a lost American frontier, a yearning to go back to the simpler, clearer days when a man knew what was right and what was wrong, when survival dictated behavior. But what, Ken wondered, could the frontier mean to anyone in New Jersey in the twentieth century? Could the customers who trekked out from the urban wasteland identify with a technicolor, staged vision of life two hundred years ago?

Standing at the entrance to the rodeo bleachers, he felt the ground shake as pounding hooves galloped into the arena. Astride a white stallion, Dan Reynolds, star of the television series "Bronco," threw his rope into the air and executed basic lariat tricks for a spellbound audience. Television stars from westerns packed the crowds in at Olympic Adventure, even though some of them approached public performances terror-stricken. Most rode horses about as well as they acted—which was to say not well at all. People wanted to believe in their heroes, though, and the stars earned extraordinary amounts of money for short appearances. Ken had met Reynolds two weeks earlier, when the deal to have him in the Western Arena on opening day was closed. For ten appearances, the star's total fee, before expenses, came in at just under fifteen thousand dollars. What most surprised Ken was that Reynolds, in person, seemed a rather obvious homosexual. He traveled with another television star with whom, rumor had it, he was intimately involved. Both men, with Reynolds's agent in tow, had appeared for the contract signing, touching each other frequently, exchanging exaggerated glances and flourishes. On stage and on television, Reynolds was the epitome of a he-man, a cowboy. Of course, Ken knew Hollywood was no stranger to such alliances, but confronted with the reality of Dan Reynolds and at the same time his public image, Ken couldn't help staring. Twice Hawkins had jabbed him in the ribs. Masters wondered if any of the hero's fans suspected. Not likely, he thought. They needed to believe.

Satisfied that all was running smoothly, Ken turned sharply on his heel and crossed the lawn to the Temple of Heavenly Delights. From across the midway, he could see Tommy and Alan and Sarah through the glass panels separating the fiberglass cream puffs covering the building's pillars. The design was Gabriel Bloome's, planned to the most minuscule detail, and Bloome hadn't used architects. Without telling Bloome, Cole Cunningham had hired an architectural firm nonetheless, just to make sure the building wouldn't collapse.

Sarah jumped as Ken pushed through the doors and ran to hug him. His youngest son, Alan, stood on a chair, tugging at his tie.

"You see what I mean, Ken?" Sarah said.

"What? What did you say?" Masters was distracted by boisterous hippies at the counter. He wanted to throw them out with his bare hands.

"Look at how they jump all over you," his wife said. "They really miss you."

"They're just playing," he told her, and walked to the counter and ordered a hamburger. Maybe they did miss him, but she didn't have to paint this picture of him neglecting his own children. How did she expect to live the way they did without him working hard? Did she want him to be a neighborhood cop, like his father, home every day at six? All right, he had been working too hard, but he had no choice.

"The kids want to ride the Sky Chariot," Sarah said when he returned. "Can you make time to go with them?"

Uncomfortably he remembered the shortage of mechanics and the problem with the Chariot engines. "I really don't have time, honey, and I wish you wouldn't take them on it, anyway. There's some problems with the engines and I'd feel better if you stayed away from it. Take them on the big wheel."

"Don't be silly, Ken. Pete wouldn't let anything happen to the Chariot." She was probably right. Toscani would close the ride before there was any danger. He was debating whether to take the children himself when the buzzer on his walkie-talkie sounded, attracting the attention of those around him. He turned the volume low before answering and used the small earphone.

"Masters, station one roving."

"A-seventeen. Richardson. Ken, there's a woman having a heart attack or something on the Bobsled. I sent a stretcher and Doc Gordon's on his way. I thought you might want to check it yourself."

"Right, will do, Sheila. Thanks." For Christ's sake, couldn't these idiots read signs? All of the thrill rides were prominently marked with luminescent red warnings. THIS RIDE IS NOT RECOMMENDED FOR ELDERLY GUESTS, GUESTS WITH HEART CONDITIONS, OR EXPECTANT MOTHERS. NO CHILDREN UNDER 48 INCHES ARE ALLOWED ON THIS RIDE. But as Hawkins repeatedly pointed out, inevitably someone ignored the instructions. It happened at all the parks, and attendants were reluctant to refuse admission to anyone.

"Sorry, honey," he said to Sarah. "Got to run. Some biddy is having a heart attack."

"Good Lord," she said quietly. "We'll see you later." He heard the disappointment in her voice. He leaned down, hugged the two boys, kissed Sarah on the forehead, and strode quietly into the crowd.

He met Doc Gordon crossing the park from the main gate. Gordon looked like everyone's image of the family doctor—graying at the temples, faint lines around his deep blue eyes, an unmanageable cowlick, and a gait that bespoke an amiable bedside manner; you didn't have to see Gordon's black bag to know his profession.

"Do you believe?" Gordon asked. "Do you believe some fool took his sixty-two-year-old mother on that thing? This joker has to be one of the major jackasses in the Western hemisphere."

"You don't seem real worried, Doc," Masters said as Gordon quickened his pace.

"She's my age. At your age, I'd be worried. Old people have better odds of living through a heart attack, and besides, we don't even know what's wrong with her yet. She may just have fainted from the excitement. And if it is a heart attack, odds are she'll make it."

"How can you be so sure?" Ken asked, finding himself taking longer and longer strides to keep up with Gordon.

"I'm not, but the body doesn't administer as strong a kick when you get to be as old as I am. A weak heart, an old heart, does less damage to itself. Look, I've already survived one and if I keep up at this pace I'll probably have another."

"You?" Ken asked in surprise. "You had a heart attack?" Gordon was so healthy looking, so robust, it was hard to imagine he'd ever had a common cold.

"You bet. Type-A all the way. Just like you and Hawkins. I had mine three years ago. Laid me up for a couple of months. My doctor told me if I didn't quit smoking and quit working so hard I'd have another. Well, I quit my practice and I kept smoking. Now all I do is run after crazy old ladies who go to amusement parks and ride roller coasters." He chuckled. "Beats making hospital rounds, that's for sure."

By the time they arrived, the woman was breathing normally, but her face was ashen. Doc Gordon checked the oxygen tanks, listened to her heartbeat, and took her pulse.

"She'll live," he said. "Might be a coronary infarction and might not be. Let's get her out of here." He beckoned to the men standing around the stretcher. "Cardinal Hospital's expecting her. There's an ambulance at the front gate."

They walked slowly, Doc Gordon regulating the oxygen supply. Masters steered the men to the edge of the Aqua Arena, out of sight of the crowd. The old woman's son, his wife, and their three children followed. Suddenly the man ran up alongside Ken and began shouting.

"I'm going to sue you bastards," the man screamed, shaking a finger at Ken's face. "She might die."

Masters felt helpless and angry. What the hell did this idiot expect him to do? Not only could this fool kill his own mother, but he could hurt the park's reputation at the same time. Masters found it difficult to feel sorry for the old woman, so furious was he at the man's outburst.

"Did you see the sign? Did you see the warning?" Ken asked quietly, restraining his temper. "What did you have in mind when you put her on that ride in the first place? Didn't want to stay with your kids, is that it? So you sent her along while you went for coffee? Is that it?"

Masters' barb struck home, and the man's face reddened. "Don't give me any lip, buster. That damn thing was moving too fast. I'll sue you bastards for everything you're worth."

Arguing with this idiot would get him nowhere. "You do that," he said. "We'll see you in court." Then he walked away. Stupidity was common enough. He dealt with it every day. But he was weary. Dreamily he envisioned a tall glass of boubron—Hawkins's drink. He was still seething at Hawkins's absence, at Sarah for bringing the children. And at this old biddy for having a heart attack in *his* park. Oddly enough, he suddenly felt proprietary about Olympic Adventure.

The grove of oaks bordering the Bobsled railing blew full in the wind, seeming to beckon him. His hair fell into his eyes and languidly he brushed it away. He lit a cigarette, inhaled deeply, realized he was chain smoking. In two hours, he'd gone through almost a pack. Slumping against a tree, he slid down and rested his head on his knees. More than ever, he appreciated Gabriel Bloome's determination to leave as many trees standing as possible. His walkie-talkie buzzer brought him back to reality.

"Damn," he said aloud. "No peace."

"Me again, Ken." Sheila Richardson's voice quavered, frantic. "You better get over to the Chariot. Pete's not there and I can't raise him on the radio. They've got real trouble."

"Pete's at the flume," Masters said. "Probably has his radio off. Use the house phone. What's with the Chariot?"

"I don't know, but I can see from the tower it's stopped running."

"I'm on my way." He slapped the radio into its holster and for a short moment leaned his head against the tree. Peering across the plaza, he saw long lines at the Chariot, drifting out into the arcade. He searched the crowd for Sarah, trying to make out her bright blond hair at the rear of the line. She was not there. He broke into a sprint toward the base of the concrete mountain. Sweat poured down his neck. His pulse raced. On his left, hundreds of schoolchildren blocked the way, yelping and laughing as they waited for their turn on the Bobsled. The cars at the top rounded a right-angle turn and clattered straight down. The faces blended to a blur, the voices into a screeching roar. His temples pounded. Blood surged in his legs. Goddamn stupid, Masters cursed himself. Should have shut the damn thing down the minute there was trouble. Should have told Toscani no risks. Should. Should. Where the hell was Hawkins? Should have let them riot, damnit. Damn Cole Cunningham. Damn Hawkins. No chances. No risks.

But it was too late.

3

Dreaming is like breathing, Gabriel Bloome thought while he waited for his wife to join him on the sun porch for breakfast. Involuntary. The difference lay in utility. Breathing kept you alive. Dreaming made breathing worthwhile. The rest of the syllogism, the deduction, flitted through his mind, and then he lost it. The yellow chintz wallpaper flashed at him like a flickering lamp, reflecting the sunlight.

On the first floor of the duplex apartment he heard workmen: furniture dragging across the floor, hammering, a waxing machine. He buttered a roll and mused on the summer party season. The year before, New York had been barren by Memorial Day. This year, for reasons Bloome neither understood nor cared about, society people were staying in town. Just as well, Bloome thought, for he would have remained no matter what the current fashion. Once Olympic Adventure opened, Gabriel Bloome did not leave New York. No social event, no importuning, could pry him away from his favorite toy.

Not that he was needed. The park ran itself. Or rather, Hawkins ran the park, which suited Gabriel Bloome. He had, in fact, been pleased when Cole Cunningham hired Hawkins. What a triumph to lure the man from Disney's camp! Hawkins understood Olympic Adventure. He understood Gabriel Bloome's dreams. The price for Hawkins had been high, but so what? Anyone who had trained with Walt Disney was good enough for him. Helluva guy, Disney. And a helluva funeral, Gabriel Bloome recalled.

No, it wasn't that the park needed him so much as he needed the park. Despite his partners' dominance, he secretly considered Olympic Adventure his own. He designed it. He created it. He *dreamed* it.

Bloome watched a gangly, bearded old man in a wheelchair on the street being pushed toward Central Park by a paunchy woman with short red hair, a color of red, Bloome thought, so distinctly not a creation of nature it must have come from a bottle. The old man bore a disconcerting resemblance to Lionel Barrymore. Gabriel Bloome was fourteen when Lionel Barrymore died, and he remembered his father crying at the news. The woman below steered the wheelchair past a cluster of privet hedges onto the path heading toward the Sheep Meadow, and instantly Bloome was transported, in his mind's eye, down to the ground, pacing Frederick Law Olmsted's miraculous island in the city. *If only,* he thought, which was how he thought a good deal of the time. If only the Board of Estimate would allow construction of a small amusement arcade in Central Park. If only Abe Beame could be convinced to get behind the idea. Rapidograph fine-point in hand, Bloome drew on the lime green tablecloth—a conical silver spire with steel rods flaring down from the point, strung with banners and marquee bulbs. Easy to assemble and disassemble. Then, around the circle, tulip gardens. Crystal globes laid like a rock path, lit from underneath. A hopeless prospect, Bloome knew. Any attempt to encroach on Central Park spawned dozens of citizens' groups, angry crazies with picket signs and petitions. He remembered what happened to Robert Moses, the great builder, another brilliant dreamer, when Moses announced the most insignificant extension of a parking lot. The crazies were out in droves then. And that was the beginning of the end for Robert Moses. Better forget about Central Park. It was, for New Yorkers, the equivalent of the Mormons' church in Salt Lake City. A sacred shrine.

Bloome put his pen down and returned to his grapefruit. His daughter Stephanie charged into the room and plopped herself next to her father. She was six years old and looked nothing at all like Gabriel Bloome. With precociously pouting lips like her mother's and straight auburn hair, Stephanie seemed already to have learned the devil-may-care affectation of the debutante she would someday be. Bloome considered the possibility of her becoming an actress, in the family tradition. Bloome's mother, Regina, had been an actress before marrying his father. Stephanie had a little of Bardot around the eyes, he thought.

"Daddy, can I ask you a question?"

"Any time, tot," Bloome said.

"Why doesn't Aunt Alexis have a little girl like you and mommy have me?"

Oh no, Bloome thought. Not time yet for the birds and the bees. Such lessons were not in his realm. That was Pinky's job.

"Well, tot, it's like this. Pinky and I, rather your mother and I—" Bloome had problems thinking of his wife as a mother or himself as a father "—we decided we wanted a little girl and so we had you. Now Uncle Cole and Aunt Alexis haven't decided yet. See? They're too busy right now."

"But daddy, they've been . . . um . . ." She bit her lip.

"What is it, tot?"

"I can't remember the word." She thought a moment longer. "Married," she exclaimed. "They've been married . . . um . . . aren't they like you and mommy?" Hardly, Gabriel Bloome thought.

"Yes, tot, they are, but, you see, they have too many other things to do."

"But you and mommy are busy. Mommy is always busy. She says she's busy every day."

"Tot, do me a favor."

"Yes, daddy."

"Eat your grapefruit before it gets warm."

The child lowered her eyes. Another topic on which she had failed to elicit any information from her father.

Pinky Bloome, carrying a clipboard, entered and sat next to her husband. Her hair was tied into a bun and piled on top of her head, held in place by several green rubberbands. Her husband thought the makeup she was wearing accentuated, instead of diminished, the dark beauty mark on her left cheek. For neurotic reasons that Bloome no longer tried to explore, his wife tried to cover the beauty mark.

Pinky Bloome sat with a sense of occasion, the occasion being a party she was throwing that evening, and she prepared herself for such events by thinking about them the moment she awoke.

"Gabe, who's Peter Welch?"

"A banker in St. Louis. Why?"

"Cole just called. He wants you to come over to the office right away. Something about a telephone call from Welch. There's a board meeting at ten o'clock."

"A board meeting? On a Saturday morning? On opening day? Today? What?"

"A board meeting," Pinky Bloome said. "This morning."

"Did he say why?" Bloome asked his wife. He slurped a section of grapefruit and the juice dripped onto his satin robe and soaked through to his bare knee.

"He didn't say, not exactly. But he sounded worried, and he was rude, as usual."

"What did Welch want?"

"I said I don't know," Pinky said, pretending nonchalance. She was actually quite worried. "How can I think of anything when I've got a crew of carpenters downstairs? Stephanie, use a spoon. You don't eat grapefruit with a fork."

"Yes, mommy."

"Jesus Christ," Bloome said. "And on a Saturday morning, no less."

"Cole said right away, Gabe. He wants you there now. He was fairly huffy about it."

Bloome gulped one more chunk of grapefruit, kissed his daughter on the nose and his wife on the cheek, then walked down the hallway to the bedroom.

Pinky Bloome was disturbed. Throughout the spring, she'd had the terrible sensation, a premonition, that Cole Cunningham was losing touch. Losing touch with the business, losing touch with the world in general. As far as

48

Pinky could tell, Cole and Alexis were finished. She was betting privately with herself that Alexis would leave him before fall. If Alexis left, Cole would crumble. She felt particularly awful because she had introduced Cole and Alexis when she and Alexis were at Wellesley together. Pride in matchmaking flawed her otherwise sensible attitude toward human relationships, and in the case of Alexis and Cole, there was a special stake. Not only had she introduced them to each other, but it had been her idea for Cole to build Olympic Adventure. That was one match she strenuously regretted. Over the nearly fifteen years they had known each other, her affection for Cole had diminished to the point of nonexistence. As a young man, his brashness had charmed her; now that he was middle-aged, it offended her. His seamless self-confidence looked more and more like sick self-deception to her. She preferred her husband's honest fantasies to Cole Cunningham's dishonest reality. Equally disturbing was the possibility that Olympic Adventure might slip from Cole's hands, for he held the corporate reins. Dreading to think what would happen to Gabriel if Olympic Adventure sank in a morass of Cole's financial ineptitude, she had cautiously discussed the situation with Gabriel's mother. Regina was adamant. She was not digging into the Bloome fortune to bail out Gabriel's toy. Money to live on, yes. Money for schemes, no. Absolutely no.

Gabriel Bloome was less disturbed, although he, too, was beginning to wonder. A board meeting? On a Saturday? But he brushed aside his concerns as he searched for a pair of brown shoes. The valet had put out black loafers, and Gabriel Bloome did not wear black loafers with tan slacks. No, he thought, let Cole take care of the numbers. If I worry about that nonsense, I'll worry myself into my grave.

The numbers. Bloome had once actually hoped to understand numbers, balance sheets, loan agreements. He had even gone so far as to ask Cole Cunningham for lessons. By the time they had struggled past the concept of mortgages and plunged on toward subordinated debentures, Bloome was hopelessly lost and mentally crippled. His head would not function. Debentures left him cold. He read the *Wall Street Journal* and *Barron's* for six months, comprehended practically nothing at all, then switched to *Business Week, Dun's Review,* and *Institutional Investor.* A paralytic enterprise. On reflection, he considered himself lucky to have had Cole as a friend.

Pinky's suggestion that Cole build Olympic Adventure, along with the fortuitous appearance of the Duke of Hampshire and his money, had seemed a bit of destiny. Cole had bubbled about "packaging the deal," as he called it. Bloome had never thought of Olympic Adventure as a "deal" or a "package." But if Cole wanted to call it one, that was fine with Gabriel Bloome, as long as it was built. For what was finally most important to him was escaping the one label he most detested: Lyman Bloome's son.

For as long as Gabriel could remember, he had been introduced as Lyman Bloome's son. Working at the studio was part of the problem, but what else had he been suited for? To be the son of Lyman Bloome was at best a trial, the son of a man who remained after his death a legend as vital and palpable as the living man himself. Lyman Bloome had produced the most grandiose musicals Hollywood had ever seen. To the faithful celebrants of filmdom, Lyman Bloome was more than a director or producer— Lyman Bloome was the supreme creator, the man who virtually gave birth to the movie musical. No matter that he stole cinematic tricks from Eisenstein and Griffith. What are great artists for, Lyman Bloome used to say, if not to steal from? Lyman Bloome performed miracles. *Sunshine Melody, Trumpets in the Sky, Angela, A Night of Passion*—each more opulent and grand and glittery than the one before. And then he made *Wonderland,* which, released and released and released over and over again, would become the largest-grossing movie ever made. Year after year, it found a new audience, new members of the Bloome cult who would say his name softly in short breaths, new film students who chattered over his stunts with mirrors, this or that camera angle. Never had *Wonderland* been shown on television, but it was said in the film magazines and at the studios that somewhere on the planet, on any day of the year, in some movie theater at the remotest corners of the globe, you would find it playing. Of his acolytes, Lyman Bloome said on his deathbed, "Bunch of baloney. I was just making movies."

And if having Lyman Bloome for a father was difficult, having Regina Spence for a mother did not help. When she retired from the screen, thousands wept. Regina herself cared little for her fans; she found acting tedious work and was content to withdraw and help her husband plan his next project.

Gabriel Bloome remembered his father's funeral as if it had been held the day before. Ten years, a second, a film dissolve. His mother weeping on the arms of Fred Astaire. Darryl Zanuck, a cigar in one hand, a casket handle in the other. The Forest Lawn groundsmen standing silent, their eyes glazed by the procession of stars. Bette Davis, Joan Crawford, Debbie Reynolds, Ginger Rogers (tough old Ginger, he loved old Ginger), Tony Martin, Frank Sinatra, Mel Torme, Julius LaRosa. And Judy Garland, crying unabashedly, with Vincente Minelli. Gabriel remembered all the stars crying, and the singular fact that he himself had not shed a tear until later. Years later, as it turned out.

He searched through his closet and selected a powder blue double-breasted blazer, discarding the kelly green jacket his valet had chosen. Powder blue and off-white were his favorite colors. Try as he might, however, he could not address sartorial questions and keep Peter Welch's face out of his head. A slack-jawed countenance, marked by the sort of eyebrows one might imagine were tweezed had they appeared on a woman's face. Colorless eyes, gray, he thought, to match a colorless, toneless voice. Narrow lips, pursed liked a deacon's. And gray suits. Bloome remembered Jim Welch as essentially gray. What kind of man, he wondered, wore only gray suits? Then, again, the doubt. What could Welch be calling about on a Saturday? Did bankers even work on Saturday? Bloome didn't think so. Suddenly he remembered a telephone call from his accountant. Regina's accountant, actually. What was his name? Dandruff, something like Dandruff. Woodruff, Rand Woodruff. He'd needed some information, which Bloome couldn't fathom, to file his tax returns. They were already late, Woodruff said, and complained that Cole Cunningham was lax in supplying records from Olympic Adventure's corporate parent, Hampshire Industries. It was unexplainably strange, since if Cole was good at anything, he was good at the numbers.

Pinky Bloome stuck her head in the doorway. "The car is waiting, Gabe," she said, then swirled around and down the hallway.

Bloome straightened his tie and pulled his shirt cuffs out from his jacket sleeves. He walked downstairs purposefully. By the time he reached the elevator, he had nearly forgotten about Rand Woodruff and what it was that had bothered him about the numbers. Confusion over a man who wore only gray, however, remained. Only gray, he thought, as a clumsy workman in the hallway came perilously close to dropping a brass bust of Queen Nefertiti on his head.

Then the image of his father returned. Gabriel Bloome's problem with his dead father, as his psychotherapist had once repeated over and over for two entire sessions, was his refusal to let the old man die. True enough, Bloome allowed. The difficulty with parents, an unsolvable dilemma, he thought, is that no matter how old you get, and no matter how long they've been gone, they never die. They never die and we never grow up, forever their children. Had he not known that, Bloome often told himself, how would he function as a showman? If the art of making people have fun consisted of finding the child behind every adult's masquerade, then you had to be a child first, just to exploit the mask. The hell with psychiatrists, Bloome thought, and the hell with people who kept reminding him of who his father was. The hell with them all, he thought. He paused at the Cadillac's door, then stepped from the curb and looked west on Eighty-sixth Street. He took in the view across Manhattan to the Hudson River and the New Jersey shore beyond the island. Once the Palisades Amusement Park, one of the oldest and greatest, had occupied the opposite shore. Bloome had been taken there as a child on visits to New York from California—a regular stop following an afternoon at Radio City Music Hall to view one of his father's films. Now Bloome saw only high-rise apartment buildings, white columns egregiously out of place on the green bluffs flowing from the bank of the Hudson. Bloome pretended he was a comic-book hero, the one with long-distance vision—Superman, perhaps, or Batman or the Flash, he couldn't remember which—seeing Olympic Adventure seventy miles away. He watched the ferris wheel turn, listened for the music of the carousel, gazed at the crowds. Crowds. He hoped there were good crowds today.

He stepped into the limousine and collapsed into the rear seat. Bloome was always relaxed in automobiles, simultaneously in motion and at rest, a phenomenon that intrigued him. He used the paradox in designing thrill rides, and on that illusion rested the three patents he held for new rides designed for Olympic Adventure. Now they were being constructed at a foundry in central Pennsylvania, the location of which Bloome never clearly remembered. Flying there to watch the work was another illusion. Into the airplane, an indefinite time in the air, again motion without noticeable motion, and then down to the mill town. Flying in an airplane was not felt, he decided. It was all in your head.

The car turned onto Fifth Avenue, past the General Motors building and the Plaza Hotel. Years before, when Bloome's vision of Olympic Adventure had existed only in a packet of drawings, he had been in an office on the twenty-third floor of the GM Building, nervously holding his sketches, trying to raise money. A painful experience for Bloome, approaching his father's friends for money. They treated him courteously, even deferentially, but reacted coolly to his presentation. Gabriel Bloome was not a salesman. These same men had lounged in his father's home, kowtowed to his imperious mother, but they had scant use for a man with drawings. They wanted the numbers. Where would Olympic Adventure be built? How much would the land cost? Who would lend the development capital? Bloome returned their questions with a dumbfounded stare. *Numbers!* Numbers were their department. Ideas were his department. What did he know of numbers, and what did he care? He decided he would try to care.

On the same day, he told his chauffeur to drive south into New Jersey, and at the edge of the Pine Barrens he was suddenly alert. He stopped at a real-estate office and said he was searching for land to build a house. He was an unconvincing liar, and not quite aware of the reason he had lied. The real-estate agent, sensing this, played along, assuming that whatever this man in the limousine really wanted might someday rebound to his benefit. All Bloome wanted, of course, was a simple idea of what land actually cost. Never having bought any property in his life, he dutifully took notes as the agent spoke. Later, riding back to New York, he calculated the cost of three thousand acres based on the price he had been quoted for twenty acres. The result was, naturally, inaccurate, but Gabriel Bloome doggedly computed the costs. And then Pinky told Alexis and Alexis told Cole, and the Duke of Hampshire allowed how he and his friends hoped to sneak their money out of England before the socialists destroyed the country.

The car stopped at a light and Gabriel Bloome turned to look at the General Motors building over his shoulder. I showed them, he thought. I showed them I'm not just Lyman Bloome's son.

4

"One-thirty in the goddamn morning, Gabriel. Can you imagine?" Cole Cunningham was yelling. "Can you believe that? Peter Welch calls me at one-thirty in the morning. All right, twelve-thirty in St. Louis, but one-thirty here."

Cunningham sat at his desk on the thirtieth floor of Olympic Tower at the corner of Fifty-second Street and Fifth Avenue. A steward served him breakfast: buffalo shell steak, medium rare, lightly spiced with tarragon; three soft scrambled eggs so liquid they had to be served in a bowl; pan-fried potatoes *au gratin;* three cold asparagus spears; orange juice and coffee.

Cunningham was thirty-eight years old and looked at least five years younger. His dark black hair was thinning at the back, but every Monday morning he walked seven blocks up Fifth Avenue to Sassoon, where it was cut and styled to hide the balding. His wide violet eyes moved constantly, bouncing his graying eyebrows as he talked. Over ten years, he had spent six thousand three hundred dollars capping his teeth, and would have had a perfect mouth were it not for an overbite into which he could fit the tip of his index finger. The overbite gave him a charming smile, beaverlike, and he used that smile to great advantage. The way Cole Cunningham figured, the dental work had cost him a lot and he wanted it to show.

"Cole, what the hell—"

Putting a piece of steak in his mouth, Cunningham stretched out a broad, hairy hand to keep his partner, Gabriel Bloome, from talking. "Quiet, goddamnit. Let me chew the food and then I'll tell you." He stood, patted his lips with a linen napkin embroidered with the Hampshire Industries corporate logo—an *H* and an *I* in Old English type laid on top of each other so as to be almost unreadable—sipped his orange juice, and lit a cigarette. He turned to the window behind his desk and stared down at the spires of St. Patrick's Cathedral.

"You could almost touch them," he said. "You know, it's like I could step out the window and touch them."

"Touch what?"

"The spires," Cunningham said. "The spires of St. Pat's."

"Cole, what the hell did Welch want?" Bloome was a soft, fleshy man, shorter than his partner. His face was round and so smooth, like brushed cotton, that one suspected he never had to shave. His index and baby fingers were decorated with matching rings: on the left hand, emeralds in platinum; on the right, sapphires in silver. He gripped the edge of Cole Cunningham's desk, drumming his fingers nervously on the marble top. Looking at him, Cunningham thought that the older Bloome got, the more he looked like his father.

Cunningham dropped his napkin on the desk, then rang for the steward. The white-coated Haitian man appeared and loaded the breakfast dishes onto a tray. With a silver-handled brush and small glass dustpan, he brushed crumbs from the leather desk pad, then wheeled the tray out of the room.

Cunningham held the coffee cup to his lips and blew, rippling the surface. The coffee was Jamaican Blue Mountain, of which he had a private stock. His cigarettes were hand-rolled in Virginia. In his desk, he had a box of Havana cigars, Montecristos, brought by way of Caracas and London, personally selected for him by a Venezuelan businessman with friends in Castro's government for whom he had once performed an elegant, complicated favor.

"Cole, would you *please* tell me what Welch wanted?"

"I was just getting to that, Gabe. Just getting to it." Cunningham put his cup down. "At one-thirty in the morning, our time, Peter Welch was in his office at First Saint Louis Trust. Don't ask me why he was in his office because I haven't the damnedest idea. I mean, who the hell ever heard of a banker in his office on a Friday night,

56

anyway? The bastard would have woken me, except I was waiting for Alexis to show up from L.A., which she didn't."

"Where is she?"

"Who the hell knows with her? She was supposedly coming in last night and I sent the car to the airport and she never showed. I don't know where the hell she is and I couldn't care less at the moment. Welch wanted to know what the damn consultants were forecasting in the way of attendance at the park this season. He wanted me to send him the report. Can you believe that?"

"Did you send it?" Gabriel Bloome was sitting on the edge of his chair.

"By air express, this morning. He'll have it tonight." Cunningham drained his coffee cup and rang for the steward.

"Was that all he wanted?" Bloome asked. *"That's* why he called you at one-thirty in the morning? Cole, I need some coffee. I didn't get to finish my breakfast."

"Where the hell *is* the coffee?" Cunningham leaned over the intercom and buzzed his secretary. "Helen, would you please find Renaldo and tell him I would like some more coffee and that Mr. Bloome would like some, too. Thank you, dear." He got up from his desk and settled into the couch at the opposite end of the room, forcing Gabriel Bloome to turn his chair around.

"Does Helen mind working Saturdays?" Bloome asked.

"For what she's getting paid, she ought to work eight days a week, thirty-six hours a day."

"All right, tell me—what else did Welch want?"

"I'm getting to that," Cunningham said, bending down to straighten the Khalabar rug in front of the couch. "It seems he heard some bad news around the bank. Apparently the sentiment on the board is not to extend our notes—which, in case you haven't read the last financial statement, are due next Friday."

"Cole, you know I can't read a financial statement."

Precisely, Cunningham thought. That's why I'm taking

all this trouble to explain it to you. Toad, he thought. His partner and friend reminded him of a toad.

"I know, Gabe. I know that." The steward entered, refilled Cunningham's cup, and set a fresh cup on the edge of the desk for Bloome. "Renaldo, please put a coaster under Mr. Bloome's cup."

The steward obliged, then backed out of the room.

"Not only did Welch want the consultant's projections," Cunningham continued, "but he also wanted to get hold of Jenkins at Price, Waterhouse. Our accountants, Gabe. He wanted to talk to our accountants."

"At one-thirty in the morning?"

"He said he'd call Jenkins today at home. I gave him the number. Then he said he didn't quite understand the sentiment against us at the bank and wanted to know if I understood it. I told him I didn't have the vaguest damned idea."

"Cole, what happens if they don't renew the notes?"

"Well, just for starters, we can't meet the payroll next Friday."

The payroll! Gabriel Bloome was out of his seat as if he'd been shot. "The payroll! We can't meet the payroll!"

"You get the message, Gabe. Now sit down before you drop your coffee and burn yourself." Cunningham lit a fresh cigarette. "Welch says he's going to recommend to the board that they extend the loans, and he says maybe he can even get some more cash for us, which he says we're going to need. But I'm not counting on it. The fact is, Gabe, we are being squeezed. Somebody wants the park. Either we sell off the park to pay the notes, or they take the whole damn business."

"We could sell off everything else and keep the park," Gabriel Bloome countered.

"Don't be stupid, Gabe. At least the importing subsidiaries are making money. It's the damn park that's soaking up all the cash." He paused to inhale, then stood and walked back to his desk, again forcing Bloome to turn his chair around. "Gabriel, how much cash have you got right now?"

"How much do we need, Cole?"

"Eleven million dollars," Cunningham said flatly.

"Eleven million dollars!"

"Gabriel, why do you repeat everything I say? And stop shouting, damnit. Yes, eleven million. I think we could get by with seven if we had to. But I wouldn't bet on it."

"Cole, you know I don't have that kind of money."

"What about Regina?"

"My mother? Every dime of it is tied up in trust. I don't get a penny until she dies. And her mother lived to be ninety-four. All I have to do is wait twenty-six years and I'll get the money." Bloome grinned.

"What about Pinky?"

"Hers is all in trust, too. She tried to break the will last year. I want to tell you it cost us plenty in legal fees. First we tried to prove that the will was written under duress. Then Pinky claimed hardship. Then she—"

"Skip the details, Gabe. You haven't got any dough and you can't get any."

"Well, I could ask Regina if—"

"Forget it. Your mother doesn't like me. Never did."

"So what do we do?"

"So what do we do?" Cole Cunningham repeated. "Why do you think I dragged you in here at this ungodly hour on a Saturday morning? I've called a board meeting. You, me, the Duke, and Hawkins." He looked at his watch. "In twenty minutes. I don't want you to say a word—I just want you to agree with me. All right?"

"Whatever you say, Cole. I don't want to lose the park, that's all."

Lose the park, Cunningham thought. We'll be lucky to walk out with our shirts. "Neither do I. But there is one thing, Gabe. We don't know who's squeezing us."

"What do you mean, Cole? You just told me that Welch—"

"Welch is a snot-nosed kid who thinks he's David Rockefeller. He's a goddamn glorified clerk, trying to impress his goddamn secretary. You could put everything Peter

Welch knows about banking into an eight-dollar-a-year safe-deposit box."

"But Cole—"

"Think, Gabe, don't talk. Somebody is leaning on that bank. Welch said that all he heard was talk—loan officers talking about our lousy hundred million dollars. Nobody talks in a bank about anything unless someone wants them to, and I want to know who that someone is."

"You're being paranoid, Cole."

"Paranoid my ass." Cole Cunningham stood and carried his coffee cup to the window. For a few moments, he stood silently, fixated on the spires of St. Patrick's. The best thing about churches in New York, he thought, is the value of the property beneath them.

"Paranoid, maybe," he said, "but there's this little twitch I've got behind my right eye, and when my optic nerve starts to twitch, then I know somebody's getting ready to smack me in the head." He blew two oblong-shaped smoke rings. "The hell with it. We'll raise the dough ourselves. You just back me up, Gabriel. Agreed?"

"Anything you say."

"Good. I'll see you in twenty minutes in the boardroom."

Gabriel Bloome padded to the door.

"Gabriel?"

"What is it, Cole?" Bloome said, turning around.

"Leave the coffee cup. I don't like the set separated."

Bloome set the cup down on the marble-topped sideboard and left.

Cunningham sat with a yellow legal pad on his knees, poising a thin amber pen over the paper. Eleven million dollars. The digits were practically engraved on his eyeballs. Two ones and six zeros without commas. The last time this had happened, he had simply picked up the telephone and called the president of United Foods and told him how much money he needed, and a day later the papers appeared. The good old days, when he worked for somebody else. Don't start thinking like that, he told himself. Eleven million dollars.

He started his list and in five minutes he had six names. He lifted the blue telephone from its cradle and held it in the air for a moment. Then he dropped it back into place with a loud crack. Not now.

Eleven million dollars, he thought. Why me? he wanted to know. Why now? The accidents of life, he thought, although he wasn't certain anything was truly accidental. His maternal grandfather, George Cole, had made and lost two fortunes in real estate. His paternal grandfather, Shooting Jack Cunningham, was an Irish rascal who had made and lost only one fortune, but before the crash had arranged to set aside a handsome chunk for Harvard University. Cole always suspected it had paid off in his own admission. Accidents. His brother Anthony committed suicide at the age of nine, six weeks before Cole was born, by putting his father's .45-caliber revolver in his mouth and pulling the trigger. In a sense, Cole replaced Tony in his mother's life, replaced the brother he never knew. Until, that is, she had her first nervous breakdown, after which she couldn't remember who Cole was.

The boy genius, they called him. Cole Cunningham, chairman of the board of Hampshire Industries. Alexis hated the "boy" part, loved the "genius." She put things into perspective. And without her, he knew, he wouldn't have survived. He knew it all too well. He brushed away the dust from a silver-framed photograph of the two of them standing together after he signed the incorporation papers for Hampshire Industries. Her blond hair hung full on her shoulders. Her squarish, broad face—the society columnists compared her to Jacqueline Onassis—was caught off-guard by the camera, and her eyes were wide, stunned by the flash. In a jersey dress that clung to her body, she seemed to Cole not the least bit changed from the June day when they were married in Harvard Chapel. Fourteen years ago. He had loved her very much then, he thought. *Then.*

Before he graduated from Harvard, he invented the frozen TV dinner. Earthshaking, the food industry said. A revolution. But Cole Cunningham thought it all quite simple. How smart did he have to be, he asked himself then, to sense that most people were essentially lazy. Nobody liked to cook in the suburbs any more. How much easier it was to keep screaming children happy by shoving an aluminum plate in the oven and bringing it out twenty minutes later. Mother could spend the afternoon playing Mah-Jongg or drinking. This, according to Professor Galbraith, was the affluent society, one that would offer more leisure than work. By the time he was twenty-seven, Cole Cunningham sold Mother's Pre-Cooked Dinners to United Foods for fourteen million dollars. Then he spent three years at United, discovering his born salesman's knack. He knew the territory, and his territory was the grocery store. Before long, he was making more money for the food conglomerate than he'd ever earned for himself. That seemed unfair, so he moved to United's largest competitor, International Brands.

What could he do after the frozen dinner? Again he went to the marketplace. He walked the aisles of the supermarkets, peered into shopping carts looking for staples, the items appearing in every food basket. And he found the product he was looking for: coffee. He would do something new for instant coffee. From the supermarkets, he went to the laboratories. What, he asked the scientists, could they do to make instant coffee taste better? Freezing, they said. Could they freeze it, he asked, then dehydrate it, and market the residue? The men in the white smocks nodded, set to work, and soon Cole Cunningham's prodding produced freeze-dried coffee. In the process, International Brands surpassed United Foods. The appellation "boy genius" stayed with him.

But the corporate world didn't suit Cole Cunningham: too many bosses. Why, he asked himself, should I line their pockets, when I can line my own? And so he opened a chain of fast-food restaurants, not built of cinderblocks and packed twenty to a suburb, but quiet, tasteful, glass-walled structures surrounded by shrubbery. Elegant, simple, cheap to construct, they were another way to get mother out of the kitchen, and this time Cole Cunningham would be on top. Someday he would be bigger than McDonald's. The franchise business quickly paid its bank loans and Cole Cunningham changed tracks, began to import cameras from the Far East and Germany, then started manufacturing them. He imported stereo equipment from Japan through the same channels he'd created for cameras. Evenually he had offices around the globe, in Tokyo, Geneva, Munich, Paris, London, Los Angeles, Chicago, New York. He was his own conglomerate until the capital shortage of the late 1960s. Suddenly the world economy weakened and tottered on the edge of collapse; European labor costs caught up with those in the United States, and he was forced to sell off his manufacturing subsidiaries to raise money.

Then, one fall day in 1974, Pinky Bloome told Alexis Cunningham about her husband's dream. The Duke of Hampshire was in town for a week, thinking of moving to New York for three months of the year, and the three men met at one of Pinky Bloome's parties. The Duke and his aristocratic friends wanted to get money out of England. Did Cunningham have any notion of investment opportunities? How might the British nobility get their fortunes away from the hands of their greedy, incompetently run government, which taxed them so heavily that their accountants had exhausted their wits trying to hide foreign profits? The noblemen had grown nervous watching their family inheritances shrink, family fortunes centuries old eaten away.

For Gabriel Bloome, the Duke and Cole Cunningham could not have met at a more opportune moment. Bloome was a man possessed by an overwhelming dream—to build the world's most magnificent amusement park, a pleasure palace beyond imaginable dimensions, to carve out of raw earth a playground rivaling the celluloid fantasies his father had bequeathed to America decades before. Gabriel Bloome lived in a separate reality, conjured opalescent visions, reveled in the chambers of his childlike mind alive with rainbow colors and lights and soaring monuments surrounded by manicured lawns. He built scale models in his lavish apartment and joined his wife in elaborate parties, building make-believe wonderlands for his guests. But a larger scale beckoned—reality. Rides, by the dozen. A safari park with thousands of animals of every species and size, a veritable Garden of Eden.

To the rest of the world, Gabriel Bloome seemed more than a little crazy. He was, of course. He spent long, sleepless nights drawing plans, sketching rolling hills with glittering carousels and ferris wheels and band shells, and at the bottom of every sketch, he lettered, in block capitals: OLYMPIC ADVENTURE. CREATED BY GABRIEL BLOOME. Like the film credits with his father's name in red script type—the Lyman Bloome trademark.

The day after his conversation with Cunningham, Gabriel Bloome summoned him to the midtown office he kept to house his numerous schemes. After the pleasantries, he led Cunningham to the rear of the suite and drew a chain from his pocket. He inserted a key into a hidden socket beneath a light switch and, as if by magic, the entire wall was sucked into the ceiling. There on a door behind the wall were two more locks, thick cast-iron bolts. It was then that Cunningham suspected Gabriel Bloome of being more unbalanced than he seemed. All those locks and bolts—it was demented.

"Close your eyes," Bloome said.

"Don't be ridiculous," Cunningham answered. "Open the goddamn door."

"Close your eyes!" The two men hardly knew each other and already Bloome was shouting. Cunningham understood: Bloome was a child, and this was show-and-tell. He closed his eyes.

"No peeking, now," Bloome said. "Put your hands over them."

Cunningham complied and heard the bolts being thrown. Bloome led him into the room. It smelled unmistakably of dirt, fresh sod. For an instant, he thought he had been taken outside, which was altogether impossible on the twenty-first floor of a building without terraces.

"Smell it?" Bloome asked.

"Dirt," Cunningham said. "Can I open my eyes now?"

"Just a minute." Suddenly loud music blared. Animals roared. Automobile horns honked.

"You can open them now," Bloome said. Cunningham opened his eyes and involuntarily let out a short, stifled gasp. His eyes blinked. The room was about forty feet square, and except for a small pathway around the edge, it was entirely covered by a detailed scale model of an amusement park. Every ride was in motion; tiny mechanical animals moved in what looked like real grass. Water tumbled over mountainsides. Cunningham touched the grass and discovered why he smelled dirt. The grass was real.

"Now watch this," Bloome gleefully cried, shouting over the music. He opened a panel on the wall and leaned on a bank of switches. The lights dimmed, and the room was transformed into a small planetarium. The ceiling lit up with stars. Lights blinked on the ferris wheel, waterfalls glowed from beneath. Animals stopped in their tracks —real tracks. And across the room, on a recessed wall, neon letters five feet high spelled out OLYMPIC ADVENTURE. In smaller letters below, CREATED BY GABRIEL BLOOME.

"Follow me," Bloome shouted.

They proceeded around the room, Bloome talking frenetically, describing each of the park's five sections. Better than Disney, Bloome screamed. Bigger, taller. Here, he pointed, the control tower, at the top of the ice-cream cone. There, the carousel, from Austria. There, see the car coming down the Bobsled. And see here, the Aquatic Arena. Over there the Land of Monuments. The Eiffel Tower, Mt. Olympus. We'll have shows, swimming and diving exhibitions, whales, dolphins, rodeos, horses, bronco busting, stagecoach robberies. We'll have television stars. And there, the Sky Chariot. The Alamo. Room for shops, the Olympic Bazaar. See there, the Pyramids. Around the room they walked, Cole Cunningham hypnotized by the sublime insanity of it all. He was face to face with a man whose capacity for wonder and illusion exceeded his own. Every few minutes Bloome turned more knobs, meshed additional switches, and new sections of the model sprang to life; spinning wheels and spurting water, more music blaring in an almost unbearable melange of sounds. Bloome led Cunningham to two chairs under the neon letters. For nearly an hour, they sat in silence, as Bloome worked the controls, taking Cunningham's eyes across the sweep by changing the lights, decreasing and increasing the level of action. No detail was missing, no fine touch neglected, no part left immobile. And then the music faded and the room was bright with fluorescent light and a cover rolled across the top of the model. For two minutes, neither man said a word.

"I picked the land," Bloome said. "In the Pine Barrens."

"Where?" Cunningham asked quizzically.

"The Pine Barrens, in New Jersey—thousands of acres of untouched land. A highway is coming through in two years. Two hours from Philadelphia, an hour and a half from New York, maybe less."

"How big?"

"Over three thousand acres," Bloome said, guessing.

"How much?"

"For the land?" Gabriel Bloome was ready with his numbers.

"For all of it. The whole thing. Land, construction, rights of way, everything."

"I'm not really . . . I'm not good with numbers," Bloome said.

"Two hundred million," Cole Cunningham said, "if it's a dime. I'll talk with the Duke."

They left the secret room. Cole Cunningham glanced over his shoulder as the wall descended from the ceiling. Deranged, he thought.

Within two weeks, they began to buy land, setting up dummy real-estate corporations so the farmers and other land owners would not have an inkling that a single force was behind all the purchases. Otherwise, Cunningham explained, prices would zoom. It took them nearly a year to assemble the package, and for six months after that they fought for zoning clearances. The Duke's money, however, was not enough, and Cole Cunningham's money was not enough, and eventually they had to borrow more than a hundred million dollars from the First National Trust Company of Saint Louis. Eleven million dollars of those loans was due in a week.

Eleven million dollars, Cole Cunningham thought, remembering Bloome's passion at the showing of his toy. In one week were the fifth anniversary of breaking ground for Olympic Adventure, and his thirty-ninth birthday, and his fourteenth wedding anniversary. All were marked in a cluster on his desk calendar. Birthdays and holidays and anniversaries didn't much affect Cole Cunningham any longer. New Year's, Christmas . . . he was unsure just why these events no longer mattered to him, as they once had, but they did not, and the longer he thought about it, the more he realized he had irrevocably lost something.

Who was putting on the squeeze? That mattered. And then suddenly he knew. All night it had been bothering him and then he knew. The talk around the bank. The bank. The words came into focus. Squire Hotels and First National Trust Company of Saint Louis. Toolco and First Saint Louis. Sunlife Orange Groves and First Saint Louis. All were tied to the bank and all were Brodky companies. And what had he seen yesterday? Something about Armco and First Saint Louis? Where?

"Helen, bring me in yesterday's *Wall Street Journal.*"

STEELS IN DECLINE, the headline said. Steels, Cunningham thought. Why the hell single out steels? Everything was in decline. The whole goddamn world was in decline. And there in the news summary column was the item he remembered—a $112-million housing project to be built by First National Trust Company of Saint Louis and Armco Housing. Another Brodky company. The nerve behind his eye twitched. No wonder Welch had heard talk around the bank. Max was putting on the squeeze. Max Brodky—acquiring, empire building. But Olympic Adventure? Why, Cole Cunningham wondered. Why?

5

The blue Mercedes 450 SLC passed under the Saarinen Gateway Arch on the St. Louis waterfront and joined the traffic flowing onto the Eads Bridge, heading east across the Mississippi. The bridge suggested its nineteenth-century engineer's fascination with armor and the arch suggested its twentieth-century architect's fascination with hyperbolas. The dome of the Old Courthouse flashed briefly in the rearview mirror, and Max Brodky thought for a moment he could see the roof of Union Station, uptown. Imagining its wasted interior, once crowded daily with soldiers returning from the war, its marble-columned space now an empty shell, Max reminded himself to think again about how it might be used. The city would accept any reasonable plan. There was money to be made.

Just across the river, he coasted down the exit ramp into East St. Louis, stopping at the stockyards. The smell of freshly slaughtered steer flesh was so thick it seeped through the closed windows, permeated the air conditioning. Then he drove on, through streets of sludge furnaces belching softly in repose. He slowed, dabbed a single tear from his cheek. He was near the spot where a trailer truck had jackknifed in the snow six months earlier, smashing down onto another Mercedes, the one his son had just purchased and was driving into the countryside to his farm.

Max Brodky was going to the farmhouse for one last look before it was torn down and a housing complex erected in its place. For sentimental reasons, Max had been unable to sell the property, but he was not so sentimental as to let it lie fallow. After the holiday weekend, construction was scheduled to begin on two apartment towers flanked by tennis courts and swimming pools, and Max fully expected the entire project to be erected and rented before the year was out. When he reached the farm, another Mercedes, this one white but otherwise identical to his own, was parked in front. His oldest son, David, sat in the farmhouse's arched doorway, with blueprints laid out on the porch in front of him. His face was deeply tanned and his thick red hair was damp. He shared his father's features: a short, broad nose; a deeply clefted chin; dark blue eyes. As Max Brodky approached, his son looked up, dropped a blueprint, and the two lanky men reached for each other and embraced. Max stared at the reflection of himself in his son's mirrored aviator glasses and thought David looked a little ridiculous in them.

"You're up early, David." A fine boy, he thought. Works hard.

"You have to get up early in the morning to be up earlier than you," the younger Brodky said. They smiled at each other. "You want some coffee, papa? I've got a thermos. My foremen are coming out later to check the site once more before we start."

"I'll have some coffee," Max said.

David Brodky poured his father a cup of coffee and passed it across the blueprints. As Max sipped, his son stared out at the two cars parked amid clumps of dry grass on the dirt road. He plucked his glasses off and rubbed his eyes.

"It would have been a beautiful place," he said. He paused, then went on in a lower voice. "I figured you'd be out today."

"He was a fine boy, David. I still miss him every day. I miss him almost as much as I miss your mother."

More, David Brodky thought. "Me, too, papa. The kid and I were . . ." The old man looked up at his son. "We were close, papa. I loved the kid."

Max turned, looking east over the peaceful farmland. The sun seemed to be balanced on the horizon, balanced like a man on a circus wire. Max shielded his eyes with his palm and held back tears. Nobody ever said life was fair, he thought.

69

His son touched his shoulder. "Papa, are we all set on the financing?"

"Financing?" Max asked, lost in memories. "Yes, financing." He walked over to the blueprints. "You understand these things, don't you?"

"I didn't spend six years at Cal Tech for nothing. Did you sign the mortgages yesterday?"

"All taken care of," Max said.

"Tell me something, papa."

"Anything, David. What would you like to know? Your father is a fount of wisdom."

"How much of First Saint Louis do you own?"

Max Brodky flinched as if he had been slapped across the face. "*I* don't own any of it," he said. "You know that."

David Brodky laughed. "I know *you* don't. I mean how much do you control through mother's estate? Have you gone and bought more of the bank without telling us?"

"Well, you *are* curious, aren't you?" Max asked, his voice light again. "My own children, spying on me. That's gratitude for you."

"Come on, papa. We just thought it was sort of funny for you to be buying a bank without telling us. Are you?"

"Well," Max said, stretching the word out for effect. "It never hurts to own a bank. You get very favorable loans that way. Money comes cheap when you're lending it to yourself."

"You tipped us, you know," David said. "With the housing market the way it is, we figured you wouldn't be building this project without some awfully inexpensive cash. And then when you didn't dip into reserves to finance even part of it but went to the bank instead, well, Jeff and I figured either somebody over there owed you a big favor or else you'd gone and bought yourself a bank. Sort of obvious when you think about it."

"Smart-ass kid," Max said, playfully, punching his son's arm. "Bunch of smart-ass kids I raised."

Max stepped off the porch and his son followed. They walked around the empty farmhouse, its windows boarded up. The side was only half-painted white, a job that would never be finished. A lone tractor rusted in the pasture. Mice scampered through the field. Nothing else moved. A stone wall, crumbling from neglect, separated the pasture from the adjoining farm, which Max now owned as well.

"Unfair," Max said. Against the sky, a small figure moved in the distance. At first, they could not make it out, then it neared—a small boy carrying a stick against his shoulder. When the boy came closer, they could see a pouch tied to the end of the stick. A piece of sailcloth. The boy stopped, seemed to notice the two men watching him, then turned back.

"Unfair," David Brodky said. "He's dead, papa. That's all there is to it."

"I know," Max said. "I know, David." Max's voice was suddenly hard.

"Papa, I know how you feel."

"No," Max Brodky said. "You don't. Don't presume." A Lockheed Tri-Star zoomed above them, drowning out his voice.

"But I do. Jerry was the smart one. Jeff and I know that. He was smarter than both of us and he looked like you and he thought like you, and when you were both in the same room it was like being with one person instead of two. He was a real special kid, papa, and we all loved him. But he's gone and you're tormenting yourself thinking about him all the time."

"I had a big thing planned for that boy," Max said. "I had a special job for him, something he would have loved."

David Brodky lit a cigarette, then held the lighter for his father's cigar. Max snapped the thin gold object out of his son's hand.

"A Dunhill, all gold," Max said. "You have expensive tastes, just like your mother."

"A gift, papa. One of my foremen gave it to me when we finished the Lake Forest job. To celebrate."

"If your foremen can afford such nice gifts," Max said,

71

smirking, "then you're paying them too much." He lit his cigar, then dropped the lighter in his son's hand.

The younger man laughed. "You get what you pay for, papa. That's what you taught me."

Max, despite himself, laughed too. "You want to join me for breakfast?"

"God, I thought you'd never ask. I'm starved."

"You were waiting here for me," Max said, "weren't you?"

'Why the hell do you think I got up early on a Saturday morning?"

"What about the foremen?" Max asked.

"They're not coming until noon."

"Smart-ass kid," Max said.

They got into David Brodky's car. Neither man spoke. On the sides of the nearly deserted roads, farmers plowed their fields. Cows dotted the plains. Orange-gray smoke from the furnaces spread in the western sky. The road surface changed from dirt to asphalt, and then to concrete. Shacks nudged the roadbed. Burnt-out auto hulks, like stranded travelers collapsed from exhaustion, lay in the gullies. They passed an abandoned Kentucky Fried Chicken storefront, and then a row of machine shops closed for the holiday. Past the rail yards they found the Blue Note, a coffee shop in which they used to sit and talk after spending a day at the farm. David got out of the car, but Max hesitated.

"This all right?" David called.

Max peered through the windshield. He had not been to this place in more than a year. The memories were at once pleasurable and painful.

"Okay," Max said, stepping out of the car.

The waitress recognized them, addressed them by name. Max and his three sons had spent many Saturday afternoons in the Blue Note and, without fail, had left substantial tips. David ordered for both of them, steak and eggs and apple juice.

"What is it, papa?" David asked. "What was this special job for Jerry? It's bothering you."

"I've had my eye on something," Max said, "for a few years. A good operation that's badly run."

"Your specialty. What is it? Lumber?"

"We've got enough lumber companies. Something different. I hoped Jerry would swing it for me. I wanted him to do the deal and then run the company."

"What is it? Why all the suspense?"

"Have you heard of Hampshire Industries?"

"Hampshire," David Brodky said. "I know the name. Importing, isn't it?"

"It's more than that. A little conglomerate with a bunch of unrelated pieces."

David sipped his juice. "Hampshire. Now I've got it. Cole Cunningham's mess. What do you want with that?"

"Well, in that mess is a money machine, if somebody would run it right—Olympic Adventure."

"The amusement park? Cunningham owns that? I thought a guy from Disney, Hawkins, ran it for Gabe Bloome."

"They're all partners," Max said. "They gave Hawkins stock to get him to leave Disney."

"Papa, what do you want with an amusement park? You need an amusement park about as much as you need another publishing company."

"I just want it, that's all. I wanted Jerry to run it for me." Max stood. "Got to make a call."

David Brodky watched his father stride to the telephone booth in the rear of the restaurant, mystified. He thought it strange that his father wanted to buy anything at all from Cunningham, considering how little respect he had for the man. And why an amusement park? Had Jerry wanted it for some reason? No, he had wanted to spend time on his farm, raising prize cattle and grooming racehorses. That's why he'd bought the land in the first place. David vaguely recalled hearing his brother mention the boom in amusement parks and how much fun it would be to own one, but David had never taken him seriously. Amusement parks? Not a very stable investment. Not the

73

sort of thing his father would tie up money in. Unless Jerry wanted it. He'd have done anything for Jerry.

Max returned to the table, less solemn. David cut a large chunk of steak and waited for his father to explain his interest in Olympic Adventure. But Max said nothing.

"Well?" David said.

"Well what?"

"What is going on?"

"Going on," Max said. "Nothing is going on."

"This isn't like you, papa. I can't remember the last time you made a phone call without coming back to complain about somebody's stupidity. You know, I have a stake in this business, too. What gives?"

"Are you questioning my judgment, son?" Almost imperceptibly, Max's voice grew more distant.

David threw up his hands, resting his elbows on the table, thrusting his head forward. "Your judgment, for chrissakes! How can I question your judgment when I don't even know what you're doing?"

Max pulled a cigar from his pocket and David fished for his lighter.

"You like that lighter, don't you, David? What if you'd been born poor? Like me. You'd carry matches, like I do."

"Knock it off, papa."

"David, my bright and shining engineer. Your father is having a little fun right now. So let me have my fun and I'll tell you everything. Don't worry about your senile father piddling away his children's inheritance. I've been cooking deals since—"

"I know, papa. Since before I was born. Whatever you say. It's your money."

"I'm so pleased you realize that, son. You were beginning to worry me." A faint smile creased Max's face. The two men finished their breakfast, and then David, annoyed and still wondering, drove Max back to the farm, where he immediately got in his car and headed west, toward St. Louis.

6

Marital infidelity bothered Alexis Cunningham. She was aware of Brad Hawkins's smell the minute she awoke. In his apartment. In his room. In his bed, where she lay. Musky, wet, the smell drenched her body. She turned instinctively and reached across the bed for him, but he was gone. What time was it? Then she remembered the phone call. What time was that? It had been Cole on the phone, Brad had told her. He was calling a board meeting. The collapse was coming, she had thought then, only half-awake. Arnie Jacobs, after all, knew the score. Whatever else Arnie Jacobs might not know, Arnie Jacobs always knew the score. Now, remembering the call, she thought it an omen. Without knowing it, Cole had found her in another man's bed.

She wrapped herself in a blanket and pulled back the drapes. Fifth Avenue was empty. Not a single car. Across from the apartment building was an empty reviewing stand. Of course, the parade. It was Memorial Day, opening day at the park. She watched a policeman wave a limousine through the barricades. A man stepped from under the building's canopy into the waiting car. It was the Australian publisher, Rupert Murdoch. She had seen him in the elevator the previous night, and he had greeted her, remembering her last name. They had met only twice before. A thoroughly charming man, she thought as she watched the limousine speed away.

The phone rang, jarring her fully awake. She turned from the window and ran across the room, dropping the blanket.

Second ring. It could be Brad, but it might also be Cole again. Brad would not call her.

Third ring. Brad was playing squash at the New York Athletic Club. His racquet was gone.

75

Fourth ring. Or would he call? She put her hand on the receiver.

Fifth ring.

Sixth.

Seventh.

It stopped. She could hear her heart beating. Crossing the room, she picked up the blanket and began making the bed. She tucked the corners of the sheet neatly—hospital corners, she had learned how to do them at Camp Hawthorn in Wisconsin, just before a group of parents complained and the owners finally relented, hiring maids to make the beds. She tore the bedspread loose and shook it, looking for a single gold earring. An anniversary present from Cole. A twinge of guilt caught her off-guard. You could shift values over the years, even change them on a whim, from week to week, but some burned too deep. Marital infidelity, that was the toughest, no matter how rotten the marriage, how dead the marriage. Of some restraints, she thought, we are never entirely free.

She finished making the bed, then emptied the ashtrays and washed them, retrieved every item of her clothing from the floor, and stepped into the shower. Rubbing her body with soap, she began a familiar litany. She was thirty-five years old, but she felt as if time were speeding past her, leaving her tired and aged beyond her years. I have lived too fast. Too long. It has passed me by. I must pay for it all. It was as if life itself presented her with a bill of particulars, debts to be paid, as if her past were filled with unmet obligations. Each lie and self-deception to be paid for. She remembered when she had first met Brad Hawkins. Cole was showing off his latest acquisition: the man from Disney. That was three years ago. She had thought herself impervious to romantic illusions then. Nothing was left between her and Cole. No feeling. No love. No sex. Their marriage was a charade. It surprised her now to recall the rush of emotion she'd felt when Brad Hawkins had walked into the apartment that night three years ago with Cole. She had looked at him, their eyes had met, and she had felt her face flush. She had thought no man could excite her the way Cole once had, and she was cautious. No more illusions. No more succumbing to the charm of successful men. No more believing in counterfeit power. Too many powerful men had invited her attention. After all, she thought, I am a beautiful woman.

But she had turned them down, all of them; out of loyalty, she had convinced herself, to Cole. It was a useful lie, the marital bond. As long as she believed it, no man could touch her and no man, therefore, could hurt her. She had thought she would use the lie to protect herself from Brad Hawkins. There was, however, a problem: the lie was good only so long as Cole believed in it, too, as long as he played the same game. And Cole, she'd found out, had stopped believing.

Still, she'd seen little of Hawkins that first year. When he came to the apartment for business meetings, she avoided him. On those few occasions when she went to Olympic Adventure without Cole, she traveled with an escort. Pinky, usually, or Gabriel. And while she imagined that Hawkins, too, was avoiding her, she could read a certain message in his eyes. It was a confused message full of conflicting signals, but one of them undoubtedly said, I want you. Then came the trip to Africa last year to gather new animals for Olympic Adventure's game preserve. Cole hadn't wanted her to go and she had fought with him. Strictly business, he had said. No, she had answered, she had galavanted around the world with him on business, and this trip she would not miss. It was the rage: African safaris. It would give her something to talk about, she said, and at the last moment, Cole had relented.

They had left New York at the end of January, on a night so cold Alexis's lipstick froze and cracked on her lips. With Pinky and Gabriel, she sat in the lounge before takeoff while Hawkins and the Commodore and Cole checked the loading of the equipment. She had never been so attracted to Hawkins as she was that night. Love, she had told herself, was only a romantic notion for ritual and security, and while waiting to board the plane, she had admitted, against her will, that love was neither of those things. Perhaps Cole had suspected that she, too, could no longer tolerate the lie, the marital bond, and in retrospect, she decided that was the reason he had wanted to leave her in New York. Cole had seen what both she and Brad had preferred to keep silent and buried because they could not face the truth. They were moving inexorably toward each other.

On the plane to Nairobi, Hawkins sat across the aisle from her. What they had talked about she could not remember; the words had merely filled the space between them. Their eyes, their hands spoke a truer language. Even then she could not imagine giving in, for indeed it seemed a weakness, succumbing to another dream. During the two days in Nairobi before they left for Lake Victoria, Hawkins was constantly on her mind. She would find herself listening to the Commodore's tales of British explorers in the Dark Continent, only to discover that she was not listening at all: she was thinking about Brad. Someone would ask her a question and she would not hear it. When they reached Kisumu, near the shore of Lake Victoria, Cole was called away to London. It seemed an omen. Late that same night, encamped in the jungle on the way to Lake Victoria, she was sitting in her tent, unable to sleep, drinking warm gin from a bottle, reading a novel by flashlight. Outside, shadows cast by torches hung around the campsite flickered on the side of the tent. Watching the shadows, she thought she would fall asleep; then she heard footsteps on the tarp near her tent. She sat bolt upright.

"Who is it?"

"Brad Hawkins. Just checking on everyone before I turn in for the night."

She invited him into the tent and offered him the bottle of gin.

"It's the best I can do," she said. "I don't have lime or tonic."

"For one of New York's finest hostesses," he said, smiling, "you ought to be ashamed. How could you not pack tonic?"

She laughed, watched him lift the bottle to his mouth. Again he smiled. His cheeks dimpled. She could smell him—sweat and dirt and the sweet tang of the jungle itself. Her heart missed a beat. She thought she knew what he was thinking—that he wanted her and she wanted him. She felt pure animal need. Reason reasserted itself. What am I doing, she thought, in a tent in the middle of Africa, drinking warm gin from a bottle, about to make love with a stranger? Cole was gone. She thought for the first time in her life that she might believe in fate.

Hawkins passed the bottle back. Alexis, nervous, did not know what to say. "Where are we, exactly?"she asked.

"Don't you know?" he answered, a touch of irony in his voice.

"All I know is we're in a jungle."

"I thought you came from a long line of explorers," he said. "Didn't I hear something about the *Mayflower*?"

"That's Cole's family," she said. "If I had any ancestors on the *Mayflower,* they rowed."

"It was a sailboat," he said, laughing. "Where we are is on the shore of Lake Victoria, sixty miles north of Kisumu in the northern plains of Kenya, East Africa. Sitting on the equator in the middle of nowhere."

"You could have told me that we were at the South Pole," Alexis said, stretching out on her cot, "and I would have believed you. I have no sense of . . . of direction."

"You seem to have done all right until now, Mrs. Cunningham. Must be instinct." Mrs. Cunningham, he had called her. He was teasing.

"I do my best," she said. "And you may call me Alexis."

The flashlight tumbled from her hand and clicked off. Hawkins retrieved it.

"Switch is stuck," he said. They sat in the dark. She wondered suddenly if he would bid her good night. He was so cool; it was impossible to tell what he was feeling. There seemed to be no vanity in him. Nothing like Cole, she thought, and nothing like herself. No noticeable self-regard. He did not posture. He seemed remarkably unaware of his own power. The flashlight came on again. He was sitting cross-legged in front of her.

Leaning toward him, she said, "I understand you've done quite a number on Cole."

"What number was that?" he asked.

"Your salary demands. The stock. Naming your terms."

"My winning, you mean."

She blinked. "I suppose you could call it that."

"He doesn't like to lose, your husband. He's not used to it." He picked up the bottle and swigged the gin. "But neither am I."

"Do you ever lose?"

"It all depends," he said, "on how you look at it."

She stared at him for a moment. There was something remote, ineffable about him. "Are you enjoying yourself?" she asked suddenly.

"Yes, but that's all I'm enjoying," he said, chuckling at his own joke.

"Seriously, is this what you want to do?"

He was silent. The coo of the swaying liana swelled in the still jungle night.

"If you're asking me," he said deliberately, "whether I like working for your husband, the answer is no. But I've never much liked working for anyone. Someday I won't."

"When is that going to be?"

"Soon," he said. "It's all coming together."

"You seem pretty sure of yourself," she said. "Everything on schedule? Everything as planned?" Her voice sounded harsher than she'd intended.

"Not quite everything," he said. He bent over, then kissed her, gently laying his arms across her shoulders. She reared back, unprepared, then moved toward him and fell into his embrace.

"You're a beautiful woman, Mrs. Cunningham."

"And you're a beautiful, presumptuous man, Mr. Hawkins—and the name is Alexis." She hugged him tightly, not entirely able to believe it was happening. "Hold me," she said. "Hold me tight."

Perhaps it was her own hunger: her deadened body

seemed to come alive again. She had nearly forgotten the feeling.

More than a year later, she still clearly remembered what he had said to her that night. She remembered watching him dress in the awkward, small space of the tent, his arm muscles rippling in the half-light.

"When is Cole coming back?" she had asked him.

"Not for a few days. Why?"

"I just wanted to know how long I would have you."

He had grinned, standing and throwing back the tent flap.

"But you don't have me," he had said, and he was gone.

And now she wondered again, as she had that night, what Hawkins thought of her. They had continued seeing each other for a year, a year of secret liaisons, and then they had stopped, or rather he had stopped seeing her. For a time, she had believed that to Hawkins she was simply a woman to be conquered: the boss's wife. A cruel condemnation of him and, she knew, a dishonest one, but it softened the pain when he no longer called.

Then three weeks ago, after months without a word, he had called her again. She ran to him. In his arms, her worst fears vanished. Her fear that the world was ending for her. Her fear that she could at any given moment float from the surface of Earth and drift into the sky, evaporate, cease to be. She had gone to Los Angeles to think about him and, a week later, he followed her. Last night, when she returned and let herself into his apartment with the key she still kept, she could tell, despite his facade of seeming impenetrability, that this was no dream and succumbing was no weakness. He was strong, solid. Confident. And while that confidence was also a wall, she sensed he was ready to let her break through. Perhaps, she thought, I need to believe that. In the last few days before leaving Los Angeles, she had been consumed by the disturbing perception that she, standing outside her body, was watching, with disdain, while another woman named Alexis Cunningham, a stranger, ate and drank and exhausted herself in catty chatter. Here, now, in Brad's room, she felt whole again.

She stepped from the shower and dried herself, then picked a brown sleeveless dress from her suitcase. Applying her makeup, she faced the mirror on the dressing table. A tan face stared back at her, sideways; enticing, she thought, yet cold. It had the well-preserved, pampered look of a woman who put great stock, perhaps too much, in her physical appearance. Her face was weathered—the result of a self-imposed requirement that she be always "in season." Not a single blond hair was out of place, not a single blemish visible beneath the makeup.

She bound the waist of the brown dress with a sash of horseshoe-shaped gold links. An obelisk of jade hung from her neck on a gold-coil necklace, its tip resting in the center of her cleavage. The green of the jade set off her hazel eyes so that at first glance, as she'd planned, one saw only her hair, her eyes, and the jade against a muted brown background.

Everything in the apartment that was hers—her clothes, her makeup bag, Friday's Los Angeles *Times*—she shoved into her suitcase. I have not yet reached him, she thought. Between them still was the slightest distance. Despite herself, despite the caution with which she approached everyone, and most of all any man who might pierce *her* mask, she wanted to let someone in this time, to let herself out.

She picked up the phone to call Pinky Bloome. She wanted to tell Pinky about Arnie Jacobs.

At last, Pinky Bloome thought. They're up. She stood back from the wall. Two massive gilt masks, slightly more than nine feet tall, hung suspended from the ceiling of the living room.

"Is that okay, lady?" one of the workmen asked. "That where you want 'em?"

Pinky backed farther into the living room, stretched her arm to its full length, and sighted the masks along the edge of her hand. As far as she could tell, they were adequately centered. Backing up farther, into the doorway between the library and the living room, she blinked and looked again.

"Too high," she said. "Let's bring them down about half a foot."

The workmen cranked the makeshift pullies and the masks slowly lowered, floating free.

"Hold it," Pinky said when they were a few feet from the floor. Flipping on four spotlights mounted on tracks across the front of the room, she sighted again along her hand. The eyes in the gold faces, prisms of aquamarine, refracted the light, laying pools of rainbow colors across the highly polished herringbone parquet floor.

"Perfect," Pinky said. "Lock them right there." The workmen latched the pullies and mounted their ladders, carrying industrial chains. Pinky turned away as they attached the chains to the masks and began drilling holes in the ceiling. She sat on the floor in a corner of the living room, trying to concentrate on plans for the evening. She had been trained since childhood, or so it seemed to her, for this sort of activity: supervising carpenters, writing guest lists, planning menus. And while she took less enjoyment in the fine points of entertaining than she once had, she still achieved a measure of gratification from a job well done, no matter how pedestrian. She propped her clipboard against the leg of a chair and purposefully checked through the items on her list as the workmen finished stabilizing the masks and removed the pullies and frames. She was relieved for a moment when the heavy work was completed. But still she found concentrating on her list of tasks impossible. She could not quite forget Cole Cunningham's tone. Quavering, raspy. Desperate.

"Desperate," she said aloud, enunciating each syllable and startling the workmen around her. She was a laconic, reserved woman with rosy skin, which accounted for the nickname given to her as a child. For the name Pinky, she was grateful. She hated the name Dolores, associating it with second-rate nightclub singers. She wore a black Oscar de la Renta high-collared lounging robe, and draped around her neck was a chain with two keys on it. Occasionally when she was thinking, she toyed with the chain the way some women toy with their hair. The keys were a talisman: the doors to her apartment and her husband's office. Boundaries. The sides of her bare feet were pocked with callouses, and though she seemed unkempt, she was obviously a handsome woman beneath the disarrayed surface—not beautiful by conventional standards, but slightly regal, the kind of woman men call striking. Pinky Bloome was not unaware of how attractive she was to men, but she never exploited her appearance. Her husband, she had once told an amorous, newly divorced friend, was enough for her, not least because of her passion for order in life. Her father, a tax laywer, and her mother, a Freudian psychiatrist, had prepared her for the world by teaching her to solve puzzles. That was how *they* saw the world. For every decision, there was a process. Every problem contained a solution. All of life, in fact, was a puzzle to be solved. As a woman, she had reached out to Gabriel Bloome, who so plainly lived a disordered, irrational life. It was as if, unable to free herself from the bonds of order, she had married Gabriel to experience his chaos. Pinky Bloome believed that however anyone might characterize her husband—and there were not a few who took joy in calling him crazy—it was her duty to minister to his needs: a comfortable home, a warm and welcoming home, shelter from the cruelties of others. As for the lavish parties he asked her to orchestrate—well, she had been prepared for it, she did do it well, and she derived some satisfaction from it. As for other men, disdaining their advances was no hardship. Devotion to her husband solved the puzzle of life, and Pinky Bloome was content with it.

"Desperate," she said again, wishing she had never suggested to Gabriel that Cole Cunningham build Olympic Adventure. She returned to her list. Clean rugs lay in the parlor, the tapestries were hung in the foyer, and the flowers . . . she'd best call Christados just to make sure. And Alexis was coming. There had been a touch of fever in Alexis's voice when she called. The break-up, she sensed, was coming. Alexis was leaving Cole. Her solution to the puzzle.

Workmen carried furniture into the room. Six high-backed chairs, a velvet-covered couch, two oak end tables topped with lapis lazuli. The theme for the party was the Court of Louis Quatorze, and Pinky had been shocked by the cost of renting and insuring the furniture. Most of it was not even authentic, just copies. Good copies, to be sure, but copies nevertheless. Even so, she estimated the bill conservatively at two thousand dollars. Which was a great deal of money, it seemed to her, for one night's rental. And that didn't take account of the movers who would be returning the Bloomes' own furniture on Sunday afternoon. Sunday, a weekend, time and a half. A holiday, double time.

"Madame, excuse me." Heloise, the maid, stood beside her. "The gentleman from the florist is here."

"Yes, Heloise, I'll be right out. Thank you." Ah, Christados, so efficient. On her way to the door, she noticed in the mirror that the whites of her eyes were flecked with red. Not enough sleep. She instructed the delivery men to line the side walls of the living room with vases of white lilies, then checked with the cook and kitchen staff. The intercom chimed.

"Yes, Val, what is it?"

The butler answered in his dry, deep Jamaican voice. "Mrs. Cunningham is here, madam. In the first-floor parlor."

"Thank you, Val. Would you ask Heloise to bring in a tray of crackers and cheese?"

"Yes, madam. Shall I say you will be in shortly?"

"Right away, Val."

Pinky crossed the back of the apartment through the maid's hallway to the parlor. Alexis stood to embrace her as she entered the room.

"Sweetheart, you look *swell*," Pinky said, thinking she had never seen Alexis look so pained.

"A modest suntan covers a thousand sins," Alexis said,

sitting and adjusting her belt and crossing her long, slender legs.

The maid entered and lazily set an ironstone platter of cheese on the rattan table. The smacking of the tray on the table's glass top reminded Pinky of the time Alexis's mother came up to Wellesley to redecorate her daughter's room with a truckload of rattan furniture. If she was going to be away at college, the woman had announced to Pinky, then she didn't have to live like a pig. Alexis, Pinky remembered, had been embarrassed. But the furniture stayed.

Gazing around the room, Alexis asked, "What is going on here? It looks like they're building the Great Wall of China in your living room."

"Gabe is celebrating the opening of the season," Pinky said. "He does the celebrating. I do the party. We're having two hundred and six of our most intimate friends for dinner. Didn't Cole tell you?"

"I haven't talked to him."

Pinky's eyes widened. "But he called this morning. He said . . . come to think of it, he didn't mention you. Didn't you come in last night?"

Alexis said, "Fix me a drink, will you?"

"Lexie, where did you call me from this morning?"

"I slept out last night."

"Sounds interesting."

"Interesting," Alexis said. "Interesting is the word for it."

"Mysterious," Pinky said. She measured a jigger of Tanqueray.

"Not exactly. I got off the plane and decided that the one thing I couldn't do was cope with Cole. So I hid in the ladies' room until the car left and got a cab." She chewed her lip. "To Brad's."

Pinky held a glass in her hand, poured the jigger, and tried to imagine Alexis hiding in the ladies' room of the TWA terminal at Kennedy.

"I'm not altogether surprised," Pinky said. "How long has this been back on?"

"Awhile," Alexis said. "It's not really what I came to talk about." Pinky passed Alexis her drink, and Alexis downed it in one gulp, a habit Pinky had observed in other difficult times. "He was in L.A. last weekend. We spent three days at the Beverly Wilshire. In bed." She coughed, lit a cigarette. "Christ, what a disaster I've made of my life."

Pinky waited for Alexis to continue. Alexis crossed and uncrossed her legs, smoothed her dress, tugged at her necklace. She nibbled on a sliver of cheese, leaned her head back, rubbed her eyes, and breathed a deep, bronchial sigh. Finally she stood and crossed to the bar, where she poured more gin into her glass, straight, and returned to the couch.

"I guess I do want to talk," she said finally. "Especially if I'm going to get the silent treatment. I know what you're thinking. If I were any kind of decent woman, I'd stick by my man. Right? He's losing his grip, he's losing me, and he's losing the park. So maybe I'm not such a decent woman, okay? Because not only don't I want to stick by him, I can barely stand the sight of him."

"Slow down," Pinky Bloome said. "Just for starters, what about the park?"

"That's what I wanted to talk to you about. Arnie Jacobs told me. He wanted to be first in line with condolences."

"Arnie Jacobs," Pinky said, gritting her teeth and remembering the pass the slovenly movie producer had once made at her, "is a despicable slime." She ran the keychain through her lips. "But he might be right. Cole called a board meeting this morning. Something about a banker in St. Louis."

"I don't know anything about bankers in St. Louis. But what do you know about Max Brodky?"

"I've heard the name. Gabe's mentioned him. Who is he?"

"He's a very rich man who lives in a nice little castle on a nice little plot of about five hundred acres in St. Louis

County and who has enough money to buy and sell half the United States. That's who he is."

"I give up. What's this got to do with the park?"

"Arnie says Max wants it," Alexis said. "He wants the park."

"Does Arnie know why? He seems to know everything." Just talking about the man made her squeamish.

"No, and neither do I. It seems to me Cole borrowed some money from Max a long time ago. Paid it all back, as far as I can tell. It was strictly business. Max is a sneaky sonuvabitch, though, and he never liked Cole much. And Max always gets what he wants."

Pinky Bloome stood and leaned on the bar, staring into an empty glass. "It'll be murder on Gabe. It's his life."

"I'll let you in on a secret, honey," Alexis said. "Gabriel will do just fine. He'll build himself another toy, bigger and better than this one. It's Cole who'll curl up and die. He built Hampshire from scratch. He's tied up every dime he ever earned in it. And if it caves in, you can call the little men in the white suits and they'll cart him away to Bellevue in little pieces."

"And you want me to tell you it's all right not to worry about Cole."

"I didn't come for absolution," Alexis said. "We sinners never do anymore. It's out of fashion." She dug into her purse and produced a cigarette. "He keeps saying he needs me. But he doesn't. I've suffered all his deals. I've watched him destroy the one thing he really wanted in life. Jesus God Almighty, they're running out of money and Cole is *building* out there. He's building more rides. Isn't it time I started worrying for me and stopped worrying for him?" She inhaled deeply. "Damnit, I haven't slept with him in six months. He can't even get it up anymore."

Pinky thought that if Alexis stepped out of her marriage and into another without coming up for air, she would never come up again. It was at times like these that she believed Alexis was the most unhappy person she had ever known.

"And what about Brad Hawkins?" Pinky Bloome asked. She thought it interesting that she had met Hawkins the day he was hired three years earlier and yet he remained as much a stranger to her as if she had met him yesterday.

"What about him?" Alexis asked.

"Are you sure?"

"Am I sure?" Alexis repeated, raising her voice. "Am I sure? I'm sure of one thing. He treats me like a woman and he cares about me, and behind that brick exterior is a man who wants to love me."

"You've loved Cole for fourteen years," Pinky said, playing devil's advocate.

"Past tense. *Loved.*" Alexis ran her hands through her hair. She wanted Pinky Bloome to tell her that Cole was a rotten human being and a louse and that Brad Hawkins was the most ideal man who ever walked the earth. She had told herself so dozens of times, but she did not believe her own voice. "What am I supposed to do? Go on living with Cole and hating him at the same time?"

"You wouldn't be the first," Pinky said in a measured cadence.

Alexis wanted to tell Pinky about Cole's worst behavior, but she had bathed in too much garbage for one day.

Pinky found it difficult feeling sorry for Alexis. She believed that people must somehow lie in the beds they make. People who changed beds too often had the unfortunate luck of ending up with no bed at all. She changed the subject. "Are you going to tell Cole about Max Brodky? What Arnie said?" Again the thought of Arnie Jacobs turned her stomach.

"I'll try," Alexis said. "If he'll listen."

"From the way he sounded this morning," Pinky said, "he'll listen." She took Alexis's hand. She suspected that in the most important ways, she did not understand Alexis, that the pretense of understanding any human being was a luxury. "Lexie, I'm bad at these things. I abhor change. I like absolutes. But I hope it goes all right." She paused. "I really do."

"No, honey, you probably don't, but that's okay, too."

"I don't understand any of it," Pinky said. "You. Cole. Any of it."

Alexis stood and closed her purse. "You know," she said, "I keep thinking of my mother through this. On the day she died, she was breathing like a steam engine and was so damn blitzed by the drugs she couldn't even talk. She was already half gone and I was standing there and she looked me straight in the eye and whispered. I had to put my ear next to her mouth to listen. She said, 'It's not how far out you go, or what you see out there. It's what you bring back.' "

"I don't get the point," Pinky Bloome said.

"Neither do I, honey. I think that's the point."

They walked to the door, not saying a word.

"Good luck, Lexie."

"Thanks for that, anyway. If only luck were all I needed." She was out the door and it closed without a sound. Pinky Bloome began mental notes for a long vacation with Gabriel in the sad event that Arnie Jacobs, the slime, turned out to be right.

7

When the duck fell, Everett Morgan could barely believe it. He had never been adept with guns. But there it was, and the girl was asking him which prize he wanted. He blinked at her, not comprehending.

"Sir, you've won. What animal would you like?" She pointed behind her at the array of stuffed toys, bears and dogs and other pastel shapes he could not distinguish. What animal would he like? Why, he didn't want any of them. The girl smiled, revealing two chipped front teeth. Her finger was still pointing.

"Sir, you've won a prize. Have you decided which animal you want? Surely your children would want one."

"Don't want anything," Morgan grunted. Why didn't she leave him alone? He was only passing time. Then he understood: he had hit the duck and was entitled to a prize, and she was forcing him to take one.

"But you've won it, sir."

"Just shooting for the fun of it," Everett Morgan said. "Don't want a prize."

A woman standing next to Morgan tapped his shoulder. He flinched. "Mister," she whispered, "my little boy's been shooting and he hasn't hit anything. Would you give it to him, please? *Please?*" The woman reached for Morgan's hand. Her reddish hair clashed with her pink rouge. Her eyes searched his face hopefully.

"Would that be all right?" the woman said to the girl behind the counter. "Could you tell my boy he's won and give him a choice?"

Morgan looked down at the little boy, standing at the far end of the shooting gallery. Gripping the air rifle tightly, the boy fired wildly, hitting nothing.

"Give it to him," he said to the gallery attendant. "Let the kid have it." The woman took his hand and pumped it, thanking him profusely. He tried to pull away, but she hung on until he yanked his hand free and turned to leave.

"I'm sorry, sir," the attendant said. "We can't do that. You'll have to choose the prize yourself. We aren't allowed to give prizes except to people who've won them. Those are the rules."

"Okay, give me that blue teddy bear over there," Morgan said, sputtering and waving his arms. Damn the rules. What the hell did the rules have to do with this?

The attendant handed him the toy and he shoved it at the distraught mother. "Here," he said, "take it." Again she grabbed at his hand. He pushed the toy at her roughly and it fell to the ground. The woman bent down to get it and Morgan quickly walked away.

Threading his way through the crowd, past the arcade railing, and out into the sun, Morgan eased himself into the stream of people. He put his hands in his pockets and relaxed, moving evenly and slowly to the other side of the fountain. Morgan felt free. Free from A. W. Albright & Company. Free from his morning drudgery, free from the subway ride to work and the clattering trucks carrying him from one Manhattan building to another. Never again, he decided, would he work for anyone else. When they reached the West—Kansas, he fancied, although he'd never been west of Pennsylvania—he would set up his own business.

He thought of Albright—a squat, red-faced man who wore suits too small, whose shirts pulled out from his waist, baring blubbery rolls of flesh—and just thinking about Albright made him laugh. Fat ass, he thought. The day before, as Morgan was cleaning out his locker, Albright had come over, laying a greasy hand on his shoulder. He told Morgan what a good craftsman he was. "Solid," he said. "You're solid. You ever need work, you just call old Archie Albright." Morgan had thanked him meekly. Good worker. Valued employee. Well, it had been nice to hear.

The tower clock above the arcade chimed. It was only ten o'clock, but Morgan was hungry. He had awakened at three that morning and his stomach was churning. He edged his way along the wall of the Western Arena, noting the show times. The announcer's voice boomed over the walls, drowned in the echo of galloping horses. The sound sent Morgan into a reverie: the plains, the West, horses.

Escape.

Beyond the arena was the Wagon Train, a restaurant with high, white, canvas domes simulating the Conestoga wagons which had carried American pioneers. Screaming children blocked the entrance ramp. Morgan waited in line impatiently, craning his neck, wanting to shout. Stop talking! Stop dawdling! Move faster! Can't you see I'm hungry? Move faster! He drummed his fingers on the aluminum rail, pulled at his collar. A small girl ran across his feet and he nearly reached out to swat her, restraining himself just in time. No time to start a scene. Inside, he looked back at the crowd struggling up the ramp. Through two half-circle windows, he saw four green-shirted guards approaching. Quickly he forced his way through the line and, glancing over his shoulder, walked to the other end of the huge hall. He ducked out the door and watched through the windows. The guards stood in the center of the restaurant for a few moments, then joined the cafeteria line. Slowly Morgan backed down the ramp, heading across the plaza for the Western Arena. Preoccupied, he bumped into a guard. The man nodded and smiled, saying, "Careful there." Morgan smiled back and kept on walking.

Down the middle of the steaming engine case ran a greasy, bulging crack. Masters leaned over it, shaking his head, disbelieving.

"I'm really sorry, Mr. Masters. Honest, I was watching the engine, but I couldn't tell. I thought I was . . ." David Thompson was on the verge of sobbing.

"Relax, Thompson," Masters said, trying to hold his own voice in control. Turning to search the crowd for Sarah and his children, he brushed his hands against the steaming engine and let out a yelp. He pulled the babbling boy away from the Sky Chariot's crowded entrance. Where the hell was Sarah?

"It seized up, sir. It didn't make any noise or anything. It didn't seem all that hot to me, really. I mean, we were running it real slow. But it just stopped. There wasn't much we could do—"

"Quiet," Masters said.

Attendants were still loading the parallel Chariot with passengers. Ken stopped the car from leaping onto the cables before the gears meshed. "Sorry, folks," he said calmly. "We're shutting down the Chariot for a while." A couple already in the car climbed out; the dozen others lined up to enter turned around, grumbling about not getting their money's worth, and walked down the steps. Ken stepped to the edge of the loading platform.

"We've had a minor technical problem, folks," he said, raising his voice so those far back in the crowd could hear him. "We'll be shutting down the Chariot for the morning. Be running again in a few hours." Wishful thinking, he thought. The crowd drifted away; a few people at the front of the line complained to the attendants that they had been waiting in line for half an hour. Putting his injured hand in his jacket pocket, Ken pushed his way to the front.

"I said we're sorry, folks, but we can't take any more passengers right now. We should be running again in a few hours." Angry stares. More complaints. Ken slammed the gate to the platform, then turned to the young girl who had been loading the other car.

"Get on that phone," he said, "and tell them to stop loading on the other end. If they've got anybody up on number two, you tell them to reverse and bring the car back slowly and stop loading. Then as soon as they're cleared over there, kill this engine. You got that? Now move. Fast."

"Yes, *sir*," the girl said.

Pete Toscani bounded over the railing behind Ken. Ken turned just as Toscani landed on his feet.

"Good Christ Almighty," the engineer said. "What a

fucking mess!" Wiping sweat from his eyes, he stood over the engine, then inserted a wrench under the crack in the engine casing and pried the top up to look inside. "Seized, seized up," he said. "You can scrap this engine for a couple of weeks. Have to rebore and grind the whole damn thing." Toscani looked tired. He, too, had been awake since four in the morning. His eyes wandered across the platform to the control booth, where David Thompson was sitting. Thompson was a slight boy with black, curly hair. This was his first season working at Olympic Adventure. "Thompson, what the hell do—"

Masters stopped Toscani. "That won't solve anything, Pete. The kid just didn't know what he was doing."

"My mistake," Pete said. "I should have shut the damn thing down and the crowds be damned."

"Don't blame yourself, Pete. I should have made the same decision and I didn't, and for the same reasons. Let's forget about that. What do we do now?"

Toscani lit a cigarette, then slipped under the pulley system and looked up into the trees. Ken followed him.

"We've got one car up," Pete said quietly. "Just by the first stilt. If you crawl over there, you can see it. Christ, we're lucky it's only one car."

Ken slid off the platform into the gully below. Through the tops of the trees, he saw the car's outlines near the edge of the steel strut holding the cable in place. Ken listened for voices from the car, but he heard nothing. It was too high. Then he looked out at the park and realized that the car was entirely hidden from view, covered by trees. He climbed back up to the platform; his hand was throbbing with pain.

"Kenny, you better get on the horn and tell those people up there what's going on." Pete handed him the intercom.

Ken paused a moment; his mind clouded as he searched for the right words, as he sought to clear the nervousness from his voice. He would have to be calm. And that was not how he felt. He blamed himself for not acting decisively. It was not Pete's responsibility to shut the ride down. Pete was not in charge of the park. Toscani busied himself with removing the top of the engine block. David Thompson sat, as if struck by paralysis, his head down. Ken heard the boy whimpering.

"Ladies and gentlemen," he said solemnly into the intercom. "We've got a minor technical problem down here and our chief engineer is working on it right now." No, that was wrong; chief engineer sounded too ominous. "We'll have you on the other side shortly." No, too positive. He had no idea how long it would be. It could be minutes. Or hours. "There's nothing to worry about." Wrong. That'll just make them worry more.

Toscani shouted across the platform. "Get one of them on the phone. And turn off the damn speaker. It's echoing the whole way down here." Toscani was covered with grease. Black smudges on his face made him appear ghoulish.

"At the front of the car," Ken said, speaking again into the intercom, "is a phone in a small red box. Would the person closest to it please pick it up so I can talk directly with you?" Ken switched off the car's speaker and put the phone onto a direct line with the intercom. He waited for a reply.

None came. Had they heard him?

"Pete, is this damn thing working?"

Toscani looked up from his work. Two of his staff were dismantling the engine. "Should be," he said. "Runs on electricity, not motor power. Give them a second to find the phone." He turned back to the engine. Masters chastised himself for holding up their work. Calm down. Be cool.

"Kenny, it's me." Sarah was on the other end, in the stranded car. Masters gasped.

"Christ, honey! How the hell did you get on so fast? I thought you were at the end of the line."

"The boy at the gate recognized us and let us ahead. What's going on?"

"Pete's working on the engine right now." Damn her. Why hadn't she listened to him an hour ago? Why had she

96

come out in the first place? And damn that Thompson kid. He had broken Olympic Adventure's rules: nobody gets ahead in line, no matter who it is. No park staff, no dignitaries, nobody. The boy had tried to curry favor with Masters by letting his wife onto the ride ahead of the paying customers. "I told you not to get on the Chariot, damnit. Why didn't you listen to me?"

"I see, Ken, I see." What? What kind of answer was that? Then he realized: she did not want to frighten the other passengers in the tram car.

"Okay, you're right. There's no point arguing now. How's Tommy? How's Alan?"

"Fine, Ken, they're just fine. Alan's half-asleep." Her voice was carefully neutral.

"Sarah, is the car full? How many people are there?" Of course the car would be full. He realized that as he asked the question; the lines were long.

"There are fifteen besides the three of us, Ken. Nine kids and six parents." Capacity. Eighteen people. Over a ton.

"All right, I want to talk to Pete. Sit by the phone and keep those people calm. Masters, out."

The sign-off echoed in his ears—the result of habit, of months spent talking to people he didn't know. It reassured him, this ritual; it was a sign that he was functioning on some level other than the purely emotional, that he had distance on the problem. Masters here. Masters out. Simple.

Toscani had removed the engine casing. "Shot clean through, just like I thought," he said, walking toward Ken. "Useless. Kaput."

"Pete, I don't want this news all over the park," Ken said. "We'd have a mob here and everybody else would go home. Tell your staff to keep it quiet, okay? And keep those kids from spreading it. I think the car's pretty well hidden. Now what do we do? Can your men climb up on that strut and slide it down?"

"Not a prayer, son. It's clamped onto that cable. We've

got to get this engine unhitched and move the other one over." Pete watched the mechanics at work. "It's going to take half an hour at least."

"Pete, what about that cable? Will it hold?"

Toscani looked up—the cable was taut, vibrating faintly from the tension of the hanging car—and he suspected that the weight of the car, pulling at an angle, would eventually snap the cable if the car was moved without motor power.

"Kenny, you just get on the horn again and tell them to sit still."

"Pete, will it hold?" Ken asked, raising his voice, "Or won't it?"

"I don't know, kid," Toscani said flatly. "Maybe. If they sit still. I just don't know."

Masters said, "Sarah and the kids are up there."

Toscani whistled softly. He had been so engrossed in dismantling the engine that he hadn't heard Masters talking with his wife in the stranded car.

"All right, kid. You might as well know. I tried to get Cunningham to replace those frigging cables a month ago. I told him—and I told Hawkins—that I didn't want to run this damn ride the way it was. Cunningham said no, that we couldn't afford to replace them. I also told that bastard I wanted these engines completely overhauled, and he wouldn't pay for the damn parts. These cars are heavy and it takes a lot of power to move them. I damn near quit on the spot last week, but I figured it was better for me to be here than some grease monkey from the local gas station. And Hawkins wanted me to stay, so I said yes. Damnit, I knew we were going to have trouble with the Chariot. I should've shut the damn thing down."

Masters was still not satisfied. "How long, Pete? How long?"

"Damnit, son, I told you I don't know. Your guess is as good as mine. Look, if the cable snaps, the clamps will hold the car anyway, but those people are going to get roughed up. Now get on the horn and tell them not to move around up there." Toscani returned to his work, feverishly turning the bolts holding the ruined engine to the platform.

Masters reached for the intercom phone. Then he saw Toscani stop working. His men gathered around him, leaving their tools on the platform. Above him, Ken heard the cable creaking. It shook violently now, like a giant violin string that had just been plucked. A whining roar filled Ken's head. In his mind's eye, he saw his children flying through the air, landing, mangled, in the trees. His chest heaved. He thought he would retch.

"Masters, damnit, get on the horn and tell those people to stop moving around up there." Pete passed him in a blur, jumping over the railing.

Ken pushed the button on the intercom.

"Yes, Ken," Sarah said, her voice clear and calm. "What is it?"

"Honey, you've got to keep them still up there." His voice was unsteady. "They're swaying the car."

"The kids are running up and down the aisle, Ken. It's hard to stop them."

"Well, try, damnit!" Ken yelled. His knees buckled and he struggled to stay on his feet. "Sorry, honey," he said quietly, "but Pete says you've got to keep the car from moving so much."

"I'll try."

"Masters, out."

More of Toscani's men had arrived. Some continued working on the engine, dismantling the frame quickly, littering the deck with slabs of metal. Across the deck, four used electric rotors to unfasten bolts. Above their heads, the cable swayed, vibrating more loudly inside the loading bay.

"Pete," Masters screamed, "It's creaking like crazy. Can't you see it won't hold? Do something!"

"I got ears, boy," Toscani shouted irritably. "Now shut up. We're working as fast as we can." Toscani leaped over the barrier between the two engines to supervise the second team. A gusty wind rolled over the treetops and the cable's creaking grew louder. Transfixed, Masters stared up, his eyes darting from the mechanics to the cable and back again. The teeth on the pullies tore into the cable, eating strips of rubber as they turned. The fibers strained under the weight of the hanging car. Toscani crossed the platform and slowly fed slack into the cable, loosening the pullies. Hurry, Masters thought. Get the damn thing working. To him, it seemed that the mechanics didn't realize that lives were at stake. The creaking grew so loud that Masters covered his ears. The entire platform shook.

"Pete," Masters screamed again, his eyes now fixed on the pullies, "it's going to rip the building down!"

"Shut up, Kenny." Toscani knew the cable would give long before the beams supporting the building cracked. A ton of weight pulling on one cable couldn't tear a building apart.

Ken's heartbeat increased. His mouth went dry and he coughed. The tension of the cable grew. The rubber began to stretch. Ken lit a cigarette, choked as he inhaled, then noticed he had left two burning cigarettes on the railing in front of him.

"We ain't going to make it," Toscani shouted. "Not a rat's chance in hell we're going to make it." His men continued working. "Get me Glenwood," the mechanic called into his walkie-talkie. He crossed the platform and stood next to Masters. "Good," he was saying into the radio, "and don't waste time, Dexter. I'll need every inch of ladder you can find."

Then he was talking to Masters, but Masters did not hear. The roar in Ken's head blanketed all sounds; he opened his mouth but words would not come. Suddenly Toscani's greasy hands were shaking him. "Damnit, son, listen to me. Get over to Glenwood and supervise the loading of those ladders. Do you understand me?"

"Right, Pete," Masters heard himself saying, but his own voice seemed far away, disembodied. The rafters of the deck shook and the cable swung more wildly, stretching visibly with every tremor.

"It's giving way," Toscani said. The crew rushed to the

railing. First one pulley tore loose from its molding, then another. The vibrating stopped for a moment, and then the wind picked up, shaking the car. Mutely the men stood by, moving their eyes from the pullies and gears to the quivering loop of rubber over their heads.

Then, crisply, and with surprisingly little noise, the cable snapped. "Oh my God," Toscani said, crossing himself. The car dipped into the trees and hung, dangling, from the broken cable, swinging gently in the breeze.

8

The Hampshire Industries boardroom reeked of tobacco, a rich aroma that reminded Cole Cunningham of Havana before Castro. Those were the days, Cole thought. Through high windows half-covered by brown brocaded drapes, shafts of light shone on the long oak table. Bookshelves filled with bound leather volumes lined the walls. A glass-doored walnut case displayed original strikings of Audubon's drawings of North American birds, faced at the far end of the room by an Empire settee and four Victorian chairs. Eight-foot Ming vases on marble pedestals showed intricately glazed scenes of fourteenth-century Chinese gardens. Eighteenth-century Sèvres porcelain plates rested in gold trivets on the mantel, capping a hand-carved oak Edwardian fireplace. Around the conference table were four chairs, and at each place was a small silver coffee pot and a note pad, all arranged with the unerring exactness of a skilled but unimaginative painter of Flemish still lifes.

Cole Cunningham sipped coffee and chewed on his cigar, waiting for the Duke of Hampshire. The Duke would arrive first. Proper bastard was probably out of bed before sunrise. At least the Duke, who was planning his departure to spend the summer in England, would want the meeting over as soon as possible. And the more the Duke wanted to get away, the easier it would be persuading him to let Cole handle the details. It was just as well, he thought, that the Duke refused to tolerate New York summers.

Soon the Duke's Rolls Royce, chilled inside almost to freezing, would cruise down a nearly empty Fifth Avenue and stop at the corner of Fifty-third Street, and the Duke, no doubt having slept during the trip from his Long Island estate, would alight from the back and walk to the polished aluminum doors of Olympic Tower, tapping his gold-topped cane on the glass to attract the doorman's attention. Cole Cunningham counted on the Duke to give him carte blanche, for the Duke had never paid more than passing attention to the financial matters of the conglomerate bearing his name.

Hawkins, however, would arrive at the last minute. To keep us waiting, Cunningham thought. To make an appearance. He would come from a squash game at his midtown club, and he too would want the meeting finished quickly, so that he could reach the park before noon. He would want to check the crowds.

"Crowds," Cunningham said to the empty room. "Overflowing crowds."

"What's that, sir?" his secretary asked, entering from the anteroom.

"Nothing, Helen. Where are my cigars?"

"Right here, sir," she said, putting the cigars down on the serving cart.

"And Helen, tell Renaldo to make sure there's more coffee."

"Yes, sir," she said. "Naturally."

He thought of Hawkins and the name stuck in his craw. Hiring Hawkins had been the one move he'd thought would save Olympic Adventure. He had hired Brad three and a half years ago, and gotten rid of that idiot Bill Jeffers, who had ruined the park's reputation nearly beyond repair. The place had been sloppy, inefficiently run, gobbling money from Hampshire Industries' coffers. Cole had thought then that Olympic Adventure might generate more money than all the other subsidiaries combined. He needed a man who could redeem the park's promise. But such men were rare. Parks on Disney's scale had just begun to boom. The field of possibilities comprised a mere handful of men, men skilled as administrators, with knowledge of finance, with the ability to oversee large staffs, to understand organizing a modern electronic circus. Cunningham had decided then that if Disney had the best, he would raid Disney. Hell, he'd raided companies before, for their talent, for their capital.

He'd been in Tokyo negotiating contracts for a new camera to compete with Polaroid. On what seemed a whim to his Japanese partners, he booked a flight to California, hired a car immediately on landing, and called on Brad Hawkins at Disneyland.

Brad Hawkins had showed not the slightest interest in Olympic Adventure. "Your park is in trouble," he had told Cunningham, reciting Olympic Adventure's attendance figures. "You had five million last year, and you lost money on them. The grapevine is small, Mr. Cunningham. Everyone knows your problems." Hawkins had turned down his offer, saying that no amount of money would budge him. He had told Cunningham that he was planning to move from Disneyland to Disney World and then to the film company. It had been a game on Hawkins's part, Cole thought now. He had been playing unavailable, waiting for Cole to make a different kind of offer. And that was precisely what Cole had done.

No interference in running the park and seventy-five thousand dollars per year for five years.

Hawkins said no.

Eighty thousand dollars per year, Cole had said, and Hawkins had simply stared past his face through his office window.

Ninety thousand dollars per year, Cole had said.

And then Hawkins had leaned across his desk and spoken very quietly. This, he had said, is what I want. A seat on the Hampshire Industries board of directors. Ten percent of Hampshire's stock, undiluted. A five-year management contract at an annual salary of $125,000 per year.

Cole had been flabbergasted. Even he had not been drawing that kind of salary, not then. It was an odd experience—finding the tables turned. Cole was accustomed to setting conditions and waiting for others to meet them.

"That's *my* offer," Hawkins had said to him. "Take it or leave it."

Cole had flown to New York and pondered the condition of the business he'd built. He'd ignored the pile of messages stacked on his desk, relegated telephone calls to his staff. Isolating himself from the Duke of Hampshire and Gabriel Bloome, he'd spoken with virtually no one—not to his partners and not to the banks to which he owed enormous sums of money. He'd thought only of the gray penciled numbers on the light green ledger pages; gray numbers that, but for the accounting profession's taste, might just as well have appeared in red ink. He'd considered the slippery slide from top to bottom, how much smoother and quicker it was than climbing in the opposite direction.

He remembered the day he made the decision as one of the ugliest in his life, marking some sort of personal failure. He needed Brad Hawkins, this steel-eyed, square-jawed Southerner with his soft voice and his demands. Demands, Cole had finally realized, he had to meet. The time had come to play someone else's game or the game would shut down, like a poker party stopped by the law. In the end, he had called his partners, extracted part of their stock, and met Hawkins's conditions.

There had been a time when succumbing to others' demands seemed no more likely to Cole Cunningham than selling off divisions to pay debts. But that, too, had come, and after that, Cole's capacity for self-doubt increased at seemingly geometric proportions. He had crossed a line, a thin but discernible line, into a private irrationality.

At precisely fifteen minutes before ten o'clock, James Whitlam, the Duke of Hampshire, casually pushed his way through the door of the boardroom. Dressed as usual in a dark gray suit, one of the several dozen seven-and-a-half ounce wools he favored in the spring, he had the look of a man who comforted himself with the belief that old age need not be a disgrace. He was a slight man, and his thinning silver hair was neatly trimmed. A narrow scar faded into the creases around his right eye, becoming visible as it extended outward to his temple. The eye fluttered occasionally, a tic, the result of a war wound in the African campaign under Montgomery.

"Good morning, James," Cunningham said, standing.

"Good morning, Cole," the Duke said, sitting and unfolding the *Times*. "What, pray tell, are we doing here on a Saturday morning?"

"All in good time, James. All in good time." Cunningham returned to writing on the yellow legal pad in front of him. The Duke pretended to read the *Times*, turning to the Friday stock closings. But he'd read them in the car en route to the city and instead fixed his eyes on the center of the page, allowed his vision to cloud, and thought about Hampshire Industries' balance sheet. There was something dreadfully odd about the numbers, and he'd been asking himself since the evening before how Olympic Adventure could be spending less money this year than last. The figures also indicated a drastic turnabout in the profits of Hampshire Industries' major importing subsidiaries, and that was totally unexplainable. Yes, the Duke thought, it was most odd indeed. All costs had risen: labor, food, entertainment, maintenance. Three managers had resigned in Europe. And the projections for Olympic Adventure's cash flow seemed ridiculously out of line.

The Haitian steward entered, filled the four silver coffee pots, then exited with a clatter. Cunningham looked up, glanced at the Duke, and once again thought his plan through. He had considered one option after another, doubting his judgment each time. Perhaps it was not Max Brodky. Perhaps he was overreacting to Peter Welch's call. Whatever the case, he had concluded that protection from a takeover bid, whether the bid came or not, would not be wasted. If he were right, only more money from outside the corporation would prevent Max Brodky, or anyone else, from squeezing him out. That meant, Cunningham admitted to himself with resignation, a new partner, *another* new partner. Preferably a silent, uninvolved partner.

Exactly where he would find eleven million dollars overnight, Cunningham was far from sure. Neither commercial bankers nor investment bankers moved that quickly. Contacts must be made, figures laid out at length, sacrifices offered. And bankers were notorious for taking time about such things. Boards must meet, ponder, give the appearance of reaching wise and solemn judgment. Scratch their heads, quibble with accountants. Before they finished maundering—well, by then, someone would have moved in and swallowed up Hampshire Industries. Cunningham could barely contain his contempt for Peter Welch; of all those he'd dealt with, none impressed him as more slow-witted, more pompous, more stupid than bankers.

At five minutes before ten, Gabriel Bloome left his office, three doors away from the boardroom, and tramped down the hallway, his fleshy body shaking noticeably as he entered and claimed his seat at the far end of the table, across from the Duke of Hampshire. The two men made small talk—summertime in England, the proper attitude toward servants, a party they'd attended the weekend before. A routine litany.

Cole Cunningham listened with one part of his mind while computing and recomputing the figures on his pad with another, counting the minutes to ten o'clock. Nine million might do it, he thought for a moment. Pay the notes and stave off the creditors for another month. Then the park would be producing enough cash to cover current expenses. Maybe. He wondered what the crowds were like today, and reached for a phone.

Uptown and three blocks west, Brad Hawkins was waiting for a cab on Central Park South in front of the New York Athletic Club. His hair was still damp. A tall, broad man, Hawkins stood as if his back were taped with splints and his shoulders pinned upright by an invisible force.

A beggar knelt on the curb in front of him, holding a cup, and Hawkins, with hardly a thought, reached into his pocket for a five-dollar bill. Beggars made him nervous. They reminded him of poverty, and poverty made him nervous. Born in the Texas fields surrounding the two-street town of Hillsboro, population six thousand, Hawkins had grown up on the plains of the Texas panhandle, hearing talk of the dry years, when the Midwest and Southwest had been the great dust bowl. His parents and grandparents reminisced about the bad times, and from them he had absorbed a fear of poverty and hunger, absorbed their fear as if it had been passed through their genes. It was then he had developed the blank stare of fear that others would someday come to see as control.

His parents were tenant farmers. As a child, Hawkins had labored in the fields, gone to school in the morning and picked melons in the afternoon, worked in the peanut and peach and potato patches and cotton fields. Until, that is, the schoolteacher in the rough-hewn one-room schoolhouse, a woman he would never forget, had asked him to stay after class, had told him to study hard and apply for admission to the state university. His parents had resented the woman and attempted, without success, to bring their son back to farming, where he would earn money. But Brad Hawkins knew better.

On the day the notice came from the University of Texas, the news buzzed through Hillsboro like one of the dust storms to which the farmers had once been so accustomed. Through the dry dirt streets—to the tailor's shop and the doctor's office and the general store, and the lumber yard, and finally to Betty Jean Foster's desk in the schoolhouse—the message moved. Willie Hawkins had a boy going up to the state university. On a scholarship. Damn, ain't that something, the farmers said. Always knew Willie Hawkins's boy was real smart.

Brad Hawkins packed up—packed the sepia photograph of his parents, packed his harmonica, packed his precious books—and bought, with his scrupulously tended savings, a train ticket for Austin. It was an opportunity the significance of which did not escape seventeen-year-old Brad Hawkins. He had made the natural comparisons a child makes between those who have and those who do not. The university was the road out of the dust bowl, away from the back-breaking labor that had kept his parents and their parents in bondage. Brad Hawkins had seen the fruits of knowledge long before being given the chance to taste them. He had seen the big, white clapboard houses far outside town, where Doc Benjamin lived, where Charlie Watson the lawyer lived, where Mr. Meehan from the general store had his ranch. All these men had gone up to the state university and had come home. Secretly, though, Brad Hawkins knew he would never come home to Hillsboro, knew the day he left on the train that he had seen the last of these dusty streets. Never again would he drag himself from the dusty fields, too exhausted to read. Never again would he bend and pick to the chatter of the field hands, panting with hunger until after the sun had set.

He plunged into academic work, and he was a good student. Long afternoons under the tutoring eye of Miss Foster, after the others had gone, had taught him discipline: how to think, how to read, how to question. In the library at the university, he sat hunched over books until his eyes were numbed with pain. And, with a canniness that might have been inborn, he slyly cultivated his friends, found those who would make their way in the world on their own and those already equipped—by birth, by money—to clear the path for themselves and others. He married an oilman's daughter, who put him through law school, where he continued building relationships that promised the most for his future. On the day he received his law degree, his wife left him. They had hardly spoken in months. He did not mourn her absence. He could not feel it.

After graduation, he worked in a large Houston law firm, where all the partners had a stake in Texas politics. They told Hawkins he could eventually become a United States senator. But senators, Hawkins learned, were men owned by other men, as were, for that matter, presidents. Hawkins preferred to own rather than be owned, and he preferred the raw power of money to the ephemeral power of politics. Too often he had watched his clients call Washington; too often had senators and congressmen jumped to

109

do their bidding. Brad Hawkins would jump for no one. And so as the years passed, he waited for the right offer, one far from Houston, Texas. Discreetly he let it be known that he was available.

When Walt Disney, already an old man, called, it seemed to Hawkins he had spent enough time practicing law, sitting behind the desk helping people avoid taxes. With Disney, he saw the chance to get out, to eventually escape from the demands of others, be beholden to no one. Perhaps his chance would not come with Disney; perhaps his chance would come later. Patient, persevering, he could wait. Leaving Texas, he'd left his past behind—his family, his nearly forgotten childhood, the wife who had left him—he left it all behind, never, he thought, to be remembered.

At ten o'clock exactly, when the clock on the mantelpiece of the Hampshire Industries boardroom chimed, Hawkins strode in. Cole looked up at him and Brad felt a twinge of guilt. He could imagine Alexis being drawn to this man who, fifteen years before, must have been in many ways not unlike himself. He wondered what she had been like then, exactly what she had found in Cole. Cole was a flawed, weak man, but he must have possessed an extraordinary power. The power, however strong it had been, was gone now, and although Hawkins no longer strictly believed, as he once had, in a world of winners and losers, in Cole Cunningham he saw a loser. At the least, Cole had lost Alexis. Hawkins remembered the first moment he had seen them together; their every gesture testified to their separateness, to her desire to leave him. In bed, she had the manners of an aged prostitute; she was so starved she begged to be ravaged. He had always obliged and eventually she awakened in him a deeper sexuality than he had ever experienced. They were beasts, turning human.

Sleeping with another man's wife, he thought, was a minor sin, negligible; he never met the husbands of the women he seduced. It was easier that way—it allowed him complete distance. Those were the rules: no expectations on either side. But with Alexis, there had been no rules, and he had chased across three thousand miles to spend a weekend with her. Not only had he met her husband, he worked for him. If he had a moral code—and he wanted to believe he did—then it prohibited kicking a man when he was down. He had, for a time, been able to justify his affair with Alexis by thinking of it not as his salvation, but as hers. It had helped her tear herself away from Cole. But it was a false justification for a nonexistent accusation. Cole did not know and he would not know because he refused to know. Cole ignored the signs. Hawkins thought, if it had not been me, it would have been someone else. No, of course that wasn't true. She had told him he was the first. She had never before been unfaithful to Cole. And I, Hawkins thought, have never become so involved. No woman ever mattered as much. No woman before Alexis had ever captured him so completely. They were leading each other out of the past, he thought, but neither had any idea of where they were going.

He took his place at the end of the table across from Cole. He had not liked Cole from the beginning. Partly he still disliked him and partly, more than he would have thought possible, he felt sorry for him. Cole was like a plant prematurely gone to seed. And so whatever he felt about Cole, he decided that he did not have to feel guilty anymore. Cole had let Alexis go as surely as if he had pushed her out the door.

"Well, gentlemen," Cole said, "we are all here."

"Cole, I have a brilliant idea," Gabriel Bloome said, his voice squeaking with excitement. "I've just sketched out a new section for the park. It's called The Magic of Time."

"Gabriel, please," Cunningham said sharply. What is the matter with the fool, he thought. He knows why we're here. Okay, you're a genius; so be quiet, creative genius, while I save your goddamn dreams. Always a new idea; a vaster, more bizarre design for carving up the Pine Barrens. This morning he had no patience for designs.

"Exactly what is the situation, Cole?" Hawkins asked.

"Yes, let's attend to business," Cunningham said. "We have a busy day ahead." Anxiety pervaded his thinking, but not his voice. "I'll set it out as clearly as I can." He was about to play for an audience of one, for Hawkins alone, knowing he had the Duke and Gabriel Bloome in his pocket. He needed Hawkins to outvote the bank and the insurance companies, the minority stockholders. Gabriel Bloome, the Duke, and he himself each held sixteen percent of the stock in Hampshire Industries. Hawkins's ten percent was crucial. Without it, Cunningham could not hope to sustain a battle against the board of First National Trust Company of Saint Louis. Or, as he suspected, against Max Brodky.

"I've had some bad news," he began. "The bank may not renew our notes."

"What does Peter Welch say about this?" Hawkins asked. Why tell us about the bank, he wondered. He was certain Cunningham would talk about Max Brodky.

"Welch was the one who told me. He called last night. It seems there's talk around the bank. Welch doesn't know why, but apparently there's some strong sentiment against us. Now we've got to plan, just in case. I think the bank wants to take control." He paused and looked directly at Hawkins, not noticing that the Duke's head had risen slightly, that his eyes were lifted slightly from the newspaper folded in front of him. "I think there's someone behind all this—someone who's forcing the board's hand."

Gabriel Bloome was not prepared for this. "Who, Cole?"

"I was getting to that. Mind you, I'm not sure. It's just a feeling, but I'm betting it's Max Brodky. I'm betting that Max will come in after the bank turns us down and offer us fifty cents on the dollar. Buy us all out."

Congratulations, Hawkins thought. He had to give Cole credit. The news Alexis had heard was right and Cole had figured it out himself. He reprimanded himself for not paying closer attention to the balance sheet. But damnit, who could have known the bank would balk at renewing the loans?

112

"Brodky," Hawkins said innocently. "What's Brodky got to do with it? What does Welch say?" He wanted to know how Cole had reached his conclusion.

"Welch doesn't know shit," Cunningham said. "I think it's Max because this is Max's pattern. Every time First Saint Louis swings a major deal these days, Max is in on it. You can call that coincidence, but I don't think so. Max will waltz in here like a disinterested party, just like he did with Marty Meeker's publishing company. Pretending to rescue us. In return, we give up our stock to him instead of to the bank. I'll tell you what I think. I think the whole damn thing smells. There's no damn reason why the bank should refuse to renew. We're turning the corner. The park will do a hundred thousand today. You know what I think, Brad? I think Max Brodky *is* the bank. We give up our stock, settle for a couple of years' salary, and then we're out on our asses." He looked around the table.

"A hundred thousand?" Hawkins asked. "Where did you get that number?"

"I called the gate five minutes ago, that's where."

Gabriel Bloome doodled on his note pad, drawing a sunken globe surrounded by sundials. The center of The Magic of Time. "That's a nice crowd," Bloome said. "How can you be so sure it's Max? He wouldn't do that to us. My father always got along with him. They were pals."

You are a lovely, sweet man, Cole Cunningham thought, and a fool.

"I'm not sure," Cole said. "I'm just trusting my intuition, and my intuition tells me Peter Welch could fall asleep during an atomic blast and wake up wondering what happened. He's missing the signals out there, that's all."

Hawkins stood up. "Let's assume you're right, Cole," he said, knowing that he was. "How much money do we need?"

"We could get by with as little as nine million, but I figure eleven million would do the trick," Cunningham

113

said. "It's got to come in one chunk, and from one source; someone out of Max's reach. Someone who'll vote with us against the bank." He stopped, watched Hawkins, wondered what he was thinking.

"It's not that simple, Cole," Hawkins said.

The Duke shifted in his chair. Cunningham saw that he was, in fact, listening. The Duke's dry, dull eyes seemed to reflect the world back on itself, as if they were mirrors.

"If Max Brodky is aiming for a takeover," Hawkins went on, "it might be worth talking to him. If Welch turns out to be right, we can't even meet the payroll next Friday."

"The payroll!" the Duke said. "Is that correct?"

Sonuvabitch! Cunningham thought he saw a smirk on Hawkins's face. Paranoid, he told himself. Relax.

"Yes, James," Hawkins said. "The payroll. Until this morning, we accepted the bank's renewal of our notes as a given. Of course, we can shift money from other divisions, if necessary, but then we start constricting everybody. Is that right, Cole?"

"Not exactly," Cunningham said.

"*How* not exactly?" the Duke asked.

"Well, we're a little short everywhere this week," Cunningham said.

"*How* short?" the Duke asked.

Cunningham was now certain Hawkins was smirking. Bastard. I *made* you!

"Short enough," Cunningham said, "that even if we don't pay the notes, we'll have trouble meeting the payroll."

"What Cole means," Hawkins said, "is that next Monday morning Tishman is locking up our Jericho warehouse unless we pay the rent. Which cuts off our supplies for the park."

Cunningham jumped to his feet, shouting. "That is not true!"

"Sit down, Cole," Hawkins said. "It is true and you know it. We could get a new partner in time, but what's the point? Sure it's possible, but what's so terrible about merging into a Brodky holding company, if you're right about that? We get their cash and their management help." Hawkins spoke from strength, knowing, after all, that he was a valuable resource. In any takeover, he would be most likely to survive. Cole Cunningham, of course, might not.

"What makes you so sure Max wouldn't just push us out?" Cunningham asked. *Not this time, Mr. Hawkins. No deals.*

Nothing, Hawkins thought. But he won't push me out.

"Because the Brodkys want to make money," Hawkins said, "and they don't know anything about amusement parks. We do."

You do, Cunningham thought. Not me.

Hawkins stood, filled his cup, and pushed his chair under the table. Leaning on the back of the chair, he towered over his partners. "Cole, we're in deep trouble. And you know *how* deep. Did you think the bank would hold out on us? No. Did I? No. But damnit, do you have any idea what I've been going through, holding off Con Ed by telling them fresh money was coming? We're lucky our power hasn't been cut off. Do you know what it's like to search for new suppliers because we haven't paid our bills? We owe everybody in the whole damn country. We're two months behind with everything. And it's my name that's on the line, gentlemen, my reputation." He paused to let his message sink in. Cunningham glared at him without saying a word.

"Now I'll tell you what I think," Hawkins went on. "I'm prepared to listen to other arguments. If you think you can raise more money in three days, Cole, I'd be glad to hear how you plan to do it. But if the bank is backing off, I don't see how the hell you can raise cash elsewhere."

That was not quite what Hawkins was thinking. He did not believe for a moment that Cunningham could raise eleven million dollars in three days. He picked up his cup, moved to the window, and sat on the sill. Light poured in as the drapes spread around him, and he was silhouetted in a haze of smoke.

"The bank is backing off," Cunningham said, raising his voice, "because Max is telling them to. And there are lots of people who'd be glad to help me. Especially against Max Brodky."

"After they see our balance sheet?" Hawkins asked.

"What's *wrong* with our balance sheet?" Cunningham shouted.

That, Hawkins thought, is what I'd like to know.

"Just a moment," the Duke of Hampshire said, his sonorous voice unexpectedly filling the room. "Might I raise a few questions?" All heads turned. "I'm rather in the dark here. Exactly what is involved with bringing anyone into the company? Will our investment be protected? How much control must we relinquish? Can we truly raise additional capital, Cole? Where might we find eleven million dollars on such short notice?"

Cunningham could not believe the Duke's interest. Since when was the old coot so damn curious? He answered the questions in order. First, they couldn't know what anyone would demand. But Max Brodky, if it was Max Brodky, had a pattern: everybody was booted out. Second, each man in the room would have to release about one-fifth of his holdings, enough to make a block of Hampshire stock for a new investor—a total of about twelve percent. The new investor would hold shares on a dollar-for-dollar basis, without diluting the number of shares. Third, as for finding an investor, that was why he had called this meeting—to ask them to consider all the personal financial avenues open to them—without strings, without a take-over threat. And finally, Cole Cunningham said he could find the money himself, if they would give him authority.

Not damn likely, Hawkins thought.

Brodky, Gabriel Bloome thought. Max Brodky and his father had been friends. Cole had to be wrong.

"I shall have to think further," the Duke said.

"Well, one thing's for sure," Hawkins said. "We're not going to raise any money this morning. And I have a park

to run. So why don't we sleep on it and talk tomorrow."
Let him try, Hawkins thought. Alexis says he can't win.
Not against Max Brodky. Hawkins was looking forward
to meeting the powerful Mr. Brodky.

"Well, that's fine, Brad," Cole Cunningham said. He
had hoped to close off a Brodky family takeover altogether
this morning, getting approval to search for a new investor.
That would have to wait. "But let's be careful, gentlemen,"
he went on. "If our problems become known, it will only
make raising money more difficult. We can't let anybody
get the idea we're running a fire sale here."

"Good God, Cole," Hawkins interjected. "We can't lie
to a new investor. I'm not about to let anybody—your
friends or my friends or anyone else—invest without giving our financial picture down to the last dime. We have
enough trouble without being sued for misrepresentation."

"Without question," Cunningham said. "I wasn't suggesting we lie. Only that we be *careful,* that's all."

His tone threatened, and Hawkins resented it, and said
so. They bickered for half an hour, the Duke and Gabriel
Bloome listening, piecing together a common front, a story
that was true but exposed serious problems as undramati-
cally as possible. Hawkins was willing to play along with
Cunningham, assuming that the battle could not be won.

As they were finishing, the telephone rang. It was Ken
Masters, calling for Hawkins.

"Hawkins here, Ken. I'm leaving right now."

Masters quickly related the story of the disabled engine
and the snapped cable. He did not explain the advance
warning or admit his indecisiveness about closing the
Chariot. He simply begged Hawkins to come, and fast.

"Relax, Ken. I'm on my way."

The three men around the conference table looked at
Hawkins apprehensively.

"An engine kicked a rod at the Sky Chariot," Hawkins
said abruptly, staring at Cole Cunningham. "I'll see you in
the morning. Here. Same time." He rushed through the
door and told Cunningham's secretary to call the heliport
on an East River pier, twenty blocks south.

117

In the boardroom, Cunningham sat impassive. Gabriel Bloome was the first to speak.

"Didn't Pete want to replace those engines, Cole?"

"Shut up, Gabriel, will you please?"

"But Cole—"

"Shut up, goddamnit." Cunningham gathered his papers and left the room. Gabriel and the Duke stared at each other, then headed for the elevator without saying a word.

Bands and baton twirlers clogged Fifth Avenue. Sprinting toward Madison, Hawkins hailed a cab. Barking his destination, "Thirty-first and the highway, the heliport, my friend, and make it snappy," he settled into the taxi's dilapidated rear seat and listened to his heart beating. Not in the condition you once were, Hawkins. You're getting old. He held his breath for twenty seconds, closed his eyes, and exhaled to the count of ten—a yoga exercise to calm himself.

The meeting had not gone quite as he had expected, but it was obvious that Cole couldn't keep Hampshire Industries afloat. It was like asking an alcoholic to tend bar. Cole seemed to have lost his talent for making money and developed a new talent for spending it. The look on Cole's face when I mentioned the warehouse, thought Hawkins; what else had he been hiding? Cunningham might get Gabriel Bloome's vote, but the Duke was wavering. He made a mental note to call the old man that evening, before tomorrow's meeting. His own mind was made up, and not least, perhaps, because of the Chariot breakdown— Cunningham's refusal to allow proper maintenance, the oil shipment Pete had complained about the week before. Hadn't the oil arrived? Was that why the engine kicked a rod? How could Pete have let it happen? Then he remembered: Pete had wanted to replace the cables as well. Hawkins had agreed with Cunningham—yes, they could get through another season—and now he regretted it. The cables were fine; four years old, but fine. Or were they? Yes, Hawkins thought, without an engine breakdown, they were.

Christ, he had gotten caught up in saving money, and damnit, the park could make money. They were turning the corner. Without Cole's interference, Olympic Adventure could mint money. Cole, the damn supplicant, who had come to him three years before on a day etched in his memory. Cole, who had come in a long chauffeured car, making a point of announcing that he had flown in from Japan. Cole, trying to impress. Wearing a confident smile. All pretense, Hawkins had thought. Why not admit your park's in trouble? It had given Hawkins great pleasure to watch Cole sweat.

"Here you are, bud. That's two and a quarter," the cab driver said. Hawkins gave the cabbie three singles and darted for the waiting copter.

"Captain, let me borrow your radio for a minute, will you? Got some serious messages to send. Matter of life and death." The copter pilot regarded his passenger curiously, then handed him the radio's microphone. Waiting for answers to his calls, Hawkins began sketching on a pad he had pulled from his briefcase. First a long, rectangular form composed of cross-hatched lines. Then, on top of the rectangle, several smaller boxes, a sort of pyramid. Then a straight line of narrower crosshatches. Maybe we won't need it, Hawkins thought, but if we do, it will work. Damn, Cunningham doesn't know what he's doing. He's playing games, not making money. Disneyland—now there was a business, not just an exercise in spectacle. Spectacle, to be sure, but not for its own sake. Hawkins thought: I should have watched Cole more carefully.

The helicopter crossed the Hudson in a rush of green and swept over the Palisades. Hawkins turned his attention to the passengers stranded in the tram, and to the drawing on his lap.

9

Six miles from the main gate of Olympic Adventure, Jake Slocum spoke to nine farmers gathered in his barn.

"Can't wait any longer, boys," he said. "We've got to take this thing into our own hands." Slocum had farmed his family's 830 acres for forty-two years. In southern New Jersey, he was the equivalent of landed gentry. He played the role of country bumpkin, but this particular hayseed operated a group of businesses that brought him some two and a half million dollars a year in gross revenues. His dairy business was one of the most modern and most successful in the entire country. From his cows came enough milk every week to supply every man, woman, and child in nearby Glenwood with six quarts a day for an entire year. Whatever remained after bottling under his own label, Slocum Farms, went to Sealtest in bulk. With his apple orchards, a dry-goods store, the Harvester tractor dealership, and the manure business, Jake Slocum was a tiny rural empire unto himself. Before him, his father had farmed the same land, and before him, Jake's grandfather, who had emigrated from Norway, had cleared away the trees and built the rambling farmhouse in which Jake Slocum was born and still lived. Jake had built two smaller houses on the property, and when his two sons finished agricultural school, they planned to return to the farm, live in those houses, raise their families, and carry on what their great-grandfather had begun. With the latest in agribusiness techniques, they would increase Jake Slocum's yield.

That, at any rate, was how Jake Slocum saw the future until Olympic Adventure arrived. Too late he had discovered who was buying up the farmland and forests bordering on the state park. Then his taxes rose, developers gobbled up land throughout the county, and soon, if the

Regional Plan Association approved their applications, Slocum's farm would be surrounded by tract housing. Eventually he would be forced to sell, when the value of his land rose so high that farming wouldn't support it. At the last equipment dealers' convention in Kansas City, the Missouri farmers complained about developers, about that West Coast outfit, Redwood, and the cheap ranch houses they were scattering across the Midwest; and about Armco, the St. Louis company, chewing up the plains. And for them, the problem was actually years away. For Jake Slocum, it was already here. He had seen the future, and he didn't like it.

"No sir," he said to the men in his barn, "we can't wait no more." Normally a boisterous man, he spoke with a rough sort of dignity. "Them damn congressmen can talk about protecting family homesteads until the goddamn White House is buried in peanut shells, and by then we'll all be gone. I'm telling you, we should have stopped that damn a-*muse*-ment park"—he parted the syllables, twanging purposefully for emphasis—"before they built it. Now we got no choice."

The others in the barn nodded as if agreeing, but Slocum's inflammatory tone made them fidget. Picket lines and demonstrations were for the kind of people they read about in the newspapers and saw on television—longhairs, hippies, perverts, Communists. These farmers had never protested anything. They rarely ventured beyond their fields and farms, barns and feed lots, silos and land markers, family and friends. Above all, family. Solitary people, they had little interest in the public maelstrom. But family, Slocum knew, was the cutting edge. By appealing to the center of their lives, he thought he could drive his friends outside their narrow boundaries.

"What can we do," one of the men asked, "when we ain't got no power?"

"You vote, don't you?" Slocum shot back. "You pay taxes, don't you? Well, we've got rights, too, and I'm saying it's about time we used them."

"Jeez, Jake," the man said, astounded at Slocum's

vehemence. "We already told the commissioners what we thought. We paid them lawyers to write it up. Now what do you want us to do?" It had been difficult for Slocum, forcing his neighbors to hire lawyers, to testify at Regional Plan Association hearings. Taking time away from their work meant longer days, and most of them were short-handed. Now he wanted more of their time.

"Crap," Slocum said, spitting a wad of phlegm and chewing tobacco over his shoulder. He grabbed a pitchfork and threw it across the barn into a bale of hay. "Crap, I say. We got our case in, but that damn amusement park's got the power. Why, they filed papers ten times as long as ours. They got the commissioners in their back pocket. We got to get them behind us because they can stop the developers. And if we're going to do that, we got to force that damn amusement park onto our side." He paused and scratched his chin. "You know, they just might join us. They got enough trouble over there without developers pushing up their taxes, too."

"I don't see what the big hurry is," said Barney Smith, Jake Slocum's neighbor. "Congressman Tate says we're going to get a bill through Congress this year to protect our farms. President Carter himself is behind it; that's what Tate said."

"More crap," Slocum said. "I talked to George Tate last week and he says that damn bill won't even get out of committee this year. And I told him it better get out, or he was going to be short campaign money next time around. The mouse-brained idiot yapped about this reality and that reality and the poor damn fool begged me to give him another year."

Slocum strutted across the barn and yanked the pitchfork from the hay. "You count on Uncle Sam, boys, and you're counting on dreams. Any of you have the damndest idea how many family farms went under in this country last year? Well, just a damned minute and I'll tell you." He picked up a thick volume lying on the ground. "This here is the United States Bureau of the Census Statistical Abstract. Says right here three thousand two hundred and six farms went under in 1974. Who do you think is next, friends? If you want to be a number in the Statistical Abstract in 1980, you just sit tight. Because that's what you're going to be unless you take this thing into your own hands: a bunch of statistics."

He had shaded the facts a bit. The numbers were high because the government had redefined the size of family farms, and many smaller operations were not included as real farms in Census Bureau figures any longer. So while the farms seemed not to exist, they were still in business and Jake Slocum knew it.

Barney Smith was the only other man in the barn with as much land as Jake Slocum, and his family had been in New Jersey as long as Slocum's. Smith stood in the center of the group, hooking his thumbs around the straps of his coveralls.

"You're one hundred percent right, Jake," Smith said. "We *do* got to do something. Why don't you go over and talk to them people at the amusement park and see if you can't get them behind us? You're a good talker. You take care of it for us."

Smith was goading Slocum. The two men stood on opposite sides of a long-term family feud. Smith's father had fought with Slocum's father over grazing rights, and the feud, although essentially settled for more than twenty years, had nevertheless spilled over into the next generation. Barney Smith didn't care one way or the other what Slocum wanted the men to do; he just didn't want Slocum to look like a hero.

"Talk to them, hell!" Slocum shouted. "Before we talk, we show them we mean business. I'll tell you what we do. We go over there this afternoon and we picket. We block the damn road until nobody can get by, and they'll talk to *us*. Or we'll threaten to picket them every day until they do."

"Picket!" Barney Smith exclaimed. "You lost your mind, Jake? We'll get arrested."

"Oh, crap, Barney. Nobody's going to arrest me. We get our pictures in the paper if we get arrested and that damn amusement park gets a lot of bad publicity. Now I ask you, how the hell would that look? A big, bad corporation having a bunch of poor farmers locked up! They'd look real silly."

"You ain't poor, Jake," Barney Smith said. "And neither am I."

"Shee-*it*, I know that," Slocum said. "I'm just telling you what the papers would make of it. We'd be poor little guys getting pushed around by a big corporation. If them damn hippies can do it, why can't we?"

"They'll call state troopers," Barney Smith said.

"Damn, state troopers," Slocum answered. "Let 'em. Let 'em call the troopers and haul us away. Then we'd see some attention real fast. I can see the headlines now. We'll tell 'em the price of milk is going up if they force us off our land. We'll tell 'em how the natural beauty of the land's going to be destroyed by all those tract houses and trailers and mobile homes. Don't you see—we can't lose."

The nine men looked around the barn at each other with their eyes lowered, and then at Slocum.

"You ought to be a politician," Barney Smith said. "Count me out of this whole damn thing." He stalked through the barn and the men sat, quietly, listening as his truck started and pulled away. Slocum tapped his foot on the dirt, then threw the pitchfork across the barn again. He wasn't certain that talking with the owners of Olympic Adventure would help. He had tried that a year ago, just about the time the Regional Plan Association was taking testimony from home builders. Olympic Adventure had wanted nothing to do with his fight. He'd called the park's New York office and talked to Cole Cunningham, who had called him a hick and said the park couldn't do anything. Slocum had been in business long enough to know that wasn't true. Money meant power. Land meant power. And Olympic Adventure had both of these, with political influence to boot.

"Okay, gents," Slocum said. "Do we mean business or don't we?"

"I'm with you, Jake," one man said.

"Me, too," said another.

"Count me in," said another. Seven voices joined in the chorus. Horace Taggart stood aside from the group, saying nothing.

"Well, Horace," Slocum said, "are you with us or against us?"

Taggart, a cautious man, hated to think he was being railroaded into a decision.

"Are you sure you know what you're doing?" Taggart asked.

"You just listen to me, Horace. My daddy and your daddy had to fight the unions when they tried to stop the trucks, you remember? Now I'm telling you we've got—"

"Jake," Taggart interrupted. "You are forgetting one thing—they *lost* to the unions. My daddy damn near got himself killed."

"I know that," Slocum said. "But it took eight goddamn years and by then it didn't matter no more. The important thing is standing up for your rights." He dug his fingers into a pouch of tobacco and tucked a clump into his cheek. "Now here's what we do. We get the wives in here with some pieces of cardboard and some paint. You call 'em up and tell 'em to get over here. Then we start calling anybody who's got harvesting help, anybody who can get away for a couple of hours, maybe less. We've got to convince them how important it is for them to be here. We'll meet about half past twelve and drive over there and block that damn road until they come talk to us."

Horace Taggart snorted. "You know what, Jake? I think you've gone power crazy. You're just like your daddy, thinking you can run the whole world. They ain't going to talk to us. This whole damn thing is stupid."

"You listen to me, Horace. You got any idea what's happening here? I mean, do you have any goddamned idea at all?" Slocum was preparing to use his last bit of ammunition to whip the men into line. "Some land company from Colorado was here two weeks ago. They wanted to buy me out. Can you imagine that? Buy out the Slocum family? You know what would happen to you if I sold? I ain't going to sell, but what if I did? I'll tell you, you'd be looking out your window one night and there off your back porch would be a split-level ranch house with aluminum siding, probably pink or some damn color. Your cows'd stop milking because the noise would scare them half to death. Rock-and-roll music all night long. Cars coming and going till all hours of the morning. Ain't it bad enough with all those cars from the amusement park? What do you think it'll be like when they start plowing roads through the middle of our land? There'll be so damn many people here you'll think you're living in the middle of New York City. Then we'll get ourselves a couple of high-rise towers and maybe a few shopping centers and before you know it, Horace Taggart, you'll be the last goddamn farmer in the state of New Jersey. What do you think of that, Horace? Huh?"

Taggart snorted again. "Colorado, you say?"

"Colorado," Slocum said. "Land developers from the middle of nowhere."

The men grumbled about developers and shopping centers and traffic. Slocum's threat was real, they knew, because offers had come their way as well.

"Okay, Jake," Taggart said, standing. "I'll get the little woman over here and she can paint your stupid signs." He turned to go. "Damn thing is stupid anyway," he said. Followed by the others, Taggart headed out of the barn and up the hill toward the big white house. Slocum sat for a minute, moving the tobacco around his mouth, thinking about a television show he'd seen the week before. In the program, a bunch of women picketed to stop a highway. Slocum clasped his hands around his neck and leaned back against a post.

"Sumbitch," he said aloud. A broad smile creased his face and he broke into laughter.

10

The helicopter finished its foray deep into the Pine Barrens. Hawkins saw, far in the distance, the ferris wheel gleaming in the sunlight and the top of Mt. Olympus. As they descended closer, thick traffic burst into view, filling the tarmac around the park. At the northeast corner, cranes stood out against the gutted, dusty pit where new sections of the park were rising. In another week, turf would be rolled over the ground, and the long strips of grass would transform the dust into thick lawn. Hawkins found it unbelievable that even as Cunningham's empire collapsed, he was still building.

Screw Cole, he thought, then turned his attention to the stranded car. For a nervous moment, he wondered if there was any possibility that the passengers couldn't be saved. He rejected the thought. He saw from the copter that Toscani had carried out the orders he had sent to Operations by radio. Every hook-ladder in the park had been trucked to the edge of the new construction site. He could see the flatbed trucks as the copter approached the makeshift landing pad. Two mammoth winch cranes, moved from the center of the site, stood side by side along the fence.

The request for cranes had puzzled the Operations supervisor, because Olympic Adventure had no roads. It was a pedestrian's land: no vehicles allowed. That was how Gabriel Bloome had wanted it. Fanatical about trees, Bloome had hired a consulting ecologist and biologist long before the park's foundations were dug. Tree by tree, Bloome and the scientists had walked through the forest, carrying cans of paint—one yellow, one red, one white. Trees marked yellow were dead or dying and could be cut with impunity. Those marked red were secondary growth, important but not essential to the forest's leafy roof. They, too, could be cut if necessary. Then came the strongest and healthiest and oldest trees, the tallest pines interspersed with maples and oaks, whose full, expansive crowns determined the forest's growth pattern. Cut down those trees and no forest would remain. Open the ground to direct sunlight by cutting these trees, the scientists warned Bloome, and you would redistribute the topsoil water, priming the ground for scrubby underbrush. The Pine Barrens would be destroyed. And Gabriel Bloome revered nature sufficiently not to destroy thousands of years of evolution. It was this natural backdrop that now set Olympic Adventure apart from the Disneylands, from Six Flags Over Georgia, from all the other products of park developers who thought only in terms of money and ease of construction. Which was fine with Gabriel Bloome. "People come to escape cars," he said. "No cars. No trucks. No golf carts. No motor scooters." You did not ride golf carts in fantasy land.

The lack of roads added myriad problems. No storage facilities marred the park's facade; no hulking, useless buildings to disturb any view or waste precious open space. Every night more than thirty tons of garbage left on small park jeeps—the only vehicles that could be accommodated on the narrow paths. Every morning as the sun rose, new supplies arrived in identical fashion, since no gate was wide enough, no path strong enough, to allow large trucks.

As his copter touched ground, Hawkins saw Masters running toward the pad. Toscani's crew was unloading the ladders, carrying them down the hill toward the base of Mt. Olympus, under the stranded tram. Harry Mullen, the construction foreman, was already at work on his cranes, attaching extensions to lengthen their reach. Hawkins stepped out of the copter, briefcase in hand, and waved to Mullen. The foreman raised his hard hat in salute. Ducking under the whirring copter blades, Hawkins saw the barriers around the Sky Chariot's loading dock.

At the fence bordering the construction site, Masters stood, breathless, his lungs heaving.

"Got to get yourself in shape, Kenny," Hawkins said as he vaulted the fence with one hand.

Masters was stuttering, unable to form a sentence. "Brad, the cable . . . snapped. Ladders stacked . . . the car is hanging." Sweat dripped from his forehead.

"Calm down, Ken. Get hold of yourself. Let's go talk to Pete." Setting the pace, he jogged toward Mt. Olympus. If anything, Hawkins thought, Masters was even more nervous than he had been on the telephone. Toscani waited for them, mopping his face with a grease-stained rag.

"Okay, wonder boy," Toscani said to Hawkins. "We ain't got much time. What's the plan?" Only Toscani could address Hawkins with that mixture of sarcasm and affection. Their relationship had begun with respect for each other's reputations and had grown stronger over the years.

"Take a look at this," Hawkins said, kneeling and opening his briefcase. He pulled out two sheets of paper, folding one into his pocket and laying the other, a sketch of crosshatches representing ladders, in front of Toscani. Masters leaned over Hawkins's shoulder.

"Sarah's up there," he said, interrupting Hawkins.

"Quiet, Ken, and pay attention," Hawkins said sharply. He turned to Toscani, who knelt beside him. "If you build the ladders from the gully starting at the bottom of the shed and branching out at an angle, you force the base into the ground as an anchor. Then you put a pyramid on top to save ladders. It'll take about three hundred feet, maybe three-fifty at most. How much have we got?"

Without taking his eyes from the paper, Toscani replied, "About three-sixty, I think, give or take ten feet. I had the base figured before you got here, but the top was bothering me. I couldn't see how we'd make it. A pyramid, huh?" Toscani examined the plan. Hawkins's drawing called for a stack of rectangles seven feet wide and twelve feet high. Lashed together with rope, the pyramid of ladders would be built upward from the gully beneath the Chariot's loading platform. The drawing also showed a horizontal line of ladders running from the lowest rectangle to the side of the fiberglass mountain, to which the whole structure was anchored. The ladders made a sort of scaffolding.

"You want us to break through the mountain?" Pete asked.

"Just two little holes," Hawkins said. "Right at the junction of the I-beams."

"It might work," Pete said, "if the ladders are strong enough."

"Don't worry about the ladders, Pete. I've used them before. They'll hold. But I am worried about the ground down there. How soggy is it?"

"Dead dry, son. Damned good thing it didn't rain out here this morning."

Hawkins leaned closer to Toscani. "How long have we got? Are those clamps going to hold?"

Toscani looked worried, pursing his lips, swallowing hard. "I don't know, son," he said quietly. "Twenty minutes, maybe. Half an hour at the outside." They held each other's eyes for a moment, and Toscani added, "My fault, son. I should've closed the damn ride down. But I could murder that idiot Cole for holding back on the cable replacement."

"Don't blame yourself, Pete." Hawkins thought, Cunningham will get his due. Someday. "Let's hop to it now."

Toscani instructed his crew on assembling the ladders. Hawkins, watching the men jump from the platform to the shallow gully below the loading platform, took the intercom for the cable car.

"You talked to them yet, Pete?"

"Ken's talked to Sarah," Toscani said, sliding off the platform to join his crew.

Hawkins signaled the car. "Hello, Sarah. Are you there?"

"Brad, thank God you're here," she answered breathlessly.

"God had nothing to do with it," Hawkins said, trying

to put her at ease. "How are things up there? Anybody hurt? In shock?"

"Nothing serious," she said, glancing around the car at the other passengers. "A couple of scraped knees. One sprained ankle." She lowered her voice. "One woman's been screaming, but I think she's okay. The kids are pretty scared."

"What about you? Holding up?"

"Pretty well," she said. Her voice quavered. "Actually I'm kind of getting used to looking at the world from an angle."

"That's my girl," Hawkins said. "Now in about twenty minutes—"

"Brad," she interrupted. "Where's Kenny? How is he?"

"He's helping Pete. He's fine, Sarah, fine." It would do no good telling her Ken was slightly hysterical.

"He *isn't*, Brad. I could tell. He's barely holding himself together."

"He's worried about you, Sarah. He probably feels responsible for this."

"Well," she said, "he . . . he should have shut the Chariot down."

"Forget it, Sarah. None of us handled it right. Including me. Ken did what he thought best. Listen to me now, because we don't have a lot of time. In about twenty minutes, or less, I hope, you'll see a ladder poking through the trees. I'll be on the end of it. I want you to tell everybody there to keep absolutely still. No one is to move until I signal. If you don't all shake that car too much, it's going to work out fine." Hawkins talked slowly, with a touch of sternness. It was important that Sarah Masters continue to cope, to stay calm.

"Everybody's stopped moving around," she said. "They're too scared to move."

"Good. I'm coming up to visit. Sit tight."

"I'm not going anywhere until you get here," she said, almost laughing. "I promise you, Brad." Hawkins was pleased that she could find humor in the situation. It would make his work easier if at least one person in the car could take charge.

"That's my girl. See you soon."

Masters and Toscani trudged up the hill, both covered with dirt and sweat. Now that the area was roped off, they had also succumbed to the heat, removing their shirts and ties. Leaves clung to Toscani's damp back.

"All right, boys," Hawkins said, "let's take a look at this other drawing." The two men drew up close beside him and Hawkins unfolded the yellow piece of paper.

"You crazy bastard," Toscani exploded. "You've got to be kidding. You want to fix this thing today?"

"Absolutely, Pete. If we've managed to keep news of the breakdown from spreading around the park until now, then let's do better." The rough diagram showed the two cranes side by side, their long metal snouts aimed between the two struts where the stranded car now hung. Drawn between the cranes' teeth was a dark line—Hawkins had sketched an unbroken cable.

Toscani was doubtful. "I just don't see it, son. Those cranes won't reach over here."

"You're right, Pete," Hawkins said. "They won't. But Harry Mullen is adding extensions to those grippers, and then they'll reach with a couple of feet to spare. The new link of cable is on the way. All I have to do is get up there, unlock the ends of those two struts, and thread it in. That'll do for the afternoon, and tonight we'll change the whole damn cable if it takes all night. I managed to get the manufacturer to give us a new one on my good name. I'll pay for it myself if I have to."

"Okay, son, slow down," Toscani said. "So maybe you can get a new piece of cable in there. So maybe those cranes got tiny fingers as good as a surgeon's. Maybe they can even hold the car while you do it. But in the meantime, you've got a dead engine here. Can't run the car without power."

Hawkins took a long drag on his cigarette. "Pete, in about forty minutes, with any kind of luck, a truck will be rolling up behind those cranes. While I'm bringing those people down, you get a couple of your men over there and unload the engine that's in it. And be careful with the damn thing. It's costing a fortune on this kind of notice."

"Where the hell did you get an engine today?"

"Harry Mullen's boss. He's bringing it in from Jersey City himself. It's a winch engine, bigger than we need. But it'll do."

"Okay, wonder boy, I'll buy it," Toscani said, smiling. "Maybe we can do it."

"Not maybe, Pete. I want that car rolling by one o'clock. You'll have your oil by then." He turned to Masters. "Isn't that right, Kenny?"

"That's what Dexter told me," Masters said. "From LaGuardia by one."

"There you go, Pete," Hawkins said. "One more thing. Have you called for ambulances?"

Masters flinched. *Ambulances?*

"Waiting at the gate," Toscani said. He leaned against the dismantled engine block, bent down, and massaged his legs. They were stiff from work and tension.

"Getting old," Hawkins said with a smile.

"Not me, Hawkins. I get younger every day," Toscani said, playfully slapping Hawkins on the back. Both men laughed.

"The minute those people are down," Hawkins went on, "I want them out of the park. *All* of them. Some will be in shock." The clatter of ladders falling into place caught his attention. "Go stick with those guys, Pete. Those hooks'd better be tight."

"Don't worry about it, son. They'll be tight."

"I hope so, because I'm the one who's going to be on them, and since I'm rather fond of my tired old body, I wouldn't want a couple of dozen spikes driven through my chest. Got it?"

"I got it, son, I got it." Toscani returned to work. Hawkins sat and beckoned to Masters.

"You know about the oil?" Masters asked. "Why it's not here?"

"I can guess. Check got there too late."

"That's it."

"No time to worry about it now," Hawkins said. "The important thing is that we get those people down and that cable in place." Hawkins bent closer, resting a hand on Ken's hand. "I know you're worried about Sarah. I understand that. But start worrying about how we're going to get those people out of the park without a scene. You'd better get Sheila down here. You'll need help."

Masters watched the crew of men carrying ladders into the gully. Sweat dripping into his eyes clouded his vision. Rubbing his eyes, he half-expected to wake from a trance, to find the broken cable and the hanging car inventions of his imagination.

Hawkins also watched the procession of laborers, but his mind was on the cable car, on whether the clamps would hold long enough. His phlegmatic calm was an act, a successful one, and it had reassured Masters. In truth, Hawkins doubted the cable's strength. Through his memory flashed a scene from years before, when he was skiing in Gstaad, in Switzerland. A jammed ski-lift pulley had dangled two cable cars above a deep gorge. With alarming clarity, he recalled how the cars had hung for hours as the cable was hauled in, inched back by hand. Just as the cars had passed the edge of the gorge and were over solid ground, the cable snapped. A few minutes earlier the skiers would have careened hundreds of feet into the chasm below. Now he thought, without letting the memory break his serene profile, that this cable was weaker, could give at any moment; that this car was held so tenuously that it might break loose, smash to the ground, and injure and perhaps kill not only its passengers but the men assembling the scaffolding as well. Or—and he could not help shuddering at the possibility—kill him if he were climbing when the car's clamps gave way. He had already decided to take that risk.

Masters was trying, vainly, to hold onto his control. "Brad, I don't know about that car. I've been watching and . . ." His face seemed to collapse; his cheeks sagged. His voice broke off. He cupped his ears with his hands to

134

close off the sounds of the park. Inside his head, a din pounded, the sound of his own blood pumping. Hawkins grabbed him by the shoulders and shook him.

"Now listen to me, damnit. Get hold of yourself." Ken looked up into Hawkins's burning eyes, at tight wrinkles bulging on his forehead. Again Hawkins was acting, seeming angrier than he was, but he needed Masters to take charge. He needed help.

"I'll . . . I'll be okay, Brad," Masters spluttered.

"You think the car's going to rip through that cable. Do you think I'd be standing here if I didn't know it was going to hold? Do you think I'd be cavalierly waiting to climb those damn ladders if I thought it wouldn't hold? The cable isn't going to tear any more, Kenny. Now get a grip."

"But, Brad, it's happened . . . it's already torn once."

"Of course, the pullies ate into it. But the only pressure now is coming from the wheels on the struts and they're rubber. The clamps are faced with rubber. That car could hang for an hour without sliding." Hawkins was lying, and again reassuring himself. "Now get down there and help those guys with the ladders and we'll have Sarah and the kids down in no time."

Toscani came up behind Hawkins. "Okay, son. They're getting up there."

"How's it look, Pete?"

"You're going to climb it. Come check it yourself."

Hawkins jumped off the edge of the platform. At the base of the mountain, the crew was lashing the bottom section to metal stakes. Hawkins walked from one end of the base to the other, tugging at the hooks, knowing his life depended on how strong they were. From far above, he heard the sound of the ferris wheel and the melody of the carousel's air-pumped organ. The workmen stared at Hawkins as he passed, knowing he intended to climb, alone, to the top. Hawkins yanked at the lashing between the hook-ladders, tugging at each juncture. He looked at the men, noticing their stares, sending a message as if by telepathy: this is no time for mistakes.

"Pete, what's going on out there?" he called. "Any snoopers?"

"The crowd's gone."

"Pete, I don't want any rumors starting. You make sure those kids keep their mouths shut."

"Taken care of," Toscani said. "Did it already."

Hawkins hopped onto the lowest section of the ladders. The ground sucked the stakes tightly. Walking from one ladder to the next, forcing his feet down hard, he bounced slightly to test the lashings. He swung through the openings easily, as if on a child's jungle gym, feeling the tension of the ropes each step of the way, then he sprang down, apparently satisfied.

"How much longer before you're near the car?" he asked the crew's foreman.

"Fifteen minutes, I'd say. Not much faster. Are you going to do the last couple of lashes?"

"Right, at the top." He called to Toscani. "Pete, let's go look at those cranes."

Hawkins boosted Toscani up to the platform with his hands and, without pausing, pulled himself up and rolled to his feet. As they reached the steps on the opposite side, Sheila Richardson ducked under the restraining barriers.

"Brad, thank God you're here!"

"I think I've heard that before."

"We're ready to move when you are," Sheila said. "The ambulances are waiting."

"Fine," Hawkins said, turning to Toscani. "Okay, Pete, let's see the cranes."

The ground under their feet, dry and dusty, crunched as they walked. When they reached the fence, the crane operator was waiting to let them in. Without saying a word, he pushed the gate aside, then walked beside Toscani and Hawkins to the towering cranes. Workmen were still attaching twenty-foot extensions to their snouts. In the shadow of the machines, Hawkins felt small. By their very size, they seemed to speak, to remind him of his fragility.

"When I get the last kid out of the car," Hawkins told

Toscani, "the first crane is going to latch onto the front car's cable grippers." The crane operator listened intently. "If it comes in gently, there shouldn't be any trouble picking the car up without damage. Then the second crane will swing up underneath and leverage it."

The operator looked dubious. "No good, Hawkins. Got to go underneath before we try to grab. If we miss on the first run, the car will be on the ground."

"Whatever you say, Harry," Hawkins answered. "Come under first. But I want to be on top of that car as soon as it's secure. Then I'll string the cable loop on the first strut. They can take me across to the second strut and I'll patch it in."

"Not good," the operator said. "How do you get the cable out there? We've only got two rigs."

Hawkins thought a minute, breathing hard. The cable would be too heavy to carry up the scaffolding with him; the extra weight wouldn't be worth the risk. "Right, Harry. All right, you've got two sets of grippers on the car. First you move under to support it. You get it steady, then lay the cable down on top of the car with the second rig. Then you move the second rig around and grab the other set of grippers. It's not as safe, but I'm not waiting for another rig. For damn sure."

"Might work," the operator said.

"*Will* work, Harry. Now there's one other thing. You've got to come in low and quiet. I don't want those damn snouts visible from the ground. Move in real carefully. You tell your other man to take his time. The damn operation's pointless if we make a sideshow out of it. Got that?"

"Sold," the man said. "Are you sure you don't want us to try it now, before you climb? I think we can get under while they're still in the car and give you a little more security."

Hawkins had already ruled out using the cranes with the loaded car. One slip and they'd tear it off the cable. He considered the possibility again, knowing he'd feel more comfortable climbing the scaffolding if the car were stable.

But he reached the same conclusion as before: the risk was too great.

"Thanks, Harry, but no thanks. You might shake it loose. There's no way to tell how tight it is now."

"Do it your way," the foreman said. "Let me know when you're ready."

Hawkins and Toscani walked down toward the gate.

"Talkative fellow," Toscani said.

"Harry doesn't say much," Hawkins answered, "but he can work those rigs in his sleep. Best damn construction foreman in the state."

"I hope so," Toscani said. "For your sake."

"Don't worry about Harry. Just watch from the platform. I'll signal you when the last kid's down and you wave to Harry, but don't make a show of it."

"Son, are you sure you want to do this? Let me do it, with a couple of my boys on the side to help."

"Absolutely not, Pete. I wouldn't ask you to do that."

"Son, I'm *offering*."

"No, Pete. This is my baby."

They stopped at the fence and Hawkins draped his arms over the slats of wood. He strained to hear the ladders meshing in the underbrush. He heard nothing. They must be nearly done.

From the edge of the ferris wheel, lit from behind by the sun in sharp relief against the sky, sparks seemed to fly. Hawkins was entranced by the view. Hundreds of afternoons like this one had gone by, and hundreds more would come, but today Hawkins felt a special passion for his work. For a brief, hypnotic moment, the midway crowds appeared to freeze, the omnipresent rush of sounds faded like a dying wind, and Hawkins's past rushed into his mind, throwing him back suddenly to the vast, haunted plains of his childhood. A quiet night descended. He heard the whistling whir of prairie birds. The song of the dark called to him, and he could almost feel the harsh grains of dust blowing against his face. This feeling did not come often, and when it did, it seemed to shoot through his skull blindingly, a remembrance of a remembrance, enlarged by time. And then there was the park in view as before, still silent, empty, and Hawkins felt a burst of pride for a moment—about the park, about himself. The scene changed again, and there was Alexis beside him, in his bed, her blond hair covering the pillow, her naked, thin, brown arms across his chest. Then, only shadows.

A truck's whining motor interrupted his reverie.

"Engine's here," Toscani said.

"Right on time. Get some men to unload it. I want to check that ladder." Hawkins threw the gate aside, then picked up his pace heading down the hill. "Here we go."

When he reached the platform, he saw the scaffolding rising through the trees. Time to finish the job, he thought. In a matter of minutes, the ladders would break through the treetops to the stranded car.

Inside the car, Sarah Masters waited apprehensively. All were calm except one couple, a Mr. and Mrs. Hendricks, who could talk only of how much money they would win in a suit against Olympic Adventure. The woman had sprained an ankle when the car unexpectedly gave way, and her foot was swollen. In the center of the car, Harold and Rose Faulkner were completely silent. They took turns closing their eyes and meditating while the other watched their three children. At the far end of the car, nearest to the ground, Terry and Jane Cohen sat with their two young sons. Keeping the boys' heads below the windows so they would not see how far away the ground was, Jane read to them from a storybook she had carried in her purse. Considering the car's awkward angle, the passengers had remarkably subdued their fear.

Sarah was stretched out on a bench to keep from sliding. She held her younger son in her arms. Somehow the child had managed to remain asleep. Through the trees, she saw the outlines of the ferris wheel as before, but it seemed to have moved. With a start, she realized the car's angle was changing. Earlier the incline had been slight, not much more, she guessed, than ten or twelve degrees. It was more pronounced now. The car was slipping on the cable. Craning her neck, she looked behind her and saw the pillar which the car had nearly passed before it stopped. In less than half an hour, the car had moved a foot farther away from it. Her momentary panic registered in her hands, and the child opened his eyes; she smiled at him, pushed his hair back, and held him tighter. He closed his eyes and slept.

She tried to lean past the window to see the end of the cable, but the car's angle was too sharp. If the car was sliding, as she suspected, then it could not have much farther to go before the cable ran out and it slipped free. The ground seemed far away. She could barely discern men moving below her through the leaves. They were only tiny specks in the mass of ladders.

The buzzer sounded on the phone. Everyone in the car turned toward Sarah as she picked it up. It was Brad Hawkins.

"Sarah, can you see the ladder?"

"Not yet," she said.

"We should be ready in about five minutes. Keep a lookout."

"Brad, I think . . . the angle . . ." Hawkins heard a change in her voice.

"Sarah, don't say *anything* to disturb anyone."

She lowered her voice. "I understand that, but—"

"I *know* the car is sliding on the cable. We can see that down here. But don't worry about it. It was bound to move a little from the shifting weight. But we'll be up there before it gets much farther. You've still got at least fifteen feet of cable under you."

Sarah could see the car inching away from the pillar. The movement was slow, but now visible. Suddenly she was more afraid than ever before, frustrated by her inability to stop the inexorable motion. The top of the ferris wheel was almost completely obscured now by the trees. In just a few minutes, the car had slid perhaps half a foot. None of the others in the car seemed to notice the gradual movement.

40

"Brad, it's sliding faster."

"I know. We're working as fast as we can. Listen to me now. I'm coming up, but don't get out of your seat. Tell the others not to move until I call for them. If they redistribute the weight, it's liable to pull it down faster. We've got time and we've got to do this right. Understand?"

"I understand," she said quietly. "Do you expect them to climb out by themselves? There are some kids here who are too young."

"I'll lift them out one at a time. Just keep them still."

Sarah lay the phone down beside her. It was an effort to summon her remaining strength. "Everybody, please listen to me," she said, raising her voice. "They're coming up to get us. But don't move until they tell us. When they're ready—"

Herman Hendricks interrupted. "My wife should go first. She's hurt."

"Mr. Hendricks, *please*. We'll be taken off in the order they think is safest. Now would you let me finish?"

"We're going to sue," Adele Hendricks said abusively. "We're going to sue them for every cent we can get."

Sarah was exasperated. "That kind of talk will get us nowhere."

"That's easy for you to say," Adele Hendricks snapped. "Your husband works for these crooks."

Jane Cohen rose to Sarah's defense. "Why don't you just *shut up?* Sarah's doing everything she can to help and you're making things worse."

Herman Hendricks stood, grabbing onto a window brace. The car swayed. "You can't talk to my wife like that, you little—" Before he could finish, the car lurched downward on the cable, sliding another foot. Jane Cohen's children began to whimper. Alan Masters awoke, crying.

Sarah shouted. "Sit down, you stupid ass. Do you want to kill us all?" The car's angle was now severe. Adele Hendricks's purse had spilled open, sending its contents rolling down the aisle. A makeup compact, loose change, and three ball-point pens clattered toward the door. The compact's plastic case shattered when it hit the door's frame. Suddenly the car was quiet except for the children's crying. Herman Hendricks, sprawled in the middle of the aisle, sat immobile, his arm caught around the leg of his wife's bench.

"Mr. Hendricks, don't move," Sarah shouted. "You've endangered us all."

"Don't talk to my husband that way, you little tramp," Adele Hendricks hissed. "He wanted to help me."

"Mrs. Hendricks," Sarah said fiercely, "the car is slipping on the cable. If you'll look out your window, you can see that. If we shake the car any more, we'll slide right off. We've got to stop moving around. Do you understand?"

"Who do you think—"

"I know what I'm doing." Sarah cut her off. "We're going to get out of this safely if we follow instructions." Now authority and anger unmistakably filled her voice. "We don't need any more outbursts. And I promise you, Mr. Hendricks, if you sue Olympic Adventure, I'll make sure there's testimony about how your stupid theatrics made things worse." She paused to regain her composure.

Jane Cohen asked, "Sarah, is there anything we should do before they get here?"

"I think Terry should try to unlatch the door to see if it works." Terry Cohen sat next to the door and could most easily reach it without standing. Leaning over the back of his seat, he tripped the latch. The door popped open, and all could see straight down into the gully.

"Jesus," Terry Cohen mumbled. "We must be fifteen stories up, at least. If we fall . . ."

"Don't, Terry," his wife said. "Don't look."

"The general manager is coming to get us," Sarah said. As she spoke, she heard ladders clinking below her. She peered out the window and saw metal shining through the trees. They were almost there.

"Ready, Ken, I'm going up." Hawkins pulled him-

142

self into the maze of steel. He climbed cautiously, checking the strength of the labyrinth as he went. With his knees, he tested the side braces. Below, Masters stood in the center of the structure, surrounded by six of Toscani's men, ruefully looking up at Hawkins's ascent. Hawkins glanced down and saw Doc Gordon's shock of white hair and Sheila Richardson, carrying stretchers, joining the group. All of their heads were tilted backward. Hawkins, satisfied with the third tier's steadiness, eased around the edge of the pyramided layer of ladders. Surrounded by leaves, he could see only vague shapes on the ground. Through the tips of the treetops, the park spread out below, and at a hundred feet everything was beginning to look small to him—the Fountain of Earth visible on the horizon, the ferris wheel circling in front of it. Sunlight the color of grapefruit filtered through the branches, and he experienced an odd sensation of power, the same power a child feels when looking down from an unnatural but manageable height. King of the Hill.

The park's sounds diminished to a hum, like the city's hum in his apartment. Underneath the surface of his thoughts, he worried, but he concentrated on climbing. Two lengths of ladder hanging over his shoulder butted the edges of the structure as he moved, clinking. Nearing the top, he saw the open door of the car hanging through the leaves. Suddenly he lost his footing. The last tier of ladders had loosened under his weight and, staring up, he nearly slipped through the gap between the two uppermost levels. Balancing the two lengths of ladders he carried with him on the hooks beneath, he swung into the center of the pyramid. Again he lost his foothold, caught without support. He stopped to rest, then heard the car creaking above him and set back to work. Laboriously he untied the ropes holding the outside frame together and lashed them again, then reached out with his foot and, fearful, pressed hard. The ladders held. Climbing back onto the outer edge of the pyramid, he began working his way toward the top. Suddenly the car appeared in front of him, hanging threateningly, directly over his head. Sarah Masters saw him through the window.

"Brad!" she shouted.

"Ready to unload, Sarah?"

"Ready as we'll ever be," she said.

He had reached the last rung and yet was still more than a yard from the door. Taking the two lengths of ladder from the hooks below and mounting them on top of the pyramid, he tied them stoutly with nylon cord. The door was still too far away, two feet from the top rung. He waited, looked up, saw a row of frightened faces staring down at him. For a second, he contemplated shaking the car to move it down on the cable, but the clamps themselves might be loosening. No, it could slam into the ladder, bringing everything down. *And me with it. Fuck Cunningham.*

"Are you ready, Brad?" Sarah yelled from the window.

"Just a minute. I've got to get another piece of ladder."

He backed down the single shaft onto the pyramid below. Knowing he might weaken the sides, but having no choice, he unlashed and removed two six-foot sections from the matrix, holding them between his legs. The first he pushed sideways as a brace, forming a triangle near the car's door. The other he carried to the top and laid across the two uppermost rungs, pulling the hooks together and hoping the ropes would hold just long enough to get the children out. The adults would be able to climb.

"Children first," he called. "Give me the youngest."

"No, no!" Herman Hendricks shouted. "Take my wife. She's hurt." Hendricks stood and the car jumped on the cable, settling just inches from the ladder.

"Sit down, you idiot," Hawkins bellowed. "You'll kill every goddamn one of us." Herman Hendricks froze.

Sarah passed her youngest son down the aisle, from hand to hand, over Herman Hendricks's head, to Terry Cohen. The boy cried vigorously, his arms and legs flailing wildly. Damn, Hawkins thought. This will take forever. Then he heard a rustling in the leaves behind him. Pete Toscani stood on the tier below.

"We decided this would be faster," Toscani said. "We'll pass the kids down the whole way. My men are on the edges. They figured if you could risk it, so could they. Let's move 'em."

"Thanks, Pete," Hawkins said. "I appreciate it." He had avoided asking Toscani or his men to climb with him. They knew, as well as he did, that the car could crash down without warning. Well, in a crunch, he thought, it paid to have the best. They began the tortuous hand-to-hand carrying of the children. Terry and Jane Cohen followed the last of them, their two sons, climbing without help. Hawkins crawled into the center of the pyramid to let them by, then unfastened the hurriedly assembled ladders at the top. Adele Hendricks slid to the edge of the car. She was a chubby, overweight woman, and it would be difficult to move her. The car swayed as she slipped into the doorway.

"Help me," she cried. "I can't move."

Hawkins reached out for her. "Listen to me, madam. Fall this way. Stretch your legs out."

"I can't. I'm afraid." She was crying.

"Confound it, woman. Lean this way and fall forward."

She fell out of the car into Hawkins's arms, slamming him back into the ladder. He held her unsteadily, feeling the ropes straining against the hooks.

"You get me down from here and get me down right now," the woman screamed. "Do you hear me?"

Hawkins set her down on the vertical ladders and her fat buttocks squeezed through the rungs, holding her in place. Then, finally, he lost his patience. "Now you hear *me,* woman. You keep your fat trap closed and we'll get you down in good time. There are other people in that car and they can move a lot quicker than you. So you just sit tight. You hear?"

Herman Hendricks climbed down from the car, nearly sailing straight through the ladders. "You watch how you talk to my wife, mister!"

Hawkins fought to avoid losing his temper. An urge to push the man off the ladder almost overtook him. "Okay buster," he said viciously, "why don't *you* carry her down yourself and make it easier on the rest of us?"

Hendricks struggled past Hawkins, his face flushed. "Goddamnit in hell, that's exactly what I'll do."

The woman, looking up at Hawkins's bulging muscles and then glancing toward her husband's flabby arms as he reached down toward her, spoke meekly. "Wait a minute, Herman. Maybe he's right. Why don't you go down and he'll carry me when he's done."

"*I* can carry you, Adele."

"Really, Herman. Maybe you ought to leave it to him." In spite of himself, Hawkins was grinning. Herman Hendricks could no more carry his wife down than he could lift the cable car.

"You sure you'll be all right, Adele?" Herman Hendricks asked solicitously.

"I'm fine, Herman," she said, adjusting herself on the ladder, unable to move. "Now you go on down."

The man turned and began climbing down, past Toscani and the other men on the scaffolding. Under his weight, the ladders creaked, and by the time he reached the bottom, he was huffing and puffing every four rungs. The others ignored him as they continued to pass the children along the chain of men. Hawkins directed the remaining passengers, watching horrified as the car shook when each person slid from the car, inching downward on the cable. Only a few feet remained. Hawkins called to Toscani.

"Pete, you'd better send word to Harry. We're running out of time."

Toscani waved in acknowledgment and rapidly swung down, using his arms and skipping most of the rungs. The last passenger in the car was Sarah Masters. As she fell from the car into Hawkins's arms, she slipped. Hawkins caught her, but the long morning had taken its toll, and she fainted.

Above him, Hawkins heard the whine of the cranes. Hurry, Harry, not much time. The car was dangerously close to sliding off entirely and falling into the ladders. They would all be crushed. He edged down slowly, carrying Sarah until he reached the second tier, where one of Toscani's men took Sarah from his arms. Hawkins waited, holding onto the frame as the man laid Sarah on a stretcher. Not knowing whether the cranes would reach the car in time, he ordered the area beneath the scaffolding cleared. Alone, he stood at the bottom, in the center, waiting for the crash. Masters, exhausted, knelt by his wife while Doc Gordon waved smelling salts under her nose. She came to, starting to sit up, but Gordon gently pushed her back onto the stretcher.

"Easy now," he said. "What's your hurry?"

Beyond the fence, past the Chariot, the other passengers were loading into the ambulances. Hawkins crawled under the ladders and leaned over Sarah, brushing dirt from her cheeks.

"Is everybody all right?" she asked.

"Everybody's fine, Sarah," Hawkins said. "Thanks to you."

"Thanks to *you*," she said, then saw her husband on the other side of the stretcher, blushing.

"Ken, get the release forms," Hawkins said abruptly, "and try to get as many signed as you can." In case of accidents, it was common to ask whoever was involved to sign statements agreeing that they would not sue the park and would settle for having their medical fees paid.

Toscani returned from the cranes. "They've got it ready, son. They're ready for you."

"I'm going up." Hawkins was on the first level of ladders when he heard Sheila shouting at him.

"Brad, the release forms. Where are they?"

"In my office. Let Ken take them. You check on that oil shipment. Pronto." Without waiting for an answer, he began climbing the ladders again, several steps at a time. Vaulting to the top, he found the cranes already in place. Well, he thought, so far, so good. He worried for a moment about Sarah and Ken, the look on Ken's face, but then the cranes began to move in on top of the car. In a mechanical ballet, one snout gracefully clasped the cente of the car, the other spreading its flaps underneath. Wh all seemed secure, Hawkins leaped into the car and pushed through a roof panel to the top. At the center, between the cable grippers, was a coil of shiny black rubber. And a tool kit. Good old Harry, he thinks of everything.

Toscani, now in the cabin of the crane, watched with alarm. "Easy, boys," he called to the operator, "take it slow." Toscani realized how fond he was of Hawkins, and thought him foolish to undertake the cable repair. It was so damn dangerous. Why not let it wait? But he knew why—because foremost in Hawkins's mind was the park's reputation. Toscani could hardly see through the trees, but the car seemed steady, securely horizontal.

Methodically Hawkins set to work repairing the damage. First he unlocked the cable from the car's clamps and dropped the new section into place. The broken cable fell onto the ladders below, and he looked down to make sure no one was standing on the ground, but the cable caught on a hook. Then, with the precision of seamstresses threading needles, the crane operators, high in their cabs, carried the car to the strut farthest from the fiberglass mountain, taking care not to bump it. Hawkins removed the cable shield and cut through the end. Inserting the new piece of cable in the socket, he tightened the shield and, with a wave of his hand, signaled the crane operators, thumbs up. As the car was carried, the cable unwound, and approaching the second strut, the cranes slowed. Deftly Hawkins stretched the heavy rubber across the car's roof, with less than six inches of cable to spare.

The car jiggled now, and Hawkins threw his arms up to warn the operators against moving. If the car struck the pillar with enough force, the entire foundation of the loading platform might give way. Inch by inch, the car moved closer. Two inches from the torn shreds of the old cable, hanging from the strut, the car stopped. Hawkins sawed through the edge of the damaged section, leaving a clean 'ge, and dropped the new cable into the strut's socket. ' it wouldn't hold. The shield had been ripped apart by the strain of the snapping cable. Good God, Hawkins thought, why the hell didn't I think of that?

He pawed through the tool kit, then smiled. Thank God for Harry: there was a spare. He tightened the cable into place, then cut through again to remove the excess and clamped on the new shield. Securing the cable to the car's grippers, he signaled again, the claws released the car, and the metal snout rose up from beneath, raised into the air. Let's hope it works. Leaning back, Hawkins eased himself onto the edge of the crane and stiffened, spread-eagled in the snout's claws. High above the trees now, he saw a red panel truck driving past the gate of the dusty construction site. Lower, Harry, Hawkins thought. No sideshow. The crane operator, proud of his exact execution of a dainty maneuver, brought Hawkins across the edge of the field, lowering the snout as he moved, and cleared the fence by a matter of inches. Then he set Hawkins down by the crane's cab, at Toscani's feet.

"Nice way to travel," Hawkins said, grinning, as he crawled from the crane and stretched his legs.

"Yeah," Toscani said, "in a pinch."

A red air-express truck rolled up behind them. The driver hopped out, clipboard in hand.

"One of you guys named Toscanini?"

"Sorry, friend," Toscani said, "the conductor's dead."

"Huh?"

"Never mind him," Hawkins said. "I'll sign." And then to Pete: "Let's get that oil."

Together they carried a case down the hill to the Chariot's loading dock. The rest was to be delivered to the warehouse in Glenwood. The driver had balked at making two stops for one delivery, but was persuaded by Hawkins's offer of ten free passes to Olympic Adventure for his family. The new engine was fully assembled when they arrived, and Toscani's men had just finished filling it with gasoline. After pouring the oil, Toscani punched the starter. The engine grunted, then hummed to life.

"Ain't that a beautiful sound," Toscani said. "Okay, son. Now what?"

"Let 'er rip, Pete. Bring that car in."

"That's what I'm afraid of. That it'll rip."

"Off your professional high horse, Pete. I'm no engineer, but I *can* fix a cable. It'll hold."

Jerkily Toscani threw the lever meshing the engine's gears to the drive shaft, and Hawkins, at the other end of the platform, tripped the switch sending power to the cable. The car shimmied into motion and pushed up through the trees. Toscani smiled at his crew, sitting on the railings around the dock, raising his thumb and index finger over his head. The Sky Chariot was running again.

"Zeus is back on the job," Toscani said. Suddenly Sheila Richardson appeared at the edge of the platform.

"Brad, the Commodore's calling you. There's a gate jammed in the lion section and he's yelling his head off."

"Let him yell," Hawkins said. "What do you hear from the hospital?"

"No serious injuries. One sprained ankle, a couple of scraped knees. That's it."

"What about Sarah?"

"She's fine. I just talked to her."

"Pete, get this thing moving," Hawkins said, gesturing to the cable car. "Take down the ropes. We'll rethread the new cable tonight." He turned to Sheila. "Call the Commodore and tell him I'm on my way. And send Ken over as soon as he gets back from the hospital." Would nothing go right today, he wondered as he stepped from the platform. He looked at his watch. It was exactly one o'clock.

11

"Hello, Bernie." Cole Cunningham was on the telephone, pacing his office with the receiver in one hand and a bicarbonate of soda in the other. "Send me somebody, will you?"

"What would you like? Adam or Eve?" The pimp's mellifluous voice belied his business. He might just as convincingly have been promoting stocks and bonds, real estate, or picture frames.

"Eve," Cunningham said. "Not too tall. Blond."

"How soon do you need her?" the pimp answered. "If you can wait half an hour, I'll send a surprise. On the house." What the hell is he talking about, Cunningham wondered. A surprise? Well, at least it would be free, and he already owed the man more than a thousand dollars.

"Fine, Bernie. I'll be looking forward to it."

Half an hour. Enough time for a call to Brill. His stomach was tense. He suffered from indigestible rage. He took his pen firmly in hand and finished his list. Not many people could raise eleven million dollars in less than a week. Georges Delacroix? Unlikely, he thought. The French banker guarded his money irrationally. He wrote the name Delacroix, then crossed it out. Who else? The Tigress, perhaps. If he could find her in that Spanish hole where she summered. Where was it?

Syndicates. There was Cheyne-Slotes in Brussels. A possibility. And Wolfgang Tenzer's group in Berlin. Now he needed Laurence Brill's advice.

He dialed direct to London. The call went through instantly.

"Hello, Larry, good friend, how are you?" There was silence on the other end for a moment. The time lag, Cunningham thought, or Laurence Brill's surprise at hearing his business line ring on Saturday.

"Cole!" the man in London exclaimed. "How are you? Where are you?"

"In New York, Larry. I know how you hate to talk business on Saturday. But I'm in a bind."

"I *despise* dealing with money on weekends."

Which is fine, Cunningham thought, if a provincial bank sends you a fat check every month and you're a lucky gambler besides.

"It's life or death, Larry. I need eleven million dollars clean and cooperative by Wednesday morning." He could risk waiting until Thursday, but that would be cutting it close.

"Just a minute, old man," Laurence Brill said. "Let me get to my desk for a cigar. This sounds serious and I never talk about anything serious without a cigar."

Cole Cunningham waited impatiently. A cigar. He needs a goddamn cigar to talk money. But Brill was trustworthy and he delivered the goods when you needed them. Cole had known him since their freshman year together at Harvard.

"All right, Cole. I'm ready now. What is it this time? A hot property you're lusting for?"

"For properties, Larry, I can always find investors. This is . . . let's say it's a personal problem. I've got to call in some favors and I've made a list. They all owe me. But I need your advice."

"If it's not an acquisition," Brill said, "what is it?"

"I'd rather not say, Larry. Just tell me who can get the cash."

"Really, old man, you don't have to play games with me."

"Notes, Larry. Due next week."

"As I assumed," Brill said. "Whom do you have in mind?"

"First, Triple-D, but in Berlin through Wolfgang. Second, Bank of Tokyo. Third, Cheyne-Slotes in Brussels. Fourth, Candy Bollinger—though I haven't the fuck of an idea where she is. And fifth—though I'd hate to resort to him unless I have to—Walter York." To the press,

Walter York was a financier. To financiers, he was a hoodlum. A rich hoodlum, to be sure, but a hoodlum nonetheless.

"Look here, Cole, I'm willing to talk, but only if you promise not to call York or I'll ring off this instant. He's probably smelling your flesh already and moving in for the kill. Don't let him get too close. Understand?"

"If that's the way you want it, Larry, then that's the way it will be. But what about the others?" Cole heard Brill inhaling at the other end of the line. "What are you smoking?"

"DeSantoras. Just arrived this week. Quite marvelous."

"Larry, you get me through this one and I swear on my mother's grave I'll get you a case of them."

"Your mother's grave," Brill intoned, "is quite unnecessary. Otherwise, I accept your offer. They're awfully dear. Cost me two quid apiece." He paused. Cole heard the flint scraping in his lighter. "Now, to business. I wouldn't call Nicky Cheyne for that sort of money. He has a terribly big mouth and everybody on the Continent would know you needed cash—in which case you'd never get it. The vultures would descend as soon as the first drop of blood was shed."

"The blood's about to flow," Cole said. "Who else?"

"Well, I'd try Candy myself. She's somewhere on the Costa Brava . . . that little town she summers in. Arenys, that's it. Arenys de Mar. Quite splendid little place. Candy will give you a flat yes or no and she won't tell a soul. She'll just forget you called if she says no. And she can get *that* kind of money without straining."

"What if Candy says no?"

"Probably won't. She owes you a few. Who's the competition?"

Cole did not answer. If he told Brill that it was Max Brodky, he knew what kind of advice he would get.

"Hello, Cole, are you there?"

"I'm here, Larry. I'd rather not say who it is."

"Come, come, old man. We've known each other too long to deal like this. Now who is it?"

"I'm guessing. Brodky. Max."

Laurence Brill clucked. "Oh my. Oh my, indeed. I should think you would want to pull out right this second, old man, before you're bloodied and mauled. Musn't play with Max Brodky. You'll lose. It's a bad game. A losing game."

Cole ignored this advice; he'd expected it. "And what about Mitzu Noshumi? Can he get the money personally, or does he need the bank?"

"You *do* want to play rough," Brill said. "Mitzu doesn't have that kind of money, not as fast as you want it, and even if he did, his wife wouldn't let him touch it. New-style Japanese woman, you know. The bank? Perhaps. He hates Max. So does Candy. You have that going for you."

"What about Triple-D?" Cole asked.

"Lord, Wolfgang certainly doesn't have that sort of cash. Besides which the bloody kraut would just as soon gobble you up as bail you out."

"Larry, this isn't bail money. This is for keeps. I'll walk out with Hampshire intact or I'll walk out with nothing at all."

"That's what I'm afraid of," Brill said. "Max will let you out with a few dollars if you don't put up a fight. Think about giving a little, Cole. Save a few pieces. Build again. I've done it. What did that dear British lady say? Tomorrow is another day. Some such rot."

"So you think it's Candy or Mitzu," Cole said, studiously ignoring the advice he hadn't asked for.

"You're going to do it," Brill said. "You're going to hang yourself. All right, call Candy and tell her you talked to me. If not her, then Mitzu. He could do it if he tried. Eleven million dollars is just so many yen to him. But listen here, friend. How bad is it?"

"It's bad, Larry. Very bad. The park alone lost eleven million last season. We have notes to pay and the bank won't refinance. And then we have a payroll to meet and I've got too much dough out for acquisitions by the importing subsidiaries. There just isn't enough cash in the

154

bank beyond next week. And we're getting the squeeze. Max is squeezing the bank. I'm sure of it."

"Max Brodky did not get where he is today," Brill sermonized, "because he's a gentleman and a scholar. He happens to be neither. And if this is a straight money game, if it depends on who can tie up the most favors at once, Max is going to win. The old man's been around for a long time. He has never lost. *Never.*" Brill paused. "He did lose once, but that was only because all the money in the world couldn't buy him a new son. Your life—that's another matter altogether. Mostly because when he gets finished with you, you won't *want* to live."

"We'll see, Larry. We'll see."

"Cole, it's a battle. Lose the battle, win the war."

"I'll put a tracer on Candy. Meanwhile, I have company coming. Thanks for the advice."

"I wish you'd listen to it."

"I said I'd call Candy."

"That's not all of my advice."

"Damnit, Larry, I won't give in to him."

"You needn't curse at me, old man. Totally uncalled for."

"I'm sorry," Cole said. "I understand what you're saying and I appreciate it. But the sonuvabitch has won too often. He can't buy my life, either."

"Most unkind, Cole. You are getting bitter. Well, good luck, and have a pleasant day and a pleasant lay."

"Thanks, Larry." Cunningham hung up. Christ, the man was perceptive. Reading my mind three thousand miles away. Company coming. A pleasant lay.

He stripped down to his underwear and slipped into a brown velvet robe. He wanted to forget Brill's advice, but the words *bloodied and mauled* stuck in his mind. Lose the battle? Never. He was not a happy man, Cole Cunningham, and he, more than most people, was aware of that. But then again, as he told himself many times each day, who was happy? He'd had his share.

To his public—he thought of the world that way, as his

public—he was a model of grace and charm. They would not know, as he stood on the greeting line at a Democratic Party fund-raiser or at an opera benefit for the March of Dimes, what transpired behind his closed office doors. Why, even John Lindsay had been charmed by him, had asked him to serve in city government. "If bullshit were money," Alexis had once whispered to him over dinner at Gracie Mansion, "you'd never have to work another day in your life." He had turned the mayor down that evening, pleading the demands of business, and discovered the mayor's respect for those who refused a chance to serve, and by virtue of his refusal joined a large group of men who met occasionally over drinks at the Yale Club to assess the mayor's performance and send him their verdict. He missed those days, most of all because he had been so impressed with himself.

The elevator bell sounded. Bernie's girl was early. He watched the white numbers change—click click click—excitedly.

The elevator opened and his wife stepped out.

"Hello, sweetness and light," he said, pecking her on the cheek. "When did you get in?"

"Cut the hearts and flowers, Cole. You are about to run into a stone wall." She flopped onto the couch.

"I just kissed one. When did you arrive?"

"Just now," she said, lying. "What are you undressed for?"

"I was about to take a sauna."

"You're waiting for one of Bernie's girls. Or is it boys today?"

"You're drunk."

"Maybe," she said. She walked to the bar and opened a can of club soda. "Pinky tells me you called a board meeting this morning. What do you think is going to happen to Gabriel when you lose the park? He'll flip out."

"I have everything under control." He sat behind his desk, twirling the belt of his robe. Alexis thought he looked foolish.

156

"Bullshit," she said.

"Your language, my dear, is so colorful. Los Angeles does wonders for your vocabulary."

"Cole, you are so full of shit it's nauseating."

"What is the *problem,* Lexie? Your tan is exquisite. Your tired old body has never looked better." This was the game they played—insults, endlessly repeated. The rules never changed. The game was beginning to wear on Alexis.

"Nothing's wrong, dear," she said. "Nothing's wrong except that everyone on the Coast asked me how we planned to get along in our years of poverty. That schmuck Belasco asked me how much you wanted for the Model T and Whitbred said he'd like to look at the Pierce Arrow. Arnie Jacobs—who's getting divorced, by the way," she used the word *divorced* only to hear how it sounded, "wants to know about the Packard. When did you buy a Packard?"

Cunningham was taken aback. He got up from the desk and sat down across from his wife. "About six months ago," he said quietly. "Arnie Jacobs is a moron. To think he'd talk about me that way in public."

"It wasn't in public."

"I don't want to hear about it." He stood up and paced the room, twirling the bathrobe belt. "I want you to go over to Parke Bernet and buy a couple of antique chairs. And then send the Bentley out to the country and get a small Jaguar to run around town in. Show those idiots I can still spend money. That'll make them talk."

"Cole, you are stark raving mad."

"That's beside the point. Go out and spend some money. I don't want them to think I buckle easily. Pretend nothing is happening."

"*Them?*" she asked.

"Them," he said.

"You mean *him,*" Alexis said. "Max Brodky."

Cole sighed. So the news had spread that far. He was right. "What do you know about Max?"

"Only what Arnie told me. That he wants the park."

"What else?"

"Nothing else. What else is there?"

"I don't know," Cole said, "but I wish I did."

"Have you told Gabriel?"

"I told him Max is not getting the park."

"Gabriel is a child."

"He certainly is," Cole said. "What else did Arnie tell you?"

"Just that Max wants the park. Period."

"Did Arnie say why?"

"That's what Pinky asked me. No, he didn't know why."

Not good, Cole thought. Not good at all. Not good if they were already talking like that on the Coast. It's not like Max to leak his plans. He's trying to spook me, that's all.

"You run along, dear," Cole said. "I'm expecting company."

"I thought you were taking a sauna," she said, signaling for the elevator. "By the way, are you still using Bernie Thompson? He's a dangerous man."

Cole sneered. "Would you please go shopping or something?" He turned away from her, focused his eyes on his desk.

"Yes, King of the Western World. But don't say I never did anything for you. I've tried to warn you."

"I can take care of Max Brodky by myself, thank you."

She looked at him sadly. The emptiness of their life together was there, between them, dead.

"I tried," she said to him.

The doors of the elevator opened and she stepped in. He did not look up until the doors closed. Why would Max talk, he wondered. Well, his intuition had been right. The time had come to call in a series of long-standing favors. Mitzu and Candy *owed* him. They owed and he would collect. If only Lexie would calm down. If only she would sleep with him.

The intercom buzzed. "Yes, Helen."

"No, dearest, it's me," Alexis said. "I wanted to remind

you of something. It's a lesson I've been learning lately. Life is not a game. Remember that. It'll come in handy in a tight spot. And your creatures are on the way up." She hung up and the elevator bell sounded. Cole rang for his secretary.

"Yes, sir, Mr. Cunningham, I'm sorry about Mrs. Cunningham coming up without being announced, but she—"

"Forget it, Helen. I want you to get hold of Candy Bollinger. And do it discreetly. She's in Arenys de Mar. In Spain. I want to talk with her this afternoon."

"Yes, sir."

"And I'm not taking any calls for an hour."

"Yes, sir, I know. Will that be all?"

"No, try Mitzu Noshumi in Tokyo right away. I'll talk to him if you can reach him."

"Yes, sir. Your guests are on the way up, sir."

"All right, Helen. Hop to it, now. On the phone."

The elevator doors parted and a tall, buxom blond stepped out. Directly behind her was a tall, blond young man. Both were dressed entirely in white. Two sets of dark blue eyes flashed at Cole.

"Do you come together?" he asked.

"Sometimes," the young woman said. "Sometimes we do."

The two of them stepped around him and took his hands. With their free hands, they reached across his chest and began massaging his thighs. Leading him to the couch, they pulled off his robe. Cole flipped a switch cutting off the telephone. He would not be disturbed. By the time they were lying down, Cole was quivering feverishly. They lay on either side of him, pressed their bodies against him, and he began to moan.

The end, Alexis thought as she stepped into the Bentley. The chauffeur closed the door and eased in behind the wheel.

"Home?" he asked.

"No, Charles, I don't think so." She knew now what she had known for months—that she was on the edge. Balancing herself. All possibilities with Cole were exhausted. When they were young, they had shared their innocence. Afternoons at Bailey's off Harvard Square. A picnic in Harvard Yard. Walks by the Charles, listening late at night, waiting in the fog, to the bells of the Old North Church. Saturdays at Haymarket, buying vegetables for dinner with Pinky and Gabriel in Cole's bright apartment on Trowbridge Street. They thought they would never grow old, that they would be together forever. I believed, she thought, in fairy tales. I would cherish, honor, and obey. She cherished him now not at all, was incapable of honoring him. The golden rhythm was broken. Forever, she thought. Now I know what forever means. Nothing is forever. Once they had shared innocence and now they could not even share memories. When, six months ago, she had slept with him for the last time, she had felt nothing. Not anger or coldness. Nothing.

"I'd like to go out to the park," she said to the chauffeur. "Don't take the turnpike. Go the long way." She took a glass from the bar built into the back of the front seat and poured herself a shot of gin.

"Yes, ma'am," the chauffeur said, and pulled out onto Fifth Avenue. The Memorial Day parade was already past, on its way downtown.

12

Peter Welch rarely spent the night in his office. He had done so only three times in the past year. When he opened his eyes, he couldn't remember where he was or what he was doing there. The first thing he saw was the clutter of ledgers and adding-machine tapes spread out on the conference table at the end of the room. Then he remembered: Hampshire Industries. The loans. The loans were due and couldn't be paid.

He reached above his head and switched open the panel door to the kitchenette. Good Lord, it was almost noon. How long had he slept? He couldn't recall when he had dozed off, but he remembered calling Cole Cunningham. The forecasts should be arriving from the airport soon.

He hoisted himself off the sofa, stripped off his suit, jammed a filter into the coffee machine, and stepped into the shower. The hot water woke him and he reveled in the status of having his own private bathroom. That had come with his promotion to vice president. Today, however, he had to ask himself: is it worth it? Is it worth living like this? His bones ached from sleeping on the couch. Until three in the morning, he had pored over the figures, realizing, and yet not admitting, the hopeless state of Hampshire Industries. Cunningham had made a mess of it, all right. The importing subsidiaries were having a decent year, but the amusement park, the crazy amusement park that First National Trust Company of Saint Louis had paid for, consumed money faster than the smaller companies could produce it. That was the trouble with conglomerates—all those separate pieces, unmoored and feeding on each other.

Welch tugged the towel around his middle. It was

possible, just possible, he thought, that Cunningham might turn Hampshire Industries around. But that meant giving him more money. Ten or eleven million, for starters. Renewing the notes. Should he press the bank's board to refinance? To approve a new loan? They were in too deep to back out. And he had taken the bank there. The loans were made on his recommendation. How had he let himself tie his own fortunes to Cole Cunningham? He didn't even like the man. Why had he let Cunningham's mistakes become his? Cunningham's pleading, his assurances that they were rounding the bend, that this year the park would make money, not soak it up—what was it all worth?

He put on a clean, thin cotton suit and resumed his audit. Total capital investment in Olympic Adventure alone: $182 million. Nearly $100 million had come from the bank. He read the accountant's footnotes: First National Trust Company of Saint Louis, $98,475,000. Now there was a mistake. The whole damn venture was a mistake. Welch thought, I'm not the only one responsible. The board approved these loans.

He contemplated selling the notes at a loss to a consortium of larger banks. Let them clean the assets for what they're worth and get out. First Saint Louis would show a small loss, a blip so small the bank's balance sheet would hardly be marred. Welch rejected that option. It was one of the largest accounts he had, and he would look incompetent. And Brad Hawkins was trustworthy. Hadn't Disney's people said he was the best?

Cunningham had come close to convincing him that the park would make money this year, enough to meet the note payments if they were deferred. If it didn't work out that way, he would have to ride it out to the conclusion. Even if he decided to unload the loans at a loss, he was by no means certain of finding a buyer. Money was tight. The only remaining chance was to find another conglomerate to absorb Hampshire Industries. ITT, perhaps. But ITT wasn't buying this year. Not amusement parks, anyway.

The coffee pot purred and Welch poured himself a cup, then drew open the blinds. Eighteen floors below, the city was coming alive. He sipped his coffee and attempted once again to make a decision. But his mind kept returning to his own track record. He'd made a few too many bad loans, costing the bank too much money. Senior lending officers were like ball players—traded to the minors when their batting averages dropped. This deal would make him or break him. When the going gets tough, he thought, the tough get going. That's what they said around the bank. What a stupid expression! Get going where?

In half an hour, Max Brodky was coming to talk. You had to hand it to the old man. He didn't summon you to his house on the outskirts of the county, didn't call arrogantly and demand your presence. He called politely—on this particular occasion at seven o'clock in the morning. And if you were the senior loan officer on Max Brodky's account, then you didn't ask why. Still, Welch thought it strange that Brodky would want to talk business on a holiday. The papers for the housing project were already signed.

Only recently had he glimpsed the shadows of Max Brodky's power at the bank. In a seemingly inconsequential lunch in the executive dining room on the twenty-sixth floor, he'd heard two vice presidents arguing over changes in the trusts and estates department. Finally one said to the other, "That's the way Brodky wants it." At that level, bank officers did not take orders from outsiders, no matter how powerful. Or was he an outsider? Welch had begun to sense a power he couldn't quite see.

Max Brodky and his two sons did not look powerful. They faded into a crowd. Newspapers did not print their photographs, not like the Kennedys or the Rockefellers, although the Brodky fortune was said to be

163

larger than both of those. Only once had the family strayed from its anonymity, when they'd purchased a publishing house and unexpectedly found themselves in the news with a spate of stories about the Brodky fortune. Reporters demanded interviews. *Publishers Weekly, Editor and Publisher,* the journalism reviews— all wanted to talk with Max Brodky about his new acquisition. No one had warned him of the petty jealousies aroused in publishing when an old family business was acquired by someone like Max Brodky. Max had lost his temper, in fact had shouted at his sons for talking to reporters. *We don't need publicity. No more damn publishing houses.*

Max Brodky demanded privacy for his family. Housewives did not connect the Brodky name with the Sunlife oranges on their breakfast tables that had ripened in the Brodky family's Florida groves. Nor did businessmen connect Max Broadky with Squire Hotels or Toolco Building Supplies. The Brodky name, except for family holding companies, did not grace the corporate empire's logos.

And it truly was an empire, spreading across the United States, into Europe and South America. There was hardly a spot on the globe to which Max Brodky's influence had not traveled, hardly a country or a commodity or a venture to which Max Brodky paid no interest. He cared not at all for politics; it didn't matter who was in power, what sort of government a country had. Brodky was there, buying and selling. Max Brodky, in his quietly tailored off-the-rack suits. Max Brodky, who traveled modestly in his small Mercedes, without a chauffeur. Max Brodky, who had not even been born in America. He had, in fact, been brought to the United States from Austria in 1916, when he was four years old. His mother and father were tailors—gown makers and suiters to Emperor Franz Joseph. They had heard the stories of wealth and opportunity in the new land, how a man might make a fortune if he worked hard enough. When they arrived at Ellis Island in New York in the midst of the first great wave of European immigrants, the squalor of the city amazed them. Was this the golden dream for which they had suffered the degrading journey? Was this the land of hope, of freedom?

Max Brodky read the disappointment in his parents' eyes as they unloaded their trunks onto the dock. As a child, he understood that this trip had not worked out as expected. But Max's father, Abel, had been luckier than most. Shunted about in the vast processing machinery for the hordes of new Americans, bewildered by the customs and immigration officials, lost without a language, he had two possessions negotiable in the promised land: money and relatives. Abel Brodky's brother, Louis, had lived in America for ten years. Unable to sustain the trip from St. Louis to New York, he sent word through friends: Abel and his wife and young son were to come to St. Louis by train. The tickets awaited them when they stepped off the boat on the island in New York harbor.

They opened a tailoring shop next to Louis Brodky's grocery store on Franklin Avenue. The young Max was sent to public school, where he quickly learned English. By the time he was thirteen, he was running numbers for the Italians. When he was eighteen, he was smuggling bootleg liquor in from East St. Louis across the Mississippi. It was 1930. Men starved in the streets. But Max Brodky earned eight thousand dollars that year, and he hoarded his money. Never letting on to his parents that he had begun amassing the promised land's fortune, he still wore the clothes they made for him. He lived simply, did not flaunt his wealth. For Max Brodky knew that visible wealth encouraged jealousy, and jealousy erupted into hatred, and hatred into violence.

The young man settled into the life of the neighborhood. His parents, visiting him in his comfortable flat, asked how he managed to live so comfortably. Surely his small lending business could not support even this simple life. He evaded their questions, and soon they no longer asked. They did not understand, but this was the new wealth they had heard of—and their son had discovered it.

Max noticed the increasing flow of immigrants pouring across the country, living at first as his parents had, in tenements, while the wealthy Scottish and Irish merchants built their mansions on Lindell Boulevard at the edge of the city. The city was growing and would not be long contained in a strip along the Mississippi. Out into the farmland around St. Louis Max made his way, offering to buy farms. Already the farmers' children were leaving for the cities, and the farmers were wondering who would operate their farms after they were gone. This young man with the strange accent, in his dark, handmade suits, offered to pay generously. The farmers would be permitted to live on their land and reap its profits. But Max would own it. He paid them slowly, delivering checks each month. He paid their taxes, and his lawyers came with papers guaranteeing them the right to live on the land until they died.

And then, when the country began to boom, as Max Brodky had predicted it would, Max was ready. They had chuckled, his Italian friends, when he hoarded money in the grimmest days of the Depression. What good would farms do, they asked him. During the war, others made money in armaments, but Max kept buying land. Finally, when the war was over, when GIs were building houses with government loans, the builders came to Max. He owned all the land surrounding the city, had bought every acre that would eventually become St. Louis County. Years later he told the story to his sons as he instructed them on managing one of the world's largest private fortunes. Look ahead, he told them. Where is the country going? Be there early. Before the others. Remember that all you do today has consequences for tomorrow.

Peter Welch stirred in his chair, swung around, and stared out the window. The sky was soft purple with pollution from the mills, and across the river, clouds

166

blossomed in the midday light. Behind him, he heard the double French doors open. He turned, extending his right hand as he stood.

"Good morning, Max," Welch said, gritting his teeth into a narrow smile. "You're looking well." The old man was vibrantly healthy, Welch thought, awesomely preserved for a man his age.

"You're looking tired," Brodky said, smiling. "Peter, you're working too hard."

"Well, you know, Max, all those jokes about bankers' hours. I'm a living contradiction, a one-man advertisement for hard-working bankers. Totally dedicated to my clients. Did you get the final papers on the mortgages?"

"Yesterday afternoon," Brodky said. "Very efficient. I just came from the site. Beautiful land. We're breaking ground Monday, you know."

"That's not wasting any time," Welch said.

"Time is money, Peter."

Welch wondered when Brodky would get to the point of his visit. This was certainly not a social call. Max Brodky did not come to chat.

Max walked to the littered conference table across the room. "You've been looking at the Hampshire figures, I see." There was not a trace of interest in his voice; he might have been remarking on the weather.

"Practically the whole night," Welch said.

"They need cash, don't they?" Max asked.

"I didn't know you were interested, Max. Friends of yours?"

"I'm interested," Max said flatly.

Welch suddenly wished he'd been more curious about Max Brodky. Was he merely one of the bank's larger clients?

"Actually," Welch said, "I've still got a lot of work to do on the audit. What did you want to talk about? No problems with the housing project papers, are there?"

"No, Peter, everything's fine. I wanted to talk about Hampshire. You see, I'm joining the bank's board on

Monday, and I wanted to bring myself up to speed on their loans."

The board? Well, he certainly was more than another large client. Dimly Welch began to understand the talk he'd been hearing about Brodky.

"I had no idea," Welch said.

"It'll be announced first thing Monday morning. I would have told you last week, but you know how these things are. Now about Hampshire Industries—what's your judgment on the loans?"

There was something unnerving in Brodky's tone, not quite condescending, but not friendly, either.

"I'd really rather wait to make my presentation to the board, Max. There's more to be done."

"Peter, I know the men involved. I've studied the situation. Just tell me what *you* think."

Now his tone was threatening, and Welch was mentally making connections. If Brodky was joining the board, he must have recently bought a substantial amount of the bank's stock.

Welch understood Brodky's manner well enough to perceive his impatience. Perhaps it was Welch's inability to conceive of himself as an underling that made him hesitate. He resolved to go only so far with Brodky— just remember, he told himself, you're the loan officer on this account.

"I think Hampshire will make money this year," Welch said. "Not a lot, but eventually they'll break into the black."

Brodky's face clouded. He considered Welch, turned and walked to the refrigerator. He poured himself a glass of juice, pulled a chair toward Welch's desk, and sat.

"So they'll make money," Max said. "Well, they might. They might. If it never rains. If the temperature sits the whole summer at seventy-two degrees and there's a nice breeze every day. If they have no accidents. If there are no breakdowns. If the rest of the economy cooperates. If there's enough gas, but not too much. If Cole doesn't buy himself another airplane or more limousines or antique cars and hide them in the books as park expenses." His voice was like a beating drum. "And if every other subsidiary turns a profit of fifteen percent."

He set his glass down, leaned on Welch's desk, and stared at him. The hairs on the back of Welch's neck stood up, alive with electricity.

"On the other hand," Brodky said, almost in a whisper, "on the other hand, Peter, they can't meet their payroll on Friday."

At first glance, Max Brodky did not appear threatening. He looked as harmless as a schoolteacher. He was, as his secretary had once said, as retiring as the poor old men who played checkers in the park on Art Hill, near the museum. But Welch felt as if the temperature in his office had suddenly been lowered ten degrees, and he felt a damp chill all over his body. It was not Brodky's presence, nor his stark face, but the dry coldness in his voice, the distance, the frightening calm.

"And so," the old man continued, "what do you propose to tell the board on Tuesday morning?" Brodky rose, smiled, and moved across the room to the couch where Welch had spent the previous night.

Welch sucked in breath quickly. His pulse quickened. "I'm going to ask the board," Welch said slowly and directly, "to extend the current notes without penalty for six months. We should refinance them if we have to. We've got too much money tied up here to do anything else. And I'm going to recommend that the bank approve Cunningham's request for a short-term note, say four or five million at nine and a half percent. After all, the cash flow from the park alone should be about three million a week. I think they'll pull through this year. No doubt about it."

Brodky stood. "That," he said, spitting the word, "is very stupid. Very stupid indeed."

Welch did not move from his seat. He lit a cigarette and inhaled deeply before answering.

"Look, Max, you have to consider—"

"Let me tell you a story, Peter." Entirely aware that

169

he had cut Welch off, the old financier walked to the center of the room. "Take some wisdom from an old man. When I was very young, growing up on Franklin Avenue, a fellow came to me and told me he wanted to open a movie house. He was convinced movies were the wave of the future. They were doing well, the movie people. I admitted that. But this young man had big ideas. He had an instinct. He wasn't guessing, you understand. He *knew*. One large movie house and he would be a rich man. Now I asked him why he wanted to build a movie house. There were plenty of empty buildings around. Use them, I told him. No, he said, there was a vacant lot on Grand Avenue, and he wanted to build a giant amphitheater. He showed me long blue sheets of paper, rolled up in a tube, and then he spread them out in front of me. I didn't understand them. They were architect's drawings. I couldn't read them." Brodky threw his hands up. "In fact, I'd never seen one before."

Welch sat rigidly upright in his chair. Brodky moved closer. "But the man had vision. Any fool could see that. So I told him these drawings meant nothing to me. I wanted to know how much it would cost to rent movies, how many people he could seat, how many shows a day he planned to run. Why did he want this big building, and how much would it cost? You see, there are many men with vision, but I wanted to know if this fellow could make money. He understood me, because he was a bright young man. He rolled up his drawings and put them back in the tube. Out of his briefcase came a folder with a stack of papers. He had all the answers to my questions, Peter. So why, I asked him, did he need my money? Surely there were others who would lend him money. Banks. Real-estate brokers. No, he said, they want me to rent a hall and show pictures. He said any idiot could do that."

Brodky walked to the desk, picked up the juice, sipped, and continued.

"But to build an elegant palace—big, special. That's what he wanted to do. He would serve refreshments. He

170

could make as much money on the drinks and candy, he said, as he could on the movies. He would have blue-coated young men to direct the people to their seats. With programs, fancy color programs. You see, Peter, this was a natural showman, this man, but he was also a businessman. He had *sechel*. You know from *sechel?*" Brodky tapped his forehead. "Brains, but more than brains. Every cost was worked out to the last dollar. That's a rare combination, a showman and a businessman in one person. You don't run into such men every day, let me tell you that. How many P. T. Barnums are born in a day? In a week? In a year? Not so many, I can assure you. So I said to this man, I won't give you a loan. But I'll build your palace for you, and I'll give you the money to rent movies. I told him, you own twenty-five percent. You do the work. I own the rest. And we made money, lots of money, showing motion pictures. And we built more theaters—big, fancy places.

"And then one day he came to me and he said we should make pictures, too. Everybody was doing it, making pictures and showing them in their own theaters. So I gave him more money and pretty soon he was one of the biggest. The building we built together was the Fox Theater, Peter, and the young man's name was Lyman Bloome."

Lyman Bloome! Welch sighed. Gabriel Bloome's father. Now Welch knew how Max Brodky had come to own the country's largest chain of movie theaters. He had not just acquired it as another corporation in distress. And now Welch was beginning to think there was another reason Max Brodky was so interested in Hampshire Industries. It had something to do with Gabriel Bloome. It was not only money, not only the balance sheet. This was more than business; this was personal. And he had just joined the bank's board. Incredible. It was incredible.

"Now Gabriel Bloome, he's a nice man," Max went on. "A nice, stupid man. He hasn't inherited his father's abilities, Peter. Maybe you can't inherit that. My own sons, I've had to teach them what they know. They're bright boys; they learn pretty well. My David, he learns by instinct, by smell, like his mother. My Jeffrey, he has to play close attention to feel what I feel. He learns with his head. Sweet Jerry, God rest his soul, he was the smartest, my best. He knew what I meant before I did. He could finish my sentences, complete my thoughts before I myself knew what they would be." The old man bowed his head. "It saddens me," he said without looking up, "it saddens me that he is dead. He was such a good student. He would have been a very successful man."

Welch was stunned by Brodky's personal revelations. For a moment, he thought the old man would cry. But Brodky looked up and went on.

"But I have lost my story. Gabriel is an inventive man, and he has some vision, but he's a dreamer, and he's no businessman. Cole Cunningham, he looks and sounds like a businessman. But the man doesn't know his own limits. There are things he can't afford and he buys them anyway. Cars, boats, airplanes, houses, office buildings; and he expands the park when he is losing money. He is buying these things with money borrowed from this bank." Brodky paused to breathe; his chest swelled, and when he spoke again his voice was fuller, louder. "The man has no sense of proportion. Do you see what I mean? *Proportion*. He wastes."

Welch did not blink. He knew the man wasn't finished. He thought: I am getting what they call the Brodky Treatment.

"To give these men more money, Peter, is like flushing it into the Mississippi. It would be foolish. It would be stupid. When a child touches a hot stove, he learns what it means to be burned. He doesn't touch it again when it's hot. Now these children in New York—Gabriel and Cole—they don't understand what it means to be burned. And I tell you as a friend, Peter, if you don't recognize a hot stove when you see one, you're going to get burned yourself."

Welch cautiously rolled his chair forward and leaned toward Brodky. The old man seemed to have grown taller.

"And what do you suggest, Max?"

Brodky looked enormously satisfied. "I'm glad you asked for my advice," he said without a touch of sarcasm. "I suggest you recommend this to the board next week: the notes are to be paid in full on schedule, or the bank will take possession of the park. Mr. Cunningham is a man with many resources. Let him try to tap them. But the bank should accept cash only, not other divisions of Hampshire Industries. If they cannot pay, Gabriel and Cole get five-year management contracts at seventy-five thousand dollars a year. With the Duke and Brad Hawkins, you could negotiate separately. Hawkins you will need to run the park. The bank would put its own trustee in charge of Hampshire Industries, with complete power over acquisitions. I think that's the wisest course, Peter; wisest for the bank, and wisest for you."

Welch clumsily reached across the piles of papers on his desk and retrieved a pack of cigarettes from a silver box. Withdrawing one, he noticed the date engraved on the box's lid. He had been a vice president for exactly one year. As he lit his cigarette, Brodky pulled up a chair beside the desk.

"Well, Max, I suppose I'll have to do some serious thinking."

"What, may I ask, will you be thinking about?"

The old man was so excessively polite that it made Welch uncomfortable. *Does the crafty old bastard expect to influence every decision just because he bought himself a seat on the board?*

"I want to think about what's best for the bank in light of what you've said."

"So you don't agree with me?"

"I didn't say that, Max. You know how much I respect and value your opinion."

"So what is there to think about?"

"The board meeting is three days away," Welch said. "I just want to think about it, that's all. I want to talk to Cole about how the weekend went, about the forecasts, about his current cash situation. I want to talk with the accountants."

"Peter, you've lent Olympic Adventure a hundred million dollars."

"No, Max, the bank has. Approved by the board."

"On your recommendation."

The morning light, growing brighter, reflected into the old man's eyes. Welch turned involuntarily to look out the window. Cars filled the streets. Tourists crowded the base of the Gateway Arch. Light shimmered from the pale metal like heat rising from the pavement.

"Have you talked with the other members of the board about this?" Welch asked, his voice faltering.

"That's not really relevant, Peter."

Welch drew himself up in his chair. It's relevant to me, you crafty bastard, he thought. Welch surprised himself. He was getting angry. The old man, sitting far forward on the corner of his chair, seemed to press a physical advantage. "Max, it's not my style to think this way, but I get the distinct impression you're threatening me."

"That's quite absurd." He pronounced it *ab-zurd*, the Austrian accent lingering in his voice. "You do what you think is wise. I simply explained to you what I think is the inescapable logic of the problem. And I suggest you look at those books again. Check them carefully."

From moment to moment, Welch could not tell whether Brodky was growing more patronizing or more polite. Was he lecturing, as a teacher? As a kindly parent? Never before had Welch noticed the arrogant immigrant assurance, the security of a man who knew his place because he had created it himself.

"Yes, of course, Max. I'll do that. I understand your logic quite well. I'm not sure I agree with it, that's all."

Brodky thought, *Goyim, goyim*. Will the fair-haired boy not learn? I am trying to save his neck.

It had gone on long enough. Brodky sensed he had

174

reached Welch's breaking point. Nothing would be served by pressuring him further.

"My plane is waiting, Peter," Brodky said. "I'm going to New York. Perhaps we'll talk later." And before Welch had a chance to reply, Max strode through the double doors and was gone.

13

Far back in the line of cars, sitting in her cream-colored Bentley, Alexis sipped cool gin. Traffic stretched for miles on the three-lane blacktop. Beyond the tops of the cars, the coniferous green of the Pine Barrens swayed against a robin's-egg blue sky, shimmering in the heat. Alexis shaded her eyes and peered through the rear window. The line of steaming metal hoods reached as far as she could see. She turned and slid aside the partition separating her from the chauffeur.

"What's holding up the traffic?" she asked.

"I don't know what the trouble is, ma'am," he said. "Shall I step out and see?"

"Please, Charles."

The red-faced old man opened the door and a cloud of hot air poured in. Alexis closed the partition and patted her cheeks with a tissue, then checked her makeup in the mirror. She had steeled herself for this confrontation with Brad and, as ever, her appearance seemed overwhelmingly important. She thought it a mistake now, rushing out to the park like this, unexpected and uninvited. The heat, the traffic jam, and the blinding sun chipped away at her alcohol-induced serenity. I should have called, she thought. Perhaps he would resent her intrusion today. She no longer pretended to understand his moods. Once he had joked about her money, her education, her manners. She was a privileged woman of a privileged class, he had said, and asked her if she had ever chopped wood with an axe or furrowed a field. She had laughed, then tried again to make him talk about his childhood. He'd grown inexplicably sullen, then withdrawn entirely. Any hint of vulnerability, any sign that she wanted to know more than he was prepared to tell her, drove him back on himself, away from her.

"There seems to be some sort of political demonstration, ma'am," the chauffeur said. "The road is completely blocked. There are men carrying signs."

Now what? Who, Alexis wondered, would be protesting at Olympic Adventure.

Suddenly the thought of leaving Cole swept over her, sending a chill up her back. Good God, she said to herself, I might actually do it. But then what? For a moment, she was tempted to tell the chauffeur to pull the car out of the line and return to the city. This might be the wrong time to lean on Brad, too soon after their reconciliation. She should let him move at his own pace. He did not like being pressured—not about his past, not about whether he loved her, not about anything. The evening before, she had tried, as obliquely as she could, to force a commitment from him. "I don't make promises," he had answered, "unless I can keep them."

She had gone to Los Angeles the week before to get away from both of them, from Brad and from Cole. She could not bear to be in the same room with Cole. And Brad's attempt at reconciliation worried her. If he had left her once, he could leave her again. She thought she could clear her mind by going away, separating herself from them and from New York. But leaving did not clear her mind at all. After a week in Los Angeles, she knew exactly as much as she had when she left New York. She knew that sustaining any semblance of a relationship with Cole was hopeless and she knew that the thought of leaving him frightened her. She knew that Brad would not commit himself to her and she was not altogether sure she wanted a commitment.

When, after a week, she found Brad waiting for her at the hotel, she began to suspect that separating herself from him would not be as easy as getting on an airplane. But then she knew she needed a promise from him if she was going to give herself up to him—she wanted a commitment, even if its precise form eluded her.

She watched the automobiles around her, strung more than three miles to the east and farther to the south, barely moving. Their windows were sealed tight against the mugginess. Air conditioners groaned. Angry drivers stuck in the long lines revved their engines to keep them from stalling. The tarmac congealed, turned damp and soft. Groups of teenagers, impatient with the delay, abandoned their cars on the shoulder and walked, tearing through a field of blue chicory and dandelions, toward the main gate and into the parking lot. At the head of the line, at the intersection in front of the gate, Jake Slocum and his friends marched, blocking the entrance by parading in a circle across the road. Occasionally a car squeezed past them, and people paused to read their signs. DOWN WITH AMUSE-MENT. UP WITH FARMS, they said. And OLYMPIC ADVEN-TURE DESTROYS THE WILDERNESS. A few frustrated drivers harassed the farmers, but Slocum's men paid no attention.

Directly across from Alexis was a battered Chevrolet. Coats of cheap paint had flaked off, revealing pitted spots of rust. Long since torn away were the chrome decorative strips, and in their place scars remained. Not unlike people, Alexis thought, except you can't see our scars. The car's vinyl roof peeled at the edges. It re-minded her of Cole, of his passion for antique cars. One of his last passions, she thought.

Through the window of the car across the road, she could hear, even in her closed cocoon, a little boy's laughter. She saw the boy's mother, no older than twenty, bounce the child on her knee and feed him from a thermos.

Alexis shivered. She realized that she wanted children before it was too late, before she was too old.

"Thank God that's over," Ken Masters said as he pushed through Cardinal Hospital's revolving door, holding Alan in his arms. Sarah followed with Tommy.

"I hope that bastard Hendricks does sue. It would be a pleasure watching you testify to what an idiot he is."

Ken held signed releases from everyone who'd been injured—except Herman Hendricks. He felt enormously relieved. At least he had done *this* right. Hawkins would be pleased.

Sarah could think only about the car sliding down the cable. Where had Ken been? They had hovered between life and death, waiting for Brad Hawkins. Then, loading the children into the back seat, it occurred to her that she was petty to condemn him so quickly. She, after all, had not been down there, couldn't know what Pete or Ken had done. Now she had more important things to talk about.

"I'll take you back to the park," Ken said abruptly. "I've got to get back. One of the crew will drive you home."

"I'm all right," she said. "I'm perfectly capable of driving."

Ken backed the car from the lot without looking. He sped through the winding roads, avoiding the highway. Tommy and Alan fell asleep in the back seat, exhausted by their adventure but not, strangely, much upset by it. Sarah thought, Children handle these things better than we do. They're more flexible.

"The kids are taking it well," she said, trying to ease the obvious tension between them. "You'd think nothing happened."

They rode in silence, Sarah absorbed in the flow of trees, orderly in their height and color, straight and reassuring. Ken drove the winding road almost recklessly and the children shifted, sliding into one another on the back seat. Sarah reached across to them, her arm squeaking on the plastic cover, and brushed her hand across Tommy's head. His eyes opened and he smiled at her, then drifted back to sleep.

Watching the countryside recede past them, the stands of trees giving way to farms, tractors briskly chopping through high grass that would become hay,

179

wire mesh fences reining in grazing cows, Sarah smelled the thick, raw stench of manure and freshly plowed dirt. She looked at the children and suddenly realized how close they had come to death, how alone Ken would have been without them, and how glad she was to be alive. It was a commonplace thought, but for the moment it stayed with her, and she regretted raising her voice to Ken in the hospital, embarrassing him in front of the doctors. But she thought it immoral to force people to sign forms releasing the park from responsibility, especially after what they had all been through. Poor Terry and Jane Cohen had both fainted. It wasn't fair, she thought; after all, it *was* the park's fault. It was somebody's fault, anyway, but certainly not those who'd been stuck in the tram.

They were only a mile away now, and Ken pressed harder on the gas pedal. The silence between them—Sarah's silence—carried the weight of a rebuke more powerfully than anything she might say. In the hospital, he had avoided her eyes as he gathered the signed forms. *It's my job, damnit.* He tried to explain to her how an unscrupulous lawyer might drag Olympic Adventure into court, not in the hope of winning, but to extract a settlement. I have to do this, he thought, Hawkins wants it done. And then, I was worried about you. That's why I couldn't do anything. That's why I waited for Hawkins.

He was driving very fast now and she was worried. "Slow down, Ken, please. I'm sorry. I didn't mean to shout at you. It's just that—"

"It's all right," he said sharply. "You're upset. You have a right to be upset. Let's not discuss it."

"I *want* to discuss it," she said. "I don't have any idea of the pressure you're under. You've been working hard and you're tired and I haven't been as understanding as I should've been, and I'm sorry. It's just that you haven't been home much and—" She broke off. "I'm sorry, Kenny."

"You don't have to make excuses for me," he

answered. "You shouldn't have been here today, anyway. I told you not to come. What the hell was so important? What couldn't wait?"

She opened her mouth, but couldn't speak.

"Well, what the hell *was* so important?" he repeated.

She spoke very softly. "Kenny, I'm pregnant."

"You're preg—"

"Pregnant," she said. "I was going to tell you last night, but I fell asleep, and you were gone this morning and I didn't want to leave you a note. I had the protein-agglutinization test on Thursday. They called yesterday. I didn't want to tell you over the phone."

"God, Sarah, that's wonderful. I wish you'd told me." He pulled over to the side of the road and kissed her passionately. She took him into her arms and caressed his face.

"I wasn't sure," she said, "that you wanted another child. You seem so . . . so burdened."

"Don't be silly, love. The kids aren't a burden. But what about—"

"The pill?" she asked. "We just broke the odds. A hundred thousand to one." She'd had the strangest feeling Ken would ask her to have an abortion.

"I can't think of any odds I'd rather beat," he said.

"Mommy, where are we?" Tommy had awakened.

"We're on our way to the park, dear," Sarah said. "Daddy and I just stopped to talk for a minute, and then he has to go back to work."

Ken started the car and for the first time that day felt calm. With all of the park's troubles, he thought, he'd nearly forgotten what was most important.

"Do you forgive me?" Sarah asked as they pulled back onto the road.

"*Forgive* you? For what?"

"For coming out today?"

"Of course I do," he said. He tapped her stomach. "That's reason enough."

As they approached the park gates from the west, Ken saw the farmers blocking the intersection, impeding

181

traffic so that only by creeping around them onto the shoulder, nearly off the road altogether, could a car pass through the main gate. A child! He hoped for a girl. Closer now, the farmers looked peculiarly out of place. In paint-spattered overalls, denim workshirts faded nearly white, and bandannas of varying colors around their necks, they might have been actors from the Western Arena performance. Carrying their signs diffidently, they shuffled in a circle. Ken pulled around the line of traffic and parked on the shoulder.

"Would you look at that?" he asked rhetorically. "As if we didn't have enough problems today." He watched the men for a moment. At most, they numbered twenty-five. Seeing how they walked, their crudely lettered signs, their apparent lack of determination to block the road entirely, he decided that none of them had ever done this sort of thing before. He nearly laughed at how foolish they looked.

"Stay here," he said to Sarah, jumping out of the car. Halfway across the road, he was intercepted by one of the park's zebra-striped jeeps, driven by Sheila Richardson.

"Look what they've done," she called to Ken. "The roads are backed up to the thruway. I was just about to call the state police."

"Don't," Ken said. "Let me try talking to them first. Where's Brad?"

"Over at the safari. Something about a jammed gate."

"How long have these yokels been here?"

"About ten minutes, I think."

"What's this about a gate at the safari?"

"I don't know. The Commodore called for Brad just after you left."

"I felt it when I got up this morning," he said. "Nothing is going to work right today." Cunningham again, he thought. Cutting back on maintenance to save money. "All right," he said, "let's see if we can't get these fellows to move."

Merely from standing in the hot open air, Ken began sweating. Damp circles under his arms widened to the middle of his chest. The air pressed against him, a barrier to movement. Tugging a sleeve across his forehead, he approached the farmers, suspecting that persuading them to leave would not prove difficult. Even from a distance, he could see that they were chagrined by their own boldness.

"Afternoon, gentlemen. What's the problem here?" Friendly, he thought, not gruff or belligerent. That's the best manner—although he knew, and supposed they knew, that he could have them arrested and carted away. Jake Slocum stepped out of the circle. Ken was struck by his weather-worn face. Darkly etched lines spread in rivers to his narrow green eyes and up to the top of his forehead. His teeth gleamed white between dry, cracked lips. A faded blue bandanna stuck to his veined, muscled neck.

"Slocum," he said crisply, extending a hand to Masters. "Jake Slocum."

"Ken Masters. I'm the assistant general manager here. What can I do for you? What seems to be the problem?"

"You know what the problem is, sonny," Slocum said harshly, surprising Masters. "You people are spreading this a-*muse*-ment park of yours into more of our countryside this year, and every time you do that our taxes go up. Why, just last week some jackass from Colorado or some damn place offered me a million dollars for my farm. Now what do you think the county assessor's going to think of that, huh? We're getting pushed off our land and pretty soon we'll all be gone." He stopped, cleared his throat, spat. "Now we aim to stop that, sonny."

"Now look, Mr. Slocum, we're aware—"

"You can call me Jake, sonny," Slocum said, throwing Ken off balance.

"We're aware of your problem," Ken continued. "You have to understand, and your friends here have to understand, there's a great deal of money tied up here and I'd be lying if I said we're not going to expand. The county governments knew we were coming seven years ago. And they were glad to have us. We bring in a lot of business and we pay a lot of taxes." He could feel

Slocum's eyes taking his measure, taking in his plain white shirt and blue tie, the conventionality of dress that in itself defined him as the enemy.

"Yep, sonny, that's right; but nobody asked *us*. And we've had enough. We've made up our minds. You people aren't going to drive us out. We're staying. And you better help us."

"Or what, Mr. Slocum? Is that—"

"Jake, sonny. Name's Jake."

"All right, Jake. Is that a threat?"

"No, sonny, not a threat. But we've got to protect ourselves and we can make things mighty tough for you."

Ken measured Slocum for a minute. Perhaps calling the police would not be such a wise idea. They would come back, these farmers. Or they would find other ways to hinder the park's operations. People forced from their homes could lose all sense of reason. It was going to be a long, difficult, important season for Olympic Adventure, and they didn't need more trouble. Ken heard a car door slam behind him. Sarah, carrying Alan, walked around the farmers and joined Sheila Richardson in the jeep.

"Jake, for the moment there isn't much I can do. I don't have the authority to make any deals and I wouldn't know what to say if I could." Ken knew the park could use its political muscle with local officials; he'd heard Brad and Cunningham talk about it. But, damnit, he had no right to commit the park to anything.

"Well, then, you're just going to have yourselves a traffic jam here all day. Or else you can call the cops and put our picture in the newspapers." And with that, Slocum turned to leave.

"Now just a minute, Slocum," Ken said angrily. "There's only one man who can promise you help and he's tied up right now. In the meantime, you've got to let these cars in. You're breaking the law."

"We sure are, sonny," Slocum shot back. "If you're gonna call the police, I'd say you ought to do it mighty soon."

What Olympic Adventure did not need was a picture on the front pages of local newspapers showing the farmers being handcuffed and carried off in police cars. Ken knew that. And he knew that Jake Slocum knew it.

"Look, Jake, let's be reasonable. Suppose we set up a meeting between your men and the park's general manager. I promise you we'll do whatever we can about the tax bite. Maybe we could have some effect."

"You bet you can," Slocum answered. "You can swing some of your fat legal money into helping us hold onto our farms. You can get these people off our roads by building an extension from the highway running right up to your front door. Then our kids won't be afraid to walk without getting run down. You can get the Regional Plan Association to turn down all the developers' zoning applications so we won't get hemmed in by tract houses and mobile homes. And there's a few other things you could do. I got a list right here in my pocket." Slocum started to reach into his overalls.

"Wait a minute, Jake," Ken said, throwing up his hands. "I said I can't promise anything. We'll try to do something about the tax assessments. I don't know about the Regional Plan commissioners. Brad Hawkins, the general manager—he's the one to talk with. Why don't we set something up for Monday? Monday morning, first thing? We'll see if we can't work something out."

The farmer considered him briefly, as if studying a new threshing machine. Slocum was gauging Masters's honesty. Without saying a word, he spun on his heel and joined the other men. They had stopped marching by this time and stood awkwardly in a circle, resting their signs on the tips of their boots. They huddled just long enough for a few cars to sneak by. Slocum quickly pushed them across the lane to block the traffic.

"Goddamnit, Jake, if we're going to give . . ." Then, "You dragged us out here, Jake. Now we're here and that slick-talking city boy will promise anything to . . ." And then another, "Damn, Jake, he's already got us moving. Now they'll . . ."

Ken could see they would not leave as politely as he'd expected. In an odd way, he admired them. He admired men like Slocum, who took charge of their lives when pushed. Naively, romantically, he thought of them as the salt of the earth. And he sympathized with their plight, even if he didn't understand an enemy as remote as rising property taxes.

Sheila Richardson crossed the road to Ken. "What did they decide?" she asked in a low, conspiratorial voice.

"Nothing yet. I think I can get them to knock this off until Monday, when Brad can deal with them. What's happening at the safari?"

"Haven't heard." She paused, looked over at Sarah. "We've been listening to you. You've been very good with him." She took his hand. "And congratulations, pop. Baby makes five."

Just then, Slocum left the group of farmers and returned to the other side of the road.

"Sorry, sonny," he said loudly, so the others could hear him. "They just don't buy that. You've got to promise something besides promises." Slocum crossed his arms on his chest. His jaw was clamped firm. Ken thought: He's performing for them, playing the tough guy.

"I guess I'd best talk to them myself, Jake."

"I guess you ain't got no other choice, sonny."

The traffic jam swelled. Occasional honking horns set off a chain reaction, a cacophony of horns. Ken approached the farmers respectfully. This was no time for bullying.

"Friends," he said, taking a deep breath, "Mr. Slocum has made your case and I sympathize. And of course, we'd like to be able to help you. But you must understand we can't do a thing today."

"When *can* you do something?" Horace Taggart shouted.

"As I've told Mr. Slocum, we can set up a meeting for Monday morning. I'm sure the general manager of the park will use whatever influence he has, within limits, to solve this development problem."

"Limits!" another man shouted. "What limits?"

"Really, we're just another landowner. Just like yourselves," Ken said.

"You're not just like us," Taggart answered. "We're farmers. We're not tearing up the land. And you've got three or four times as much land as the rest of us."

The group was growing unruly. An ugly tension filled the air. Ken decided to risk committing the park. He would answer to Cunningham himself, if necessary. Anything to get the road open.

"I'll make you this promise," Ken said, and the farmers quieted. He sensed that Sarah was listening. "Olympic Adventure will submit a brief on your behalf to the Regional Plan Association for restricted development growth in the Pine Barrens and the surrounding two counties. That's the best we can do."

No one said a word. Slocum gathered the men around him.

"You see, I told you," he said to Taggart, jamming his forefinger into the man's chest. "I told you we got them just where we want them."

"Don't you point at me, Jake Slocum." Taggart's face flushed.

"Oh, damn you, Horace." He spat. "Well, what do the rest of you think? I say we go back to work. We spent enough time here already for one day. If they don't deliver, well, we just come back and picket again until they do."

The men mumbled agreement, encouraged by Ken's promise, and in a group, all except Slocum, ambled across the tarmac. The traffic picked up speed instantly and whizzed by them.

"Well, sonny," Slocum said, "we've decided to take you up on your offer. Today the cars go through. But you see how we can make trouble for you, and we'll be here bright and early Monday morning." He looked around. "Some of us will, anyway. To meet with this Hawkins fellow. And he'd better be ready to talk serious."

Slocum was trying to sound important. Ken understood.

It was something all men had to do. They shook hands and Ken thought he saw Slocum wink. Perhaps not. One by one, the farmers put their signs in Slocum's truck, then hoisted themselves into the cabs of their pickups. Ken joined Sarah and Sheila Richardson and watched while they backed out into the rushing traffic. The trucks' gears strained to jump the curb. Ken waved, shook his head, and pushed strands of damp hair behind his ears.

"Can you really do that?" Sarah asked.

"Thank God they've gone," Ken said.

"Kenny, can you really get Cunningham to file a brief for them?" Sarah asked.

"I don't know. I think so. Brad and Cunningham have been talking about it anyway. We knew we'd have to face this sort of pressure eventually." He picked up his children, one in each arm, and put them in the rear seat of the jeep. "Besides, what the hell was I supposed to do? They weren't going to leave without something definite, and I gave them the only thing I could."

"You gave them your word," Sarah said.

"I know. And I'll stick to it. We ought to do it, anyway." What was she accusing him of now? He'd said he'd try. "Sheila, I'm going over to the safari. Would you bring my car in?" She took his keys and crossed the road. As Ken was steering the jeep into the park, Alexis Cunningham's Bentley pulled alongside him.

"Hello, Ken," Alexis said, rolling the window down.

"Good afternoon, Mrs. Cunningham," Ken said, smiling formally and with ill-concealed distaste. He still seethed with anger at Cole Cunningham's maintenance cutbacks. The tram accident was Cunningham's fault, he thought. The lives of his wife, his children, and his unborn child had all been placed in danger because Cole Cunningham wanted to save money. His dislike of Cunningham extended to the man's wife. He didn't like Alexis, her expensively groomed hair, her permanent suntan, her Bentley, or her manufactured smile. He would not have liked her if she were the most gracious woman in the world. Her name was Cunningham, and that was enough.

Alexis did not misconstrue his veiled tone, regretting at the same time that she could do nothing about it. She said to herself: *I don't like my husband any more than you do*. Not missing a beat, she complacently returned his smile and said, "Do you know where Brad is?"

"He's over at the safari," Ken answered in his most brusque, businesslike manner. "Some sort of trouble with a gate. We're on our way there now. I've really got to go."

Alexis attempted to be cordial and disarming. "Would you mind terribly if I joined you?"

"You can follow us down if you like," Ken said. He sent the message as clearly as he knew how: she was not wanted.

"No, I meant could I come along with you?" Alexis wanted to know these people, Brad's people. They could tell her about him, she thought, let her see him through their eyes. Never did it occur to her that Brad was close to none of them.

"There's not much room in the jeep," Ken said, although Alexis could obviously fit in the front seat.

"I'm not very big," she said. "I don't take up much space."

She's forcing herself, Ken thought. Her name is Cunningham.

"Hurry, then," he said. "I should have been there by now."

Alexis leaned over to the chauffeur and told him to drive the Bentley back to the city, assuming that if all went as planned, she would be leaving that night with Brad. She nearly stepped out of the car with her drink in her hand, then thought better of it.

"I appreciate this a great deal," she said, squeezing into the front of the jeep with Ken and Sarah. "I really do." She smiled her hardest, coolest smile. Ken shrugged, nodded to Sarah, and wheeled around into the park.

Everett Morgan stood stiffly in line and fidgeted with a strand of plastic-coated wire. His hands quivered as he formed a cat's cradle, jerking the wire back and forth through his fingertips. The line in front of him did not move, and the children who were crowding him, tugging at their parents' arms, only exacerbated his nervousness. He toyed with the wire, kneading it, wrapping it around his thumb and then unwrapping it, tying slip knots and untying them, finally twisting the wire so tightly around his knuckles that they turned white. Hoofbeats echoed inside the Western Arena. Quickly he stuffed the wire into his pocket, suddenly fearing there would be no more seats.

"Have we missed the show?" he shouted, too excitedly, to the guard at the entrance. His voice cracked. "I've got to get inside. My wife and children are waiting for me."

"Relax, mister," the guard answered. "The show doesn't start for ten minutes. You'll get a seat."

"Thanks," Morgan said, regaining control. The guard looked at Morgan for a moment, then turned and continued talking with the gate attendant.

It had been years since Everett Morgan had attended an amusement park. Not since his childhood, when his father took him to Coney Island. The memory was not quite clear, but then much of his childhood wasn't. He didn't care to remember and spent a great deal of energy not remembering. When the memories broke through, they came in fast, flashing rushes. Waking up in the middle of the night, lying in his rickety bed with the itchy wool covers pulled over his head, listening to his father chase his mother through the crumbling Newark housing-project apartment. Slipping out of bed, opening the door, peeking while his father smashed a bottle against a table and slashed his mother's arms. Blood spurting. Police arriving. Hearing his father curse his mother. Lazy, filthy whore. Whore, his father yelled. A lamp flying, crashing through the window. Just as quickly, the memories shut off, like a television screen going dead. A white, sparkling dot. Then only darkness.

The gangs had taken him out of Newark, the street gangs of roving black thugs. In the first street gang he had joined, he was the only white, and he proudly acccpted lessons in survival from the blacks. How to fence stolen cars. How to clip the wires of a burglar alarm. He saw himself reflected only in the gang's identity. But that reflection disappeared as, one by one, the gang members were caught by the police, and he, too, was finally sent to a prison vocational school for juveniles. He learned his trade in the reform school shop, and when he got out, he attended a state training school.

The state found him a job with the Albright company. Louise was a bookkeeper there when he married her. She thought his quiet determination a sign of strength. It was only after Matthew was born that he began to change, becoming irrationally violent, hitting her for no apparent reason, becoming threatening even to the child. "You're no good for him," Louise had said the night in March when she moved out, taking Matthew with her. *No good for him? No good for my son?* What did Louise know about raising a boy? She was a whore. She'd turn him into a mama's boy.

Still waiting in line, he told himself about the fun they would have together. The night before, on television, he had seen Alan Ladd and Brandon De Wilde in *Shane*. That's how it would be with Matthew. He imagined the two of them on a ranch, where they would fish and hunt together. He saw them on horseback, in a field of high grass waving in the wind, riding toward a setting sun, a red sky. They would be dressed in leather, herding cattle, and at night sit at a campfire with the other ranch hands. Just like in the movie.

"Move along, please," a young girl in a uniform said. "The show will be starting in a minute." She stared into Morgan's eyes; they were focused somewhere across the stadium, clouded. "Sir?"

Morgan had forgotten where he was. Then the crowd swept him into the arena. He ascended the concrete steps haltingly, scrutinizing the people encircling him. His legs buckled at each successive step, as if he were carrying a load of bricks on his back. Losing touch, thinking he was at a baseball game with his son, he reached down for Matthew's hand and lost his balance, nearly stumbling forward to the pavement. "Matthew," he called, drawing stares. He climbed the steps to the last row and walked unsteadily along the circular wall until he found an empty seat.

Hawkers' voices bellowed, resounding in the arena's open expanse. "Peanuts, popcorn here." The hawkers jumped up and down the steps. Morgan was personally offended by their vigor. Brats. "Cold beer, here. Getcha cold beer." His throat was dry and he stood, frantically waving a dollar bill. A blond girl raced up to him, smiling. "Yes, sir. Budweiser or Miller?" Morgan didn't answer, but reached into the cooler and grabbed a bottle. The girl made change, smiled again, and turned down the steps. Morgan swigged the beer, gazing out at the mass of people sitting expectantly in the midday sun. Fifteen thousand people; they made him feel small.

"And now, ladies and gentlemen . . ." A horn sounded. Riding the perimeter of the Arena floor, a man dressed as a Roman warrior drove a chariot chained to four white horses. Covered in silvery metal, his legs wrapped in spangled leather, the warrior held the horses' reins and, pointing his horn to the sky, peeled long, drilling, clarion notes.

"Call forth the gods of war," the announcer said.

The warrior leaned back, his body arched, his legs spread apart. Darts of light bounced from his breastplate. Around the arena he rode, conjuring up the illusion of battle. Dust swirled, dirt flew sporadically; turning at sharper and sharper angles, the charioteer swayed back and forth until he reached the arena's center. The horses reared on their forelegs as if to dance. Again the horn sounded. Morgan's spirit changed as he felt himself to be a warrior. Stirred by the charioteer, he was sucked into the fantasy of the performance.

From gates on the rim came dozens of chariots and men on horseback, all costumed in metal and leather and gold helmets plumed in red, orange, and green, raging across the dirt floor, propelling clouds of brown into the air. With spears glinting in the sun, they raced toward each other, and men flew from the chariots onto the ground with thuds so loud the crowd gasped. Metal crashed against metal as the men slammed into one another. Helmets sailed, showering feathers. Horses whinnied, seemed to roam madly out of control. The battle had occurred before and would occur again, choreographed to the last flinging spear, to each horse's moment of flight. Every helmet had sailed at the same time earlier that morning; each truncheon had hit the same breastplate. The animals, so well trained they could have galloped through their paces wearing blinders, precisely avoided the men on the ground.

Transfixed by the theatrical charade, suspending disbelief, the audience roared as the battle progressed. Cheering when a magnificent silver chariot pulled by six stallions entered the arena followed by two hundred soldiers on horseback, the spectators released themselves to a ritual as old as history itself.

Frenzied, the army of horsemen in their flying green capes charged into battle. Bodies lay strewn across the ground. At the rear of the regiment, soldiers stood on a broad, grassy hill, sounding the clarion call on five-foot brass horns. The leader, in the silver chariot, had come to save his troops. Waving his spear as he rode through the fray, knocking one man after another from his horse, emerging triumphant at the opposite end of the stadium, he directed his men to dismount, and they gathered their wounded compatriots and victoriously paraded, surrounding the vanquished army, raising their green flag. As they marched off the field, their leader stood high in his chariot, circled the arena, and held high above his head a flowing green-and-gold banner. The crowd cheered. His soldiers closed in formation around him, their horses prancing; the men saluted the charioteer with their spears. Unseen by the crowd, a patch of ground opened up behind them and the chariot was lowered into the earth. Horses moved toward the exits as the earth closed.

Again the audience cheered. The magic, so reminiscent, intentionally, of a Cecil B. DeMille film, had worked.

"And now, ladies and gentlemen, we move forward in history," the announcer's stentorian voice boomed when the cheering stopped. "A wagon train of families is moving west to California, on the American frontier." The field filled with covered wagons, but Everett Morgan was only half paying attention, scanning the crowd.

Commodore Alfred Windsor paced across the road leading to the lion section of Olympic Adventure's safari game preserve, muttering at his assistant, Chuck Graham. "Where is that bloody fool Hawkins? Where are those bloody mechanics?"

"On their way, Alf," Graham answered. "Don't get in a snit about it. Hadn't you best get on the radio and hold back the flow of autos?"

"Not just yet, thank you," the Commodore said archly. "No need for alarm." Graham tolerated the Commodore's manner. After six years of partnership, Graham remained subdued and the old Commodore fell more frequently into intemperate rages. Few men would have accepted the Commodore's abuse or temper, but Graham understood: Alf Windsor was getting on in years; he was no longer the adventurous hunter of his youth.

The Commodore had long since retired from the jungle and specialized in designing commercial game preserves. Olympic Adventure's safari was his finest creation. It was equipped with its own internal radio-transmission network. In the fences and buried in the ground were wires carrying recorded messages to car radios. Different messages were broadcast in each section of the five-hundred-acre preserve, all on the same frequency. Those passing through the wooded area where the bears were heard descriptions of their feeding habits, how they cared for their cubs, their geographic origins. As cars entered the flat, grassy plain where broods of lions roamed, visitors heard about the different species, African and Asian, and the viciousness with which the two species were likely to attack each other. And always the warning: "These animals are dangerous. Do not try to feed them. Keep your windows closed."

Because the recordings in each safari section lasted only a few minutes, cars drifted slowly from the beginning to the end at exactly the speed required to prevent crowding. While every driver might set his own pace, stopping in some sections longer than in others, the total trip varied little from one car to another— between thirty and forty-five minutes.

The incongruous concrete road through the sculpted jungle was hardly noticed by the drivers. Alfred Windsor had designed a hilly, rolling ride to keep the spectators' attention on the animals, not other cars. The animal collection was the most extraordinary ever assembled in the United States. More lions were in captivity at Olympic Adventure than at any zoo or game preserve in the world. Its thirty-one bears had cost nearly a million dollars. Who could suppress fascination?

Ostriches pranced directly up to the cars, their heads bobbing. Waddling as they walked, they frightened no one. Until, that is, they leaned over and snapped, like woodpeckers, at the windows, reminding the sightseers that the long-legged birds could tear a human finger from its socket with one bite. Without warning, the ostriches would spin away from a car and race into the grass at such enormous speed that their legs were barely visible, their entire egg-shaped bodies bouncing violently as they ran. Orangutans, the largest weighing several hundred pounds, seemed equally warmhearted. Until, that is, they bounced on a car's roof furiously enough to dent it. The previous summer anyone foolish enough to ignore the signs warning away vinyl-topped cars discovered that baboons and orangutans relished the taste of whichever plastic Detroit automakers chose to cover hardtops. With their naillike claws, the ape-family creatures dug into the vinyl, peeling off long strips. This summer the park had simply stopped allowing vinyl-topped cars into the ape section. It had been the Commodore's decision; he was less concerned, he admitted to Hawkins, about the cars than the animals' health. Plastic did not help their digestion.

"You are now in one hundred and seventy acres of African jungle," the announcer's voice said as the cars passed the double gates into the lion preserve. "But in Africa the animals were never treated so well as they are here at Olympic Adventure. We've built shelters for them, one for each species. And the animals are never hungry here. We've duplicated their natural diets perfectly, and these animals survive better in captivity than they do in their natural habitat . . ."

Around the lions, most spectators were careful. With the elephants, however, they invariably broke the rules. The announcer on the tapes might pause in his story to repeat, "These animals are dangerous," but still everyone wanted to feed the elephants. Park rangers patrolling the preserve shouted into bullhorns, "Keep your arms inside your cars," but the lumbering gray creatures nuzzled against the cars and soon arms reached out with peanuts. Despite their size and lethal power, the elephants unfailingly treated children gently, never attacking or biting the tiny outstretched hands.

Shortly after one-thirty, Hawkins rode past the safari's entrance, heading for the jammed gate. When he arrived, Commodore Windsor was already lecturing the mechanics, who had begun work just before Hawkins appeared. Stepping from his jeep's running board, Hawkins caught the end of what he assumed was a sustained tirade.

"You bloody fools, hurry up," the crotchety Britisher was saying, his voice carrying the extreme disdain for which he was famous among park employees. "What were you hired for? Can't you make things work? Bloody fools!"

Hawkins took the Commodore by the arm and pulled him away from the gate. "Relax, Alfred," he whispered

196

quietly. "They know their jobs. Now tell me what happened."

Windsor bristled visibly at Hawkins's reprimand. From the beginning, since Hawkins's first day at Olympic Adventure, the two men had fought a pitched battle for authority. "Good heavens, Bradford," Windsor said, "I don't know how these things work. Somehow both gates opened at once and now they won't close. My men are at both ends of the road with their firearms. We could forget all this nonsense if your idiots would just get this gate closed."

"Yes, Alfred, I know," Hawkins said soothingly. He inhaled deeply on his cigarette, scanned the horizon, then knelt beside the electrician who was working with the three mechanics. "What's the problem, George?"

"That's the question of the day," the electrician answered. "Some sort of short in the wiring. But I can't find it."

Hawkins was annoyed. "George, I thought all this stuff was checked last week. Didn't you do it yourself? Your name is on the service report."

The man did not look up from his work immediately. He fiddled with his tools and continued probing the lock mechanism's circuitry.

"George?" Hawkins asked impatiently. "Did you or did you not check this last week?"

"Take it easy, Hawkins," the man said, standing. Brushing his hands together, he led Hawkins away from the mechanics, out of hearing range. "Okay, I didn't want to tell you. I ordered new parts for all the gates in February, maybe March. The orders never went through. Last week I told Operations we absolutely needed new locks for the double gates. Half the contacts are corroded. Some of the wiring is rotted from the rain. I couldn't get a damn thing out of supply. They said I was over budget."

"Well, are you?" Hawkins asked.

"The only reason I'm over budget is that New York

cut the damn budget by twenty percent. I screamed that it was ridiculous. What the hell am I supposed to do?"

Hawkins rubbed his chin. "When did they tell you about the budget?"

"That's the bitch of it," the man said. "I'm waiting for the damn parts and they tell me last week. They don't give me time to rewire the locks myself. If I'd have known, I could have done it. Would have taken maybe two weeks."

Last week, Hawkins thought. When Cunningham had to present the balance sheets to the bank. Cunningham was cutting corners again—the wrong corners.

"I understand, George. I'll get the budget increased this week. In the meantime, can we get these gates closed?"

"Sure," the electrician said, "if you want to saw the gate apart, you can close it. You'd have to cut through the tracks. Cost you a fortune to replace them."

"What's the alternative?"

"Give me half an hour to rewire this one circuit and I think we can swing it."

"Do your best." Hawkins watched the electrician return to his work.

Four of the safari's rangers stood by the open gate, holding their rifles at their sides. Alfred Windsor paced behind them, reminding them not to shoot unless he gave the order.

The gate system was designed to prevent the predators from roaming freely in the game preserve. Those sections with the most dangerous animals—the lions and bears—were protected with two gates at either end of the road. The first opened onto a short stretch of tarmac with fences on either side. After passing through the first gate, the cars reached a second gate, which opened only after the first had closed. Only six cars fit in the narrow space between the two gates. In order to pass from one lion section to another, or into the open grass where the giraffes mingled freely with gazelles, nyalas, elands, zebras, and water bucks, all cars had to clear the first gate before the second would open. Thus no lion could escape into another animal's terrain. The protection was not so much for the cars or their passengers as for the other animals. The gates were large and heavy, sixteen feet by twenty-five feet, riding on tracks embedded in concrete. The electronic system opening and closing them had failed, and with both gates locked open, rangers stood at the top of a steep hill leading down to the African lions. The animals rarely climbed the hill to the gate, and when they did, park jeeps, with wire mesh cages to protect the rangers, butted them back into the valley. Hawkins pulled the Commodore away from the rangers, who were by now easing their guns off the ground and into their hands. They were trained to shoot, and they would not hesitate if animals crept over the ridge.

"Alfred, let them do their job. I don't want any foolish risks." Hawkins was still nervous from the tram accident. They had come all too close to the sort of catastrophe that was capable of doing the park irreversible damage. Now Hawkins thought of every incident in which an animal had escaped from a park. Just the previous season, a lion in one of the Florida game preserves had mauled three children after leaping a barrier. One of the children had died, and the publicity was so widespread that the park had ultimately closed. That the children had been taunting the animal with sticks and throwing rocks behind the barrier hardly mattered; news reports spoke only of a dead child. Television films showed battered young bodies being carried into a hospital. And that was enough: parents were scared. They took their children to zoos.

"Bradford, these men are *not* to shoot," Commodore Windsor said. "Not until I give the order."

Windsor's reputation for capturing animals without harming them, eschewing the use of tranquilizers because it often took animals days, and sometimes weeks, to recover, accounted for his being in demand among park managers. After the war, when he'd left England to join his two brothers as territorial governors in Africa, he'd led shooting safaris for wealthy adventurers hunting for trophies. He was renowned as a man who knew the jungle as well as the natives did. But eventually he became sickened by the slaughter and catered only to those who wanted to capture live animals. He developed elaborate cages to trap the animals without hurting them, and with the passing years, his fanaticism among hunters became the subject of sour jokes; they said he cared more about animals than people.

"Damnit, Alfred," Hawkins said, "they'll shoot if a single lion comes near the gate. That's how it's going to be. We're not taking any chances."

Windsor tried a different tack. "Bradford," he said tonelessly, "do you know what it will cost to replace one of these lions?"

"Alfred, I damn well do know. But I'm less worried about the lions than I am about our rangers or the other animals. Do you have any idea what would happen if a lion got loose in here and attacked one of our own men? I won't have that on my conscience."

"Now, Bradford, really—"

"Really *nothing,* Alfred. The rangers shoot if one lion comes up the hill. Not to kill it, but to drive it back or stop it. No more arguments."

Windsor resigned himself to Hawkins's decision, but with angry misgivings. He listened, scowling, while Hawkins instructed the rangers: Don't kill if you don't have to, but don't hold back.

Chuck Graham joined the Commodore. "Did I hear the bloke correctly?" he asked.

"Yes, of course. Bloody fool."

"It's to be expected," Graham said to his boss. "You heard what happened this morning on their cable cars."

"What?" the Commodore asked.

"Some sort of power failure. A cable snapped. Why, they nearly lost twenty people, I hear. Hawkins flew in from the city just in time."

Windsor sighed. "That explains his attitude. Quite

understandable, I suppose." Graham offered him a cigarette and lit it for him.

Hawkins was coming toward them now, looking grim. Several cars passed as he approached. "They've shut off the other end now. Cars are being routed around," he said. "As soon as they're all out of this section, I won't be so worried."

"Look here, Bradford," Windsor said. "I hadn't heard about your cable car problem this morning. You should have said something. It's much clearer now why you're so on edge about—"

"I don't want any talk about the tram. Where did you hear?"

"Why, from Chuck here."

"What about it, Chuck? Who told you?"

"I was over at Operations picking up meat for the lions. Some fellow there mentioned your needing all these ladders. The word is you took a rather large chance with your life there."

"I don't want it discussed, Chuck," Hawkins said harshly. "Not with anyone. Are we clear on that?"

"Absolutely, Brad. Quite right."

"Have the lions been fed yet?" Hawkins asked.

"Not yet," Graham answered. "We've been so caught up with this gate problem I haven't attended to it."

"How long can they wait?" Hawkins asked.

The Commodore cut in. "No problem, I should think, if we're half an hour off."

"Won't they attack if they're hungry?" Hawkins asked, remembering again the Florida incident.

"But there's no one to attack, Bradford," said the Commodore. "You said yourself the section is nearly empty now."

"Just the same, I want the men to know." Hawkins switched his walkie-talkie to the safari circuit. "This is Station One, roving. Calling gate four." It was the gate at the opposite end of the lion section.

"This is B-11," came the answer. "Gate four, Watson."

"Watson, this is Hawkins."

"Yes, sir. I know."

"How many men have you got down there?"

"Five of us, sir, including me."

"Arms?"

"We've all got rifles, sir. Scopes and cartridges. But none of us has ever used them."

"Well, you might have to. I want your men to know the lions haven't been fed. And that if any of the beasts get close, they're to shoot. Let's not kill them if we don't have to, but those animals are going to know the gate is open. They can smell trouble better than we can. Is that clear?"

"Yes, sir. Shoot to wound."

"Unless you have no choice."

"Yes, sir."

Hawkins turned to Graham. "How many cars have come out?"

"Just a moment," Graham said. "I'll check."

"Watson, you've got the outside gate closed off down there?" Hawkins said.

"Ten minutes ago, sir."

"How many cars were in then?"

"Sixteen, sir."

"Can you see any from where you are?"

"No, sir. They're all in the jungle by now."

"Very good. Stay alert. Station One, out."

Graham returned. "Fifteen cars out, Brad. Looks like that's all of them. I can't see any more from the guard post."

"Watson says sixteen went in. There's still one car left."

"Should be out any minute," Graham said, checking his watch. "Unless they're dawdling. Shall I go down and check?"

Hawkins thought a moment. "Better to feed the animals first. Why don't you—"

"Fire!" one of the rangers in the raised guard post shouted. "Smoke! Down there!"

Hawkins scurried up the ladder to the guard post. Wisps of gray smoke rose from the foliage far down the road. "Get me a gun," he called to the ranger below. "And a cage." The rangers moved quickly to install a mesh frame on the top of a jeep. One of them tossed Hawkins his shotgun.

"Bradford," the Commodore yelled as Hawkins headed for the jeep. "You are not going to shoot any of my animals! I won't allow it!"

"Damnit, Alfred, I'm not planning to shoot. But I'm not going in without a gun." The Commodore climbed into the jeep with Hawkins as Chuck Graham boosted the old man onto the seat. "Chuck, get another jeep," Hawkins said. "And get on the radio and call the main gate. Tell them to stop all cars. Get the fire engines down from the helicopter pad."

"Right. What about the program network?"

Hawkins did not want to risk a panic by broadcasting news of the fire to all the cars in the safari. "Let it go," he said. "They're routing them around anyway."

Already the safari's small water truck, striped black and white like the jeep, was rolling down the hill. The larger fire engines, equipped with pressurized tanks, were normally stationed at the helicopter pad, as required by state law.

"Careful, gentlemen," the Commodore called to the rangers on the truck. "Don't spray directly at the animals. They'll charge if you do."

Two other jeeps lined up behind Hawkins and Windsor.

"Alfred," Hawkins said, "you drive." He heard Chuck Graham on the radio to the clerks at the safari entrance. He decided not to wait for him. Switching seats with the Commodore, he called out to the men in the other jeep, "All set?" They yelled back that they were ready. In the second jeep, they were just clamping down the last corner of the cage.

"Let's move, then," Hawkins called. He perched himself on the seat back, leaning his rifle through the wire mesh. The lions had already noticed the alarm, and as the jeeps reached the bottom of the hill, Hawkins saw them standing, lined at the side of the road, watching intently as the convoy of vehicles rolled deeper into the veldt.

Far down the road, in the middle of the lion preserve, Anne and Thomas Fleming drove slowly in their station wagon. They had turned off their car radio and were no longer listening to the recorded description of the lions. In the seat behind them, their son Todd listened, with his face pressed against the window, as his father talked about the lions gathered around the car.

"Li-ons," said three-year old Daisy, the Flemings' daughter, who sat in the back seat facing the rear window. "Big li-ons."

"These are the real rulers of all the other animals," Tom Fleming was saying as he eased his foot down on the brake. "The kings of the jungle. There are stronger animals in the jungle, and fiercer ones, but all the animals fear the lions."

"Li-ons," Daisy said.

"What about the birds, daddy?" asked six-year-old Todd. "The lions can't scare them."

"Except the birds, Todd," Tom Fleming said, laughing.

"The lions look friendly, daddy," Todd said. "Just like big dogs."

"Cats," Tom Fleming said. "And they probably wouldn't hurt anyone unless they were bothered. They don't attack other animals except when they're hungry."

"Yecch," Todd said. "They eat other animals!"

"Only when they're hungry, Todd. That's how nature works. Some animals eat other animals to survive."

"Yecch. I don't want to eat any animals."

"But you do," Anne Fleming said. "You eat fish and chicken and cows."

"I don't eat cows," Todd said. "I never ate a cow."

Anne Fleming decided against trying to explain that hamburgers came from cows. Tom Fleming lifted his foot from the brake and the car coasted forward.

"Look there, Todd," he said, pointing ahead. "See how

204

they play." Two lions were pawing friskily, swatting each other on the head.

In the back of the station wagon, Daisy Fleming had pushed the button operating the rear window and it slid down noiselessly. She had played with the car's gadgets—the electric windows and push-button radio especially fascinated her—ever since it was purchased. She bounced her rubber ball on the seat and watched it fly through the window to the pavement. Leaning against the door, she followed the ball with her eyes as it rolled toward the grass. A fat lioness, standing near the side of the car, moved toward the ball, pushing her cubs along.

"Are they fighting, daddy?" Todd Fleming asked.

"That's just play, Todd. Just like you and Daisy do."

Preoccupied with their son's questions, Tom and Anne Fleming did not hear as Daisy crept onto the hump over the spare tire. With surprising agility, she worked her way to the top of the tailgate. Staring at the lion cubs playing with her red ball, she leaned through the window to reach it, then turned around and climbed down onto the bumper, then onto the road.

Hawkins, more than a mile from the jammed gate, stopped the jeep convoy. Smoke had seemed to be rising from this part of the valley, and yet he saw no fire. Around him, lions gathered all along the road. The chirping of birds had risen to a squall. Outside the fence, baboons and orangutans scrambled erratically over the bushes, squawking a warning to the other animals. Fire was a threat, and instinct told them to flee. Hawkins was still far from Anne and Tom Fleming's station wagon when the park jeep bearing Ken and Sarah Masters and Alexis Cunningham reached the gate at the opposite end of the lion section. The guards told Ken about the jammed gate at the opposite end, but they had not yet seen the fire. Barely a hundred yards past the gate, driving toward the opposite end, Ken saw Daisy Fleming crawling over the station wagon's rear door.

"Holy shit, there's a kid in the road!" He jumped out

of the jeep, grabbing a pistol clipped inside a door panel and a bullhorn hanging from the dashboard. He slung the bullhorn over his shoulder, but paused as he stepped from the running board, deciding he needed a whip.

"Take the jeep back," he said to Sarah, "and send one of those rangers down with a prod."

As the gate closed behind him, Ken saw the fire spreading in the grass to his right, several hundred feet from the station wagon. "Be careful!" Sarah screamed.

Alexis was goggle-eyed. She had never heard Cole talk about the daily business of running Olympic Adventure, only complaints about costs: food cost this much, gate figures were low, vendors were asking for more money. Sarah had driven the jeep through the gate and a ranger returned to Ken with a rifle and a thin whip-prod with a padded truncheon at one end and a ten-foot nylon cord at the other; he tossed the whip to Ken as he approached the car, then stood behind Ken, his rifle poised to shoot. The fire was spreading slowly down the hill toward the road, burning a stream through the small patch of open, dry grass. Already a few of the lions were running from the heat, bolting across the road, oblivious to Daisy Fleming. Only two lions remained at the edge of the grass, ten feet from the car. The little girl was crying and her father turned at the sound of her voice. When he realized his daughter was not in the car, Tom Fleming opened his door and stepped out.

"Get back in," Masters screamed. He ran at breakneck speed toward the station wagon. The two lions lolled between him and the little girl. Fleming got back in his car and crawled over the seats to the rear window. By this time, the fire had attracted a crowd at the gate. Cars being routed around the lion section stopped when they saw rangers kneeling with their guns aimed through the wire. Within a matter of minutes, more than a hundred people leaned against the fence alongside the road.

"Look over there," one man screamed, standing on a friend's shoulders. "There's a little girl in the road."

A group of rangers attempted to pull the crowd away, but they did not move. They had come for excitement, and this was the real thing.

"Move on, now," the rangers were saying, pushing to the front of the crowd. "Back in your cars." Still the onlookers clung to the fence, attracted by the smell of danger.

Hawkins and Alfred Windsor, followed by two other jeeps and the small truck with water tanks, rolled to a stop ten feet in front of the station wagon.

"Take it easy, Ken," Hawkins shouted to Masters. "They haven't been fed yet." He called to the other rangers to get the hoses ready, and again the Commodore warned that spraying would only excite the animals further. Daisy Fleming, despite pleas from her father, had shifted onto the grass, aimlessly searching for her rubber ball, crying loudly.

Hawkins cocked his rifle and rested its tip in the wire mesh of the jeep's cage. "Don't shoot," the Commodore whispered. "You can't kill them with one shot and they'd be on top of Masters and the child before you could get off another round. They *are* rather fast animals, you know." He ducked under the cage and out of the jeep.

"Where the hell are you going?" Hawkins asked.

"Bradford, they're my animals. I know them better than any of you. Your young assistant needs help." He ran back to the second jeep, took a rifle, and walked slowly around the station wagon.

"Careful now, Masters," he said. "These brutes are hungry."

Hawkins rapidly punched the main park circuits on his walkie-talkie. "Station One, roving. Are you there, Sheila?"

"Station C–16. What is it, Brad?"

"Where the hell are those fire engines?"

"The tanks were down. They're on the way now."

"Damnit, they should have been here already."

"They're on the way, but we've got another problem.

The governor's helicopter can't land without fire engines at the landing pad and—"

"Forget it, Sheila. I can't worry about it now. Tell the goddamn governor to wait. Station One, out." He had forgotten about Governor Lloyd Birdwell's visit. To hell with that. He couldn't worry about public relations now.

Tom and Anne Fleming leaned over the station wagon's rear door, reaching frantically toward their daughter. Both were in tears. Ken could see them crying but he paid attention only to the lions, both males with manes so smooth and long one would have thought they were groomed. Faces impassive, unaware of the threat they represented, they stared at Masters with wide, liquid eyes. Other lions, females, ran past them, away from the fire, but these two did not move. Resting back on their haunches, they waved long, tawny tails, flexing their chest muscles as they breathed. Masters held the whip in his left hand and the pistol in his right. At this close range, he didn't dare shoot; he couldn't hit both in time.

"Why aren't they moving?" he asked Windsor without taking his eyes off the lions.

"They're hungry. And they scent a meal." He said it dispassionately.

"What if we fired over them?"

"Don't," Windsor said. "One shot and they'd be on you. They're fast and not as stupid as you think."

The lions still did not move, their lean chests heaving slightly with each breath. Masters surprised himself with his own lack of fear. He moved only to brush hair out of his eyes, to shift weight from one foot to the other. In the distance, a macaw screeched, sending the other birds into flight. The shrill noise echoed with a cadence, and Ken realized the birds, flying directly overhead, were fleeing from burning trees. He heard an engine start behind him, but he did not turn.

"What is it?" he called to the Commodore.

"Fire trucks. I'll see to them." The Commodore backed off with a measured pace. "Keep your eye on the lions, Masters. They're watching you now." He turned finally and padded evenly toward the trucks. He was used to moving around animals carefully so as not to draw their attention.

"Quiet now, men," he said to the fire-truck drivers. "Stay where you are." For the moment, nothing could be done about the fire. If they attempted to extinguish it now, the lions might be excited into attacking. Flames no longer spread into the jungle, having reached a deep, concrete water trough at the edge of the field. But fire licked the grass and consumed it; the ground was dry. Masters saw the fire reach perilously close to the station wagon's gas tank, hanging near the tarmac's edge.

"You'd best move quickly," Windsor said to him quietly. "You're covered on all sides."

Daisy Fleming looked up at Masters; even she now sensed the danger. She made an effort to stand.

"Don't move, little girl," Masters said. "Stay where you are."

"Mom-my. Mommm-mmy," the little girl wailed.

Anne Fleming screamed. "Oh God, Daisy! Daisy!"

"Quiet," Masters said without looking up.

"They're not going to move," Windsor said to him. "Listen now—you mustn't give them a reason to attack."

The fire hit a patch of higher grass and flared up, spreading into the underbrush near the car. It burned feverishly, nipping the lowest branches of the trees hanging over the road. A burning cinder drifted down to Ken's feet, and he involuntarily glanced up to see if the trees were burning. They were still too moist to catch fire completely. A pride of lions now paced behind the fire, across from the water trough. But the two between Ken and Daisy Fleming sat. For a moment they did not move. Then they smacked each other and roared, baring sharp, pointed teeth. Spittle dripped from their damp, pink gums. Hawkins stepped out of his jeep and walked nervously to the gate. "Cover me, too," he called to the rangers. They leveled their guns.

When he reached the gate, a ranger in the guard post threw a switch which opened it briefly; as soon as Hawkins squeezed through, it clicked shut behind him. Sarah Masters ran to him and wrapped her arms around his shoulders.

"Oh God, Brad, what's he doing in there? He'll be killed!"

Alexis Cunningham pulled Sarah away and held her.

"Easy," Brad said. "He'll be fine." Then, to Alexis, "I didn't know you were coming."

"I had to see you. I—"

"Later."

The fire had begun to move forward in the grass, ominously near the lions. Still they did not move. Ken eased the whip from his side and haltingly backed away. He felt his shirt sticking to his sweaty chest. The aroma of burning grass, the bark of living trees gradually drying and being consumed by the fire, wafted toward him. At his left, other lions gathered across the road. He imagined them watching his confrontation with their brothers, betting on who might be the victor. Did they know guns were trained on their skulls? How much did they perceive of their man-made surroundings? How acutely did they sense, in their wild state, the impending crack of the rifle shot? Hearing its report, could they learn to run before it fired again? No, animals do not reason. It was eerie, standing with the beasts, being so vulnerable. He felt naked before their power. The gun in his hand did not steady him. Yet he could think and they could not. There are times when the ability to think seems a burden, but becomes a blessing when confronted with the alternative: power without thought, strength without reason.

"Losing your nerve?" the Commodore said in a low voice.

"I'm fine."

"You'd better be, because they know you're here now. They're ready to play."

"What are they playing for?" Ken asked.

The Commodore paused. "For food."

"What's their game?"

"Simple enough," Windsor said. "Who gets to their food first? Us. Or them? You, actually. I'm too old to outthink them."

"Think," Ken said. "They don't think."

"After a fashion, they do," Windsor said. "Careful now, they're getting ready."

"Can't we toss them some meat?"

"Too late."

The smaller lion eased up from his hind legs and stretched to his full height. It moved out from the grass, and for a moment Ken feared it would circle around him. But it stayed there, sniffing the air. Ken felt his knees go weak; he tried to remain motionless.

"Why don't they shoot?" Tom Fleming called plaintively to Ken, his voice quavering.

"The others might attack," Ken answered, his eyes never leaving the imperious gaze of the lion in front of him. "It's too much of a risk."

"We've got to do something," Fleming said.

The little girl cried out, "Mom-my." Then she wailed.

"Don't cry now, Daisy," Anne Fleming called to her child, her voice choking.

The fire leaped closer and Ken heard the truck engines humming behind him. Then he recognized the sound. Water pumps pressurizing.

"Keep back, damnit."

"Relax," the Commodore said. He was just out of Ken's sight, standing to the left. Ken could feel the old man's breath on his neck.

"Get those damned engines away," Ken said.

"Don't worry about them," Windsor said. "Watch the lions."

The smoke was thicker, drifting from the grass. Jackasses, Ken thought. Ashtrays in their cars and they throw cigarette butts out the window. Signs were everywhere: FIRE IS OUR GREATEST ENEMY. BE CAREFUL WITH YOUR MATCHES. USE ASHTRAYS. The wind died

211

and the smoke rose more thickly. The larger lion, still on its haunches, tensed its muscles, ready to spring. It was almost as if the two animals spoke with their movements. Ken forced a reminder: they do not think.

The Commodore had walked backward to the fence. Hawkins called to him. "What the hell is Ken doing?"

"He's doing fine," the Commodore said. "He's showing them he's there and they don't know quite what to make of him. Well done, actually."

"What? Well done?"

"I wouldn't worry," the Commodore said.

The smaller beast stood in the road, its head turned upward, tail flailing the air, snorting. The other, in front of Ken, pawed the ground. Violence, Ken thought. Madness. It's a question of who moves first. The standoff was over. He pushed the prod toward the slouching lion, underneath its belly. From deep in the animal's gut came a growling snarl; it waved an enormous paw at the whip with such force that Ken almost lost his grip. Chuck Graham had once told him that a trained animal, a circus animal, would attack only if taunted unexpectedly. But a wild animal, like those in the safari, attacked only when viciously assaulted. The wild lion, oddly enough, was the less violent, because of the trained animal's sensitivity to ritual. Ken pushed the prod harder, and the animal leaped toward him, then lay down. Through the muffled roar in his head, he heard Sarah scream.

"Oh God," she said, cupping her hands across her mouth.

Alexis pulled her away from the fence. "Quiet, dear," she said.

Ken concentrated on the lion's heavy-lidded eyes. To his left, the other lion marked off a small circle, sauntering back and forth, apparently unaroused by the confrontation. Again the large lion roared, and this time Ken could see its rosy gums clearly, its white teeth reflecting the sunlight. The lions were testing him, and together the man and the two animals seemed to dance.

Ken bounced forward on the balls of his feet, stretching the prod out. The lion backed away. Then it raised its front paws, gathering strength to jump, and Ken poked at it again. Now the lion was angered and lurched at him. He jumped back without taking his eyes from the animal. The lion landed at his feet and their eyes met. Ken felt as if he and the lion were enacting a duel, a testing of wills: reason and instinct. He shot his left hand down with the prod, his right hand tensely clasping the gun. The lion's wild eyes moved to the gun as Ken raised it to his side. Suddenly the lion swatted, knocking the edge of the prod and driving the truncheon into Ken's arm. As the animal jumped, Ken lifted the gun and fired into the air. He turned quickly, seeing the smaller lion flying toward him. He struck out frantically as the lion landed. Both lions roared. Dimly, he felt a pain in his leg; the lion had grazed him and he was bleeding. But then the pain vanished; it seemed not to be his leg, his blood. The lions stood to their full four-footed height, between Ken and the little girl. He thought he heard shots being fired in the distance. The lions paced toward the car, then back toward Ken, as if they were caged. Now he was the meal they sought. He walked directly around them, toward Daisy Fleming, in short steps, waving the whip in the air to hold the lions at bay.

"Daisy," he said, still looking at the animals, "reach up and take my hand." The little girl, on all fours, crawled to him and tugged at his cuffs. Stooping slightly to find her hand, he pulled her up by one arm and cradled her against his side. Unexpectedly one of the lions jumped at them and Ken staggered against the back of the station wagon, swinging the whip at the lion's chest and striking it in midair. The beast landed in front of him, snarling. He smacked it harder with the whip and lifted one foot onto the car's bumper. The animals moved closer. Now Ken could feel the heat of the fire on his legs; for a second, he feared the gas tank would explode directly under him. He pushed the little girl through the tailgate window, boosting himself up with his other leg, leaning against the roof of the car. The lions lunged again, throwing their paws over the tailgate. He pointed the gun straight down, terrified, and shot wildly, hitting one animal in the chest. The lion fell. Ken leaned back and fell into the car, landing on top of Anne Fleming, who was crying hysterically, and the other jeeps closed in.

"Drive," Ken screamed. "The fire."

Tom Fleming, in the middle seat, did not move. Ken pushed him aside and climbed to the steering wheel. He started the engine and drove a few feet into the center of the road. Lions surrounded the car. Ken groped at the buttons for the electric windows and they rose, sealing off the noise from outside. Then, as he saw fire engines speeding down the road, spouting long jets of water into the burning grass, he slumped over the wheel, exhausted. Hawkins and the Commodore, in their jeep, shouted commands to the rangers.

"Spray the lions," the Commodore ordered.

The lions scattered, hit by the jets of water. The fire engines moved closer, soaking the trees on either side of the water troughs, beyond which the fire had not spread. Within a few minutes, the flames were extinguished, leaving behind a swath of charred earth.

"More water," Hawkins called. "The ground is still hot." As he spoke, flames burst out again farther down the road. Fire engines raced past Hawkins and the Commodore. At the station wagon, Hawkins lifted the jeep's cage, got out of it and into the station wagon, and pushed Ken aside, then drove the car to the gate, followed by the Commodore in the jeep.

"He's hurt," Sarah screamed when they lifted Ken out of the car.

"It's nothing," Ken said, rolling up his pants leg. "Just a surface scratch." A crowd gathered around him. Hawkins pushed them away.

"Give him air," Hawkins said, spreading his arms to hold the people back.

214

Sarah leaned over and kissed Ken's forehead. "I love you," she said. "You were beautiful."

"Good work, Kenny," Hawkins said. "How's the leg?"

"Fine, really it is," Masters said, trying to stand.

"Take it easy, Kenny. You take the rest of the day off."

"No way," Masters said. "It's just a scratch."

"Home," Hawkins said.

"I'm staying, Brad," he said. "Look, I'm sorry I had to shoot. They got too close."

Hawkins smiled broadly. "I think that makes sense."

Alexis stood next to the jeep, waiting for Hawkins. She had told Brad she would probably spend the day helping Pinky Bloome. Now, he thought, she wanted him to accompany her to the Bloomes' party, but Cole would be there and Brad had no desire to see him tonight. Tomorrow would be soon enough. "I'll meet you at the tower," he said to her, "when we finish up here."

"Brad, I—".

"Not here, Lexie," he whispered.

"I'll be waiting," she said. Her heart was pounding as she stepped into the jeep.

Doc Gordon had arrived and helped Ken into the back seat. Gordon drove the jeep through the crowd, and Sarah watched as the rangers removed a lion from the road, the one Ken had shot. She heard the Flemings behind her, getting into a jeep, then turned back as the rangers loaded the lion onto a truck. She gasped. The lion's chest was torn open, and it was dead.

By the time Hawkins reached the tower, he was so overcome with anger at Cunningham that his resolve had finally firmed into a decision: either he or Cunningham must leave. He wondered what other corners Cole had cut without his knowing. How could he run the park this way? Gates jammed. Tanks not pressurized.

Curiously, he suspected the Duke would take his side in a vote on new investors. The wily old man didn't say much at board meetings, but his behavior that morning had suggested to Hawkins that he might be ready at last to sever his ties with Cole. The Duke was undoubtedly charmed by Cunningham, but Hawkins thought that the charm was wearing thin. With his questions about how more money could be raised, the Duke had shown he was worried about his investment. Maybe he should unequivocally lay out the morning's events for the Duke—and lay them at Cole Cunningham's feet. That ought to provoke the Duke to take sides. Only four more days remained for Cunningham to save his empire. It hung by a thread now. Hawkins was prepared to cut that thread.

Sheila Richardson was in his office when Hawkins slammed through the door.

"Mrs. Cunningham is upstairs," she said.

"I know," he snapped. She gave him a hurt, quizzical look. "Sorry, Sheila, I didn't mean to sound like that."

"It's been a rough day," she answered with resignation. "Are you up to dealing with the governor? He wanted to land twenty minutes ago, but I told his people the helicopter pad was out of commission without the fire engines. So we re-scheduled him for three o'clock."

Hawkins looked at his watch. It was two-thirty. "Fine," he said. "I'll see you at the pad."

"Are you sure you want to?"

"How important is it?"

"Well, it ought to be good coverage. Newspapers and some local television."

"Insane," Hawkins said. "Why do they do it?"

"Do what?"

"Follow politicians around like that. Reporters must have more important things to do."

Sheila laughed, glad his temper had changed. "Don't ask *me* why. Just be glad they do. We couldn't ask for better free publicity."

"I'm glad you deal with the press," he said. "I've never been able to figure them out."

"They just want a story," she said. "It's that easy."

"Flacks," Hawkins said. "Egomaniacs."

"If Murray Rothbart heard you talk like that, he'd

216

never speak to you again." Rothbart, a *New York Times* reporter, was a friend of Hawkins's.

"Murray isn't like the rest of them," Hawkins said. "He really reports. As a matter of fact, he agrees with me. Get him going on the subject of lazy journalists and you'll be listening all night."

"Thank God some of them are lazy," Sheila said. "Otherwise I couldn't feed them stories about Olympic Adventure."

"Like I said, I'm glad it's your job." Hawkins pulled off his jacket and fell into the chair behind his desk. "I suppose I should clean up for the governor. Put on a clean shirt, anyway."

"For the governor?" Sheila asked. "Or for the cameras?"

"Okay, you proved your point. I also have an ego."

"That," Sheila said laughing, "is the understatement of the year." She lingered at the door and Hawkins knew why. But he had no desire to bring up the subject of Alexis. Best to just let Sheila get used to it.

"How are we doing at the tram?" he asked.

"It's still running. Pete's worried, though."

"That's Pete's way. It'll be all right until tonight."

"I hear Ken was the hero at the safari."

"I'll tell you one thing," Hawkins said. "I wouldn't have wanted to stand there with those animals. They were literally drooling for some flesh. I can't decide if he was courageous or stupid."

"Maybe courage requires stupidity. And from what the Commodore told me, he didn't have much choice. Either he jumped in there or they'd have torn that little girl to shreds."

Hawkins frowned. "Jesus, that was a close one. A couple of more minutes and . . ."

Sheila remained in the doorway. Neither of them spoke, and Hawkins bent down to untie his muddy shoes.

"Brad, is there . . . are you and Mrs. Cunningham—"

"Sheila, I think you're stepping out of bounds. That's my private life and it has nothing to do with the park."

He regretted having to treat her curtly, but he knew she harbored romantic fantasies about him. He had tried at every turn to squelch them. Sheila was a bright, competent girl, but that was as far as his feelings went.

Sheila looked down, disappointed, and a flash of anger crossed her face. "I didn't realize . . . I'll see you when the governor gets here." She walked out and the door swung briefly, then closed with a thump.

Struggling to dismiss Alexis from his mind, Hawkins found she kept reappearing, ever present, a beacon in his consciousness. He would think about the Duke and then there was Alexis. Then about a new script for the Arena program, and Alexis appeared. About Cole Cunningham, about the meeting that morning, and then there was Alexis, standing at her husband's side. She was filling an emptiness in Hawkins, a void he had never cared, until now, to acknowledge. The night before, he had burned at her touch, melted like a candle.

He changed clothes and sorted through the papers on his desk, reminding himself with a note to increase the safari maintenance budget. His office was austere to the point of anonymity. Sheila Richardson's attempt to add cheer had failed. Fresh plants from her apartment sat ingloriously against the flatness of the room, so utterly did Hawkins's coldness dominate it. His desk top, meticulously ordered, displayed his compulsion for neatness. The sitting area next to the door was symmetrical, two light gray couches facing each other across a glass-and-chrome table, flanked by two matching gray chairs, all exactly centered on a dark gray carpet. The office might have been the waiting room of a large corporation: functional, institutional, without human touches saying, I work here. This is my space. And yet minor signs of disorder had recently crept in. A chipped ashtray. A finger-smudged spot on the wall next to the light switch. A stack of papers overflowing a bin on a worktable. A sensitive observer might notice the contrast: a room so well maintained and yet marred by imperfections. Hawkins himself, as he straightened his tie and saw the room reflected in the mirror, consciously marked the change in his surroundings and thought these flaws, which not so long ago he would have corrected instantly, symbolic of breakdown.

He continued sorting the mail, marking time, agitated by Alexis's presence in the tower upstairs.

Alexis thought, I have lived a life of lies. She wondered if this affair were not merely another cloak draped over the world, one more facade to hide an unacceptable fact— that she lacked the capacity to care. Waiting for Hawkins in the tower, she watched, hypnotized, as red and yellow lights blinked haphazardly on the control board.

Fourteen years before, on the day she married Cole, Alexis had already believed that whatever relationships she might establish would be built on illusion. Yes, she thought, I loved him. But it had been his image she loved, and not so much an image created by Cole Cunningham as one she had projected onto him to suit her own needs. Self-assured, rich, and successful, a flawless portrait, in fact, of everything her father was not—this was the Cole Cunningham she married, not the erratic, insecure child he later demonstrated himself to be. No, he was not her father, a man stupefied by his inherited wealth, drowned in alcohol, obsessed by sex with young women. But Cole was worse, partly her father and more. Perhaps, she thought, we have no choice: we are doomed to find and embrace images of our parents.

Do we become them as well? She thought of her mother: a sad, mouselike creature who did not quite *live* in the conventional sense of the word, but rather rose each day to perform the public duties required of her by training, every act an obligation. She recalled the day her mother and father brought her to Miss Porter's, the *right* school, her mother had said, although Alexis was never certain exactly what it was right for. She observed how other parents held their children, laughed excitedly. Her father was drunk. Her mother could merely smile, graciously to be sure, but that was all: a smile.

Watching her own marriage decay, she admitted the

parallels. For the first few years, it had all been fun, she and Cole jetting across the world, met in every city by his corporate minions—managers and suppliers and their wives obsequious to a fault, fawning over them, leading guided tours. One city after another, until all cities seemed alike, a permanent fog of buildings and dirty streets and auditoriums and restaurants. Was this Chicago? Dayton? And tomorrow, Hong Kong or Houston? Life in the whirlwind, she knew, was not without satisfactions, and for a time, she devoured every moment of it. Being Cole Cunningham's wife had some benefits. But increasingly, Cole had drawn away from her, and she had remained in New York or Los Angeles, tending house. He refused to have children; vaguely she understood the significance of this: how could a child have children?

Lately she and Cole had stopped sleeping together, taking separate rooms in the apartment, and now he simply disappeared for days at a time. She heard through friends that he had acquired a taste for sexual acrobatics with strangers, and after a while he no longer attempted to hide this from her. She had begun drinking heavily, as her mother had, finding herself still in bed at noon, hung over, idly thumbing through fashion magazines without reading them, waiting for her head to clear. Frantically she filled in the days at department stores and at luncheons for charity groups in which she had no interest, then into the evenings, unable to be alone, she sat in dimly lit East Side bars, holding insipid conversations with other bored women, all pretending pleasure with each other's company. Now waiting for Hawkins in the tower, she remembered this clearly, and now she knew better: a life of lies.

She opened her purse and pulled out her compact, held the mirror up, and studied her face. Her lipstick had faded and she tried to apply it again, but her hand was shaking, and the lipstick smudged. She wiped the smudge away and tried once more, but it was no use. Her hands trembled. In the bright light of the tower room, she looked pale, and despite the makeup she saw that all color had drained from her skin. She powdered her nose.

220

She had been preparing a face and a feeling and a mood for him, but the storm of anxiety did not pass and the mood she had planned did not quite come together. As she dropped the compact and lipstick back into her purse, the elevator doors opened and Hawkins walked in.

"Good afternoon, hero of the day," she said brightly.

"Very funny," Hawkins answered. He was still on edge, still wondering why Alexis had not stayed in the city. He poured two drinks and carried them to the console where she sat, then bent down and kissed her on the forehead.

"A nice gesture," she said, unable to be completely at ease with him except when in bed, and put off by his harsh tone.

"It's not a gesture," he said. "You should know that by now." He spoke neutrally. It was a fact. He cared for her, but she refused to believe him. Like him, she preferred no risks. What, he wondered, did she really want? He braced himself against the control console and sipped his bourbon. "We had a close one there. We could have lost that kid."

"Ken's wife looked happy." She regarded Brad's impassive face. "Do they get along?"

"Well enough, I suppose," he said flatly. "They're pretty happy, I think."

"Is there much damage from the fire?" she asked, glad to talk about anything except what was really on her mind. She was aware of him watching her, watching, she thought, more than listening.

"Not much damage, considering what could have happened. We can sod the grass and clip the trees. But the lion . . ." He shook his head. "It's weird how friendly a lion looks," he said, smiling, "when it's dead."

Hawkins set down his drink and ran his hands through his hair. He thought Alexis seemed unusually tense. The lines around her eyes were tight. Her back was rigid. She looked as if she were holding herself together by an act of sheer will. "I thought," he said abstractedly, "you were going to help Pinky get ready for her party."

"I stopped by to see her," Alexis said, "but I didn't want to stay. She didn't seem to need my help."

"She doesn't think much of me, does she?"

There was something challenging in his voice. She knew he would not accompany her to the party.

"You don't want to go tonight, do you?"

"There's too much work here. I've got to wait until closing before we put a new cable in the Chariot."

"Doc Gordon told me about the breakdown," she said. "Can't Pete handle the cable?"

"Lexie, you know I don't want to go. Pinky's parties aren't my idea of a good time. You said yourself you've been to too many of them."

"It's settled, then," she said. "I'd rather stay here anyway."

He didn't answer.

She touched her fingers to her lips. "How did the accident happen this morning?"

"An engine kicked a rod because we didn't have the right oil, and we didn't have the right oil because we hadn't paid our bills. And we hadn't paid our bills because—"

"It was Cole's fault, wasn't it? That's what you were going to say."

"Christ, it's not *all* his fault," Hawkins said, exasperated. "I agreed with some of the maintenance cutbacks. But he's been chopping department budgets without telling me. It's crazy. It's not the way to save money. We ought to stop construction at the new site until we can afford it. But no, Cole goes right on building."

"What happened at the board meeting?" She knew Cole was lying when he told her everything was fine.

"You were right about Max Brodky," he said. "Cole figured it out himself. I don't know how, but he did. Now he wants to raise more money himself. Can he do that? Can he put together eleven million dollars in a week?"

"He has lots of friends," she said, thinking how Cole

222

abused the notion of friendship. To Cole, a friend was someone you did a lot of business with. "I saw him this afternoon. He's running scared. It was written all over his face." For a second, she felt sorry for him.

"He ought to be," Brad said. "It's worse than I thought. He admitted we couldn't siphon anything from the European operations to pay our bills here." He lit a cigarette and flicked the match into a wastebasket across the room. "And we're completely out of cash. If the bank doesn't renew the loans . . ."

"Then what?" she asked.

"I suppose we'll find out from Max Brodky. I'm looking forward to meeting him."

"You don't seem worried about it."

"I'm not, especially," he said. "Even if we're bought out, somebody has to run the place. And I've still got my stock."

She stood and moved away from him. "Cole's doing it again," she said.

"It?"

"Hookers. Today it was girls *and* boys. Together." She stared at Hawkins. Her voice dropped. "He's pathetic."

She looked down at her hands. They were shaking. She picked up her glass and walked over to the curved window. It distorted the view, like a funhouse mirror. At the far end of the midway, she could see tram cars gliding in and out of the Mt. Olympus station. The sky was preternaturally clear. She thought about their weekend in Los Angeles, then about the night before, played back all of his gestures, as if her memory were a continuous roll of film. Lying in bed with him, riding later in the car down the West Side Highway to their favorite restaurant in Little Italy, where they went to have dinner unnoticed. She remembered the lights flickering on the Jersey shore, reflected in the murky Hudson, then remembered watching his hands on the steering wheel, their sure grip, the short, blond hairs blowing upright in the breeze.

"It was fun in Los Angeles," she said, "wasn't it?"

Hawkins crossed the room and stopped behind her. Absentmindedly he flipped through a series of safety switches, holding each for a moment while test lights flashed. He had checked them two hours earlier, and did so again only to find a place for his hands.

"Do you know," he said dryly, "I've never done that in my life?"

"Done what?" she asked.

"Run after a woman the way I ran after you."

"Do you think you've run after me? I thought it was the other way around."

"In my way," he said. "I have."

He rested his hand on her shoulder. Her thoughts raced, and fleetingly she was in touch with her sadness for Cole. Life does not change, she told herself. It gets better or worse, but it doesn't change, and we simply go on. Maybe I will no longer be Mrs. Cole Cunningham, but I will go on being whoever it is that I am.

Hawkins gestured toward the ground, at the park. "Magnificent, isn't it?" he asked.

"I suppose."

"You suppose?"

"It reminds me of Cole. It's tainted."

"When you think about it, the park's not really his. Never was. It was Gabriel's idea. It was the Duke's money. And the bank's. Cole wasn't much more than a traffic cop."

"But you work for him."

"Not for much longer," he said. "Lexie, why did you come out here today?"

"I wanted to know what happened this morning."

"You could have asked Cole."

"I did. He said everything was under control."

"You could have called me," Hawkins said. "Saved yourself the ride."

"What did you mean when you said you wouldn't be working for Cole much longer?"

He pulled her away from the window, turned her around so they were looking directly into each other's

224

eyes. He could not quite decide whether to tell her the truth, although he sensed that she already knew.

"I think I can get the Duke to vote with me," he said slowly, choosing his words with care.

"Vote?" she asked. "Vote on what?"

"Even if Cole can raise more money, he still needs a majority of the voting stock to approve a new partner. Without me and the Duke, he hasn't got a majority." He put his hands on her shoulders. "I'm going to push Cole out, Lexie. He's finished."

She walked out from under his grip. "The funny thing is," she said, "he was finished a long time ago." She felt sorry for him again, but less than she would have imagined. "What about Max? He could push you out, too."

"No," Hawkins said. "Anybody who buys the park will buy me. And on my terms. Because I'm the best there is. I've made some mistakes, and the biggest mistake was not watching Cole more carefully. I'll never make that mistake again." He walked across the room to her. "Maybe I did it because of you. Maybe I couldn't see him clearly because of you."

She took his hands, held them between hers.

"I'm not good at these things, Lexie," he said softly. All his emotions seemed to rush to the tips of his fingers and stop. He felt himself alien to his own feelings. "I've always wanted—" He broke off. "I've wanted to tell you how much I loved you, that I wanted you to leave Cole." These are not my words, he thought. "It's hard for me to say."

Her eyes widened. She was mute. She had wanted to hear this, she had come today to hear this—and yet it frightened her. So accustomed were they to making love in the middle distance, remote, that it was as if they were merely animals, nothing passing between them except the current of sex.

"We're selfish people," he said, "you and me. We like to take but neither one of us wants to give. It's a sickness." He leaned against the wall and lit a cigarette. "Do you

225

know how I feel? I'll tell you. I don't know what love is. I haven't had a hell of a lot of experience at it."

She went to him, took him in her arms. "I love you, Brad. I've loved you for a long time. Only I didn't know."

"Do you know now?"

She looked down. "I think so," she whispered.

"You thought you loved Cole once, didn't you? Maybe you still do."

"Love changes," she said, pulling away from him and sitting on the banquette under the windows. "Sometimes it grows and sometimes it doesn't. And then it dies."

He sat next to her. The tears he had been holding back welled into his eyes. He had lost his prized control, but he did not mind. She hugged him and they clung to each other until they were breathing in the same steady rhythm.

"I wonder what's going to happen to us," she said.

"We live happily ever after," he said. "Isn't that how dreams end?"

"Right," she said, almost cheerful. "King and queen of the amusement park."

"It's not mine yet."

"Why did Cole do it?" she asked. "What happened to the money?"

"He just didn't know any better. There was always somebody to watch over him before. Somebody to rein him in."

"And you didn't know?"

"I never had any time to do anything about it. I was spending all my time trying to keep the place running. And then maybe I just didn't look carefully at the balance sheet because I didn't want to know."

"What about us?" Alexis asked.

"We'll have to pay more attention to us," he said, and he kissed her. "I have to leave, to meet the governor. Business goes on."

He was stepping into the elevator when she ran to him and held him.

"I'll be back in an hour," he said.

She sat and stared through the window at the crowd,

waiting for him to come out the door downstairs. In a moment she saw him in the sun, walking up the midway. He stopped and looked up, smiled, and waved. Alexis did not believe this would last. Nothing did.

14

The train clattered along Spain's Costa Brava. A lean Englishman, wiping sweat and dust from his eyes, watched two Frenchwomen holding fiercely to the armrests across the aisle. Danes, Germans, and Americans, chattering in a low hum, crowded the single first-class enclosed coach. Poor Spanish peasants sat in the open-air second- and third-class cars. On one side of the train, over a promontory, a rough, pebbled beach swept down to the Mediterranean; on the other, the villages of rural Spain flickered past, frozen in the nineteenth century. Only Coca-Cola signs, visible from the rumbling coaches, reminded the foreign tourists of the twentieth century. The brightly painted adobe train stations could have been built a hundred years before.

"Arenys de Mar," the conductor called, and Jeremy Fitch stood and walked to the door. Although he was formally dressed in a linen suit with a small red boutonniere and carried a leather solicitor's envelope, he attracted no attention in the crowded station. Tourists no longer surprised the peasants. Wealthy foreigners came each summer, some for only a few days, others for several months, bringing with them obscure habits and raucous drinking in the streets until the early-morning hours. Storekeepers earned enough in the summer to survive through the rest of the year. *Farmacías* sold amphetamines and narcotics to young people and *commerciantes* charged ten pesetas for cigarettes instead of the three they normally cost. On the Avenida Torquemada, the single main street, restaurants and bars doubled their prices.

Fitch walked to the main plaza leading into town from the station. From there, a wide dirt road sloped gradually uphill for about two hundred yards and then rose into the mountains. Fitch threaded his way through clusters of tourists. Others jammed the sidewalk cafés, sipping wine and nibbling bread and cheese. He stopped to buy a pack of Rothmans, which cost him the equivalent of ten packs of Spanish cigarettes; then walked toward the top of the avenue to the Hotel Nacional. Its white marble facade, studded with ornate brass-railed balconies, gleamed in the late afternoon sun. The thickly waxed lobby floor creaked as Fitch entered.

"Candace Bollinger, please," he said to the dark, thin man standing at the desk.

"Bollinger?" the man answered, a bit too quickly. "We have no one here by that name, señor."

Fitch frowned, exasperated. He reached into his breast pocket and pulled out a card. Handing it to the clerk, he said, "The name is Fitch. Ring the lady up, will you please, and tell her I'm here." He turned around and crossed the lobby, set his briefcase down on a side chair, and gently lowered himself onto a wicker divan. He had sat on exactly the same wicker couch in the same lobby carrying the same briefcase on an almost identical errand two years earlier. It was, indeed, just about the same time of year, at the turn of the low season. And exactly as before, the desk clerk—this one was new, but his bogus imperial manner was interchangeable with that of all the Nacional's staff—had denied the existence of a resident named Bollinger.

It was Candy's way, absurd in light of her punctual move from London to Spain each May. Her suite of rooms at the Nacional was sealed each winter, her furniture stored in the same warehouse, and then each spring the suite was opened and the furniture brought down and cleaned and installed in the rooms when she wired from London. On his last errand for Max Brodky, Fitch had come to deliver a favor to Candy Bollinger. She had needed Max's connections to acquire a casino on the Riviera, one to which she owed such huge sums of money that it made more sense to simply buy the place rather than pay the debt. She did not, of course, want the transaction publicized. Max could be private. Today was the same. Max would do her a favor but, as before, at a price.

Crazy rich Americans, Fitch thought. Max Brodky. Cole Cunningham. It was not their extravagance Fitch marveled at. The British rich had no peers at displaying wealth. But the Americans and their dealings, their personal machinations—it was useless trying to understand them. Not that Jeremy Fitch cared. Max Brodky had made him wealthy, no small feat in an England of confiscatory taxes. Max paid him well, created channels through which money flowed to Switzerland and back to England, bypassing government tax collectors. Fitch's ostensible business—importing Italian, Spanish, and Moroccan leather—hid a vast network of Max's European concerns. All of it was legal, Fitch told himself, and it was—to the limits of the law. Well, what was one to do? England would dim its remaining glory under creeping socialism. The sun was finally setting on the British Empire, its final glow reflecting a once-unparalleled civilization in its last stages of decline.

"Miss Bollinger will see you shortly." The desk clerk was standing over him, proffering a tall glass of iced coffee. Candy had told the odious little man what to serve—the vulgar drink to which Fitch had become accustomed in America. Fitch nodded and sipped the coffee—vile, greasy stuff—but he resisted adding cream or sugar, the whole point in drinking it being the avoidance of anything fattening. Now that the clerk was informed of Jeremy's importance, he remained standing there, grinning a distasteful, rotten-toothed grin.

"Fetch me some bottled carbonated water, will you, man?" Fitch said, needing something to rinse away the bitter taste in his mouth. The tap water, unboiled, was certainly not safe to drink.

"Pardon, señor?"

Fitch thought a moment; the man's English was obviously limited. "Perrier, Vichy. *Agua mineral.*"

"Yes, señor. *Uno momento.*"

What an unpleasant task, dealing with Candy Bollinger.

Fitch unzipped his briefcase and removed a sheaf of papers labeled Hampshire. An utter disaster. But Fitch could see why Max Brodky wanted Hampshire—or rather he thought he could. Such possibilities lurked in its balance sheet. The importing subsidiaries, the manufacturing in Taiwan—but most of all, that tarnished jewel, Olympic Adventure. The amusement park was clearly the gem on which Max had fixed his eye.

The clerk returned with a chilled seven-ounce Perrier and handed it to Fitch with a bottle opener. To let him inspect, as Fitch would have in any event demanded to, the cap, to determine if the bottle had been opened, refilled with a local variety of spring water, and then closed again. Fitch would have recognized the taste, but he realized this Spanish peasant was now taking no chance of offending him. He opened the bottle, poured its contents into a glass, and cautiously drank it.

"She will see you now," the man said, deferentially leading Fitch to the elevator. When the doors opened on the top floor, a butler was waiting for him. He led Jeremy to the front parlor. Another glass of iced coffee was waiting, this one milder. Torn cigarette butts in the ashtray showed that Candy Bollinger had nervously occupied the room earlier in the day. Fitch remembered her trademark: everywhere she went she tore paper from the filters of cigarettes and peeled the layers inside, leaving a mound of yellowish fluff. She might just as well have scrawled her name in the ashes.

A shadow crossed the table and Fitch looked up. Candy had entered the room quietly, padding softly in blue velvet slippers.

"Well, Jeremy Fitch, to what do I owe the pleasure of your company?" She wore a plain white cotton dress that reached to the floor, starkly setting off her tanned complexion and dark auburn hair.

"Surely you know," he said. "Our friend has sent me to ask a favor and deliver a favor."

"Come now, Jeremy. Our friend, as you call him, doesn't *ask* for favors." She sank into the chair opposite him. "You might have called ahead. I have guests arriving tonight. It's unlike you to come unannounced." He saw her looking toward the hallway and, glancing around, caught sight of a naked figure dashing past.

"Trouble with the highway," he answered, reaching down for his briefcase. "No time. I had to run to make the train. And I left London in rather a hurry." While he talked, he shuffled the papers. A butler appeared with a tray of thin, damp wafers. With his left hand, Fitch began to eat while he continued to riffle through the case. The line of light from the mansard windows, curtained in bright green fabric, grew dimmer.

"Max," Candy finally said. "What, pray tell, dear Jeremy, can this poor girl do for him?" Poor little girl, Fitch thought, who was neither poor nor a little girl. In Monte Carlo, the croupiers called her the shark. At the diamond markets in Johannesberg and in New York's gem exchange, she was known, affectionately but fearfully, as the Tigress.

"This should explain it," Fitch said, laying a file marked Hampshire on the alabaster-topped table.

"Doesn't Max work fast?" she asked rhetorically. "I've just now put through a call to Cole in New York."

"Cancel it."

"Pardon me, Jeremy?"

"I said cancel it. Best do it now." His voice was a touch menacing, ugly despite its surface smoothness.

She picked up the phone slowly. *"Jorge, olvida la llamada por teléfono a los Estados Unidos."* She paused. "For the moment."

Candy reckoned at a glance that Cole Cunningham could, with help from his friends, survive. But how clever Max was, she thought. She had never considered Max cruel or grasping, as some did, or even greedy. Merely clever. How else could it be with money, of such minor consequence in the larger scheme of things? She looked again at the Hampshire file. How the hell had Cole allowed his fortune to slip so precipitously close to disaster? Just last spring, he'd helped her construct a lovely syndicate for disposing of the emeralds she'd bought from a distressed French countess. But now these balance sheets. Had he gone mad?

"Rather embarrassing," Fitch said, "isn't it?"

"Sad," she said. "A terrible waste."

Fitch drew himself up against the back of the chair. "You can see now why our friend would appreciate you not rescuing—"

"Stop calling Max 'our friend.' He's not my friend and you know it."

"—the slovenly Mr. Cunningham from his wretched excess. You would only complicate his problems, don't you think?"

"No, I don't." She daintily placed a thin brown filtered cigar between her lips. Fitch leaned over with a match and she held his hand briefly, bending toward him, her breasts falling free so that he found himself peering directly into her cleavage.

"Shall we attend to business?" Fitch asked.

"Am I supposed to administer the *coup de grace*? Or should I stick the knife in and twist it a few times?"

"Mustn't be bitter now. Max doesn't want anything of the kind. And he doesn't want Cole to suffer unnecessarily."

"You make him sound like someone dying of cancer."

"Apt," Fitch said. "He just wants him out; nothing more, nothing less."

Candy inhaled slowly and picked up a tea sandwich. She wasn't hungry. She ate slowly, turning the problem over in her mind, examining it from all sides. How raw, she thought. Push the poor bastard hard enough and . . . well, this was not Cole's year. His marriage was in shambles—she already knew that. A pity. She had liked Alexis. He'll lose it all at once, and then come here to take the cure. Could she risk running against Max? All is fair, she thought, in love and money.

"How *can* he ask me to do this?" Candy finally said. "Cole has been good to me."

"So has Max," Fitch replied. "More than good."

She looked at the balance sheet again. Hampshire Industries indisputably teetered on the brink. Cole had been careless. She fingered the edges of the papers.

"What shall I say to Cole—that Max called in his chips? That after fifteen years, sorry, friend, business is business, tough luck, that's the way it goes, see you at the tables?" She stared him straight in the eye. "Is that it?"

"Now let us not be melodramatic, Candy. Cole will survive. He always has. Actually, Max would prefer you not to involve his name." Fitch could see that additional ammunition would be needed.

"He'll know, of course," Candy said. "You can be goddamned sure he'll know."

"No problem. Just don't mention Max. That's the way he wants it."

"What's in it for me, Jeremy? What do I get for playing the heel of this piece?"

It was the question Fitch had been waiting for. "It's not only you. I shouldn't tell you this, but Max is leaning on a few others, from what I can tell. First of all, you get that little—" yes, she was listening intently now "—that little set of pearls you've been after and—"

"Christ on a crutch! Max knows about *them*?"

"As I was saying, the pearls. And your sister's . . . uh . . . delicate matters in Zurich get taken care of right away. Your franchise with the Fontero mines will appear shortly. Then there are those diamonds you've been trying to unload for three months. A buyer will be found. Good show, don't you think?"

She was stunned. Her face froze, the cigarette dangling from her lips. How could Max know? Every deal she was working on.

"There's something odd here, Jeremy," she said at last. "That is all going to cost Max a lot of money. A great deal of money. It's personal, isn't it? It's not Hampshire Industries at all. It's Cole—his head on a silver platter."

"Not at all," Fitch said. "You've got it wrong. Max doesn't work that way and you know it. This is purely business."

Bullshit, she thought. Max works exactly that way. And then pretends it's business. Carries grudges and swears he doesn't know the meaning of the word. So be it. How little was certain, she thought, in friendship as in love. How little was assured. She felt responsible for Cole, had once loved him. Now that he needed her, she was unable to deliver. What would Max do to her if she refused? What *could* he do? I'm sorry, Cole. My portfolio isn't as liquid as you imagine. My accountant says it's impossible. Surely you can make it without me this time.

No, she would forego excuses. She wouldn't even return his call. She wanted to blame Max, but she couldn't. It was merely money. He was merely clever.

"Business is over, Jeremy. Cable Max that all is well. That *is* what you're supposed to do, isn't it?"

"May I borrow your telephone?"

"Yes, and you can stay for supper. The guest list is quite interesting."

She stood as he picked up the receiver. Business was over, Fitch thought. Perhaps there would be time for pleasure.

All the way to his office, through the crowded Ginza swarming with the tides of newly rich Japanese workers, Mitzu Noshumi chided himself for having to conduct business on a weekend. In a promise extracted by his wife for marital peace, he forsook the bank on weekends for family, now that he no longer needed to consider his financial security. But of course he loved the bank, loved its smooth glass facade, found it as comforting as the mellifluous singing of his children's voices. Noshumi's attachment to institutions, while so Japanese in style, reflected as much how Western he had become. He dressed and talked like his American counterparts, spoke their language although few of them spoke his. During the years that he had strived to become president of the bank, his wife's family, with their money and centuries of intimate involvement with the country's ruling elite, had watched and prodded at every step; they would make him one of their own. But in so doing, they had created a hybrid creature, ill at ease in his new incarnation—a butterfly of perfect color tearing out of the cocoon, missing a wing.

The caller had asked to visit Mitzu at his home, but *that* Western he had not become. Family was family and business was business. Bankers in New York might travel to country clubs with their families and then conduct business in the locker room and bar, but if the Americans wished to behave in such a fashion, Noshumi thought, that was their business. He realized he was thinking in English, as he always did when preparing to talk with foreigners.

"Don't call Mr. Cunningham until we speak," the caller had said. Noshumi had known Cole for twenty years, and when Noshumi was being tested as a loan officer, Cole had done well by him. He remembered when Cole had come to meet the bank's senior officers. Cole had felt superior, Mitzu could see, and the bankers had regarded Cole with contempt. With all the help from his wife's family, it may well have been Cole's business that had finally solidified Mitzu's position at the bank. Mitzu Noshumi became bank president.

Tea was waiting for him in the sitting area as he crossed the threshold into his office. In a few minutes, Conrad Hamilton, Max Brodky's man in Hong Kong, would arrive. Noshumi was so burdened by guilt, anticipating the desertion of his friend Cunningham, that he nearly bumped into the weekend man as he bent over the green mother-of-pearl tray to pour tea. After the required formal greeting, Noshumi dismissed him.

Well, he thought, again in English, it is, as they say, the times. His wife had said it before he left the house. New times, she said, shaking her head, a gesture and perspective recently acquired from the tennis-playing wife of a Chase Manhattan vice president. Perhaps, Noshumi reflected, she was right. Max Brodky was the larger power, and the Brodky family also had a great deal of money in the bank. All of it in street accounts, of course; their name never appeared. Still, there was enough of his past in mental view, memories of traditional virtues: constancy, loyalty, trust. It gave him pause.

The weekend man knocked quietly on the door. Mitzu answered and the man entered to announce the arrival of the guest from Hong Kong.

"Show him in, please," Noshumi said in his round-toned English, which he had learned at Harvard. Harvard, where he had met Cole. The memory was painful. All the memories were painful. He watched through the open door. Hamilton sauntered down the row between the desks.

"Mitzu, old friend," Hamilton said as he entered. "It's been too long." The pleasantries. Noshumi recoiled to hear this man calling him a friend. How utterly false.

"Conrad, I see you. It is an honor to welcome you." He used the literal translation of a ritual Japanese greeting. It made Westerners comfortable in dealing with Orientals, Noshumi knew, if they could continue to consider them, as the American joke had it, inscrutable. Racism could be turned to an advantage—this Noshumi had learned in the United States. Let them think we possess magical powers: the wisdom of the Orient. Just as the black revolutionary had told him: let them think we are better in bed and threaten their women. Any frightening myth will do.

He passed Hamilton a cup of tea, and though Hamilton detested tea, he drank it anyway, to avoid offending his host. Noshumi himself had developed a strong liking for American-style cola, but he never consumed it in the company of Americans. Maintain the image.

"Surely this is urgent business," Noshumi said, "if you ask me to leave my family today."

"Mitzu, I told you I'd have been glad to come to your house."

"No, the drive is too long. How urgent is this problem?"

"Very," Hamilton said. "Mr. Cunningham is in serious trouble, as you know."

"I do not know. I had just received his message when your call came."

"He's in need of a large sum of money, Mitzu."

"Yes, he often calls me when that is the case. And I shall be glad to help him. But why has he sent you? Are you not still associated with Mr. Brodky?"

The verbal dancing frustrated Hamilton. He was not adept at it. For Noshumi, such conversations were dancing indeed, a form as precise as a minuet, a No drama, a style of business encompassing all the complexity of Japanese thought throughout the centuries, the delicate art of meaning what you say without saying what you mean.

"Mitzu, couldn't we do this more simply?"

"Do what, Conrad? Am I not a simple man?"

"All right, then. Let the numbers tell you." Hamilton reached into his briefcase for the Hampshire file. Sitting at the low table, knocking his knees, Hamilton spread the papers out. Noshumi fiddled in his pocket for his reading glasses, balancing his teacup between two fingers. His eyes moved involuntarily to what bankers are trained to see: the bottom line. Typed numbers. Large figures, Noshumi thought. He recalled Cole's rough laughter, his gruffness, his receding hairline; the thought made the back of his neck tingle, a feeling like a shower of tiny beads of cold water. It seemed only yesterday that Hampshire Industries had opened its Tokyo office. The champagne, food, congratulations, Americans, money . . . dreams.

"It's worse than it seems," Hamilton said. "This only covers through last month. This month he's got a cash drain so bad he can't meet the payroll. He's short with the power company, his paper suppliers, and his landlords. His camera business is way off. Next month his tax returns are going to be audited, and once the IRS starts moving, his troubles have just begun. This is not the time for you to be lending him any money, Mitzu."

"What is your phrase?" Noshumi said. "Like rats from a sinking ship? Is that correct?"

"If you keep talking English like that, Mitzu, you'll forget Japanese."

"We have similar phrases, Conrad. Different words, but they mean the same."

"We've cut him off, Mitzu. You're his last hope and you'd be crazy to waste the money, I assure you."

"Perhaps I am crazy, Conrad," Noshumi said. He refilled the teacups.

"No, Mitzu, you're not."

"It is done then, you are telling me," Noshumi said without a trace of emotion. "Max will . . . how would you say it? Max will come after me, yes?"

Hamilton sighed, weary. "No, Mitzu. Max wants you to do the right thing. What's best for you."

"What is best for me," the Japanese banker said softly, "is that I am able to sleep well."

Hamilton stood and crossed the office. He toyed with the figurines resting on the window sill, exquisite miniatures of blown glass. Frogs. Seashells. How far, he wondered; Noshumi could not be pushed too hard.

"Mitzu, this isn't pleasant for any of us. I want you to know that."

The banker said nothing and sipped his tea.

"Mitzu, listen to me. Cole is a sick man. He's lost all control. He pays no attention to business. His wife is leaving him." Hamilton paused—how to put it delicately? "He has sex with strangers." Hamilton lit a cigarette. "Of both sexes."

At this, Noshumi looked up. His lips pursed, but still he said nothing.

"He has run his business into bankruptcy. He's spent more money than he has. And . . . and he has lied to his partners."

"No, I do not believe it." Noshumi stood. "That Cole would not do."

"It's true, Mitzu. He never told them how bad things were. Bloome. The Duke. Hawkins—it's their money, too. He's off the deep end, damnit."

"Such language is not necessary here," Noshumi said.

"All right. I'm sorry. But he's out of his mind, I tell you." There, it was over. What more could he say? Hamilton could have recited a list of other sins, but he knew he had struck home. The sex and the lying. Now if only Noshumi believed him.

"He kept double books," Hamilton added, driving the point further. "One for himself and one for them. In case you were wondering how he got away with it, I can show you."

"No, no," Noshumi answered, waving his hand. "This is enough." From the bottom drawer of his desk, Noshumi drew a tattered envelope. Yellowed papers poked through the frayed corners. He handled them carefully, as if they were ancient scrolls, not mere balance sheets. For years, Noshumi had kept the working papers from his first transactions with Cole Cunningham. He put his head into his hands, then sat up and brushed the papers into a wastebasket.

Hamilton averted his gaze. Too bad he doesn't have a fireplace, he thought. Better drama. Instead, Noshumi lifted the bucket and emptied it into a paper shredder. He touched his foot to the pedal, and the torn ledgers sank into the machine's teeth. There was a barely audible whir, then the machine turned itself off.

"I will see you to your car," Noshumi said.

"Quite all right," Hamilton said.

Noshumi accompanied him to the elevator. "A pleasure to see you again, Conrad. I trust your other business here will go well."

"Thanks, Mitzu. I'm glad we could settle this so amicably." Hamilton stepped into the elevator.

Noshumi opened a can of Seven-Up, distractedly dusting the tabletop with his napkin. His wife would be waiting for him, wanting an explanation. No, he thought, he would not return Cole Cunningham's call. The times, he told himself. New times.

15

What I do not need today, Hawkins thought, standing at the helicopter pad with Sheila Richardson, is Governor Lloyd Birdwell.

The fire engines were finally in place, to allow the governor's helicopter to land. Around the pad, a clutch of reporters and photographers gathered. The pack of journalists never ceased surprising Hawkins. The *news.* A governor's movements were worthy of attention no matter how inconsequential. And the reporters and television crews, notebooks in hand, cameras rolling, tripods of lights—all to capture the governor's arrival. Scanning the crowd, Hawkins saw Murray Rothbart of the *Times.* Rothbart affected a studied seedy look common to newspapermen of the old school: shirt unbuttoned at the neck, tie askew, rumpled suit, cigarette dangling from his mouth, a pencil balanced behind his left ear. Rothbart was a pro; Hawkins had read the reporter's stories on New York's financial scandals—the "follies," as Rothbart regularly described them—and he respected the man's talent. A rope barrier around the pad held the press back, and Hawkins asked Sheila Richardson to let Rothbart through.

"I'll bring him over," she said. "Who do you want to take on the tour with the governor? Jock Constable wants to come."

Poor Jocko, Hawkins thought, endlessly infatuated with celebrities. As if the governor of New Jersey were automatically interesting simply because he was a politician. Hawkins had dealt with politicians throughout his life, had been exposed to all manner of them since his earliest days as a Texas lawyer. Some were good and some were corrupt and most were tedious—boring company, Hawkins thought, because all they really wanted to talk about

241

was themselves. As a group, Hawkins thought, they were shallow.

"I don't know, Sheila," Hawkins said. "Is Jock . . . well, would it—"

"He's sober today, if that's what you mean."

"That's what I meant."

"It'll make for better pictures, Brad. You know, you and Jock and the governor on the arcade. Jock showing the governor the stables. And the governor's sort of a . . . well, he drinks a little himself. He might feel comfortable with Jock."

Hawkins smiled. Sheila was doing her best to make a case for Jocko. Well, she had an instinct about these things; her job was to know what resulted in good press, and if she thought Constable was right, then fine. Hawkins thought he might even be able to leave Birdwell with Sheila and Jock and slip away.

"I'll buzz him," Hawkins said. Sheila crossed the ropes to the reporters, signaling to Murray Rothbart. Hawkins called Constable on his walkie-talkie.

"Constable here," the voice crackled.

"Hawkins, Station One, roving. Where are you, Jocko?"

"Just checking my storeroom and bringing on the new shift, big fella. What can I do for you?" Hawkins hated being called big fella, which Constable had done since law school. It was Constable's problem: Jock was short. And Hawkins was not ignorant of the power of his own height. Tall men made shorter men feel inadequate.

"Governor Birdwell's going to be landing in about ten minutes. Sheila said you might like to meet him and join us for the VIP tour. Get your picture taken and show the press a little hospitality. Can you get away from your work?" It would be good for Jock, Hawkins thought. Their friendship had been strained ever since Ken Masters had been hired; Constable had made no secret of his desire for the job, or of the fact that he thought he deserved it.

"Well, how about that? Sounds good to me. I'll clean up down here and be right over. Is that kid there? What's his name . . . Masters?" It was sad, Hawkins thought;

Jock had been pretending for weeks that he couldn't remember Ken Masters's name.

"He's busy, Jocko. So speed it up, huh?"

"On my way. Constable, out."

Hawkins felt bad about Constable. Even at the beginning of their friendship, in Austin, he'd protected Jock from his own self-destructiveness. Whether it was carting him home after a stumble-down drunk or paying bar owners for broken mirrors, or comforting Jock's wife when he was in the hospital for one alcohol-related ailment or another, he had been Jock's guardian. Never having had a brother of his own, Hawkins had forged a special bond with Constable. It was something they never talked about. And with good reason, Hawkins thought. You couldn't very well talk about friendship for very long without destroying whatever was precious about it. Just like love, Hawkins thought. Talk about it and it evaporates. Thinking about Jock, about the rift hiring Masters had opened between them, about the memories of Texas (memories Hawkins would just as soon have forgotten), disturbed him.

He could remember all too well a hot Austin spring night fifteen years before, the kind of night when the scent of rose blossoms permeated the air like perfume, when the wind bit through your clothes and burned your skin, when you thought you could drink cold beer for hours and still not slake your thirst. Hawkins had sat in his apartment, fighting the weather and concentrating on studying for his law-school exams. His wife had been asleep and the work was going tolerably well until Jock, who should have been studying for the same exams, burst in on him, bellowing obscenities.

"Fuck the law," he cried. "Fuck contracts. Piss on torts. To hell with the whole goddamn Code of Hammurabi." He was deliriously drunk.

Spoiled rich kid, Hawkins had thought. He'd carried him into the shower and, without taking off his clothes, turned on the cold water and held him there while he squalled. Eventually Constable had calmed down and passed out on Hawkins's bed. Hawkins went on studying. The next morning he had tried to wake Constable, but Jock refused to get up. Returning that evening, he had found Jock still there, drinking. On Hawkins's desk was one empty bottle, a cheap brand of Scotch that smelled like country moonshine, and another bottle nearly gone. Constable sat by the window, humming to himself, bouncing a glass on his knee, splashing liquor across his shirt and dribbling it onto the floor.

"Jock, you missed the contracts exam," Hawkins had said.

"Didn't I though?" Constable had answered, slurring his words. "Big fucking deal."

Hawkins said no more, pushed the bottles aside, and continued studying. Constable did not stir from his chair; he just stared out the window, rocking back and forth, and eventually dozed off. For three days, Constable drank and Hawkins studied. Hawkins brought food, which Constable didn't touch. At year's end, Hawkins left with his degree, and Constable, who did not graduate, disappeared from his life, only to return two years later, caught in a real-estate swindle and on his way to jail. Hawkins defended him, proved that Jock had had nothing to do with the swindle, and from then on, Hawkins made certain that Constable never lacked honest work. Clean work, not very difficult work, well paid and the kind where he couldn't get himself into trouble. Wherever Hawkins went, Constable and his family followed. To Disney, and then to Olympic Adventure. Of course, no man likes depending on another, and inevitably Jock came to resent Hawkins —pehaps, Hawkins thought, to hate him. Ken Masters's hiring had pushed Jock overboard, and he was drinking more than ever.

"Hello there, Hawkins. Ready to talk with the big man?" Murray Rothbart knew Hawkins's response to politicians. It was one view they shared.

"Murray, you scrivener," Hawkins said jovially, slapping Rothbart on the back. "What are you doing covering this story? Are you off the big city follies?"

"There's a lull now. We're waiting to see whether the city is going to shut down the schools, the hospitals, or the fire department this week. I'm betting on all three. Want to move to Montana?"

Hawkins laughed. "Can't," he said. "Hay fever."

"Hawkins, *you* can leave. I'm a city boy."

"Seriously, though," Hawkins said, "what are you doing covering this nonsense?"

"Needed some stuff for a column. I talked to your demonstrating farmers."

"You can put in your column that we'll do everything we can to help them, and we will. But just between you and me, Olympic Adventure didn't create suburban sprawl and we didn't build the highways. Don't forget that, huh?"

"Sure, Hawkins. Doesn't matter anyway. The best stuff is watching the governor pump hands and kiss babies. Maybe he'll pump some babies and kiss some hands and there'll be a story here yet."

"What's Birdwell like? Our public relations department found getting him out here today incredibly easy. Christ, we made him wait half an hour and he's still coming."

"I was over at the fire. Anybody hurt?"

"Just the lion. Dead."

"And the little girl and your assistant?"

"Scared and scratched a little, but okay. What about Birdwell?"

"Well, the guy's had a bad year. Two of his commissioners have been indicted for fraud, his appointments secretary has been accused of peddling favors, and now everybody's saying the Mafia paid for his election. He's got his own little Watergate." Rothbart took the burning cigarette from his mouth and lit a fresh one from its tip. "I figure the guy needs all the good press he can get, and what better way to look like a swell kind of family fellow? Spend an afternoon in an amusement park. You get *your* stories, he gets *his*."

"We're being used; is that what you're saying, Murray?"

"You're using each other. It's the name of the game.

He's just one of the boys, out for a good time. Except everybody else sits in traffic and he comes by copter."

"What about the election? *Did* the Mafia pay for it?"

"Search me, Hawkins. I'm just a reporter, I ain't Clark Kent."

"Come on, Murray. You've got more dirt on these guys than we have in all the lawns here."

"If you want my guess, I'd say no. The guy's not real lucky, and not too smart either. But *that* crooked? I doubt it. Oh, sure, he's got a lot of dough behind him, but not Mafia money. Speaking of money, did I see Mrs. Cole Cunningham over at the fire? The blond bombshell?"

"That's her."

"No shit. Now there is one beautiful broad and a bundle of dough all wrapped into one."

That's what you think, Hawkins thought. Reporters, like most people, were easily fooled. If people lived like they were rich, people thought they were. They never saw the bills and second mortgages. Hawkins was willing to bet that Cole Cunningham had less cash in the bank than the poorest *Times* reporters, the way he and Alexis spent it. The Cunninghams lived on what Hawkins called funny money: credit cards, expense accounts, company cars, other people's hospitality. And, Hawkins thought ruefully, the park was living on funny money, too, thanks to Cole.

"What's this I hear about the Brodky family buying you out?" Rothbart asked.

"Is that the truth?" Hawkins asked. Christ, how did that get around? "What *do* you hear?"

"That Max Brodky is finally getting his revenge on the ghost of Lyman Bloome. That's the scuttlebutt from a wizened old fart on the business page, and since he usually knows who's buying out whom, and since that's *all* he knows, he's probably right."

Revenge on Lyman Bloome?

"Search me," Hawkins said. "I don't know a thing about it."

"Right, you're the general manager of the place, a minority stockholder, and you never heard of Max Brodky. Who do you think you're talking to, Hawkins? The tooth fairy?"

Revenge on Lyman Bloome? Hawkins thought, What do I know about Lyman Bloome? He made movies. He owned movie theaters. He was the most powerful force in the entertainment industry for damn near half a century. He left his son a great deal of money and enough emotional problems to cripple him for life. But what the hell did Max Brodky have to do with Lyman Bloome?

"Well, Murray, I honestly don't know much. Are you really interested?"

"I'm always interested in Max Brodky. I'm always interested in rich people who don't flaunt their money. Rich people nobody's ever heard of are the most fascinating people in the world. So what about him?"

"Murray, did you come out here today to cover the governor or to talk to me about Brodky?"

"Sometimes, Hawkins, sometimes I think you were born yesterday."

"The day before yesterday, Murray. Now tell me something—what has Max Brodky got to do with Lyman Bloome?"

"Lyman Bloome, now there was one smooth bastard," Rothbart said. "I met him once, a couple of years before he died. We were talking at one of those stupid parties movie people throw and then invite everybody in town. Movie people like the kind of crowds where you put three hundred and fifty people in an eight-by-ten closet and then expect them to drink and have a good time. Anyway, I was standing next to Lyman Bloome and I didn't know what to say to the guy, and in those days I felt like I had to talk to everybody, because you never knew where your next story was coming from, right? So what did I say? I said, 'Hi. Murray Rothbart of the *Times*.' And you know what he said, this smooth bastard? He said, 'And one of the finest journalists in America.' Well I ask you, what the hell do you say to that?" Rothbart looked out toward the helicopter pad. "Where the hell is Governor Birdbrain?"

"On his way, Murray. You were going to tell me about Lyman Bloome and Max Brodky."

"I knew there was a point to that story. Max Brodky. Anyway, I ended up doing some work for Bloome—a picture about a great American newspaper that never got made. But Bloome paid me a bundle anyway. My wife celebrated for a week and then bought our summer place. Good investment, too. We bought land in Vermont for half a song and we could sell it for a whole song and retire on the profits."

"You'd get hit on the capital gains, Murray. Now what about Max Brodky?" Hawkins was losing patience. Governor Birdwell would be arriving any minute.

"Brodky, of course. Bloome flew me out to work on this picture in Hollywood. We got plastered at Bloome's place one night. Me and Bloome and his wife, Regina Bloome. The old bag's still alive. And Bloome starts to tell me the story of his life, how he was just a poor kid from the Midwest with a bright idea. Wanted to build movie theaters and make movies. Clean up on both ends. Even as a kid, he was a smooth bastard. But he didn't have any money, see. Now think carefully, Hawkins. Here's the sixty-four-thousand-dollar question. Who did he get the money from?"

Hawkins was totally mystified. What did this all have to do with Max Brodky?

"Max Brodky," Hawkins said.

"Bingo. You just won a two-week, all-expenses-paid vacation for two at the Altoona Motor Hotel in lovely downtown Altoona, Pennsylvania."

"Very funny, Murray. You ought to be a stand-up comic. You missed your calling."

"That's possible," Rothbart said. "Actually, I'm a sit-down comic. That's what the guys on the rewrite desk think. And speaking of my calling, where is Governor Birdshit?"

"I don't get one thing, Murray. What has any of this got to do with Gabriel Bloome or the park?"

"You *are* thick, aren't you?" Rothbart doodled idly in his notebook. "Lyman Bloome screwed Max Brodky out of a big hunk of dough when the government went after them with the antitrust laws. They had to split the business up. You couldn't own movie studios and movie theaters at the same time. You know, they didn't want the studios having control over distribution, or nobody else would have been able to make movies. But when the deal was closed, old man Brodky found himself short a million and a half bucks. And remember, income taxes weren't what they are today. That was a lot of dough. Some people said it was the lawyers who screwed the deal up. But Brodky always thought Bloome concealed the money. Kept it off the books, see. Max Brodky doesn't like to get screwed. As a matter of fact, from what I understand, he does most of the screwing. So Lyman Bloome is dead and Gabriel Bloome, along with his pal Cunningham, spent a lot of money borrowed from a bank in which Max Brodky has bought what the boys on the business page call a substantial interest."

"So he bought the bank to . . . that's preposterous. He bought the bank just so he could—"

"Bingo again," Rothbart said. "You hit the jackpot. Two weeks in lovely downtown Peoria, Illinois. All expenses paid."

"You're telling me he watched them spend themselves into a pit just so he could start shoveling the dirt in on top of them." Hawkins whistled.

Rothbart eyed him suspiciously. "You really didn't know any of this, did you? Where the hell have you been, Hawkins?"

"Too damn busy running the park, that's where."

"So what about it?" Rothbart asked. "What do you know about the Brodkys taking over? Where does the story go from here?"

"Is it your story, Murray?"

"Who gives a damn whose story it is? What's next?"

"I'll tell you. Off the record."

"Nothing's off the record."

"Either it's off the record, Murray, or I can't tell you. I've got a stake in this, remember?"

"Okay already. Off the record."

"Cunningham is looking for more money to ward off a Brodky takeover. We've still got a couple of days. But it *is* Brodky, as far as I know, and Cole knows it, too. Everything will be out in the wash before the end of the week."

"That close, huh?"

"That close, Murray."

A whirring noise filled the air and both men looked up. A huge blimp of a helicopter—an Eagle 1200, Hawkins thought; the governor travels in style—swooped down through the sky and hovered over the makeshift pad. The rush of wind sent television cameramen racing toward their equipment.

"Governor Birdhead has finally arrived," Rothbart said. "Tell me one more thing, Hawkins. What *is* your stake in this?"

"I'm not sure yet, Murray. I'll let you know."

"You do that. Remember your friends." Rothbart turned to leave. "Look sharp now, Hawkins. You're on *Candid Camera*."

Hawkins grinned and walked toward the craft as it set down. Jock Constable ran up behind him.

"It's about time," Hawkins said. "I thought maybe you didn't want your picture in the papers."

"Doesn't mean anything to me," Constable said, shouting to be heard over the helicopter's whine. "Just doing my job."

"Cheer up, Jocko. Let's show the governor how real people spend their Saturday afternoon."

Governor Lloyd Birdwell stepped out of the helicopter with his staff, several men in dark business suits, all of whom seemed to look alike: nondescript; fashionably long hair, but not too long; vacant eyes, focused on their boss; well scrubbed, tanned faces. Birdwell was in his mid-fifties, Hawkins guessed, and he had the sort of polished, dignified mien in which middle-aged politicians specialize. His brown hair, streaked with just a bit of silver and gray at the temples, was cropped close and appeared fuller than it was. Hawkins noticed that the hair did not blow out of place when the governor ducked under the copter's blades. Governor Lloyd Birdwell's hair was sprayed stiff against his skull.

Cameras were turning now. Hawkins and Constable walked toward the governor, but Birdwell, his attention drawn by the photographers and cameramen, didn't notice them. Flashing a toothy smile, he moved straight for the cameras, forcing Hawkins and Constable to reach him. Then the governor saw them and seemed to recognize Hawkins. Flashbulbs popped as they shook hands.

"Hawkins, isn't it?" the governor asked. "Brad Hawkins, is that right? A pleasure to see you."

"Thanks, governor. I'm glad you could make it. Sorry about the landing delay. State law, you know. The fire engines were tied up and they have to be here when you come down."

"Nothing serious, I hope," the governor said, continuing to walk away from the whirling copter blades, smiling all the way. Hawkins noticed that the governor was carefully placing himself in direct line of the cameras.

"All under control," Hawkins said, thinking that a man would have to practice smiling and talking simultaneously in order to do it well. "This is Jock Constable, who's in charge of—" Hawkins didn't know how to introduce Jock. "Jock's one of my right arms."

"I'll bet you need a spare right arm now and then," the governor said cheerfully. Reporters crowded around. One shouted for the governor's attention. "Just a minute here," Birdwell said to Hawkins. "The gentlemen of the fourth estate are always in a hurry. They have to ask their questions."

A reporter scrambled forward with a microphone in his hand, trailing a camera crew and a maze of wires.

"Tom Patterson, WCNJ, sir. Could we get a question in here?"

"Sure, Tom," the governor said. "Shoot."

"Could you turn a bit, sir, so we can get the park behind you?" The governor obliged. "There's some question," the reporter quickly went on, "as to how good Olympic Adventure is for central New Jersey. As a matter of fact, there were some farmers here this morning protesting property-tax increases. They say land developers are going to force them off their land. What's your opinion?"

Not stopping to think, the governor leaned into the microphone, looked directly past the reporter into the camera, and launched into his reply. "I'm very pleased to be Olympic Adventure's guest today, and I'm happy they invited me. This amusement park has been very good for our local economy. It employs several thousand of our young people every summer. It pays large state taxes, and it's been a boon for the entire region. It's my view that such protests as the one you refer to are common in these changing times, but perhaps a few people have overreacted. All things considered, I think one would have to be shortsighted to say this area of the state is over-developed." The governor bared his teeth and smiled and looked earnestly at the camera.

"Sir," the reporter went on, "what about the state's farming industries? Aren't we in danger of driving the family farm out of business with industries like Olympic Adventure?"

"Absolutely not," the governor said. "That is uninformed opinion not substantiated by the facts."

Absolutely yes, Hawkins thought. He and Cunningham had already talked several times about local complaints. Still, the politician's performance impressed him—Birdwell was prepared for this. Virtually everyone in the state understood that industrial development threatened farmers, and Hawkins himself had cautioned the Regional Plan Association against zoning variances for tract-house builders. The governor blandly asserted the opposite.

"We will do all we can," the governor was saying, "to prevent growth that would endanger the family farm. You have to strike a balance and that's what this administration will do."

Another television reporter had pushed his way to the front of the crowd. "One more question, governor," the man said, turning toward his technicians. A cameraman waved and the reporter began his question in a measured tone. "Governor, your real-estate commissioner was indicted last week for taking bribes from contractors. Reports indicate that the entire real-estate department has been taking part in widespread abuse of the state's building codes. What do you plan to do about it?"

"I believe in our system, young man; a man is innocent until a jury says he's guilty, and we'll have to wait before we know anything about guilt, won't we? In the meantime, I've ordered a full investigation of the state's policies and the attorney general will report directly to me. But I won't cast any aspersions on my own real-estate department or on the commissioner. We may find out that these charges are politically motivated. And that's all I have to say for now." He waited for the camera to stop and then continued. "Gentlemen, I'm here to visit Olympic Adventure and that's what I'm going to do."

The governor turned back toward Hawkins and Constable while other reporters yelled questions. "Gentlemen, please," the governor said, a touch of frost in his voice, "you are being rude to my hosts. I'll take more questions, if necessary, later in the day."

Birdwell put his arm around Hawkins. "You get used to this," he said. "Now let's have a look at your operation." Hawkins led the governor into the park, followed by reporters and camera crews. Rothbart's judgment seemed inaccurate to Hawkins; if Birdwell wasn't very bright, he certainly put on a good show. And the number of reporters was better than Sheila had hoped for. The governor's endorsement of Olympic Adventure, more effective than a week of television commercials, would appear on several local news programs that night. As the men walked, news photographers zigzagged around them, snapping pictures furiously. Hawkins couldn't help thinking that if every amateur photographer at Olympic Adventure used as much film as the professionals did, then the Olympic Bazaar film shop would make more money than all the others combined. But park visitors clicked the shutter once or twice and hoped they got a good picture; professionals did the same shot six or seven times at different exposures and angles because newspaper editors liked to make choices.

Constable described for the governor how each of the park's sections had been designed and built. At the governor's urging, he tactlessly revealed rough financial figures for food concessions and then, at the governor's insistence, supplied crowd sizes and profit margins for the entire park. Hawkins listened, mildly disturbed. But his mind was on Max Brodky. A man he'd never met was about to take over Olympic Adventure. It angered Hawkins—not least because he hadn't seen how much damage Cunningham was doing. Well, the deck wasn't dealt yet and Hawkins thought he had one card left. If Max Brodky needed anyone, he needed Brad Hawkins. Who else could manage Olympic Adventure? Who else could Brodky use to force Bloome and Cunningham out completely? Max Brodky's maneuvering against Gabriel Bloome might be turned to his own advantage. Brodky was no penny-ante conglomerateur. This might be the chance Hawkins had been waiting for.

They reached the stables of the Western Arena, and the governor was keen on touring. He wanted to see the horses. Hawkins reconsidered Rothbart's assessment—the governor had come to Olympic Adventure because he really *did* want to have a good time. Which was fine for the governor, Hawkins thought, but he and Constable had work to do. The governor was taking his time, walking through the stables and stopping at each stall.

"Beautiful animals," he said to Hawkins. "I've got a stable full of them myself, but these are beauties."

"Just stunt horses," Hawkins said.

"Mine are fat and lazy," the governor said. "My daughter and her friends ride them for fun because they're too damn old for anything else. I'd like to get a few racehorses, you know, but it wouldn't look right for the governor of the state to be out at the track watching his horses run."

"Might seem a little improper," Hawkins ventured, trying to hold up his end of the conversation.

"A little!" Birdwell exclaimed. "Why, they'd hang me in the newspapers and then they'd try to hang me in the courts. No, I think I'll have to run for senator before I buy any racehorses." The governor chortled loudly. Hawkins wondered about the Mafia.

Constable had disappeared—where the hell is he, Hawkins thought, when I need him?—so Hawkins led the governor to the blacksmith shop. Between shows, Hawkins explained, all the horses were examined for possible damage to their shoes and injuries to their legs. In stunt jumping, no matter how well trained the horses, a few injuries were inevitable. Governor Birdwell stopped to observe a blacksmith molding horseshoes.

"Now how do you know how big to make those?" he asked the smithy with all the ingenuousness of an eight-year-old. The man looked up from his work quizzically.

"This is the governor of New Jersey, Deke," Hawkins said. "Governor Birdwell, meet Deke Harrington. Deke used to be with Barnum and Bailey."

"Got tired of traveling," the smithy said, extending his hand.

"Pleased to meet you," the governor said. He glanced down as they shook and discovered a thick film of sludge on his hand.

"Sorry," the smithy said, flustered. He handed Birdwell a towel. The photographers had caught up with them and bulbs flashed as the governor leaned over the forge.

"Nothing to worry about," the governor said. "Now how is that done, sizing the shoe?"

"Well, it's just like people," the smithy said, blinking from the flashing bulbs. "You take a mold of the horse's foot—I'm doing that mare in stall six—and you build the shoe in the mold." He gripped the hot metal in a pair of heavy steel tongs and twisted it inside the dirt mold clamped to the forge. "You've got to have good shoes for stunt horses, but it ain't hard, you know. Just got to be careful you keep 'em even. Got to be the same thickness pretty much or the horse'll stumble."

"Fascinating," the governor said. "That's just terrific." He pulled Hawkins away and said conspiratorially, "How much do you pay that man?"

A bald question, Hawkins thought. All the governor could talk about, it seemed, was money. "About twenty thousand a year. He's one of the best in the country."

"Damn," the governor said. "That's terrific."

Constable joined them and whispered in the governor's ear. The governor nodded to his staff and they quickly blocked the photographers and reporters. Jock, Brad, and the governor retreated to the rear of the shop, whereupon Jock produced two glasses and a bottle of Scotch.

"Wouldn't want to drink in front of the press," the governor said. "You understand. They start ugly rumors." He downed the entire shot. A professional drunk, Hawkins thought. Hawkins was livid with Jock for drinking on the job, but he supposed it was excusable if it meant making the governor happy.

Just as he was feeling his anger, Sheila Richardson joined them. Hawkins excused himself, turning the governor over to Sheila and Jock, and headed for the tower. He was so tired he thought he could sleep standing up. The tram, the lions, Jock, Ken Masters—all swirled in his head. Leaving the others behind, he realized that he would rather be with Alexis—it was a strange feeling, preferring Alexis over the park. But he was glad she had not spent the day with Pinky Bloome. He thought that now she was ready to leave Cole, and although he did not entirely trust his own faith in the future, he was adjusting to the idea of a future with Alexis. It panicked him for a moment. He realized he was looking forward to spending the night with her, and many days and nights yet to come.

16

The Duke of Hampshire had spent the early afternoon settling his household affairs in anticipation of leaving for England. On the drive from Manhattan, he had decided to be home by Tuesday at the latest. But while selecting his clothes to pack for the summer, his resolution crumbled. He was disturbed, thinking that however little he might understand about money, Hampshire Industries bore his name. And it had not only his name but also his money and his reputation and his friends' money. And, if his growing suspicions should by some awkward circumstance bear any resemblance to the truth, it had his signature on all sorts of documents that could tie him up in American courts for years. A dreadful prospect. An episode in the past, in which some stock in a now-defunct brokerage house had mysteriously disappeared, had left its mark on his temperament, not to mention his bank account. And it had taught him a lesson about fraud. Now again he smelled it. Fraud. Deceit. Thinking about his money and his good name, pride finally got the best of him.

Usually loath to disturb his financial lieges during a holiday, he nevertheless telephoned his accountant, whom he found, after several calls, at his beach house in the Hamptons. Apologizing, he politely requested an hour of the man's time. The accountant, Martin Pepper, was a junior partner at Arthur Andersen & Company, one of the Big Eight firms, and the Duke was not unaware that Pepper valued him as a client. Would Martin be so kind as to motor over to the Duke's estate for a short talk? Of course, Pepper said, knowing quite well that an account like James Whitlam's, while negligible compared to those of large corporations, was important for what he called its register value—the Social Register. Pepper's trip from

Easthampton to the Duke's house in Oyster Bay took less than an hour. By the time Pepper arrived, the Duke had cleared a large writing table in the library and assembled all the Hampshire Industries records he had.

Meeting Pepper's car in the circular driveway, the Duke said, "Martin, I'm terribly sorry to drag you away from your family."

"I'm sure it's important," Pepper said cordially, staring up at the house's four ivy-covered gables and imagining that as a senior partner, he might one day own such a house. He wore bright yellow slacks and a madras jacket —the Hamptons uniform.

"It is," the Duke said. "I have some of the corporation's papers I'd like you to look over."

He led Pepper into the library. A butler followed with a pot of coffee and a bottle of Armagnac. Pepper could not restrain a sigh of exasperation when he saw the ledgers piled on the long table.

"James, did you say on the phone a short talk?"

"Actually, I want you to look at the books for last year and this year, and then the projections, and the income statements, which combined with—"

"Slow down, James. It would help me to know what you're looking for. Doesn't Price, Waterhouse do these audits? They're perfectly reputable, you know."

The Duke caught the plug. Pepper was hoping to get the Hampshire Industries account himself.

"What I'm looking for is . . . actually, I suspect that if you'll just compare the figures, you'll find what I'm looking for."

"Yes, James, but what is it? Needles are easier to find in haystacks if you know roughly where to start searching."

"This is awfully difficult," the Duke said, stroking his chin. "You see, I'm afraid I suspect . . . rather, it seems to me . . ." The Duke turned and walked the length of the room, forty-five feet, to the other end. Then, slowly, he walked back, stroking his chin the entire time. The

259

soles of his feet whispered on the thick Persian rug as he moved.

"Martin, you have no idea how difficult this is."

"You're dead right, James. I don't."

"Yes, of course." He paused. "I'm afraid one of my partners has been less than forthright with me about our financial condition. I want you to tell me if everything here looks right to you. Have you seen my butler? Where did he run off to?"

"He left a minute ago. Which partner?"

"Touch that bell under your chair, will you? I'd rather not say, actually. But we have some loans coming due next week and the bank is threatening not to renew. I'd like to know why."

The butler appeared.

"Would you locate my cigarettes, please," the Duke said to the butler, then turned back to Pepper. "Something is wrong, but I can't quite imagine what. It's just a feeling, you see."

"A feeling," Pepper said flatly. "Okay, then. Let's take a look." From his briefcase, he produced a pocket calculator. He lined the ledgers up next to each other and began adding. The Duke listened to the click of his pen against the calculator keys. For twenty minutes, he sat behind Pepper and watched. Then his impatience won out.

"Find anything?" he asked.

Pepper looked over his shoulder. "Not yet. Maybe. James, it's going to be awhile."

"I'll be upstairs," the Duke said, resigned. "Ring me if I can help."

In his study, the Duke struggled to overcome his increasing resentment of Cole Cunningham. He had, after all, successfully invested and consequently sheltered from the British tax service large amounts of the Duke's money. Profits during the first two years had helped pay for the house in which he was now sitting. He should have been satisfied. Still, Cole's display of petulance that morning in the face of Hawkins's criticism discomfited him.

If all were well, why would the bank refuse to renew the loan? Why would the renewal be so crucial? The Duke wished he'd paid closer attention to business. But why ruffle the feathers of a goose laying golden eggs? He considered the metaphor for a moment, and then decided that it was apt. If his suspicions proved correct, Cole Cunningham would be a goose—a cooked goose. Flipping through his card file, he found Gabriel Bloome's home number. Then he dialed information in St. Louis to find Max Brodky's number. His home telephone was unlisted.

The telephone rang. It was the butler. Mr. Pepper was ready.

"What do you say, Martin?" the Duke asked as he walked into the library.

"I'd say I'd like a real drink. Some whiskey."

"Yes, of course." He nodded to the butler. "But what about the books?"

"If I had about two weeks, I'd be able to tell you what's going on here. Why don't you call your man at Price, Waterhouse?"

"Martin, if I knew who he was, I'd have done that. I simply haven't paid due attention to these matters. That's why I called you."

"James, let me put it this way. Either Peter Pan has been writing these income projections or someone has a vivid imagination. There's just too much money going out and your debt is too high for your income. If you wanted to take this company public, you'd have to reduce the debt by at least half. You're in water over your head and you'll drown before you swim. I'd say you have to raise some cold cash. And fast. How did this happen?"

"Interesting question," the Duke said. "I don't really know. Is there fraud?"

"Against you? Not likely. You're on the board of directors. I assume you approved all expenses."

"Of course I did."

"What can you do? Sue yourself?"

"Obvious, isn't it? I suppose I've been a fool."

"You might have a fraud case if your partners misrepresented assets to the banks. But you'd also be liable. You know ignorance and the law—no excuse."

"Thank you, Martin. You'll send me a bill."

Pepper put his coat on. "A bill? James, you pay us a reasonable retainer. We wouldn't charge you for this kind of service." And besides, Pepper thought, if Price, Waterhouse messed up, we may get this account after all.

"Sporting of you, Martin. May I see you to your car? I can't tell you how much I appreciate this. Apologize to your wife for me."

The Duke stood in the driveway, watching the red Saab sedan wind toward the road. Whatever childish impulse had allowed him to take joy in Olympic Adventure as it was being built had long since faded. Getting out with his money would be enough. Like a pool of water in the hot sun, his loyalty to Cole Cunningham evaporated.

In the study, he sipped Armagnac and dialed Gabriel Bloome's number in the city. With Pepper's findings, perhaps he could enlist Bloome's help in unseating Cunningham.

"Get me the blond bitch goddess on the phone and I don't care if you have to install the goddamn phone lines from here to Spain. I want to talk to her and I want to talk to her *now*. And what the hell is with Noshumi? Did you try his club? Did you try the bank?" Cole Cunningham roared at his secretary, waving his hands in the air, staggering erratically around his office like a wounded bird.

"Yes, Mr. Cunningham," the woman answered meekly. "I'm trying, sir. But Mrs. Bollinger's hotel says she isn't there and doesn't know when to expect her. I had to wake Mr. Noshumi's wife, and she hasn't seen him, and I can't get an answer at the bank, sir. It's very late at night there."

"Sonuvabitch. Try Noshumi's club. The number's in your Rolodex. Call Candy's office in London. Maybe she checked in with them. I don't care who the hell you call. Just keep trying."

"Yes, sir, I will, sir." She tiptoed backward out of the office.

Candy, goddamnit. She should have called him by now. What was he doing here on a Saturday afternoon in his office trying to raise eleven million dollars? *Not so long ago I could write a check for eleven million dollars. I could buy and sell you shits, all of you.* The thought did not comfort him. For three hours, he had waited to hear from Mitzu Noshumi and Candace Bollinger, and neither had returned his calls. He had left messages offering stock and secured notes. He had explained in detail what he needed and what he was offering. He sent two wires to each of them. Rights to mortgages. Christ, he only needed the money for a couple of months, and he was willing to pay for it. Still they had not returned his calls. His friends.

Friends, he thought. What the hell is friendship worth, anyway? He chewed on his cigar. For a moment, he thought he would pray, and then he remembered he did not believe in God. He reminded himself, with a half-hearted laugh, of the small boy who said to his father, I don't believe in God. And the father who answered, Do you think God cares?

It was Cole's father who had said that thirty years before, and now he wondered if God were punishing him for blasphemy. He poured himself another gin and stood at the window. At least he had this height, could look down on the world, on the pathetic, idiotic peons marching from one boutique to another pursuing fashion, paying prices for shoddy goods; and he had his precious automobiles, in his garages, on his land, with his personal mechanic, next to his own gasoline pump. *I have transcended fashion. I make fashion. I have had too much to drink.*

The telephone buzzed. "Who is it, Helen?" he asked excitedly.

"No one, sir. I can't get either Mr. Noshumi or

Mrs. Bollinger. Mr. Noshumi's wife says he can't be reached. And Mrs. Bollinger's hotel doesn't know where she is and her London office doesn't answer."

"Keep trying. Call Noshumi's kids. Tell that spic at Candy's hotel to go up and get her out of the sack and I don't care who she's in bed with. They *owe* me, goddamnit."

"Mr. Cunningham, I've tried that. There's no way to reach them. We've left messages. Sir . . . I . . . it's Saturday and . . ." She trailed off.

"All right, Helen. Go home already, goddamnit. Leave me the phone numbers. Good night." Even my goddamn secretary deserts me.

He stood for a long time at the window, trying to distinguish out-of-town license plates cruising down Fifth Avenue, watching tourists scurrying from the paths of taxicabs. He was sentimental about New York. About the GM building and the Columbus Circle fountain, about Washington Square and the Statue of Liberty. About the mimes in Central Park and Fifth Avenue at twilight and street peddlers selling chestnuts. About the chestnuts and the smell of the streets. The smell of desire and the smell of money. He felt a message drifting up to him from those streets. A message whispering failure. He was not sure if he had given up, but he questioned whether he was losing the ability, so indispensable for hope, to fool himself.

He had known Alexis was drifting away, and he had known there was nothing he could do to stop her. *I am sinking in quicksand*. Simple pleasures eluded him; perhaps, he thought, because he had never known them, had never been a child.

At the age of seven, he'd begun failing every test significant to a schoolboy. He could not spin a yo-yo. He could not whistle. He could not hit a baseball (bad eyesight, he told himself, a lie he never believed). Unable to perform as a child, sensing as children do the inadequacy of his performance, he'd adopted quite young a different role: adult. He'd excelled in the activities of which his parents, not his peers, approved: grooming, schoolwork, earning money in part-time jobs, conversation, manners. And so he had an acutely refined radar about himself, about success in those terms and those terms alone. *Would the bitch goddess Candy not call? And where was Noshumi?*

The office closed around him, enveloped him. Stiff Victorian chairs, hard and cruel, accused him. The abstract paintings confused him. Then he realized again he had been drinking too much. He turned from the window, walked into the reception area, and rested his hands on the railing around the scale model of Olympic Adventure. Gabriel's toy. In the shadowed room, he paused, then turned on the current. The model came to life. Ferris wheels turned, boats weaved across the lake, fountains flickered. For a transitory, fantastic moment, Cole entered the world he had built: rode the tram, ate cotton candy, fired electronic bullets in the arcade, watched a rodeo show. And then, just as quickly, it slipped away. He was beyond fantasy. He opened his lips and tried to whistle, then retrieved a piece of paper from his secretary's desk, returned to his office, and picked up the phone.

"Overseas operator. Yes, I want to place two calls. One is to Spain, the other Japan."

For all his intuition, Cole Cunningham did not give up easily.

"I'm glad you could come," Hawkins said. Governor Lloyd Birdwell boarded his helicopter. "Sorry we couldn't spend more time, and again, I apologize for disrupting your schedule."

"I understand," the governor said. "You have to run your park."

If only you knew, Hawkins thought. He was glad to see the governor leave; publicity was fine, but running to the helicopter pad to wave good-bye to dignitaries was not his idea of the best way to spend his time. The helicopter quivered, then lifted and disappeared in the western sky.

The news photographers, with their press credentials flopping around their necks in the churning wind, dispersed. Brad silently wrote their captions:

Governor Lloyd Birdwell talks with Brad Hawkins, general manager of Olympic Adventure. The New Jersey chief executive toured the country's largest amusement park at the opening of its season yesterday.

Six suburban front pages on Sunday, the Bergen County *Record*, a center spread in the New York *Daily News*, a column in Long Island's *Newsday*, quite possibly the Sunday *Times*.

"Nice going, Sheila," Hawkins said. "Looks like we'll get nine or ten papers tomorrow with pictures."

"I'm sorry he came at such a bad time," she said. "But the response is unbeatable. We'll do good business next week."

"Not much we could do about the schedule," Hawkins said. "Would you take the reporters up and give them everything they need? Fact sheets, that stuff."

"I already did. But there's an old man up there who wants to see you."

"I haven't got time for reporters."

"He's not a reporter. I told him you were busy, but he said he was sure you would want to see him. His name is Max Brodky."

"Brodky!" Hawkins was stunned.

"Do you know him?"

"In a way," Hawkins said hesitantly. "Tell him I'll be there soon, will you? Put him in my office." Hawkins could have gone straight to the tower, in fact should have —to check the evening shift changes. But he wanted time to think. Brodky certainly wasn't wasting time, appearing like this.

Sheila saw the look on Hawkins's face change from distraction to concentration. "Is anything wrong, Brad?"

"No, nothing's wrong. Everything is right, I think."

266

"You have some messages on your desk. One from the Duke of Hampshire and one from Gabriel Bloome. They both said it was urgent. Do you want to use my office to call them?"

"No, Sheila. They'll wait." The Duke. Gabriel Bloome. Max Brodky. Hawkins was the central figure in everyone's calculations. Accidents, he thought, do not happen. Events occur on some cosmic schedule. Some things were indeed inevitable. Max Brodky had come to him, just as Cole Cunningham had come four years before.

The air was cooler now, the sun lower in the west. Hawkins walked down the hill to the fountain and sat on the ledge. The tram rolled noiselessly across the park above him. He heard the crowd in the Western Arena, looked across at its green concrete walls blending into the ubiquitous green of the trees and gardens. Clowns romped past, smiling, waving in salute. In front of him, people jammed the walk leading down from the main gate, spilling into the fountain plaza, past the walkways lined with flowers. A black girl tripped on high wedged heels, recovered, and kept her balance, defying, it seemed to Hawkins, the laws of gravity.

He felt a hand on his shoulder.

"What's it like being a celebrity?" It was Alexis.

"Same stuff every year," he said. "I don't have much use for politicians, but I'm glad for the publicity. We had them all today. Newspapers, television, columnists."

"Sheila says Jock handled the governor beautifully."

"Two happy drunks." He paused, looked into her eyes, couldn't read them. "Max Brodky is here."

"Max? Here? In New York?"

"No, *here*. Waiting in my office."

"You should feel honored. A command performance. He's coming to you."

"I know, but why today? What the hell does he want?"

"It isn't too hard to guess."

"Me," he said. "And the park."

"Exactly," she said.

"I know that. But why today?"

"Because he's closing in. That's how he does it."

"I don't like it," Hawkins said. "I don't like it at all. I'm not prepared. Not yet."

"Some things you can't prepare for," she said, and she stood on her toes and kissed him. "You take things as they come."

He searched her eyes. How did *she* feel? What was her reaction? Isn't she confused, he wondered, about me, about Cole, about the park between us?

"You can bet," she said suddenly, furrowing her brows, "Cole already knows. He knows these things. He always has."

She's hard, he thought. Hard to the end.

She did not say how confused her feelings were. She was in love with Brad Hawkins, and she saw now, now that he would succeed, that this, too, had attracted her, but at the same time she was bewildered, still in love with the image of Cole that she held in her memory.

They touched hands, clasped them, began walking. They were two survivors, and they walked in that knowledge, heads high.

"I think I'm going to enjoy owning the park," he said. "I think I'm going to enjoy it a lot."

STEELS IN DECLINE, CAUSE LULL IN RECOVERY, said the headline in Max Brodky's private economic summary, which he read while sitting in Hawkins's office. His secretary had delivered it to the airport before he boarded the plane for New York. Every day his staff economists prepared a report so Max Brodky would know the state of his empire. Bad news about steel worried him; if steel companies couldn't raise money, then construction industries would also suffer. He folded the papers and put them back in his pocket.

Hawkins's office impressed him. It was functional and neat. It spoke well of the man, Brodky thought. He nestled his cigar in the plain glass ashtray on Hawkins's desk. Next to the ashtray lay, sheathed in leather, a beveled silver letter opener, its thin, pointed stem topped by a dark vermeil square with a single tiny star in the right-hand corner. The Lone Star flag. Across the top of the desk, above a large, neatly filled calendar pad, were seven stacks of paper, one for each day of the week, logging personnel changes for the park's long days. An orderly desk, an orderly mind, Brodky said to himself.

Brodky was embarrassed waiting for Brad Hawkins. Max Brodky was not accustomed to waiting for anyone; others waited for him. The day flashed before him. First, his sons. Bright boys. But he thought them flawed, lacking in ambition, the result, perhaps, of a childhood too full of money. Brodky thought a man without ambition, without drive, was nothing. A need to remake the world, and the will to support that need, possessed ambitious men, men like himself. And then there was Welch, not a sufficiently ambitious man; he was taken care of, Max was sure. And if he didn't go along, well, Max would convince the bank's board himself. And if that didn't work, he would offer to buy the Olympic Adventure stock himself. No, they'd go along. And then Conrad and Jeremy, efficient men, ambitious men. Neither Candy nor Mitzu would rescue Cole Cunningham. Now, Hawkins. Max needed Brad Hawkins, and he experienced an uncomfortable sensation: Hawkins would be the least malleable. As Brodky was helping himself to a glass of orange juice from the small refrigerator in the corner of Hawkins's office, the door opened.

"Mr. Brodky," Brad said, entering, stretching out his hand.

"Max. Call me Max." He touched Alexis's hand. "And how are you, Alexis my dear?"

"Fine, Max. It's good to see you. You're looking well." How *did* the old man do it, she wondered. Face lifts? Probably not.

"And seeing a lovely lady like you is always a pleasure," he said with unmannered, genuine charm. Hawkins had no doubt that Max Brodky did delight in lovely women. Brodky looked from Brad to Alexis and back again, on the verge of suggesting that Alexis leave when, trusting his intuition, he realized that Alexis was not there as Cole Cunningham's wife. "Beautiful, this place is," Max continued. He had been expecting only Hawkins, but with Alexis present he calculated again, for the third time that day, how to approach Hawkins. He already knew that Hawkins was a shrewd bargainer, and simply seeing the man confirmed his original opinion: Hawkins was the only shareholder worth recruiting.

Max Brodky was, above all, sophisticated in the business labyrinth. Max planned mazes. His targets stumbled through them. Max did not give orders; he won people over, cajoled them, convinced them without ever speaking to the point. He led people to his position, so that others believed they had arrived at a decision all on their own. The art of negotiation consisted of making others believe they had come upon the desired solution themselves.

"Beautiful," Max said again. "You must spend freely to keep the grounds so beautiful."

"Not as much as we used to," Hawkins said. "But plenty, yes."

"I am amazed," Brodky said. "Do they not throw cigarettes on the ground? Food? Papers?"

"Psychology, Mr. Brodky. If we—"

"Max. Call me Max."

Hawkins was wary. He preferred distance to illusory intimacy, especially in business. "Max, then. If we keep the park clean, so do the guests."

"You mean the customers?"

"We call them guests. They respond to cleanliness by using wastebaskets. It's a matter of making them feel at home, making them want to have a good time, making them feel it's to their benefit to keep the park clean."

"Wonderful," Brodky said. "I don't believe it. But you say it works."

"You see for yourself."

Alexis took a seat behind the two men, swimming in memories of Cole and Max dickering, dealing, bellowing at each other years before over a small sum of money. The partnership of Max Brodky and Brad Hawkins, one that was certainly developing, seemed ridiculous. Money makes strange bedfellows.

"And Alexis, my dear, how is Cole?" Brodky asked. She snapped from her reverie.

"I wouldn't know," she said, the words flowing out before she had a chance to catch them. "I'm leaving him."

Hawkins wheeled around, shocked. Did she mean that? Was she certain? And then he read the message in her eyes. They stood, both in an imaginary embrace. Max Brodky watched, wondering, the witness to an explosion. And then he saw them smiling, sharing a secret.

"You are leaving him?" Max said. "I didn't know. I'm sorry."

"There's nothing to be sorry about," Alexis said, hoping she was right.

"A beautiful young woman should not be alone in the world," Max said.

"Oh, I won't be alone," she said. "There's someone to take care of me."

"This bright young man, may I assume?" Max asked.

Alexis laughed softly. To Max, any male under sixty was a bright young man.

"You may assume," she said. Even now, it seemed not quite possible to her that she could risk so much, could relinquish the predictable for the unknown. Hawkins studied her for a moment, feeling a rush of fear. This will work, he thought. I will make it work.

"I have a park to run, Max," Hawkins said. "Surely you didn't come here to talk about Mrs. Cunningham or clean sidewalks. So if you'll just tell me what I can do for you—"

"Oh, but I did," Max interrupted, grinning. "Of course I did. About clean sidewalks and labor costs and the high price of entertainment and employee relations. You know, I could talk about these things forever and never tire of the subject. Now tell me, how many people are here today?"

"About a hundred thousand."

"So on admission fees alone," Max said, "you grossed

about three quarters of a million dollars today. Am I right?"

"I multiply just the way you do," Hawkins said, growing edgy at Brodky's manner.

"Then could you answer for me a simple question? You're a bright young man. With that kind of daily gross, plus what you take in from food," he paused for breath, "how is it . . . could you explain . . . ah, how is it that you are losing money?"

"I could give you the answer to that," Hawkins said, "which is the answer you want to hear, and it's the truth. But you already know."

"You don't want to play my game," Max said.

"What *is* your game, Max?"

You are slipping, Brodky said to himself. You have handled this young man badly. "In three days," Max said, "I am going to become a stockholder in Hampshire Industries. A minority stockholder, because of certain outstanding loans. I will then also be a stockholder in Olympic Adventure. And since I wouldn't like my sons or my accountants to question my judgment, I would like to tell them Olympic Adventure is going to make money this season. And next season and the following season. Can I tell them that?"

"It all depends," Hawkins said.

"On what, young man, does it depend?"

"Well, it depends first on reorganizing the debt structure of the entire business. Which, I would point out, you can't do as a minority stockholder. You'll need someone else's votes on the board for that. And second, it depends on who the board could get to run the park if I should decide to quit and hold onto my shares."

"You would quit?"

"It's just hypothetical, Max. I'm not planning to quit."

"So you will continue to run the park?"

"For the moment," Hawkins said.

Max stood, lighting a fresh cigar. The wood safety match burned almost to his fingertip before he flicked it out. He walked around the desk and toyed with the letter opener, touched each stack of papers with its tip. Tactical: Max was shorter than Brad and now Brad, standing, had to look directly down on him.

"Do you want to own this park?" Max said quickly.

"I do," Hawkins said. "What of it?"

"I hear you are the best equipped to run it. You might as well own it."

Be careful, Alexis thought. She wanted to say to Brad, *Be careful of him.*

"Who says I'm the best equipped?"

"Cole Cunningham thinks so," Brodky said.

"If you're trying to take the park away from Cole, if you think he's so incompetent, why take his word? Maybe it's my fault the park is losing money."

"Is it?"

"Partly."

Max found this enjoyable all of a sudden—fencing with Hawkins. "Cole was once a financial wizard," Max said, his voice milky with irony. "Only he isn't any longer." He looked at Alexis. "He's careless." He looked at Brad. "But he could always spot talent. Always. And considering what he had to pay you, well . . ." Max shrugged.

"Aren't you forgetting a few things?" Hawkins asked.

"Such as?" Max asked in mock agony. "I never forget anything."

"The notes aren't due until next week. You've jumped the gun. Cole might raise the money."

"Oh, that," Max said, waving his hand in dismissal. "Don't worry about that. He'll never find the money. I've already seen to that."

Perhaps, Hawkins thought; perhaps you have.

"The bank might renew the loans," Hawkins said.

"No," Max said. "They won't. That is also taken care of."

Brad sat behind his desk. Max also sat, opposite him.

"Granting your case," Hawkins said expansively, propping his elbows on the desk, "there are other stockholders.

They might sell to someone else. I might sell to someone else."

"You wouldn't want to do that, would you? You'd have no guarantees you'd eventually get to own the park."

"None, but you never know who might offer us a better deal."

"Better deal?" Max said, looking hurt. If there had been balconies, he would have been playing to them. "You haven't heard mine yet."

"I'm listening," Hawkins said.

"But you aren't listening," Max said. "You're talking. What's on your mind?"

"Lyman Bloome," Hawkins said.

Max's eyes widened. "What do *you* know about Lyman Bloome?"

"Is it revenge?" Hawkins asked softly. "Am I part of the plan?"

"So you too have heard these stories. Who put such thoughts into your head?"

"It doesn't matter," Hawkins said.

"Do you believe these stories?"

"It doesn't change my attitude," Hawkins said. "I just want to know. Is this business or isn't it?"

Max knocked his cigar against the ashtray and a long ash dissolved into a pile of flakes. The end of the cigar was dead and he lit it again. Flame seared the wrapping leaf.

"I came here to talk business with you," Max said, puffing. "And you want to talk about the past. The past is past."

"The past is never past," Hawkins said. "Understand, Max, that the deal is a separate question. I just want to know why. Have you been carrying a grudge against a dead man? Are you going to carry it against his son? That's all I want to know."

Max was not grinning now. "I'll tell you something," Max said. "We were good friends, Lyman and I. So maybe he bargained better than I did once. So maybe these stories are true. But it was just business. I helped

274

him get started, but for that he owed me nothing. He owed me nothing because we made money together. He made money for me, I made money for him. His son? I hardly know his son. How could I carry a grudge against him?"

"Did you keep an eye on our loans, Max? Did you count on Cole trying to hide his losses?"

"Am I so clever?" Max asked.

"I think you are."

"You overestimate me."

"Nobody overestimates Max Brodky," Hawkins said. "That's one thing I'm sure of."

The slightest hint of a smile showed on Max's face. "I am a proud man, Brad Hawkins. So maybe my pride and my ability to make money worked together here. Maybe that is why we are here today. What do you think?"

"I think you pretend business is just business. And I think it isn't."

Max stubbed out his cigar and lit a fresh one. He twirled the letter opener between his fingers.

"Maybe," Max said. "Maybe. Let's say I am doubtful of Cole's judgment. The bank lent him some money. He spent it unwisely. He hanged himself, you could say, and I am holding the noose. I did not become a rich man without an eye for good investments."

"What's your deal, Max?"

"My terms?"

"Your *offer*," Hawkins said.

"Allow me to think aloud. I want the best man to run this park, and of course the best manager is the one with a vested interest in his company. So . . ." Brad and Alexis watched him intently. He pretended to be oblivious. "So let's say I buy out your partners and sell you half the stock in Hampshire Industries. You get the stock for a pittance—let's say you pay for it only if profits don't go up every year for five years. Let's say five percent a year. We'll be full partners, then. You and me."

275

Alexis was half out of her chair before she saw that Hawkins had made no move to close the deal. She sat.

"You need my votes to buy out my partners," Hawkins said.

"Yes, and look what I've offered you for them."

"You can do better," Hawkins said. He leaned across the desk. Their eyes met and locked like magnets coming into line. Hawkins was thinking quickly. Some things you can't prepare for. "A seat on the board of Brodky International with stock options."

"Absolutely not," Max said. No one outside the Brodky family owned stock in the family corporation. Max thought, Smart young man. He knows what he wants.

"Absolutely?" Hawkins asked. "How badly do you want Hampshire Industries, Max? How badly do you want me?" Hawkins wanted to be wanted. But neither man fully understood what Max Brodky wanted. Max partly understood, but mostly he concealed the knowledge from himself. He needed a young man to help his sons maintain his fortune.

A very smart young man, Brodky thought. "A seat on the board, yes. Stock options, maybe. We can discuss the details later."

"Max, I *want* the options. In writing."

"We are going to be partners for a long time," Max said. "Must you have everything now? Do you not trust me?"

"I trust you, Max. I want the options."

Max Brodky wondered if he had planned it this way. Had he stumbled through his own maze? Just to explain it to his sons? Was his mind playing tricks? Did Brad Hawkins resemble his dead son?

"You may have the options."

"Fine," Hawkins said. "One other thing. A two-million-dollar loan from Brodky International to fix this place up."

"You will *destroy* my balance sheet," Max said. "I mean *our* balance sheet."

"Without a loan, this park will destroy itself. Two years, no interest. It all washes out in taxes, anyway."

"Very well," Max said. "Done. Now, will you also hold me up at gunpoint? Is there more?"

"One last matter. I want Cole and the Duke and Gabriel treated fairly."

"All of them?" Max asked, swinging his head around to look at Alexis. "Is *this* business?"

"All of them," Hawkins said. "It's business, Max, just like it's business for you."

Max allowed himself to laugh. "So we have a deal?"

"Deal, partner," Hawkins said.

Max shot his hand across the desk. Brad took it and squeezed it firmly. "Partner," he said, "let's go take a look at our new property. I'll teach you a few things about making money."

Alexis smiled to herself. Strange bedfellows, she thought. Wonderful, Max thought. Who would have figured it this way? And Hawkins thought, I have it all. They walked out into an afternoon breeze. The sun was low in the western sky.

17

Twenty-one, twenty-two, twenty-three, twenty-four, twenty-five, twenty-six. Everett Morgan counted steps as he walked, etching the path in his mind like an electrical diagram. He would have to know it well. Across the fountain, through the tiled plaza, past the carousel—that was twenty-six steps. Now up the hill to the gates. Again he paced it off, mentally marking the columns leading to the arcade, the sharp turn on the graded asphalt path halfway up the hill.

He kept his eyes on Louise now. She was coming up the far side of the hill, and he ducked behind a tree. They were returning from the safari. Matthew tossed a toy giraffe into the air. How happy he looked. They would have so much fun together. Without Louise.

Morgan felt in his pocket for the maps. Tomorrow night they would be in Kansas. He would drive straight through without stopping.

He resumed counting when Louise passed. Up the hill, then sixteen more steps to the gate. Now, with the car close to the parking lot exit, he could avoid getting caught in the crush of people trying to leave. He grew impatient for nightfall. Again he felt watched. He whirled. No one was behind him. He had no reason to be afraid, yet a mere glance from a park guard reduced him to terror. Solitary in his enclosed world, projecting hatred onto objects and people, he exaggerated ordinary worries into a never-ending panorama of imagined dangers. He believed himself the target of barbaric forces. Strangers conspired against him. In an astrology magazine, he had read about the universe's negative vibrations, and he felt himself to be at the center of them, all the world's destructive intentions focusing on him. His disease was as real, as crippling, as the harshest physical ailment, a cancer eating not at his body but at his mind. With subtle turns of perception, Morgan transformed himself into a brave conqueror of black demons. Black demons surrounded him. Black, deeper black. Men, women, children, buses, buildings, the heavens and clouds—nothing could be neglected. Everett Morgan felt safe nowhere.

With his son, he had decided, he would feel safe. With his son, away from Louise, in the West; the West he had never seen but had invented as benevolent; away from the city and buildings and wicked whores. Away from Louise, who was consuming his son. For weeks after Louise left, he had thought about his son. Anger exploded in him. Anger at Louise for stealing his son away. Anger at her refusal to let him visit. He lost his temper at work. The other electricians avoided him. Only Albright understood. A man can get that way, he told the others. When a man's wife leaves, he can get that way.

Morgan wore a bitter, thin-lipped expression. His once-handsome face changed overnight, growing pale and long, pinched, prematurely aged. Louise's refusal to let him visit Matthew this weekend was the excuse he sought. "You're no good for him," she had said, and in uncontrollable passion he had swung at her. Backing off to avoid his hand, she had fallen against a table and tripped, knocking over a vase. "Whore!" he had shouted. Then she had thrown him out and told him never to come again or she would call the police. He had brooded, and then the plan came to him. "An adventure," Matthew had said before Louise silenced the boy. Morgan remembered his wife talking about the amusement park, and as she pushed him through the door, he saw the newspaper advertisement for Olympic Adventure. An adventure. Memorial Day. Louise was taking him to Olympic Adventure. He would go and watch. He wanted his son. The boy's face reared up like a ghost. His liquid blue eyes stared at Morgan, his shaggy blond hair waved across his face. He was playing with his trains, the set Morgan had bought him last Christmas. "Matthew," he whispered. He would have his son.

Every night that week he had driven to New Jersey to watch the park's crew get ready for the season's opening. Only two guards patrolled the park's perimeter. It would be easy, Morgan decided, to sneak in without being noticed, especially in darkness. The schematic drawings of the park's electrical system were easy to find; they were in Albright's files. Copying them in the office late at night, Morgan worried about being discovered in the park. Then he decided early morning would be safer, when no one would be looking for an intruder. He gave Albright notice, cashed his final paycheck on Friday, withdrew all the money he had saved from working overtime. Waking early in the morning, he had packed everything he owned into the trunk of the old Pontiac. Getting past the guards had been easier than he'd hoped. After finishing his work, he had waited until the park began to fill up, then melted into the crowd.

He had stalked Louise and Matthew since early afternoon; they were in front of him now, heading for the ferris wheel. Watching, he grew feverish, waiting for nightfall. Dusk had settled. Light from the fountain flashed across the sky. Patrols swept through the park, kindling gas lamps. Photoelectric sensors on the band pavilions boosted the intensity of the spotlights. Glittering auroras bathed the park in opalescent shadows. Halos crowned the restaurants and shops. In the amber sky, the sun receded into the pines: yellow and blue and green—a postcard sunset.

Compulsively Morgan checked the time. Less than an hour to go if his watch was right. Forty-nine minutes. He scraped in his pocket for a cigarette and matches, but caught his fingers on the wire cutters. He panicked. He could have sworn he'd left them in the car. He felt in his other pocket. His money. And the wiring diagrams. He was certain he'd left the diagrams in the glove compartment. He looked around for a place to throw them away—no, not here. He considered shredding them and flushing the scraps down a toilet. Time—there was no time. He had to stay with Louise and Matthew.

It was nearly dark. He stood for a moment in the

shadow of the glistening helium balloon, one hundred feet high. Matthew. The name rang in his ears. My son. My son. He seethed with anger again. His face reddened. His arms felt numb. He watched the ferris wheel turn. Matthew's face, framed by the lights, leaped out at him.

"I'm impressed," Alexis said. "I don't think anybody has ever talked to Max like that." Leaving the Aqua Show, they were still talking about Max Brodky, waiting for him to join them.

"I'm not sure Max didn't get exactly what he wanted."

"Brad, you're being—"

"Realistic. We pay for everything we get. One way or the other."

"Stop being so grumpy."

"I'm not being grumpy. Just realistic."

"Then stop being realistic, goddamnit."

He put his arms around her and pulled her against him. She rested her head on his shoulder and kissed his neck.

"Lady vampire," he said.

Max Brodky came toward them, twirling a noisemaker.

"All right, children. No more lovey-dovey. I'm through with my phone calls. Now aren't you going to show me a good time?"

They laughed. "Sure, partner," Brad said. "Now you get the best views."

The sky burned luminescent blue. At the center of the park, past the fountain, the ferris wheel joined the sky, absorbing the stars. The Chariot of the Gods streaked by, tripping sensors and bringing to life faces: Zeus, Pan, Apollo, Diana, outlined in red and white neon against the edge of the forest. Even the trees glowed.

"I'd completely forgotten," Brad said aloud, more to himself than to Alexis or Max.

"Forgotten?" Alexis asked.

"Six months ago. Just before we added these faces to the Chariot. It's hard to remember what nighttime does to Gabriel's imagination. Do you know he sat in the dark when he built the model for these faces? He just sat and tried combinations of colors until he got what he wanted. Look up." Hawkins pointed to the neon figures. "See that, the green outline behind the red? Gabriel built it to scale first. He knew exactly how it would shine. When I saw the mock-up, I couldn't believe it. Whoever thought it would look like that?"

"Gabriel did," Alexis said.

"Children, children," Max said. "Did you ever see *Trumpets in the Sky?* Did you see *Wonderland?* You talk about imagination? Gabriel gets it all from his father. A genius, Lyman Bloome was."

"Come on, Max," Alexis said. "Give Gabriel some credit."

"I give him credit," Max said, "for copying well. The hotel mirror in *Trumpets in the Sky?* Do you remember it? That's where he got these faces. The funhouse in *Wonderland?* That's where he got the idea for your carousel. All of this comes from Lyman. And to be cursed with that fool for a son."

Alexis was angry. "Gabriel isn't a fool. He's a child."

"Same thing," Max said.

Brad was worried that they might start shouting at each other. The subject of Lyman Bloome was undoubtedly one of the few which could set Max off. Now Hawkins thought he knew why Max called Lyman Bloome a genius: to prove to himself that only a genius could out-bargain or outdeal him.

"Enough," Hawkins said. "Let's go for a ride."

"Which one?" Max asked excitedly.

"Whatever you like, partner."

"Way over there someplace," Max said, pointing south. "I saw it from the tower. The one where you ride the waterfall."

The idea of Max Brodky on the flume nearly made Alexis laugh. She could not imagine Max capable of having fun.

"Come, let's go," Max said, and he was off down the wrong path. Hawkins ran after him, steering him around the fountain toward the Pyramids in the Land of Monuments. Max looked up as they passed the Eiffel Tower. "Not bad," he said. "But I prefer the original." When they reached the flume, Max headed for the turnstile.

"No," Brad called. "We wait in line like everybody else."

"Don't be ridiculous," Max said.

"As long as I'm general manager of Olympic Adventure," Hawkins said, recalling how Sarah Masters had gotten on the tram, "everybody waits in line. Including me. And including you."

"All right already," Max said. "Don't make a federal case out of it." He stood, with obvious discomfort, jostled on every side. Occasionally a buzzer sounded on Hawkins's walkie-talkie as supervisors throughout the park checked in.

"All this talk," Max said. "Is it necessary?"

"You've done your business for the day," Hawkins said. "I'm still running a park."

The attendant recognized Brad and Alexis and led the threesome to the front canoe. "It's more exciting this way," Alexis said. "You feel like you're alone up there."

Max climbed in awkwardly. "My feet," he said. "Where do I put them?"

"Just squeeze your knees against your chest," Hawkins said with a smile, seeing how uncomfortable Max was. He swung into the back of the gaily decorated canoe. Alexis eased down in the middle, settling back against Hawkins's chest. Around the track's rim, rubber bladders inflated, locking the canoe to the track, and they began to move up.

"Wait, wait," Max screamed. "I'm not in yet." The canoe continued traveling up the incline.

"Don't worry, Max," Brad said. "It's almost impossible to fall out."

"Almost!" Max shouted.

Behind them, a group of children yelled. When the canoes reached the top, their shouts changed to squeals of glee. From the top, they had an unobstructed view of the horizon and the lake far below. Max turned around. His face was white.

"What's the matter?" Alexis asked.

"A touch of acrophobia," he said. "Heights. Makes me sick."

Alexis and Brad laughed again. Now, at the edge of the ramp, high above the maze of troughs into which the canoes would be spilled, water rushed through the deep basin. The rubber bladder surrounding the canoe deflated and they were off, downhill. They shot straight down and Max pushed hard against the boat's side, grabbing fiercely. Alexis and Brad, knowing it was impossible to slip out of the boat, held each other. Alexis, thrown against Brad as the boat picked up speed and rounded a right-angle turn at the bottom of the first slide, fell into his arms, and he bent down to kiss her. Even as the boat gathered speed, they reached for each other and pressed their lips together. The boat slid around the bend, then down into another, steeper slide. The water rushed faster. Brad dipped his hand into the water to check its speed. The boat itself moved no faster, but the illusion—partly because of the height, partly because of the water's noise, and partly because the ground was nearly invisible at night—was of increasing speed as they plummeted toward the final trough. Max's thin gray hair blew in the wind.

Approaching the bottom of the slide, the canoe veered left, heading for the waterfall. At the bottom, the waterfall was visible—first a flat expanse ten feet long and then the fall itself. From above, the illusion was deftly horrifying, as it was designed to be. From the canoes, passengers saw only the narrow ledge and assumed, as they were meant to, that the canoe would sail off the edge into space. In fact, the tip of the platform, wedged and curved, did not end but sloped down to the last trough. The thick plastic faded from green to clear, and water cascading over it seemed to pour free. Reaching the edge, the canoe stood still for a second, then shuddered and slapped onto the magic waterfall, fitting into indentations in the plastic. Water splashed from all sides, spraying a fine, misty rain. Alexis looked down. Max whooped like a child. An unpleasant thought crossed Alexis's mind: he was an old man; he could have a heart attack. But as Max Brodky himself had said many times, he was so healthy they would have to ask his corpse's permission to bury him.

The canoe glided into the circular dock. Its rubber bladders, inflated, held it steady. Brad and Alexis climbed out, brushing beads of water from their faces. But Max remained seated. He grasped the sides, leaning toward the dock, but still his body did not budge. Then he pushed his feet against the front and arched his back, trying to slide up against the seat's back. He didn't move. Alexis resisted a laugh.

"All right, Hawkins. It's bad enough I'm wet. Now get me out of this stupid thing."

Alexis pretended concern. "You mean you didn't have a good time, Max?" she said sweetly. "You said you wanted a good time."

"Fine, fine time," he said. "Just get me out of here." Brad leaned over and tucked his hands into Max's armpits. Max was so startled he jumped. Then in one smooth, upward tug, Brad lifted Max out of the canoe and set him gently on the dock.

"Not bad," Max said, straightening his suit jacket. "When I need a strong bodyguard, I'll call."

And then it happened. Everett Morgan's transformer, tripped by a timer, let a surge of electric current break through the park's generators. Brad, Alexis, and Max stood on the bottom step of the dock's landing. Brad was reaching to put his arm across Alexis's shoulders. Max held a cigar; he had just found matches in his pocket.

Then the lights went out. Every light in the park. Every ride stopped. For one long moment, there was silence.

Brad, Alexis, and Max stood together in the glow of Max's match, speechless, the flame gleaming surreally in the blackness. Hawkins, turning, could barely see the flume canoes stuck in the center of the ramp. Behind him, other canoes glided in, sailed wildly around the dock, water still rushing around them. People screamed. Hawkins's hand hung in midair. Cole, he thought: that stupid ass. What had he done now? Con Edison wouldn't just shut the power off. Or would they? No, Cole had bought cut-rate parts. Fired an electrician. Something. Anything. Hawkins was convinced that Cunningham had once again demonstrated an almost unimaginable incompetence, or cupidity, or both.

Shouts swelled to a thundering, convulsive roar. When his eyes had adjusted to the dark, Hawkins saw the crowds below the dock racing through the park. He gritted his teeth, waited a few seconds; perhaps the power failure was temporary. No matter what happened, he thought, some equipment would be badly damaged. He heard a faint buzz, as if it were reaching his ears from far away. The sound nearly didn't register at all, then he realized it was his walkie-talkie. Of course he could not hear it clearly—there was so much screaming. Thousands of people running madly, knocking others out of their way. White noise, the whoosh of running water, a wall of sound, echoing. A screaming so loud, so insistent, it became almost no sound at all.

"Hawkins here. Station One."

"Jesus, son. I thought you'd never answer." It was Pete Toscani.

"Location, Pete." Control. Clarity returned.

"The big wheel, kid. You?"

"Western flume. What the hell is happening?"

"You got me," Toscani said. "I'm waiting for a flare now. Can't get to the power station in the dark."

Hawkins waited, thinking. Radio chatter had to be kept to a minimum. All frequencies would be busy.

"Pete, my friend, I hear a small voice telling me this is going to get worse before it gets better. Could it be temporary?"

"It's not the circuit breakers, kid. Every line in the park is out. Dead."

"Then worse is going to be bad. Post men at every aerial ride. Three men in rotation. Nobody climbs. I don't want any heroics tonight, and that means you, too."

"Look, son, I'm no goddamn hero. Have you talked to Operations yet?"

286

"Not yet. Next. What do you need?"

"Better tell someone there to bring the engine flares with him and we'll use them in our hands. My guys are almost out."

"Out? What the hell do you mean, *out*?"

"Out," Toscani said. "Empty. Finished. *Nada*. I've been waiting for flares for six weeks. And slack ropes. And cotter pins. And, you might remember, oil."

"Fuck Cunningham," Hawkins said.

"What?"

"Never mind. What about the backup generators?"

"Don't know nothing yet, son. They should've kicked in. I'll check 'em."

"Okay, let me know. Hawkins, Station One, out." He broke the channel. One of the flume attendants handed him a flare.

"How many of these do you have left?" Hawkins asked. There should have been a case.

"Three," the attendant said.

"Cases?"

"Three *flares*, sir."

Damnit. What next?

"Mr. Hawkins, sir." The attendant tugged at his sleeve. "What happened?"

"Good question," Hawkins said. "I'll let you know just as soon as I find out. Which is not likely to be soon. In the meantime, you better light this place up with those flares. See what you can do by spacing them around. And bring those boats back down before they slide and crush a few people. Right?"

"Yes, sir. Right away, sir." The attendant turned away. Hawkins punched the code on his walkie-talkie for Operations. Dexter answered. He'd already heard from Pete Toscani, he said. What else should he do?

"You've talked to the state police?"

"I've tried, sir. All the phone lines are dead."

"The phones?" Hawkins asked, surprised.

"I sent a man down to McNeely's on the other side of

287

the thruway." McNeely's was a bar. "He'll call from there."

"Christ," Hawkins shouted. "That'll take half an hour."

"Yes, sir. I know that," Dexter said. And then Hawkins realized it wasn't Dexter's fault about the phones. Why scream at him? The phone lines—why the hell were they dead?

"Sorry, Dexter. How soon will Pete have the flares?"

"I sent them up to the power station. A man should be there in ten minutes if he can get through the lot." The parking lot would be chaos.

Hawkins thanked him and signed off. Dead telephones forced him to think again. Maybe Cole Cunningham was not responsible. A simple power failure wouldn't affect the phones.

He turned to Alexis and Max. They were gone. He couldn't see very far in the dark and was pushed against the railing by crowds fleeing the flume. He shouted. He couldn't hear his own voice. A long-haired teenager brushed by him, trailing the smell of marijuana. The boy carried a metal Olympic Adventure banner, ripped from the side of the flume's dock. Looting, Hawkins thought. It's just beginning. Again he shouted for Alexis, but the din of the crowd grew and his voice was submerged in the clamorous roar. Then he spotted Alexis and Max across the plaza near the Chariot of the Gods. He pushed his way into the swarm, but he was moving against the flow. They were rushing out, toward the main avenue. Exasperated, angry, Hawkins put one hand into the air with the flare and braced the other against his waist, using his elbow as a football player would, leaning hard into the crowd. Pandemonium was spreading.

Alexis saw his face in the flare's white light, its corona near his head. His eyes burned. He loves this place, she thought, maybe more than anything, or anyone, else.

Brad, bumped from behind, stumbled as he reached her. "How the hell did you get over here?" he shouted.

Max smiled. "We just got carried away."

Brad wondered how Max could make jokes. "I want

288

you both to get up to the shops," he said. The Olympic Bazaar was at least six hundred yards away, through the main promenade, past the fountain. "See if you can shut them down before they're emptied out."

Alexis was stung by his tone: so businesslike. He saw the confusion on her face. "Look," he said, "we've got to get mobilized before this crowd rips the place apart. I'm going up to the main generators to see what happened. You've got to help."

"Of course," Max said. "Let's keep our losses down."

Then Hawkins understood how Max could make jokes. The old man, serene and unruffled, had seen calamity before, and he would see it again. This was simply another call to action: a challenge. In that way, Brad thought, he and Max were not so different. They thrived at the eye of the storm. Alexis clumsily tried to hug him. He hoisted the torch above his head and held her.

"Oh God," she said, closing her eyes. "I can't handle this."

"Yes, you can," Hawkins said. "You have to. Now go with Max." He wanted them away, both of them, in the shops, where they would be safe, away from the rides. "Go around back," he said, "through the forest."

Hawkins began fighting his way toward the generators on the opposite side of the park. More flares were lit now, hanging from posts inside the rides' maintenance areas. Many people no longer hurried toward the gates but instead wandered aimlessly, dazed. Some called names into the darkness. Some were injured, crying. Hawkins saw an elderly woman kneeling at the base of the Pyramids, nursing a gash on her leg. Another woman held a boy by the hand, huddled against a tree. Food was scattered across the ground. Looters raided the restaurants. The farther Hawkins moved from the center of the park, the more he saw that although the tumult had slowed, the crowd was not thinning. People stopped, stayed to watch. Nothing, Hawkins thought, was quite so hypnotic as chaos. It feeds on itself. It increases itself. Releases the worst in people.

Coming toward Hawkins through the crowd was Ken

Masters in a park jeep, prying people apart, it seemed to Hawkins, spreading them like a wave. As it came closer, the jeep's headlights broke the night with an ethereal, rainbow glow. Masters picked up speed. Hawkins saw only legs scrambling across the headlights, out of the vehicle's way.

"Pete's been trying to get you," Ken shouted. He pointed to the wireless radio strapped to Hawkins's side. It was smashed. Masters handed him a new walkie-talkie and Hawkins tore the broken one from its case. Wires dangled from the frame like strips of thread from worn cloth. He chucked it into the back of the jeep.

Masters spoke breathlessly. "Backup generators are out. A circuit shorted. The entire system's dead."

"Does Pete know why?"

"Not yet. He was on his way to the power station when I dropped off a jeep for him."

"Kenny, be careful with your leg, will you?"

"Don't worry about me, Brad."

"I *am* worried about you." The kid is tough, Hawkins thought. Which reminded him of Jock Constable. Jock was probably drunk. Poor bastard. "How many jeeps are out?"

"Just mine and Pete's," Masters said. "I wanted to wait until I talked to you."

The two men eyed each other. The significance of what they had been through and what they were about to experience escaped neither man: Masters, learning both the responsibility and burden of power; Hawkins, reaching out to teach and explain, and most of all to trust. Could he trust Masters now? He needed a deputy and it couldn't be Jock. Jock was either drunk or on the way to being drunk. Jock couldn't do the job, not least because so few others in the park trusted him. It was a bitter poison: Jock, his friend, a likable, blundering moose.

"The jeeps," Masters said. "How do you want them deployed?" His voice hammered; he talked as if he were striking the air. There's strength, Hawkins thought.

"What do you think?" Hawkins asked.

"There are twelve small jeeps left and five wide-bodies. We ought to keep the tankers out. Too easy to run somebody over with. I'd like to send the small ones to Maintenance and keep the wide-bodies for supervisors. I can use Bill Harrison to get them around."

"Check," Hawkins said. He rubbed his eyes with his thumb and forefinger. His face was smudged with dirt and the sweeping of his hands left gray arcs across his cheeks. "Get over to Maintenance then, and take two of Harrison's men when you come back down. I'll call him. Send Don Brossard to help Constable at the southern aerial rides." How he hoped Jock was sober enough. Just this once. "You and Bill check the shops. Tell Bill to use his fists. He may have to crack some heads."

"It's already bad up there, Brad. A mob. You can't even drive through it."

"Did you see Alexis?"

"Mrs. Cunningham? I couldn't get that close." Masters thought it odd that Hawkins called Cole Cunningham's wife by her first name; he'd never heard that before.

"Tell Bill to watch out for her, will you?" Hawkins said.

Masters let it pass. "What about the central aerial rides? The big wheel and Winged Zeus are packed. The coaster's damn near upside down."

"Empty them. They've got gas engines."

"Can't do it. Both engines choked off. The starters are electric."

"Christ, I'll call Operations. They have a couple of guys who can climb, They can do the Monuments, too. You get Jock's security crew and check the aerial rides on this side of the coaster. I'll check with Pete and pick up a jeep myself and swing south." He jumped into the jeep. "Have you talked with anybody down there?"

"All the foremen. They're coping, but they're desperate for flares."

"They're on the way."

"I guess that does it," Masters said.

Hawkins inhaled slowly. Masters, sensitive to Hawkins's authority, waited to be told where to drive.

"Drop me at the power station," Hawkins said. Masters barreled through the heart of the park, then slowed to avoid bodies on the sidewalks. Hawkins called Jock Constable and told him that relief crews were on the way. Constable sounded sober, but you never could tell. Everywhere there was rubble—baskets overturned, clothing, wire mesh, fence spikes, mounds of plastic banners. They had just crossed the plaza in front of the fountain when, from behind, there came a deafening tremor, a sound seeming to rise from a deep gorge. The Western Arena gates burst open. First hundreds, then thousands of people billowed out, heading for the fountain plaza in a throbbing phalanx. Hawkins guessed that the crowd had stampeded, clogging the gates. Now they rushed forward, trampling those who did not move fast enough. The absence of light gave birth to violence, as if violence grew organically from darkness.

"Step on it," Hawkins yelled. "I don't want to get caught in this."

Masters burrowed recklessly across the plaza, with the crowd fast upon them from the rear like wild dogs on the run, their faces open with fury, scenting metaphysical blood. Hawkins turned to look, tearing his sleeve on the jeep's windscreen. The top of the arena, triangular sheets of painted muslin stretched on dowel frames to simulate a teepee, began to sway. Then the edges began to curl and burn like ink spreading in a pool of water, and before Hawkins could tell what was happening, flames had sucked through the center, an exploding torch sending sparks into the dead blue sky.

"Good God Almighty." Hawkins threw his arms across his chest, shivering at the sight. The jeep had come practically to a standstill. Masters was driving through a solid wall of human bodies. The arena fire burned higher as the topmost muslin sheets fell outward. One by one, they tore loose from aluminum moorings, slipped over, and slammed down. Adjacent layers, forming a cupola inside the arena, were already catching. Flames shot out over the arena's concrete walls. Men standing on the ledge,

292

their backs turned to Hawkins while they watched the widening inferno, dropped off the wall in flames. Falling to the ground, ignored by those with necks craned to the sky, they writhed on the grass, continuing to burn. Hawkins turned away, sick with disgust.

"Station One, open channel. Hawkins to pad. Is anybody there?" No answer. Hawkins punched the open channel code again. "Station One to Helicopter Pad. Answer."

"Pad here, Harrison."

"Hawkins. Can you see it, Bill?"

"We're on our way, Brad. The first two engines just went out. We've got two down with pressure problems, but we're working on them."

"Pressure problems! Still? What the hell . . ." It was inevitable. He had heard it all day—things not working as they should.

"I didn't want—"

"I know," Hawkins said. "You didn't want to tell me. Bad parts?"

"The tanks. The compressors ain't got no power."

"Do your best. And look, Bill, once they're out, get on up to the garage and give Masters a hand getting the jeeps out. He'll meet you there. That's all."

"Right, pad out."

Hawkins slumped in the jeep. Weariness consumed him. He felt as though his body were stretched on a rack, being pulled apart from every side. Behind him, the arena tent burned furiously, puffing in the wind. The air underneath grew hotter, pumping waves of smoke and charred cloth through the middle, until the whole structure pulsated upward. Hawkins feared it would lift off entirely, blowing into the trees, showering sparks on the Monuments. The Pyramids were—what? Fiberglass. Did fiberglass burn? He didn't know.

More bodies, some in flames, emptied from the arena, crawling to stay below the dense smoke. A vengeful God, Hawkins thought, claiming His victims for Cole Cunningham's sins. Sinners in the hands of an angry God. He remembered the lines from Jonathan Edwards: "An

293

axe is laid at the root of the tree which brought forth bitter and poisonous fruit. Haste and escape for your lives. Look not behind you, and escape to the mountain lest you be consumed."

The tent exploded. Canvas balls of flame soared into the sky. Vibrating reds and yellows lit the horizon. A second explosion ripped through the tent. It spit shreds of cloth like a volcano. Fire tore through the cone and spread at the top, shooting clouds of dust reaching from one end of the vast arena to the other. Hawkins and Masters, in the jeep, moved faster again, past the helium-filled Olympic Balloon, which was waving on its base. In the fire's light, the words *Olympic Adventure* reflected down on them, inflated iridescent shadows on the plastic bubble. By the time they reached the power station, Pete Toscani was already there, standing in the doorway, his round, monk-like face ashen and covered with sweat. He stepped back as the jeep clattered to a halt.

"After you pick Harrison up," Hawkins told Masters, "get back to the Monuments. And make sure you get bullhorns for the jeeps. Pete will take me up to the garage." Masters backed the jeep out and Hawkins joined Toscani in the generator room. It was cool, quiet, airless.

"Tell me the worst, Pete."

"Destroyed," Toscani said. "Whoever did this knows his stuff. The best equipment. Tersa timer. Breiter clips. A Farrell PR-3 two-stage transformer." He pointed to the main electrical-circuit board. "This thing is completely shot through. Every line is shorted. And it was all done with one transformer." He held up the shiny black box and two strands of wire.

"Who?" Hawkins asked solemnly.

"The Wicked Witch of the West," Toscani said irritably. "How the hell should I know?"

Hawkins thought for a moment. "Pete, what about that guy you fired a couple of weeks ago? The one who was stealing parts. Could he have stolen this stuff from us?"

"Doug Dowling? No, he's a mean bastard, but he

294

ain't crazy. And I don't stock this kind of hardware. I couldn't afford to."

"Who, then?" Hawkins asked.

"Search me," Toscani said. "We've both pissed a lot of people off. And Cunningham's got more enemies than you could fit into the whole damn park."

"The hell with it," Hawkins said. "We're not going to figure it out now. What about the backup generators?"

"Same thing," Toscani hissed through his teeth. "The crazy fucking lunatic, whoever he is, planned it this way. Blew the whole frigging business. Main power and reserve power. That's how the damn fire started." He stepped from the concrete building and, shielding his eyes, stared across the arena. "Damn circuits overloaded and sizzled the wires." He pointed to his forehead. "You know what I say, kid? Toys in the attic. Bonkers."

Hawkins balled his right fist in his left hand and squeezed. For nearly a minute, he stood there, overcome by cold rage.

"Let's go," he said finally. "The longer we wait, the harder it'll get. What can you do about getting us some power, Pete?"

"I need parts from Operations. They're putting together a package now, but it'll take some time."

"What about your crew?"

"They're ready to work for you. I can't use them."

"Send two men to the northern aerial rides. Jock is there."

"Great," Toscani grunted. "He'll be a big help."

Hawkins ignored the sarcasm. "You take the two Chariots and Winged Zeus. Sooner or later, some jackass is going to start climbing out by himself. Try to swing the crowd down there around toward the gates. And send Sheila with stretchers."

"Stretchers?"

"And blankets. You'll need them."

"Christ, it's not that bad," Toscani said. "I just came from there."

"It is now. It's a goddamn rampage. Looting and—"

"Looting?" Toscani shouted.

"That's the least of it. There must be a couple of hundred people burned outside the arena. And when that crowd broke out, they didn't wait for women and kids, I can tell you that. Without the damn phones, we'll be lucky if the state cops get here in less than an hour."

A dream, Toscani thought. A nightmare. Crazy, fucking lunatic.

The two men jumped into Toscani's jeep. Hawkins found another waiting for him at the garage and drove toward the Bazaar. A man wearing a clown mask tried to push Hawkins out of his seat while the jeep was still moving. Hawkins knocked him aside, and the man fell into the crowd. Then the man stood and heaved a rock through the plate-glass window of the film shop. Hawkins's first urge was to stop and fight, but he kept driving. Throughout the park, flares glowed, speckling the night like lights flickering through a fog on the Manhattan skyline. When Hawkins reached the middle of the Bazaar, a mob surrounded his jeep. Teenagers and adults, men and women, all were piled together around him. They seemed to breathe in unison, an undulating mass, one organism. Shouting and rocking the jeep, a group lunged at Hawkins, dragged him out of his seat, and he found himself on the ground, his left hand bleeding from a sinuous gash. He was stepped on and, to avoid being crushed, rolled under the jeep. Then the jeep itself was turned over and one man, whose jacket hung in shreds from his arms, tossed a flare into the belly of the car, directly onto the gas tank. Hawkins crawled away and stood. Reflexively he checked his wireless. It was still intact.

Pushing through the crowd, he saw Alexis coming toward him. The jeep exploded behind him and was swallowed in flames.

"It's out of control," Alexis shouted. "There's nothing we can do."

"Let's get out of here. Where's Max?"

Alexis turned and pointed. The old man stood behind

the glass door of the souvenir store, puffing on a cigar, a witness for sanity, testifying in the midst of madness. Alexis and Brad signaled for Max to meet them in the back. They struggled around the store. Max waited for them at the rear door.

"I'd say four million, maybe five," Max said.

"You'd say what?" Alexis asked.

"Damages," he said. "As long as they don't do real structural harm to the rides, I'm betting on at least four million to put the place back together. Plus lawsuits. I hope you're carrying good insurance." Shaking his head, he laid a hand on Hawkins's shoulder. "What do we do now?"

"The south aerial rides. I want—"

"Brad!" Alexis screamed. "You're hurt."

"It's a small cut," he said, wiping the blood on his shirt. The burning jeep's glare lit the entire midway. Women swarmed through the store, loading shopping bags full of toys. "Good God Almighty," he said. "You wouldn't think . . ." He couldn't finish the sentence. "There's nothing left to do here. Let's go." They started down the path, through the woods, toward the ferris wheel.

"Move slowly. Don't rush. This way, to your left." Masters stood on the jeep's hood, speaking into the bullhorn, but with little success. Injured people lay moaning, scattered across the grass in front of him. A middle-aged man, blood streaming down his face, cradled a woman's head in his arms. A tiny blond girl limped, stumbled, and fell. A woman crawled off the sidewalk, dazed, holding her purse against her side. The stampede continued unabated. Masters heard the piercing scream of a child. Behind the jeep, a man wrestled with a little boy.

"No, I don't want to go!" the boy shouted.

A woman tried to separate the man and the boy. She cried out for help. Ken jumped from the jeep, landed on Everett Morgan, and wrestled him to the ground. Morgan struggled, holding Ken's neck in his forearm. Their legs entwined. Masters, lying on his side, jerked his knee into Morgan's chest. Morgan fell over and Ken crawled on top of him, holding his arms against the pavement with one hand, delivering rapid hammer blows to his chest. He didn't want to hurt the man. He just wanted to knock him out. Morgan was delirious now and fought violently, refusing to be subdued. "Matthew," he screamed. Ken thought the man was calling his name, stopped, leaned back. "Matthew," Morgan screamed, rolling Ken over and pouncing on him. Finally, Masters had no choice. He pressed forward with his knees, then slammed his fist into Morgan's jaw. He punched him in the stomach, taking his wind away. Morgan twisted and the wirecutters and plans for Olympic Adventure's electrical system fell from his pocket.

The woman rushed over and held the man's head.

"Everett, oh Everett," she cried. "Why?"

"You know this man?" Masters asked.

"He's my husband."

"Your husband! I'm sorry—"

"No, my ex-husband. He was trying to take our son away."

Masters picked up the wirecutters and papers. Wirecutters? The words at the corner of the schematic diagram, in the smallest type, caught Masters's eye: Electrical Plant. Olympic Adventure, Glenwood, New Jersey. A. W. Albright, Contractors. Electrical plant? Wirecutters? Suddenly he made the connection.

"What does your husband do?"

"He's a . . . what's the matter?"

What does he do for a living?

"He's an electrician. He works in the city."

"For Albright Contractors?"

"Yes, I'm . . . what has he done?"

"I don't know, lady. I don't know." Masters looked at the diagram again and then at Louise Morgan. "Do you want to press charges?"

"No, Everett's sick. He needs help."

"That's for sure," Masters said. He hesitated a second

and pulled a spool of rope from the jeep. He bound Morgan's hands and feet, then lifted the unconscious man, his dead weight straining the rope's bonds, onto the jeep's rear floor. Christ, Masters thought. Could one crazy guy . . . ? "You'd better get in," he said, motioning to Louise Morgan. She picked up her son, touched her sleeve to a faint cut on his forehead, and climbed into the jeep.

"Lay it up easy," Jock Constable yelled, "slower, you nitwits, slower." Four mechanics with Constable at the front of the line vaulted a ladder over their heads and stood it straight up, fitting the legs into bolts on the ferris wheel's deck. With the bottom moored—a little shaky, Constable thought, but it would have to do—the mechanics cranked the gears, extending the ladder. Slowly, for lack of wrenches, they forced the metal, grinding, through its turns. Foot by foot, steps pushed upward, until finally the ladder was forty feet long, nearly one-quarter of the way up the side of the huge circle. The men leaned it against the big wheel's girdered frame. With four unlit flares and a bullhorn hanging from his shoulder, Jock began to climb. His first step shook the ladder, sending a reverberating shudder through the wheel. The seats swung slightly, and the movement, combined with the darkness, frightened those near the top; in the highest car, one hundred and eighty feet in the air, three drunk college students began to shout, setting off shrieks around the wheel.

"I'm going to climb down," the boy in the middle of the top car said to his companions. "Move over." The other two boys laughed at his bravado. Emboldened by their mocking, he grabbed the girder above his seat and swung out of the car.

"Superman!" he yelled.

"Stop," one of his friends shouted. "Jack, come down."

"Bullshit," the boy shouted. "I'm going down to the ground, where the action is."

He wrapped his legs around a girder. Searching for a foothold, he lowered himself behind the seat below, stretching his body across a space between two metal bars

299

connecting the seat to the frame. Then he let his hands loose and swung to the outside edge of the wheel. He executed the identical maneuver again. He lowered his feet onto the next girder, then swung his arms to the outside.

Constable was attaching a lit flare when the wheel started to shake. He looked up and saw the boy.

"Get back in the car!"

"I'm coming down. Can't take it up there anymore."

"Get in a seat, you jackass."

The boy looked down, and then across the seat in front of him. Only two people were in it, an elderly couple, and he stepped across the face of the wheel away from the edge and leaned toward the seat.

"Move over, folks. The man wants me to sit."

The occupants of the car crushed together. At first the boy hesitated, then swung down another level. As he reached around the seat, he miscalculated and slipped, his rangy body coming within inches of missing the girder altogether. Accidentally he slapped a light bulb with his hand and it smashed. He wobbled and stood again.

"Goddamnit, kid," Constable yelled. "Get in a seat, I tell you!"

The old couple in the car held frantically to the restraining bar as the boy, looking down, put his left foot across the open space. Straining to reach, the boy slipped, lost his balance, and fell backward. For a moment, he held a girder with his hands, dangling free. He screamed. Then he fell fifteen stories to the ground, his head banging against the frame. Jock saw the body sail past. The thud was so loud when it hit the ground that Jock heard it forty feet above. His stomach churned.

"Jackass," he said aloud. Voices on the ground rose in a dull murmur. When he reached the last rung, he heard a muffled boom. By the light of the fire, he could see that horses had broken loose from the Western Arena stables and were galloping toward the center of the park. Panicked, unrestrained, the horses pulled wagons behind them, sweeping through the trees. When the horses reached the center of the park, the wagons, gyrating on cracked wheels, snapped loose, splintering apart as they hit the fountain's marble facade. The horses surged past the fountain and across the plaza, aiming straight for the ferris wheel. Constable was worried; if they hit the ladder, he thought, they'll take me down with it. He positioned himself against the wheel, to jump free if the ladder fell.

The stampeding animals cleared a swath of ground wherever they moved. Crowds spread north toward the midway in their wake. The stampede moved closer and closer, shaking the ground, the hoofbeats echoing up to Constable, and then the terrorized horses flew past in a blur below him, scattering into the surrounding trees, just missing the ferris wheel. Jock breathed a sigh of relief.

"Let's relax now, people," he said through the bullhorn. No one spoke a word. "You people in the three cars above and the six below can reach the ladder. We'll start with you up there—" he pointed to the car above his head "—number sixteen. You in the sailor's cap, can you hear me?"

A nervous, hoarse voice replied, "Yes, we hear you."

"You got any kids up there?"

No children, came the response.

"Fine, I'm on my way up."

Constable eased onto the frame. The girders on the inside, four feet apart, were wide enough to mount and climb. Jock bent over the edge of car number sixteen. A dark young man with long hair held a frightened, shaking girl in his arms.

"Evening, folks," Jock said casually. "Name's Jock. Jock Constable."

"Martin," the young man said, unconsciously mimicking Jock's tone. "Martin Forbisher. My wife Amy." The young woman's lips quivered. Around her eyes were red, blotchy spots. She had been crying.

"This is going to be real easy now," Jock said. "Do you both feel like you can make it?"

Martin Forbisher nodded. His wife looked up at him, then at Constable.

"What about you, Amy?" Constable asked solicitously. "Do you feel strong enough?"

She hesitated. "I . . . I think so." Constable wasn't so certain. She looked too scared.

The roof of his mouth was dry. Sweat dripped from his chin, around his eyes, and gathered in the folds of his neck. His throat burned. He craved a swig of bourbon so badly that the salt from his sweat, dripping onto his lips, tasted like it was eighty proof.

"If I can do this," Jock said, "anybody can. I'm all thumbs." He thought he saw the faintest crack of a smile from Amy Forbisher. He winked at her. "Just leave it to old Jock."

He took her hand, reaching through latticework surrounding the car. It was clammy and cold. She stood slowly, as if she were rising from a pool of water. Her hand trembled in Jock's. The grasp was weak. She stepped over her husband's legs and Jock had to practically yank her out of the car before she would step onto the girder.

"Oh, God," she said. "I'm going to sneeze."

"Hold it," Jock said.

"Oh no," she said. "Oh God."

He held her around the waist and braced her against the girder. The wheel rocked. Martin Forbisher stared goggle-eyed.

"Let's sit down," Jock said. He pulled her down into a crouch.

"I can't," she said. The words stuck in her throat. She gasped. "I'm scared. I'll fall."

"Nonsense. Easy does it. Easy." Her legs splayed out and she fell onto the girder. Her husband sucked in breath, stifling a scream.

"Okay, honey," Jock said. "Now's the time to sneeze." Her chest heaved and a faint wheeze of air escaped from her nose. She smiled. "See," Jock said, "I told you how easy it was. Now the simplest part. Just like walking. One foot after the other." He dragged her to the edge of the girder, in full view of those above. This'd better work, Jock thought, or the rest of them will never move. They

302

slid to the edge, hugging each other, glued together as if one body, the woman's hand digging into Jock's ribs the closer they got. She shook violently.

Jock fixed his eyes on her, fighting his own fear. "I'll step down first," he said abruptly. "Hold onto my hand." He had not wanted to do this backward, but he dared not turn away from her. Her eyes registered unrelieved terror. Dropping one leg down, locking his knee rigid, he felt his foot touch metal and realized he would need both hands to brace himself. But Amy Forbisher held him so tightly that her nails were cutting into his flesh. Well, he thought, you'll have to be lucky, Jock. If you let her go, she'll end up just like that crazy kid. Mashed potatoes. Straining at the weight on his leg, he lowered himself, feeling some external force guiding him and holding him steady, his own will mysteriously superceded, and landed squarely on the beam, the balls of his feet hitting accurately, perfectly balanced. A fly buzzed in his ear. A drink, he thought. I need a drink.

"You see," he said, "nothing to it." He wished she would relax her grip so he could swat at the fly.

"You're scared," she said matter-of-factly.

"Not so much," he said. "Let's go now." She released him then and dropped, both legs together, bending her body toward him. Praying that his arms would not break under her weight, he pushed up. She was light. In a moment so harrowingly short he could not recall it afterward, she was standing beside him, next to the ladder.

"From here on," he said, "it's a snap." They walked across the beam to the ladder. "Me first." Although she might falter and knock both of them flying to instant death, Jock decided he would risk it. Perhaps he could catch her and hold on. In any event, he thought, there are worse ways to die. But he couldn't think of any. He swung onto the ladder, holding her hand. She looked down.

"Don't," he said harshly. Her head jerked up. "Don't look."

They started their descent.

On the ground, Hawkins approached the ladder apprehensively. "Where's Constable?" he asked.

"Up there," one of the mechanics said, pointing into the darkness. In the light from the flares hanging on the ladder, Hawkins could see two figures. He had not meant for Jock to do this, but there was hardly anything he could do about it now.

Alexis winced. "I hope he's sober," she whispered.

"Quiet!" Hawkins fired back. "Be quiet."

The two forms gradually came into view. Too fast, Hawkins thought. They were coming down too fast. Despite himself, he could not help wondering if Jock was sober. A drunken man will engage in the most foolish heroics.

"He's okay, Mr. Hawkins," one of the mechanics said. "Really, he is. We wouldn't have let him go up otherwise." They had overheard Alexis.

"I know that," Hawkins said, lying.

Max Brodky tapped Hawkins's shoulder. "You can't do much here," he said. "Why don't you check the rest of the rides? Alexis and I will wait."

"I want to talk with Jock," Hawkins said. He put a cigarette in his mouth, and before he could light it Max held a match for him. Again he saw the serenity in Brodky's face. And again he was surprised.

"What is it, Max?" he asked. "How can you be so calm?"

"I practice," Brodky said. "I have to. I'm too old to get excited."

Constable reached the deck, followed by Amy Forbisher. She collapsed, weeping, into Jock's arms. He walked her to the steps and sat her down. Constable looked at Hawkins and read the doubt on his face. He took him aside, away from the mechanics.

"I know what you're thinking, big fella," Constable said. "But I'm not. I'm cold fucking sober. And I'd murder for a drink."

"Can you take it, Jock?" Hawkins asked.

"I wouldn't be up there if I couldn't."

"I can send someone else," Hawkins said. "One of Harrison's men."

"I can take it, goddamnit," Constable said. His voice was gelid with anger.

"I'm sorry, Jocko," Hawkins said. "But I've—"

"I know, I know. But I'm okay. Really, I am." He was begging for a chance to prove himself.

Hawkins's eyes moved to the gray tarp near the steps. Blood seeped from under it, forming rivers in the cracks of the wood.

"He tried to make it on his own," Constable said. "I couldn't stop him." He paused. "The kid was drunk, big fella. Reeks of booze."

Hawkins sighed. "I'd like to get my hands on whoever's responsible for this. Did you hear from Pete?"

"Yeah, he told me. The generators. Crazy bastard, huh?"

Hawkins wrung his hands and looked again at the tarp-covered body. "Jesus Horatio Christ," he said. "Jesus Christ."

"I'm going back up," Constable said. "That girl's husband is waiting."

"Right," Hawkins said. "And Jocko, I'm sorry."

"Forget it," Constable said, turning away.

Hawkins's walkie-talkie buzzed. He was now attuned to the sound or he would not have heard it over the roar of human voices.

"Station One."

"Masters here. Brad, I've found the man who did it."

"You what? Did *what?*"

"I found him. He had diagrams of the park's generators in his pocket. An electrician. Some terrible scheme about his son. I've got him tied up."

"You're sure?"

"Absolutely. The schematic, all marked up. And wirecutters. His wife is here, she told me he wanted his son. It's so crazy I don't even understand it."

"His son? What the hell are you talking about?"

305

"You can talk to him yourself, when he wakes up. He's out cold right now. Or you can talk to his wife. They're in Sheila's office. What's the picture down there? The northeast is beginning to empty out. We've got lots of people hurt. Hurt bad."

"Hard to tell," Hawkins said. What sounded like howling wolves around the platform confused him for a moment, until, walking to the railing, he assimilated afresh the rumbling of human voices. The noise had changed from screeching to screaming and, as the reality of the constant darkness set in, the commonplace din of a mob. A man bellowed in the distance. The echo of his voice hung in the air, a ricochet.

"It doesn't seem quite like a riot anymore," Masters said. The radio crackled. "How is it up there? Any luck emptying the big wheel?"

"Jock's just started."

"Jock?"

Hawkins ignored the implicit question. "The Chariot is almost clear now. Security's got the shops sealed off finally—but it was bad." He looked down at his hand. "I damn near got killed up there."

"You? What happened?"

"Got thrown out of a jeep. They set it on fire."

"My God," Masters said. "I had no idea it was that bad."

"How's your leg, Kenny?"

"I'm walking."

"We're in a lull now," Hawkins said. "One more fire will set this crowd off. They're not leaving. They're staying for the show."

"We're in trouble, then," Masters said. "Harrison's been running around putting out small fires for the last half-hour. I just talked to him. Every time they finish one, there's another. They just went back to fill the tanks."

"Who's starting the fires?"

"Nobody. It's sparks from the tent. We've got garbage burning all over."

"At least the wind's down," Hawkins said. "What else is there to do down there?"

"Not much. The crowd's moving in your direction."

"Go on up to the main gate. We ought to have some state cops soon. They'll need help." The relay light flashed on his radio. Someone else was trying to reach him. "Got another call, Kenny."

"Talk to you soon. Masters, out."

Hawkins clicked in the second circuit.

"Richardson, Station Six. Are you there, Brad?"

"It's me, Sheila. Where are you?"

"At the gate. I've got about a hundred injured people in the guest office, and a couple of hundred more in the locker rooms. Some pretty bad burns. Doc Gordon's doing the best he can, but we need ambulances."

"State cops should be here any minute. Have them radio the hospital. Check with Operations, will you, to see if they've had any word. What about the cash?"

"All locked up, Brad."

"Supplies?"

"We're running out of stretchers. Three crews are out now, but they have to carry people in."

Hawkins thought a moment. "Pull one of the crews in and have them start cutting up tarps. It'll be a while before we get enough ambulances."

"Anything else I can do?"

"Stay where you are and keep me posted."

"Good enough. Richardson, out."

The radio went silent, but Hawkins could hear indistinct conversation. The channels, overloaded, blended together. Thin yellow smoke drifted by, carrying the acrid odor of melting plastic. Small, glimmering fires shone across the south end of the park. The lambent air, heavy with the scent of burning garbage, swelled with rising voices. Against the blanched sky, the Western Arena burned sporadically, sending up reeds of black smoke. At the jeweled carousel, a mob had gathered, and Hawkins could see people cleaving strips of beaded glass from the wooden horses.

"Station One, Hawkins."

"Twelve, security. Benson."

"Benson, send anybody you can spare to the carousel. And fast. They're tearing it apart."

"On our way. Benson, out."

Insane, Hawkins thought. From what sickness did such destruction come? Why had these people remained? Why did they not go home? He thought of Coleridge: "The harlequin mask falls to reveal the madman beneath."

Hawkins reached for his wireless. "All bands open. This is Hawkins, Station One. Count off."

Voices responded in order, crisply, beginning with Masters and continuing through each section's operations manager, supervisor, and head of security. Four stations on the open band—all senior administrators—did not answer. Not bad, Hawkins thought. He checked his watch. It was six minutes before nine. Less than an hour had passed.

"We're missing gate security and concessions, Kenny. Check on them. Listen up, the rest of you. We have state cops on the way." Alexis and Max moved closer, listening. "In the meantime, we've got to do everything we can to cut down on the fires and pick up the injured. Sheila Richardson is set up to take care of injuries at the main gate. Take in anybody you can move safely, but only those who really need help. We're short on stretchers. Call Sheila if you have questions. And watch the heavy machinery carefully. We've got lots of crazies loose tonight, so keep your eyes open." That ought to do it, he thought. "Questions now, department supervisors. All circuits open and everybody stand by." Briskly and without fuss, the reports came in.

"Operations, Dexter. The state police are on the way. All my flares are out."

"Security, Benson. All arenas secured. We have men to spare, so don't try to handle looters yourself."

"Maintenance, Harrison. Two crews freed up for heavy moving."

"Main lots, Jordan. Cars are beginning to move out.

People separated from families are gathered at the western end."

"Engineering, Toscani. I need some barricades at the southern rides."

Masters interrupted. "Pete, use the tanker jeeps. We'll just have to risk it. I can't spare any of the wide-bodies now."

"Right," Toscani said. "I'll load them. What about you, Hawkins? Do you have any problems with that?"

"Whatever Kenny says, Pete."

Hawkins was pleased with his staff. From the chaos, order was emerging. He clicked three times and switched back to local channels.

Alexis took his hand. "It's not so bad, then," she said.

"Not so bad now," he said. He had not noticed before that her hair was matted and makeup smeared her face. He dropped the radio into its case. As he brushed a shock of hair from his eyes, he left a smudge of grease on his forehead. Shades of gray, brown, and green covered his cheeks. Alexis was reminded of the masks in Japanese drama: cold, lifeless.

Max said, "You look like death."

"I feel worse," Hawkins said grimly. "Sheila needs help. Why don't you both go up? Take Jock's jeep." He looked toward the ladder. "It's going to be a while before he needs it."

Alexis rubbed her face with her sleeve and kissed him. "I love you," she said.

No sooner had the jeep disappeared into the crowd than a boom sounded behind the ferris wheel, followed by a resounding, reverberating crash. Under the weight of stagnant water, the deep plastic troughs of the flume had split. Now, too late, it occurred to Hawkins that he should have ordered the ride drained, just as it was emptied each night during the season. But in the shock of the first few minutes of darkness, he had forgotten. Only one of the vertical sloping slides had given way, but hundreds of gallons of water from the upper terraces flowed down torrentially, and a yawning tear ripped further from the pressure, bouncing canoes to the bottom and tearing pieces of the trough loose, spewing wood and plastic into the air and onto the surrounding crowd. As the water showered below his line of sight, Hawkins heard the screams. He felt nauseous.

The water cascaded from the slides onto the flume's loading dock and then down to the ground. Canoes floated into the terraced pools and sailed off the edge of the highest slide, beating onto the lowest troughs near the dock. Hawkins could hear the crashing halfway across the park.

High on the ladder, Constable, mesmerized, stopped to watch. Water seeped over the flume dock's railings. In the torchlight, he saw the water's power build from a trickle to a downpour as the dock became a gurgling lake. Helplessly he watched those beneath the dock, wanting to urge them to move, wanting to scream across the darkness: Run!

Then the wooden stilts on which the dock rested high off the ground buckled. The stairway ripped apart in the flood of water. Jackasses, Constable thought: Get away!

As the stairway tore from the dock, Constable watched a park attendant carrying a flare, standing on the top step, holding to the railing. At a distance, Constable could not tell if the shadowed figure was a man or a woman, but before he could think about it, the steps gave way altogether and the body sank in a mass of timber and water and plastic and muck. The slats of the dock separated and the body was completely swallowed. The flare sailed into the air from a sinking hand.

On the ground, Hawkins looked up as the dock broke open. The troughs pulled the last of the structure down, releasing waves of water, a river overflowing its banks. The water seemed to have a life, a will, of its own; thrashing waves washed downward, unspent, ripping energy yearning to burst free. The water struck the dock's splintered remains and chunks of wood bounced and landed on the few people still able to run and, with a precision that appeared anything but random, nailed them to the ground.

"Hawkins, Station One."

"What is it, Brad?"

"Sheila, you'd better——" He stopped to find his breath. "You'd better send . . . get a crew to the flume. It's split open. They'll need stretchers."

"On the way."

The walkie-talkie was almost in its holster when he heard her continue.

"And Brad, I just wanted to say . . . well, we all think you're doing an incredible job. Pete told us about everything."

"We're all doing well," he said, thinking of Jock. "We're doing our best. Are Mrs. Cunningham"——he almost said Alexis——"and Mr. Brodky there yet?"

"Not here," she said.

"They're coming to give you a hand."

"I can use it."

"Enough chatter, then. Keep your chin up. And thanks, Sheila. Station One, out." The girl thought she was in love with him, but she was just a girl. Life with Alexis would not be so simple. It had been so many years passed alone, so many years since he had even considered the possibility of being in love. In love, that is, with anything but work, living the pulse of the park as his own. He had made the park his passion—its candy-colored buildings, its flowered and jeweled arches, its pastel-painted steel, and its spectacle. All this he could possess. It was real—even though it had its own mystery. Once the touch of a woman's hand, the silent but felt quickened breath, the meeting of lips, had been real as well, had seemed guaranteed, permanent. From that mystery, he had run. The permanent, the guaranteed, had collapsed around him. He had awakened alone one fetid Texas morning long ago, a note on the table, a rising gorge in his throat, the closets empty, the coffee cold in a cup. The doors had closed then on that particular illusion. Now, with Alexis, he was prying them open again.

He turned to watch another woman climb from the ladder. One of the mechanics helped her off the platform.

Above, Constable stepped two rungs down to the next

car, number fourteen. A middle-aged man, his face almost invisible in the shadows, stood to reach for Jock's hand. Leaning toward the man, Jock felt a muscle spasm in his side, a dull pain as if he had been kicked. His lungs pounded. His eyes widening, he gasped for air. The man in car number fourteen, unable to see the anguish on Jock's face, stood, waiting. The pain in Jock's side grew worse, but he reached out for the man. Suddenly his vision clouded and he pulled his arm back. The ladder shook and Jock's grasp on the rungs weakened. He slipped, screamed, and slid down two more rungs, then lost his grip altogether and fell backward off the ladder.

Hawkins turned at the scream, saw Jock sailing toward him. In disbelief, he reached out, frantically trying to catch Jock's body, but it flew by, slammed into the railing, and flipped over the platform onto the ground. Hawkins ran to him. Constable's neck was broken. He was dead.

"Oh God, no," Hawkins cried, falling to his knees and cradling Jock's battered face. The mechanics rushed to him, tried to pull him away from the body, but he did not move. In the shock of grief, tears would not come. He held Jock in his arms.

"The balloon!" one of the mechanics shouted, and Hawkins turned to see the helium-filled Olympic Balloon tilt in the wind. But there was no wind. Why did it move? Hawkins stood, peered across the plaza. Two men were jumping on the restraining ropes. Hawkins looked down at Jock's twisted face, and then, enraged, broke into a sprint, worried that the balloon, if it were cut free, might not simply rise but explode.

The two men, unable to snap the balloon's ropes, held torches to them. The flames ate through the ropes and the plastic mass bobbed from side to side. The men raced around it, intoxicated. Only seven of the sixteen ropes remained when Hawkins collared one of the men from behind. He knocked the man's torch to the ground and raised his fist. A voice in him shouted no, but he surrendered to violence. He wrestled the man to the ground and then pummeled his face and chest. Blood spurted from the man's mouth. The man swung weakly at Hawkins, but Hawkins threw him over and shot his knee into the man's back, sending him reeling in pain. From around the balloon came the other man, throwing a torch at Hawkins. Hawkins jumped, fell, and the man leaped on him. Hawkins arched his back and threw the man over his head, sprang to his feet, and pounced. Whipping his arm back and forth, he repeatedly slapped the man in the face until he had beat him senseless. Standing over the two men who lay on the ground, Hawkins reached to tighten the remaining ropes; but it was no use. Flames had singed the balloon's skin. It was melting slightly, and for a moment, Hawkins thought it might seal itself. But the heat was too much and it ruptured.

Hawkins backed off, shouting to people to keep away. The crowd would not listen. The enormous globe, whistling softly, began leaking. A hole opened and helium rushed out. The skin sucked inward, sagging, rending the fabric more quickly. A jet of escaping gas, released from pressure, blasted out with sudden force and a thousand square feet of plastic webbing split open, spreading as it sank to the ground. As it spread, Hawkins rushed to drag people from under it, but many were too stunned to move. He could not pull them away. Suffocating bodies writhed underneath the plastic. Choked voices cried out in terror. Hawkins, weak, clawed at the fabric, but it was too heavy to move. When he lifted his head, he saw the surrounding crowd retreating. The paths were emptying. Only the injured remained. In the distance, sirens blared.

18

An eerie quiet had descended. Sweeping the grounds in teams of four, state troopers collected the injured. From the parking lot flowed a continuous stream of cars, an orderly procession directed by local police. A fleet of ambulances, commandeered from hospitals as far away as Delaware, passionlessly accepted the human debris. Doctors tended first to the severely burned. Children cried out in the still of the night.

Hawkins slouched against the main gate. Alexis, speechless, stood beside him, one hand covering her face. She felt her own hot, heaving breath.

Park crews helped carry the dead to police vans. Hawkins could not help counting the dead as the stretchers passed. Hundreds of them. Dozens of trucks were already filled with bodies. There would be more—more bodies, more waste. He searched for reasons. There were none to be found.

"You Hawkins?" A state trooper, his brown uniform festooned with silver stripes and bars, walked toward Brad, clipboard in hand. His jaw jutted against the strap of his hat. He was a large, square man, as tall as Hawkins, with bushy, black eyebrows extending in one unbroken line across his forehead.

"Hawkins," Brad said.

"Captain Flanders," the trooper said. "We're about done here. My men are making one last run through the place. I think we have everybody, but we want to be sure."

Hawkins nodded blankly. Everybody? "How many dead?" he asked.

"Hard to tell right now. Two hundred, maybe more. Not bad when you think how many you had here. Must have been seventy-five thousand." He's seen death, Hawkins thought. It doesn't bother him.

314

"One hundred and eleven thousand, four hundred and six, to be exact," Hawkins said. The number had pleased him. "The biggest gate we ever had." Why did it matter now? Why did he still think this way?

The trooper let out a low whistle. Then he saw the grief on Hawkins's face.

"You're taking this hard," the trooper said. "But you did what you could, right?"

"One man," Hawkins said softly. "One crazy bastard."

"No," the trooper said. "He just set it off. You start a crowd going, anything can happen." The trooper unhooked the strap from his hat. "You wonder sometimes. You wonder why they do it. You see it again and again, and you wonder."

"Ever get any answers?"

"Answers?" The trooper shook his head. "Answers. Well, the experts tell us all about it. Crowds, you know. Mobs. What they do to people. Doesn't mean a damn to me." He turned to watch the loading of the ambulances. "Doesn't mean a damn to nobody," he went on. "Knowing why doesn't help you stop them. I guess it's just the way people are, you know. I guess it's there in all of us. That's what they tell me." He paused. His jaw stiffened. "Shit, you figure it out."

Hawkins started to leave. He had nothing to say.

"I hate to bring this up," the trooper said, stopping him, "but there are a couple of reporters who want to talk to you. If you don't want to do it, I'll just send them on their way."

"I'll see them," Hawkins said. "They might as well have their story straight."

"Okay, but we don't want anyone running around in there. If you want to let 'em in, it's okay by me, but my men are going with them. Otherwise they're liable to get hurt. We'll close the road off until you can get your own guards."

Hawkins thanked the trooper and, taking Alexis's hand, joined the reporters gathered on the parking lot near the turnstiles. There were more than he expected, as many as had been at the helicopter pad earlier for the governor's arrival. Bright television lamps shone across the lot.

He told the reporters that they had found the man they suspected of destroying the park's generators. An out-of-work electrician, he said. A man named Morgan.

"Where is this guy?" one reporter asked.

"You'll have to talk to the cops," Hawkins said. "They've got him now." Vultures, Hawkins thought. Listlessly he recited the statistics: two hundred dead, more than ten million in damages. One cameraman asked Hawkins to move closer to the ambulances, but Hawkins paid no attention. Newspaper photographers crowded around him. Shutters clicked. Suddenly Hawkins realized the photographs would show Alexis. Screw them, he thought. It didn't matter now.

A pack of reporters loped into the park with the troopers. Hawkins turned away, repulsed. Did they have no feelings? No, they were only doing their jobs. A voice called to him out of the dark.

"Hawkins, wait up." It was Murray Rothbart.

"Jesus, Murray, are you still here?" Hawkins asked.

"They sent me back. That was rough there, but you have to realize these guys need stories. No stories, no jobs."

"I know, Murray."

"Are you okay?"

"I'm holding together."

"Sorry about Constable," the reporter said. "Masters told me. He was a funny kind of guy. Always laughing, but real unhappy."

"Yeah," Hawkins said, "I know." Poor Jock. The full reality of Constable's death had not yet hit him. None of it had.

"What about the lady?" Rothbart asked.

Hawkins looked over his shoulder. Alexis had joined Max Brodky, a hundred yards away.

"What about her?"

"You're going to have your picture in the papers with her tomorrow. People are going to talk."

"They already talk. Right now it's hard to care what people say."

"Is that Max Brodky with her?" Rothbart asked. "Or am I dreaming?"

"That's him, Murray," Hawkins said with a touch of bitterness. "Do you want the story? Is that it? Can I help you with your story?"

"Relax, Hawkins. Just asking."

"You can *have* the story," Hawkins said, now with venom in his voice. "Brodky is the proud new owner of Olympic Adventure. He's buying himself a scrap heap. Good story, huh, Murray? An exclusive, right?"

"Calm down, Hawkins. I'll see you later." Rothbart spun around and walked toward his car.

"Murray," Hawkins called. "Wait a minute."

Rothbart stopped. Hawkins walked over to him.

"Sorry, Murray. Let's talk next week."

"Sure, Hawkins. I understand. What can I say?"

"Nothing. There's nothing any of us can say."

"That's where you're wrong, Hawkins. You can read all about it in the morning editions. As for me, I'm calling it a day."

Hawkins watched Rothbart's car pull into the line heading for the thruway. The shining taillights from the row of cars blurred, and he found himself on the verge of tears. For the dead, for the injured, for the lives broken. For Jock. And for himself. He had thought himself incapable not only of love, but of real sadness, and now he was ineffably sad. His veneer of distance, efficiency, coldness had been peeled away, and he thought, for a moment, that he understood the purpose of sadness: to help us endure.

Across the parking lot, more ambulances were leaving, sirens blaring. He walked back to Alexis and Max, waiting for him at the tower door.

"I can see it now," he said. "In the papers. Pictures before and after." *After*, he thought. What came next? He could not but wonder, in spite of himself, if Max had changed his mind. Who would want Olympic Adventure now—a dream world that had become a nightmare.

And then he realized that he wanted the park more than ever. To make it better and safer. To make it his. Even in anger and remorse, this longing did not fade; indeed, it grew stronger: to have his own. A melancholy song cut through his thoughts: *God bless the child that's got his own.* . . .

Sheila Richardson passed by the tower. "A bright young woman," Max Brodky said, shaking his head, looking for words to fill the empty space. "And Masters, a bright young man." Brodky's calm acted like a sedative on Hawkins.

"They're good people," Hawkins said, standing at his office door, watching the doctors remove the last of the injured.

Max looked out across the park. Another series of sirens blared. "You see, you don't have to live as long as I have to . . . to know madness. It is all around us."

Hawkins stood next to him, wondering what the old man had seen in his lifetime, what misery and despair. "Well, Max," he said finally, "where do we go from here? Still want to buy this wreck?"

"Of course I do, of course," Brodky said. "Worse it could have been. We can rebuild, you and me together. Maybe we will ask Gabriel for help. Yes?" He smiled, walked to the window and pushed it open. Across the plaza, Ken Masters and Sheila Richardson stood talking. Brodky's eyes, glinting, Hawkins thought, with tears, took in the whole park. Already his mind was shaping, planning, building. In the face of destruction, Max Brodky looked to the future. "A terrible waste," he said. "Terrible." He slung his jacket over his shoulder. "Well, children, I have one more appointment tonight. Mr. Cunningham is waiting for me."

"Cole? Waiting?" Alexis asked. "Waiting for you?"

"In a manner of speaking," Max said. "He has surely by now heard the bad news."

"About tonight," Alexis said.

"Yes, that, and about the future. He is a good general. He will accept defeat."

"Life," Alexis said, echoing words she had often heard but did not thoroughly believe, "is not a war."

"Of course not," Max said. "I never thought it was." He turned from her, seemed to wipe his eyes, and turned back. "It is not only in war that there are defeats." He touched her shoulder lightly and walked to the door. "We will talk tomorrow," he said to Hawkins, slipping his jacket on. Hawkins thought he looked old and suddenly very tired.

"Tomorrow," Hawkins said. "I'd almost forgotten there was going to be a tomorrow."

Max smiled, pushed through the door, and was gone.

"You don't like him," Brad said, "do you?"

"I never have," Alexis said. "He's scary."

"That's the last thing in the world I'd call him."

"I don't know what he really wants, what he believes in. I don't know what's important to him. It makes me nervous."

"Do you know what you really want?" he asked. "Do I?"

She put her hand on his chest and with her fingers drew an imaginary arrow across his heart. Then she kissed him. They walked out of the office into the park, picking their way through the rubble. Past the fountain, they stopped at the burned-out jeep in the shattered Olympic Bazaar. In the smoldering remains, a piece of metal shone through. Brad picked it up gingerly and rubbed away the damp ashes. It was a small gold pin, an *O* with an *A* in the center. Cole Cunningham had given it to him on the day he was hired.

"An omen," he said. "Things survive."

At the entrance to the Western Arena, they stopped. The green walls, splattered with soot, had cracked from the heat. Shards of glass from broken gas lamps sparkled in the muddy grass. Burnt canvas hung from the trees. A cloud of helplessness lay on his mind and suddenly claimed its momentary reward. Sadness overwhelmed him.

He slipped his arm across Alexis's shoulder and they continued walking, passing stable boys who were leading the horses into trailers. The boys told Hawkins they would stay the night, until all the horses were rounded up and cared for. He thanked them, and he and Alexis walked deeper into the wreckage. At the ferris wheel, they stopped again and Hawkins choked back a sob. Pools of blood had dried on the ground. He blamed himself for Jock's death. He should never have let him climb the ladder. Now he thought about calling Jock's wife. Senseless, he thought. Where is the meaning? The notion of futility gripped him, but he sloughed it off. Senselessness degrades. Alexis tugged him away from the ferris wheel and they walked arm in arm toward the carousel. As they stepped onto the platform, Hawkins's walkie-talkie buzzed. It was Toscani.

"Backup generators working, son. Do we need power anywhere tonight?"

"Check with the troopers, Pete. They're still running the show."

"Will do. Are you coming up?"

"In a bit. I want to see how things look down here."

"We've got some food, whenever you're ready."

"Thanks, Pete. We'll be there in a while."

He set the walkie-talkie in its case and, gazing at the carousel's horses, slaughtered wooden beasts, his sense of helplessness and his anger flared anew.

"Bastards," he said.

"We'll survive," Alexis said.

"I know," he said, "but with what?"

"With us," she said. "With what we have. Isn't that enough?"

He was grateful for her, for her strength and, more, for the weakness she had showed him. In the center of the carousel, they sat, holding each other, finally succumbing to tears. And then the carousel came to life with its wheels spinning, horses turning, music playing, and lights flashing red, white, blue.